Praise for *Mindscan*

The John W. Campbell Memorial Award–Winning Novel
by the Hugo and Nebula Award–Winning Author of *Flashforward*

"Sawyer lucidly explores fascinating philosophical conundrums."
—*Entertainment Weekly*

"A crackingly good novel; a delight."   —*SF Crowsnest*

"A tale involving courtroom drama, powerful human emotion, and challenging SF mystery. Sawyer juggles it all with intelligence and far-reaching vision worthy of Isaac Asimov."   —*Starlog*

"Sawyer's most ambitious work to date. In Sawyer's capable grasp the story positively sings with humor, insight, and depth. *Mindscan* is truly a work of literary art. With a brilliant narrative, intriguing and well-researched scientific extrapolation, and characters that are believable and utterly human, Sawyer has undoubtedly cemented his reputation as one of the foremost science fiction writers of our generation."   —*SF Site*

"This tightly plotted hard-SF novel from Hugo and Nebula winner Sawyer offers plenty of philosophical speculation on the ethics of biotechnology and the nature of consciousness."   —*Publishers Weekly*

"An intriguing and stylistically fine story."   —*Rocky Mountain News*

"Lately, I've been inspired by ideas from Robert J. Sawyer."
—artificial intelligence pioneer Marvin Minsky

"With his customary flair for combining hard science with first-rate storytelling, the author of the Neanderthal Parallax series and *Calculating God* imagines a future of all-too-real possibilities."   —*Library Journal*

"This is Sawyer at his best: compelling characters, an intriguing and involving plot, and deep philosophic themes backed by credible scientific reasoning. *Mindscan* will resonate in your thoughts for a long time after you have closed the book."   —*Kitchener-Waterloo Record*

"An exciting crowd-pleaser. Richly informed by current interdisciplinary research in the burgeoning field of consciousness studies, and alive with provocative speculation of its own, *Mindscan* is a heady brew of hard SF, blended with enough comedy, romance, and adventure to appeal to a wider audience." —*SFRA Review*

"This is high-quality, clever, and thought-provoking near-future SF. The characters are nuanced, and the plot is believable. Recommended." —*Kliatt*

"A delightful read. Grips the reader with engaging characters and cosmic ideas. Another excellent (not to mention surprising) novel from one of the genre's brightest lights." —*Winnipeg Free Press*

Praise for Robert J. Sawyer

"Robert J. Sawyer is just about the best science fiction writer out there these days." —*Rocky Mountain News*

"Sawyer writes with near-Asimovian clarity, with energy and drive, with such grace that his writing becomes invisible as the story comes to life in your mind." —Orson Scott Card

"No reader seeking well-written stories that respect, emphasize, and depend on modern science should be disappointed by the works of Robert Sawyer." —*The Washington Post*

"Sawyer is one of contemporary SF's most consistent performers." —*Publishers Weekly*

"Sawyer is Canada's answer to Michael Crichton." —*Montreal Gazette*

"A sense of wonder that hasn't prevailed in American SF since the days of Heinlein." —*Books in Canada*

"Sawyer has won himself an international readership by reinvigorating the traditions of hard science fiction, following the path of such writers as Isaac Asimov and Robert A. Heinlein in his bold speculations from pure science." —*National Post* (Canada)

BOOKS BY ROBERT J. SAWYER

NOVELS

*Golden Fleece**
*End of an Era**
The Terminal Experiment
Starplex
*Frameshift**
Illegal Alien
*Factoring Humanity**
*Flashforward**
*Calculating God**
*Mindscan**
*Rollback**

THE NEANDERTHAL PARALLAX

*Hominids**
*Humans**
*Hybrids**

THE QUINTAGLIO ASCENSION

Far-Seer
Fossil Hunter
Foreigner

THE WWW TRILOGY

Wake
Watch
Wonder

*Published by Tor Books
Readers' group guides available at www.sfwriter.com.

MINDSCAN

ROBERT J. SAWYER

TOR®

A TOM DOHERTY ASSOCIATES BOOK
NEW YORK

MINDSCAN

Copyright © 2005 by Robert J. Sawyer

Edited by David G. Hartwell

A Tor Book
Published by Tom Doherty Associates, LLC
175 Fifth Avenue
New York, NY 10010

www.tor-forge.com

Tor® is a registered trademark of Tom Doherty Associates, LLC.

The Library of Congress has cataloged the hardcover edition as follows:

Sawyer, Robert J.
    Mindscan / Robert J. Sawyer.—1st ed.
        p. cm.
    "A Tom Doherty Associates book."
    ISBN 978-0-7653-1107-8
    1. Ethics—Fiction.   I. Title.
PR9199.3.S2533 M56 2005
C813'.54—dc22

                                            2005299539

ISBN 978-0-7653-2990-5 (trade paperback)

First Edition: April 2005
First Trade Paperback Edition: December 2011

Printed in the United States of America

0 9 8 7 6 5 4 3 2 1

To

JOHN ROSE

with thanks for
a quarter-century of
encouragement,
friendship,
and
inspiration

We cannot expect to have certain, universal agreement on any question of personhood, but we all are forced to hold an answer in our hearts and act upon our best guess.

JARON LANIER,
The Journal of Consciousness Studies

proLogue
March 2018

There wasn't anything special about this fight. Honest to God, there wasn't. Dad and I had argued a million times before, but nothing awful had happened. Oh, he'd thrown me out of the house a couple of times, and when I was younger he used to send me to my room or cut off my allowance. But nothing like *this* had ever occurred. I keep reliving the moment in my mind, haunted by it. It's no consolation that *he* isn't haunted by it, that he probably doesn't even remember it. No consolation at all.

My father's grandparents had made a fortune in the brewing industry—if you know Canada at all, you know Sullivan's Select and Old Sully's Premium Dark. We'd always had a shitload of money.

"Shitload." That's the way I talked back then; I guess remembering it is bringing back my old vocabulary. When I'd been a teenager, I didn't care about money. In fact, I agreed with most Canadians that the profits made by big corporations were obscene. Even in supposedly egalitarian Canada, the rich were getting richer and the poor poorer, and I'd hated it. Back then, I'd hated a lot of things.

"Where the hell did you get this?" my dad had shouted, holding the fake ID I'd used to buy pot at the local Mac's. He was standing up; he always did that when we fought. Dad was scrawny, but I guess he felt his two meters of height were intimidating.

We were in his den at the house in Port Credit. Port Credit was what you came to if you continued west along Lake Ontario from Toronto; it was a classy neighborhood, and even then—this would have been, what?, 2018, I guess—it was still mostly white. Rich and white. The window looked out over the lake, which that day had been gray and choppy.

"Friend of mine made it," I said, without even looking at the ID card.

"Well, you're not seeing that friend anymore. Christ's sake, Jake, you're only seventeen." The legal age for buying alcohol and marijuana in Ontario, then and now, was nineteen; the legal age for buying tobacco is eighteen. Go figure.

"You can't tell me who I can see," I said, looking out the window. Seagulls were pirouetting above the waves. If they could get high, I didn't see why I couldn't.

"Hell I can't," snapped my father. He had a long face and a full head of dark hair, graying at the temples. If this was 2018, that would have made him thirty-nine. "So long as you live under my roof, you'll do as I say. Jesus, Jacob, what were you thinking? Presenting a false ID card is a major offense."

"It's a major offense if you're a terrorist or an identity thief," I said, looking across the wide teak desk at him. "Kids get caught buying pot all the time; no one gives a damn."

"*I* give a damn. Your mother gives a damn." Mom was out playing tennis. It was a Sunday—the only day Dad wasn't normally at work—and he'd gotten the call from the police station. "You keep screwing up like this, boy, and—"

"And what? And I'll never end up like you? I *pray* for that." I knew I'd hit home. A vertical vein in the middle of his forehead swelled up whenever he was really pissed. I used to love it when I got the vein.

His voice was trembling. "You ungrateful little bastard."

"I don't need this shit," I said, turning toward the door, preparing to stalk out.

"Damn you, boy! You're going to hear this! If you—"

"Fuck off," I said.

"—don't stop acting—"

"I hate this place anyway."

"—like an idiot, you'll—"

"And I hate you!"

No reply. I turned around, and saw him slumping backward into his black leather chair. When he hit it, the chair rotated half a turn.

"Dad!" I hurried behind the desk and shook him. "Dad!" Nothing. "Oh, Christ. Oh, no. Oh, God . . ." I lifted him out of the chair; there was so much adrenaline coursing through my veins from the fight that I didn't even feel his weight. Stretching out his gangly limbs on the hardwood floor, I shouted, "Dad! Come on, Dad!"

I kicked aside a waste basket with a shredder attached; paper diamonds scattered everywhere. Crouching next to him, I felt for a pulse; he still had one—and he seemed to be breathing. But he didn't respond to anything I said.

"Dad!" Totally out of ideas, I tried slapping him lightly on each cheek. A string of drool was hanging out of the corner of his mouth.

I quickly rose, turned to face his desk, hit the speakerphone button, and pounded out 9-1-1. Then I crouched down beside him again.

The phone rang three excruciating times, then: *"Fire, police, or ambulance?"* said a female operator, sounding small and far away.

"Ambulance!"

"Your address is—" said the operator, and she read it off. *"Correct?"*

I lifted his right eyelid. His eye tracked to look at mine, thank God.

"Yes, yes, that's right. Hurry! My father's collapsed!"

"Is he breathing?"

"Yes."

"Pulse?"

"Yes, he has one, but he's collapsed, and he's not responding to anything I say."

"An ambulance is on its way," said the woman. *"Is anyone else with you?"*

My hands were shaking. "No. I'm alone."

"Don't leave him."

"I won't. Oh, Christ, what's wrong with him?"

The operator ignored the question. *"Help is on its way."*

"Dad!" I said. He made a gurgling sound, but I don't think it was in response to me. I wiped away the drool and tipped his head back a bit to make sure he was getting plenty of air. "Please, Dad!"

"Don't panic," said the woman. *"Remain calm."*

"Christ, oh Christ, good Christ . . ."

The ambulance took me and my dad to the Trillium Health Centre, the nearest hospital. As soon as we got there, they transferred him to a gurney, his long legs hanging over the end. A white male doctor appeared quickly, shining a light into his eyes and tapping his knee with a small hammer—to which there was the usual reflexive response. He tried speaking to my father a few times, then called out, "Get this man a cerebral MRI, stat!" An orderly wheeled Dad off. He still hadn't said a coherent word, although he occasionally made small sounds.

By the time Mom arrived, Dad had been moved into a bed. Standard government health care gets you a space in a ward. Dad had supplemental insurance, and so had a private room. Of course.

"Oh, God," my mother kept saying, over and over again, holding her hands to her face. "Oh, my poor Cliff. My darling, my baby . . ."

My mother was the same age as my dad, with a round head and artificially blonde hair. She was still wearing her tennis clothes—white top, short white skirt. She played a lot of tennis, and was in good shape; to my embarrassment, some of my friends thought she was hot.

Shortly, a doctor came to see us. She was a Vietnamese woman of about fifty. Her name tag identified her as Dr. Thanh. Before she could open her mouth, my mother said, "What is it? What's wrong with him?"

The doctor was infinitely kind—I'll always remember her. She took my mother's hand and got her to sit down. And then the woman crouched down, so she'd be at my mother's eye level. "Mrs. Sullivan," she said. "I'm so sorry. The news is not good."

I stood behind my seated mother, with a hand on her shoulder.

"What is it?" Mom asked. "A stroke? For God's sake, Cliff is only thirty-nine. He's too young for a stroke."

"A stroke can happen at any age," said Dr. Thanh. "But, although technically this *was* a form of stroke, it's not what you're thinking of."

"What then?"

"Your husband has a kind of congenital lesion we call an AVM: an arteriovenous malformation. It's a tangle of arteries and veins with no interposing capillaries—normally, capillaries provide resistance, slowing down the bloodflow rate. In cases like this, the vessels have very thin walls, and so are prone to bursting. And when they do, blood pours through the brain in a torrent. In the form of AVM your husband has—called Katerinsky's syndrome—the vessels can rupture in a cascade sequence, going off like fire hoses."

"But Cliff never mentioned . . ."

"No, no. He probably didn't know. An MRI would have shown it, but most people don't have routine MRIs until they turn forty."

"Damn it," said my mother—who almost never swore. "We would have paid for the test! We—"

Dr. Thanh glanced up at me, then looked into my mother's eyes. "Mrs. Sullivan, believe me, it wouldn't have made any difference. Your husband's condition is inoperable. AVMs in general affect only one in a thousand people, and Katerinsky's affects only one in a thousand of those with AVMs. The sad truth is that the principal form of diagnosis for Katerinsky's is autopsy. Your husband is actually one of the lucky ones."

I looked over at my father, in the bed, a tube up his nose, another in his arm, his hair matted, his mouth hanging open.

"So, he's going to be okay, then?" said my mother. "He's going to get better?"

Dr. Thanh sounded truly sad. "No, he's not. When the blood vessels ruptured, the adjacent parts of his brain were destroyed by the jet of blood pounding into the tissue. He's . . ."

"He's what?" demanded my mother, her voice full of panic. "He's not going to be a vegetable, is he? Oh, God—my poor Cliff. Oh, Jesus God . . ."

I looked at my father, and I did something I hadn't done for five years. I started to cry. My vision began to blur, and so did my mind. As the doctor continued to talk to my mother, I heard the words "severe retardation," "total aphasia," and "institutionalize."

He wasn't coming back. He wasn't leaving, but he wasn't coming back. And the last words of mine that ever would have registered on his consciousness were—

"Jake." Dr. Thanh was calling my name. I wiped my eyes. She had risen and was looking at me. "Jake, how old are you?"

I'm old enough, I thought. I'm old enough to be the man of the house. I'll take care of this, take care of my mother. "Seventeen."

She nodded. "You should have an MRI, too, Jake."

"What?" I said, my heart suddenly pounding. "Why?"

Dr. Thanh lifted her delicate eyebrows, and spoke very, very softly. "Katerinsky's is hereditary."

I felt myself starting to panic again. "You—you mean I might end up like Dad?"

"Just get the scan done," she said. "You don't necessarily have Katerinsky's, but you might."

I couldn't take it, I thought. I couldn't take living as a vegetable. Or maybe I did more than think it; the woman smiled kindly, wisely, as if she'd heard me say those words aloud.

"Don't worry," Dr. Thanh said.

"Don't worry?" My mouth was bone dry. "You said this—this disease is incurable."

"That's true; Katerinsky's involves defects so deep in the brain that they can't be repaired surgically—yet. But you're only seventeen, and medical science is galloping ahead—why, the progress we've made since I started practicing! Who knows what they'll be able to do in another twenty or thirty years?"

CHAPTER 1

TWENTY-SEVEN YEARS LATER: AUGUST 2045

There were perhaps a hundred people in the ballroom of Toronto's Fairmont Royal York Hotel, and at least half of them had only a short time left to live.

Of course, being rich, those who were near death had mostly availed themselves of the best cosmetic treatments: face-lifts, physiognomic rebuilds, even a few facial transplants. I found it unsettling to see twenty-year-old visages attached to stooped bodies, but at least the transplants looked better than the ghastly tautness of one face-lift too many.

Still, I reminded myself, these were indeed *cosmetic* treatments. The *faux*-youthful faces were attached to old, decaying bodies—bodies thoroughly worn out. Of the elderly who were present, most were standing, a few were in motorized wheelchairs, some had walkers, and one had his legs encased in powered armatures while another wore a full-body exoskeleton.

Being old isn't what it used to be, I thought, shaking my head. Not that I was old myself: I was just forty-four. Sadly, though, I'd used up my fifteen minutes of fame right at the beginning, without even being aware of it. I'd been the first baby born in Toronto on 1 January 2001—the first child of the new millennium. A much bigger fuss had been made over the girl who had popped out just after midnight on 1 January 2000, a year that had no significance save for ending in three zeros. But that was okay: the last thing I wanted to be was a year older, because a year from now, I might very well be dead. The old joke ran through my mind again:

"I'm afraid I've got some bad news," said the doctor. "You don't have long to live."

The young man swallowed. "How much time have I got left?"

The doctor shook his head sadly. "Ten."

"Ten what? Ten years? Ten months? Ten—?"

"Nine . . . Eight . . ."

I shook my head to dispel the thought and looked around some more. The Fairmont Royal York was a grand hotel, dating from the first glory days of rail travel, and it was enjoying a revival now that magnetic-levitation trains were flying along the old tracks. The hotel was across the street from Union Station, just north of Toronto's lakeshore—and a good twenty-five kilometers east of where my parents' house still stood. Chandeliers hung from the ballroom ceiling, and original oil paintings adorned the flock-papered walls. Tuxedoed servers were milling about offering glasses of wine. I went to the open bar and ordered a tomato juice heavily spiked with Worcestershire; I wanted a clear head this evening.

When I stepped away from the bar with my drink, I found myself standing next to an honest-to-goodness old lady: wrinkled face, white hair. Amid the surrounding denial and fakery, she was quite refreshing.

The woman smiled at me, although it was a lopsided smile—she'd clearly suffered a stroke at some point. "Here alone?" she asked. Her pleasant voice was attenuated into a Southern drawl, and it was also tinged by the quaver often found in the elderly.

I nodded.

"Me, too," she said. She was wearing a dark jacket over a lighter blouse, and matching dark slacks. "My son refused to bring me." Most of the other old folks had companions with them: middle-aged children, or lawyers, or paid caregivers. I glanced down, noted that she was wearing a wedding band. She apparently followed my gaze. "I'm a widow," she said.

"Ah."

"So," she said, "are you checking out the process for a loved one?"

I felt my face quirk. "You might say that."

She looked at me with an odd expression; I sensed that she'd seen through my comment, but, although curious, was too polite to press further. After a moment, she said, "My name's Karen." She held out her hand.

"Jake," I said, taking it. The skin on her hand was loose and liver-spotted, and her knuckles were swollen. I squeezed very gently.

"Where are you from, Jake?"

"Here. Toronto. You?"

"Detroit."

I nodded. Many of tonight's potential customers were probably Americans. Immortex had found a much more congenial legal climate for its services in increasingly liberal Canada than in ever-more-conservative America. When I'd been a kid, college students used to come over to Ontario from Michigan and New York because the drinking age was lower here and the strippers could go further. Now, people from those two states crossed the border for legal pot, legal hookers, legal abortions, same-sex marriages, physician-assisted suicide, and other things the religious right frowned upon.

"It's funny," said Karen, glancing at the aged crowd. "When I was ten, I once said to my grandmother, 'Who the heck wants to be ninety?' And she looked me right in the eye and said, 'Anyone who is eighty-nine.'" Karen shook her head. "How right she was."

I smiled wanly.

"Ladies and gentlemen," called a male voice, just then. "Would you all please take seats?"

Doubtless no one here was hard of hearing; implants easily rectified that sign of aging, too. There were rows of folding chairs at the back of the ballroom, facing a podium. "Shall we?" said Karen. Something about her was charming—the Southern accent, maybe (Detroit certainly wasn't where she'd grown up)—and there were, of course, the connotations that went with being in a ballroom. I found myself offering my arm, and Karen took it. We walked over slowly—I let her set the pace—and found a pair of seats near the back at one side, an A. Y. Jackson landscape hanging under glass on the wall next to us.

"Thank you," said the same man who'd spoken before. He was standing at the dark wooden podium. There was no light directly on him; just a little illumination spilling up from a reading lamp attached to the lectern. A gangling Asian of perhaps thirty-five, his black hair was combed straight back above a forehead that would have done Professor Moriarty proud. A surprisingly large, old-fashioned microphone covered his mouth. "My name is John Sugiyama," he said, "and I'm a vice-president at Immortex. Thank you all for coming tonight. I hope you've enjoyed the hospitality so far."

He looked out at the crowd. Karen, I noticed, was one of those who murmured appreciatively, which seemed to be what Sugiyama wanted. "Good, good," he said. "In everything we do, we strive for absolute customer satisfaction. After all, as we like to say, 'Once an Immortex client, always an Immortex client.'"

He smiled broadly, and again waited for appreciative chuckles before going on. "Now, I'm sure you've all got questions, so let's get started. I know what we're selling costs a lot of money—"

Somebody near me muttered, "Damn right," but if Sugiyama heard, he gave no sign. He continued: "But we won't ask you for a cent until you're satisfied that what we're offering is right for you." He let his gaze wander over the crowd, smiling reassuringly and making lots of eye contact. He looked directly at Karen but skipped over me; presumably he felt I couldn't possibly be a potential customer, and so wasn't worth wasting his charm on.

"Most of you," Sugiyama said, "have had MRIs. Our patented and exclu-

sive Mindscan process is nothing more daunting than that, although our resolution is much finer. It gives us a complete, perfect map of the structure of
your brain: every neuron, every dendrite, every synaptic cleft, every intercon-
nection. It also notes neurotransmitter levels at each synapse. There is no part
of what makes you you that we fail to record."

That much was certainly true. Back in 1990, a philanthropist named Hugh
Loebner promised to award a solid gold medal—not just gold-plated like those
cheap Olympic ones—plus $100,000 in cash to the first team to build a
machine that passed the Turing Test, that old chestnut that said a computer
should be declared truly intelligent if its responses to questions were indistinguishable from those of a human being. Loebner had expected it would be
only a few years before he'd have to cough up—but that's not how things
turned out. It wasn't until three years ago that the prize had been awarded.

I'd watched the whole thing on TV: a panel of five inquisitors—a priest, a
philosopher, a cognitive scientist, a woman who ran a small business, and a
stand-up comic—were presented with two entities behind black curtains. The
questioners were allowed to ask both entities anything at all: moral posers,
general-knowledge trivia, even things about romance and child-rearing; in
addition, the comic did his best to crack the entities up, and to quiz them
about why certain jokes were or weren't funny. Not only that, but the two entities engaged in a dialogue between themselves, asking each other questions
while the little jury looked on. At the end, the jurors voted, and they unani-
mously agreed they could not tell which curtain hid the real human being and
which hid the machine.

After the commercial break, the curtains were raised. On the left was a
fiftyish, balding, bearded black man named Sampson Wainwright. And on the
right was a very simple, boxy robot. The group collected their hundred
grand—paltry from a monetary point of view now, but still hugely symbolic—
and their gold medal. Their winning entity, they revealed, had been an exact
scan of Sampson Wainwright's mind, and it had indeed, as the whole world
could plainly see, thought thoughts indistinguishable in every way from those
produced by the original. Three weeks later, the same group made an IPO for
their little company called Immortex; overnight, they were billionaires.

Sugiyama continued his sales pitch. "Of course," he said, "we can't put the
digital copy back into the original biological brain—but we *can* transfer it into
an artificial brain, which is precisely what our process does. Our artificial
brains congeal out of quantum fog, forming a nanogel that precisely duplicates
the structure of the biological original. The new version is *you*—your mind

instantiated in an artificial brain made out of durable synthetics. It won't wear out. It won't suffer strokes or aneurysms. It won't develop dementia or senility. And . . ." He paused, making sure he had everyone's attention. "It won't die. The new you will live potentially forever."

Even though everyone knew that's what was for sale here, there were still sounds of astonishment—"forever" had such weight when spoken aloud. For my part, I didn't care about immortality—I rather suspected I'd get bored by the time I reached, well, Karen's age. But I'd been walking on eggshells for twenty-seven years, afraid that the blood vessels in my brain would rupture. Dying wouldn't be that bad, but the notion of ending up a vegetable like my father was terrifying to me. Fortunately, Immortex's artificial brains were electrically powered; they didn't require chemical nutrients, and weren't serviced by blood vessels. I rather doubted this was the cure Dr. Thanh had had in mind, but it would do in a pinch.

"Of course," continued Sugiyama, "the artificial brain needs to be housed inside a body."

I glanced at Karen, wondering if she'd read up on that aspect before coming here. Apparently, the scientists who had first made these artificial brains hadn't bothered to have them pre-installed in robotic bodies—which, for the personality represented by the recreated mind, turned out to be a hideous experience: deaf, blind, unable to communicate, unable to move, existing in a sensory void beyond even darkness and silence, lacking even the proprioceptive sense of how one's limbs are currently deployed and the touch of air or clothes against skin. Those transcribed neural nets reconfigured rapidly, according to the journal articles I'd managed to find, in patterns indicative of terror and insanity.

"And so," said Sugiyama, "we'll provide you with an artificial body—one that's infinitely maintainable, infinitely repairable, and infinitely upgradeable." He held up a long-fingered hand. "I won't lie to you, now or ever: as yet, these replacements aren't perfect. But they *are* awfully good."

Sugiyama smiled at the crowd again, and a small spotlight fell on him, slowly increasing in brightness. Beyond him, just like at a rock concert, floated a giant holographic version of his gaunt face.

"You see," Sugiyama said, "I'm an upload myself, and this is an artificial body."

Karen nodded. "I *knew* it," she declared. I was impressed by her acumen: I'd certainly been fooled. Of course, all that was visible of Sugiyama were his head and hands; the rest of him was covered by the podium or a fashionable business suit.

"I was born in 1958," said Sugiyama. "I am eighty-seven years old. I transferred six months ago—one of the very first civilians ever to upload into an artificial body. At the break, I'll walk around and let you examine me closely. You'll find that I don't look exactly right—I freely admit that—and there are certain movements that I just can't do. But I'm not the least bit concerned, because, as I said, these bodies are infinitely upgradeable as technology advances. Indeed, I just got new wrists yesterday, and they are much more nimble than my previous set. I have no doubt that within a few decades, artificial bodies indistinguishable from biological ones will be available." He smiled again. "And, of course, I—and all of you who undergo our procedure—*will* be around a few decades from now."

He was a master salesperson. Talking about centuries or millennia of additional life would have been too abstract—how does one even conceive of such a thing? But a few decades was something the potential customers, most with seven or more of them already under their belts, could appreciate. And every one of these people had been resigned to being in the last decade—if not the last year—of their lives. Until, that is, Immortex had announced this incredible process. I looked at Karen again; she was mesmerized.

Sugiyama held up his hand once more. "Of course, there are many advantages to artificial bodies, even at the current state of technology. Just like our artificial brains, they are virtually indestructible. The braincase, for instance, is titanium, reinforced with carbon-nanotube fibers. If you decide you want to go skydiving, and your parachute fails to open, your new brain still won't get damaged on impact. If—God forbid!—someone shoots you with a gun, or stabs you with a knife—well, you'd almost certainly still be fine."

New holographic images appeared floating behind him, replacing his face. "But our artificial bodies aren't just durable. They're *strong*—as strong as you'd like them to be." I'd expected to see video of fantastic stunts: I'd heard Immortex had developed super-powered limbs for the military, and that that technology was now available to civilian end-users, as well. But instead the display simply showed presumably artificial hands effortlessly opening a mason jar. I couldn't imagine what it must be like to be unable to do something so simple . . . but it was clear that many of the others in the room were blown away by this demonstration.

And Sugiyama had more to offer. "Naturally," he said, "you'll never need a walker, a cane, or an exoskeleton again. And stairs will no longer present a problem. You'll have perfect vision and hearing, and perfect reflexes; you'll be able to drive a car again, if you're not able to now."

Even I missed the reflexes and coordination I'd had back when I'd been younger. Sugiyama continued: "You can kiss good-bye the pain of arthritis, and just about every other ailment associated with old age. And if you haven't yet contracted Parkinson's or Alzheimer's, you never will." I heard murmurs around me—including one from Karen. "And forget about cancer or broken hips. Say *sayonara* to arthritic joints and macular degeneration. With our process, you'll have a virtually unlimited lifespan, with perfect eyesight and hearing, vitality and strength, self-sufficiency and dignity." He beamed out at his audience, and I could see people nodding to themselves, or talking in positive tones with their neighbors. It *did* sound good, even for someone like me, whose day-to-day troubles were nothing more irritating than acid-reflux disease and the odd migraine.

Sugiyama let the crowd chatter for a while before raising his hand again. "Of course," he said, as if it were a mere trifle, "there *is* one catch . . ."

CHAPTER 2

I knew what the "one catch" Sugiyama was referring to was. Despite all his salesperson's talk about *transferring* consciousness, Immortex couldn't really do that. At best, they were *copying* consciousness into a machine body. And that meant the original still existed.

"Yes," said Sugiyama to the audience of which the old woman—Karen, that was her name—and I were part, "from the moment the synthetic body is activated, there will be two of you—two entities who each feel they *are* you. But which one is the *real* you? Your first impulse might be to respond that the flesh-and-blood one is the real McCoy." Sugiyama tilted his head to one side. "An interesting philosophical point. I fully concede that that version *did* exist first—but does such primacy make it *really* you? In your own mental picture of yourself, which one do you consider the real you: the one that suffers aches and pains, the one that has trouble sleeping through the night, the one that is frail and old? Or the vigorous you, the you in full possession of all your mental and physical faculties? The you who faces each day with joy, instead of fear, with decades or centuries of life ahead, instead of—please do forgive me—scant months or years."

I could see that Sugiyama was winning people over. Of course, these individuals had self-selected to come to this sales seminar, so they presumably were already predisposed to at least open-mindedness about these issues. Perhaps the average Joe in the street wouldn't share their opinions—but, then, the average Joe in the street couldn't possibly afford the Immortex process.

"You know," said Sugiyama, "there used to be a lot of debate about this, but it's all evaporated in the last few years. The simplest interpretation turned out to be the correct one: the human mind is nothing but software running on the hardware we call the brain. Well, when your old computer hardware wears out, you don't think twice about junking it, buying a new machine, and reloading all your old software. What we at Immortex do is the same: the software that is you starts running on a new, better hardware platform."

"It's still not the real you," grumbled someone in front of me.

If he heard the comment, Sugiyama was undaunted. "Here's an old poser from philosophy class. Your father gives you an ax. After a few years of good service, the wooden handle breaks, and so you replace it. Is it still the ax your father gave you? Sure, why not? But then a few years after that, the metal head breaks, and you replace that. Now, nothing of the original is left—it wasn't replaced all at once, but rather piece-by-piece. Is it still your father's ax? Before you answer too quickly, consider the fact that the atoms that make up your own body are completely replaced every seven years: there's not one bit of the you who was once a baby that still exists; it's all been replaced. Are you still you? Of course you are: the body doesn't matter, the physical instantiation doesn't matter. What matters is the continuity of being: the ax traces its existence back to being a gift from your father; it *is* still that gift. And—" he underscored his next words with a pointing finger "—anyone who can remember having been you before *is* you now."

I wasn't sure I bought this, but I continued to listen.

"I don't mean to sound harsh," said Sugiyama, "but I know you are all realists—you wouldn't be here if you weren't. You each know that your natural lives are almost over. If you elect to undergo our procedure, it's the new you that will get to live on, in your house, your community, with your family. But that version of you will remember this moment right now when we discussed this, just as it will remember everything else you ever did; it *will* be you."

He stopped. I thought it must be awkward to be a synthetic lecturer; a real person could choreograph his pauses with sips of water. But after a moment, Sugiyama went on. "But what happens to the original you?" he asked.

Karen leaned close to me, and whispered in a mock-menacing tone, "Soylent Green is people!" I had no idea what she was talking about.

"The answer, of course, is something *wonderful*," said Sugiyama. "The old you will be provided for, in unsurpassed luxury, at High Eden, our retirement village on the far side of the moon." Pictures of what looked like a five-star resort community began floating behind Sugiyama. "Yes, ours is the first-ever civilian residence on the moon, but we've spared no expense, and we'll take care of the original you there in the highest possible style, until that sad but inevitable day when the flesh gives up." I'd read that Immortex cremated the dead up there, and, of course, there were no funerals or grave markers—after all, they contended the *person* still lived on . . .

"It's a cruel irony," said Sugiyama. "The moon is the perfect place for the elderly. With a surface gravity only one-sixth of Earth's, falls that would break a hip or leg here are trivial there. And, again, in that gentle gravity, even weakened muscles have plenty of strength. Hoisting oneself in and out of bed or the bath, or walking up stairs, is no longer a struggle—not that there are many stairs on the moon; people are so light on their feet there that ramps are better.

"Yes, *being* on the moon is wonderful, if you're elderly; the original version of me is, right this very instant, having a grand time at High Eden, believe you me. But *getting* to the moon—that used to be quite another story. The high acceleration experienced during rocket liftoff from Earth is brutal, although after that, admittedly the rest of the journey, spent in effectively zero *g*, is a piece of cake. Well, of course, we don't use rockets. That is, we don't go straight up. Rather, we use spaceplanes that take off horizontally and gradually climb to Low Earth Orbit. At no time during the flight do you experience more than 1.4 *g*, and with our ergo-padded chairs and so forth, we can get even the frailest person to the moon safe and sound. And once there—" he paused dramatically—*"paradise."*

Sugiyama looked around the room, meeting eyes. "What scares you? Getting sick? Not likely on the moon; everything is decontaminated as it enters one of the lunar habitats, and germs would have to travel through vacuum and endure harsh radiation to move from one habitat to another. Being mugged? There's *never* been a mugging—or any other violent crime—on the moon. Those cold Canadian winters?" He chuckled. "We maintain a constant temperature of twenty-three degrees Celsius. Water, of course, is precious on the moon, so the humidity is kept low—no more hot muggy summers. You'll feel like you're enjoying a beautiful spring morning in the American Southwest all year round. Trust me: High Eden is the best possible retirement home, a wonderful resort with gravity so gentle that it makes you feel young again. It's a win-win scenario, for the new you down here on Earth and the old one up there on the moon." He smiled broadly. "So, any takers?"

CHAPTER 3

My mother was now sixty-six. In the almost three decades since Dad had been institutionalized, she had never remarried. Of course, it wasn't as though Dad was dead.

Or maybe it was.

I saw my mother once a week, on Monday afternoons. Occasionally, I'd see her more often: Mother's Day, her birthday, Christmas. But our regular get-togethers were Mondays at 2:00 p.m.

They were not joyous occasions.

My fingerprint let me into the house I'd grown up in, right on the lake. It had been worth a lot when I was a teenager; now, it was worth a fortune. Toronto was like a black hole, gobbling up everything that fell into its event horizon. It had grown hugely three years before I was born, when five surrounding municipalities had become part of it. Now it had grown even more, swallowing all the other adjoining cities and towns, becoming a behemoth of eight million people. My parents' house wasn't in a suburb anymore; it was in the heart of the continuous downtown that started with the CN Tower and continued along the lakeshore for fifty kilometers in either direction.

It was hard coming through the house's entryway into the marble foyer. The door to my father's den was on the right and my mother, even after all these years, had left it untouched. I always tried not to look through the open door; I always failed. The teak desk was still there; so was the black leather swivel chair.

It wasn't just sadness I felt; it was guilt. I'd never told my mother that Dad and I were arguing when he collapsed. I hadn't actually lied to her—I'm a terrible liar—but she'd assumed I must have heard him fall and come running, and, well, it was not as if he could contradict me. I could have dealt with her anger over the fake ID; I couldn't deal with her looking at me and thinking I'd been responsible for what had happened to the man she was devoted to.

"Hello, Mr. Sullivan," said Hannah, emerging from the kitchen. Hannah, about my own age, was my mother's live-in housekeeper.

"Hi, Hannah," I said. Normally, I told everyone to call me by my first name, but I'd never taken that step with Hannah—because of our similarities in age, she seemed too much like the dutiful sister doing what *I* should be doing, looking after my mother. "How is she?"

Hannah had soft features and small eyes; she looked like the kind of person who'd have been pleasantly plump in the days before drugs had eliminated obesity—at least there had been *some* real cures for things in the last twenty-seven years. "Not too bad, Mr. Sullivan. I served her lunch about an hour ago, and she ate most of it."

I nodded and continued along the corridor. The house was elegant; I hadn't understood that when I was a kid, but I did now: the hallway was paneled in dark wood, and little marble statues were set into recessed niches, with fancy brass lights pointing at them.

"Hey, Mom," I called out, as I reached the bottom of the curving oak staircase.

"I'll be down in a second," she replied from upstairs. I nodded. I headed into the living room, which was sunken and had bay windows overlooking the lake.

A few minutes later, my mother appeared. She was dressed, as she always was for these trips, in one of the blouses she used to wear back in 2018. She knew her face had changed, and even with a nip here and a tuck there, she still wasn't immediately recognizable as the woman she'd been in her late thirties; I guess she felt the old clothes might help.

We got into my car, a green Toshiba Deela, and drove the twenty kilometers north to Brampton, where the Institute was located. It was, of course, the best care that money could buy: a large, treed lot, with a modern, central structure that looked more like a resort hotel than a hospital; maybe they'd used the same architect Immortex had for High Eden. It was a fine summer's afternoon, and several—patients? residents?—were outdoors in wheelchairs, each accompanied by an attendant.

My father was not among them.

We entered the lobby. The guard—black, bald, bearded—knew us, and we exchanged pleasantries, and then my mother and I headed up to Dad's room, on the second floor.

They moved him around, to avoid bedsores and other problems. Sometimes we found him lying down; sometimes he was gently strapped into a wheelchair; sometimes, they even had him strapped to a board that held him vertically.

Today, he was in bed. He rolled his head, looked at Mother, looked at me.

He was aware of his surroundings, but that was about it. The doctors said he had the mind of an infant.

He'd changed a lot since that day. His hair was white now, and, of course, he had the wrinkled countenance of a man of sixty-six; no point in cosmetic surgery here. His long limbs were thin and untoned; despite electrical and occasional manual stimulation, there was no way to keep them muscular without real physical activity.

"Hello, Cliff," my mother said, and she paused. She always paused, and it broke my heart each time. She was waiting for a reply that would never come.

Mom had lots of little rituals for these visits. She told my father what had happened in the last week, and how the Blue Jays were doing—I'd gotten my love of baseball from my dad. She sat in a chair next to his bed, and held his left hand in her right one. His fingers always closed reflexively around my mother's. No one had removed the gold wedding band from his hand, and my mother still wore hers.

Me, I didn't say much. I just stared at him—at *it*, really, a shell, a body without much of a mind, lying there, looking at my mother, his mouth quirking occasionally into what might have been the seed of a smile or frown, or might have just been random movements. As she spoke, he made occasional sounds—he'd have been making little gurgles if she wasn't speaking, too.

My own personal sword of Damocles. I was now five years older than my dad had been when the blood vessels in his brain had ruptured, washing away his intelligence and personality, his joy and his anger, in a tide of red. There was a digital clock on the wall of his room, showing the time in bright numerals. Thank God clocks didn't tick anymore.

When my mother was done talking at my father, she rose from the chair and said, "All right."

Normally, I just dropped her off at her house on my way back into the city, but I didn't want to do this in the car. "Sit down, Mom," I said. "There's something I have to tell you."

She looked surprised, but did so. There was only one chair in my father's room here at the Institute, and, as I'd asked, she took it. I propped myself against a bureau on the opposite side of the room and looked at her.

"Yes?" she said. There was a hint of defiance in her voice, and I flashed back. Once before, I'd broached the topic of how futile it was to come here each week, how my father didn't even really know we were here. She'd been furious, and had verbally slapped me down in a way she hadn't since I was a kid. Clearly, she was expecting a repeat of that argument.

I took in air, let it out slowly, and spoke. "I'm—I don't know if you've heard of it or not, but there's this process they've got now. It's been covered on all the news shows . . ." I trailed off, as if I'd given her enough clues to guess what I was talking about. "It's by a company called Immortex. They transfer a person's consciousness into an artificial body."

She looked at me silently.

I continued. "And, well, I'm going to do it."

Mom spoke slowly, as if digesting the idea a word at a time. "You're going to . . . transfer your . . . your consciousness . . ."

"That's right."

"Into a . . . an . . . artificial body."

"Yes."

She said nothing more, and, just like when I was a little kid, I felt a need to fill the void, to explain myself. "My body's no good—you know that. It's almost certainly going to kill me"—if I'm lucky, I thought—"or I'll end up like Dad. I'm doomed if I stay in this . . ." I laid a splayed hand over my chest, sought a word ". . . this *shell*."

"Does it work?" she asked. "This process—does it really work?"

I smiled my best reassuring smile. "Yes."

She looked over at her husband, and the anxious expression on her face was heartbreaking. "Could they . . . could Cliff . . ."

Oh, Christ, what a moron I am. It hadn't even occurred to me that she would connect this to Dad. "No," I said. "No, they copy the mind as it is. They can't . . . they can't undo . . ."

She took a deep breath, clearly trying to calm herself.

"I'm sorry," I said. "I wish there was some way, but . . ."

She nodded.

"But they *can* do something for me—before it's too late."

"So, they move . . . they move your soul?"

I looked at my mother, totally surprised. Maybe that's why she still came to visit Dad—she thought, somewhere under all the damage, his soul was still there.

I'd read so much about this, and wanted to tell it all to her, make her see. Before the twentieth century, people had believed there was an *élan vital*—a life force, some special ingredient that distinguished living matter from regular stuff. But as biologists and chemists found mundane natural explanations for every aspect of life, the notion of an *élan vital* had been discarded as superfluous.

But the idea that there was an ineffable something that composes *mind*—a soul, a spirit, a divine spark, call it what you will—still persisted in the popular imagination in some places, even though science could now explain almost every aspect of brain activity without recourse to anything but fully understood physics and chemistry; my mother's invocation of a soul was as silly as trying to cling to the notion of an *élan vital*.

But to tell her that was to tell her that her husband was totally, irretrievably gone. Of course, maybe it would be a kindness to make her understand that. But I didn't have it in my heart to be that kind.

"No," I said, "they don't move your soul. They just copy the patterns that compose your consciousness."

"Copy? Then what happens to the original?"

"They—see, you transfer the legal rights of personhood to the copy. And then, after that, the biological you has to retire from society."

"Retire where?"

"It's called High Eden."

"Where's that?"

I wished there was some other way to say it. "On the moon."

"The moon!"

"The far side of the moon, yes."

She shook her head. "When would you do this?"

"Soon," I said. "Very soon. I just—I just can't take it any longer. Being afraid if I sneeze or bend over or do nothing at all that I might end up brain damaged or a quadriplegic or dead. It's tearing me apart."

She sighed, a long, whispery sound. "Come and say good-bye before you leave for the moon."

"*This* is good-bye," I said. "I'm going to have the process done tomorrow. But the new me will still come to visit regularly."

My mother looked at her husband, then back at me. "The new you," she said, shaking her head. "I can't take losing—"

She stopped herself, but I knew what she'd been going to say: "I can't take losing the only other person in my life."

"You're not losing me," I said. "I'll still come to visit you." I gestured at Dad, who gurgled, perhaps even in response. "I'll still come to visit Dad."

My mother shook her head slightly, unbelieving.

✹

I drove sadly to my house in North York, thinking.

I hated seeing my mother like that. She'd put her whole life on hold, hoping that somehow my father would come back. Of course, she knew intellectually that the brain damage was permanent. But the intellect and the emotions don't always end up in synch. In some ways, what had happened to my mother affected me more profoundly than what had happened to my father. She loved him the way I'd always hoped someone would love me.

And there *was* someone special in my life, a woman I cared about deeply, and who, I think, felt the same way about me. Rebecca Chong was forty-one, just a little younger than me. She was a bigwig at IBM Canada, worth a lot of money in her own right. We'd known each other for about five years, and saw each other often socially, although mostly with a few other friends. But there was always something special between just the two of us.

I remember the party last New Year's Eve. Like many of our little group's get-togethers, this one was held at Rebecca's place, a luxury penthouse at Eglinton and Yonge. Rebecca loved to entertain, and her home was central for everyone in our group—and her building had direct access to the subway.

I always brought Rebecca flowers when I visited. She loved flowers, and I loved giving them to her. On New Year's Eve, I took her a dozen red roses—I asked the guy in the flower shop to make sure the color was perfect, since I couldn't tell myself. When I arrived, I gave Rebecca the flowers, and, as was our habit, we kissed on the lips. It wasn't a long kiss—we were, at least overtly, just good friends—but it always attenuated a bit more than it needed to, our lips pressed against each other's for a lingering few seconds.

I'd had lots of sex in my life, but those kisses truly excited me more. And yet—

And yet, Rebecca and I had never gone any further. Oh, her hand would occasionally rest on my arm, or even my thigh—gentle, warm touches in response to a joke or a comment or, sometimes, best of all, to nothing at all.

I did so want her, and I think—no, I *knew*: I did know it, beyond any doubt—that she wanted me, too.

But then . . .

But then I'd go with my mother to see my father again.

And it would break my heart. Not just because my mother's life had been ruined by what had happened to him. But also because it was likely that I was going to have the same thing happen to me . . . and I couldn't allow a situation to develop between Rebecca and me in which she'd end up like my mother, burdened with someone whose mind was damaged, having to put her own wonderful, vibrant life on hold to look after the husk of what had once been me.

Isn't that what love's all about, after all? Putting the needs of the other person before your own?

And yet, last New Year's Eve, when the pot had been plentiful and the wine had been flowing freely, Rebecca and I had snuggled more than usual on the couch. Of course, midnight on New Year's Eve is always special to me—it precisely marks my birthday, after all—but this one was fabulous. Our lips locked at the stroke of twelve, and we kept kissing and petting for long after that, and once Rebecca's other guests all had left, we adjourned to her bedroom, and finally, after years of flirting and fantasizing, we made love.

It had been spectacular—everything I'd imagined it might be—kissing her, touching her, caressing her, being inside her. Even in January, Toronto is never that cold anymore, and we lay in each other's arms with the bedroom window open, listening to the revelers on the street far, far below, and I for the first and only time in my life had some sense of what heaven must be like.

New Year's Day this year had fallen on a Sunday. The next day, I'd gone with my mother to see my father, and it had been very much like this afternoon's visit had been.

And even though, ever since January, I thought about Rebecca constantly, and wanted her more than I would have believed possible, I'd let things cool between us.

Because that's what you're supposed to do, right? Be more concerned about that other person's happiness?

That's what you're supposed to do.

CHAPTER 4

I looked around my living room one last time.

Of course, one version of me would return here. But for the other—the biological original—this would be its final chance to see it.

I lived alone these days, except for Clamhead, my Irish setter. There'd been a few—all right, two—women who'd moved in and out of my life, and my various homes, over the years. But no one shared this particular house. Even the guest bedroom had never been used.

But it *was* my home, and it reflected me. My mother, on the rare occasions she came here, always shook her head at the lack of bookcases. I loved to read, but did it with ebooks. Still, no bookcases meant no spaces on the shelves in front of the books for knickknacks, which was just as well, because I couldn't be bothered to dust them, and yet—yeah, yeah, I'm anal, I know—whenever the Molly Maids came in, I was always upset that all the little things that did have to be dusted got rearranged in the process.

No bookcases also meant that I had lot of exposed walls, and those, in the living room, were covered with baseball jerseys, mounted behind glass. I was a demon at electronic auctions, and baseball memorabilia was what I collected. I had every permutation of Toronto Blue Jays jersey—including the lamentable ones from the zeros, when they'd temporarily dropped the "Blue" from their name; blue was one of the few colors I saw, and I liked the fact that the rest of the world and I apparently agreed on what the team's name meant.

My pride and joy, though, was an original Birmingham Barons jersey that had actually been worn by Michael Jordan in his brief stint in baseball; he'd joined the White Sox, but they'd bumped him down to their minor-league team as number 45. Jordan had signed the jersey on the right sleeve, between two of the pinstripes.

I had a suitcase open on the couch, containing some clothes. I was supposed to fill it with things that I wanted to take with me to the moon, but I found myself torn. Yes, this biological me was going to head to the moon tomorrow, never to return. But another me—the Mindscan version—would come back here in a few days; this house would be its—*my*—home. Anything the old me took from here would be missed by the new me—and the new me would have decades (I still couldn't easily think "centuries" or "millennia") to enjoy it, while the old me . . .

That was the one thing that I *had* packed. It wasn't a perfect solution, since if I did end up a quadriplegic or in a vegetative state, I wouldn't be able to administer it myself. But the little vial of drugs in that small unlabeled box would finish me off if need be.

People sometimes wondered why I didn't leave Canada and move to the States, a land with lower taxes for the rich. The answer was simple: physician-assisted suicide was legal here, and my will specified the conditions under which I wanted to be terminated. In the States, ever since the Buchanan administration—Pat, not James—doctors were legally obligated to keep me alive even if I had severe brain damage or couldn't move; they'd keep me alive *despite* my wishes.

But, of course, on the moon, there were no national laws to worry about; there were just a few scientific outposts and private-sector manufacturing facilities there. Immortex would do what I wanted. They had every client swear out an advance directive, describing precisely what to do in case they became incapacitated or ended up in a persistent vegetative state. If I could do it myself, I would, and the kit I'd packed, a kit that had lived in my night-table drawer for years, would do the trick.

It was the one item I knew the artificial me wouldn't miss.

I set up the robokitchen to take care of feeding my dog while—well, I was about to say, "While I was gone," but that's not quite right. But it would feed her during the changing of the guard . . .

"Well, Clamhead," I said, scratching the old girl vigorously behind the ears, "I guess that's it. You be a good girl, now."

She barked her agreement, and I headed for the door.

Immortex's facility was in Markham, a high-tech haven in the northern part of Toronto. I drove out to my appointment, heading east along the 407—somewhat irritated that I had to do the driving. Where the hell was the self-driving car? I understood that flying cars would likely never exist—too much potential for major damage when one came crashing out of the sky. But when I'd been a boy, they'd promised there would be self-driving cars soon. Alas, so many of the things that had been predicted had been based on the school of thought known as strong AI—the notion that artificial intelligence as powerful, intuitive, and effective as human intelligence would soon be developed. The complete failure of strong AI had taken a lot of people by surprise.

Immortex's technique detoured around that roadblock. Instead of *replicating* consciousness—which would require understanding exactly how it worked—the Immortex scientists simply *copied* consciousness. The copy was as intelligent, and as aware, as the original. But a *de novo* AI, programmed from the ground up, such as Hal 9000—the computer from that tedious movie whose title was the year I had been born—was still an unfulfilled fantasy.

Immortex's facility wasn't large—but, then, they weren't a high-volume business. Not yet. I noted that the entire first row of parking spaces was designated for handicapped visitors—far more than Ontario law required, but, then again, Immortex catered to an unusual demographic. I parked in the second row and got out.

The wall of heat hit me like a physical blow. Southern Ontario in August had supposedly been hot and muggy even a century ago. Little incremental increases, year by year, had all but banished snow from Toronto's winters and had made high summer almost unbearable. Still, I couldn't complain too much; those in the southern U.S. had it far, far worse—doubtless that was one of the reasons that Karen had moved from the South to Detroit.

I got my overnight bag, with the things I'd need for my stay here at Immortex, out of the back seat. I then walked quickly to the front door, but found myself perspiring as I did so. That would be another advantage of an artificial body, no doubt: no more sweating like the proverbial pig. Still, I might have been sweating anyway today, even if it hadn't been so bloody hot; I was certainly nervous. I went through the revolving glass door, and took a nice, deep breath of the cool air inside. I then presented myself to the receptionist, who was seated behind a long granite counter. "Hi," I said, surprised at how dry my mouth was. "I'm Jacob Sullivan."

The receptionist was a young, pretty, white woman. I was just as used to seeing men holding that job, but the clients of Immortex had grown up in the last century—they expected eye candy at the front desk. She consulted an air screen, holographic data floating in front of her. "Ah, yes. You're a bit early, I'm afraid; they're still calibrating the Mindscan equipment." She looked at my overnight bag, then said, "Do you also have your luggage for the moon?"

Words I'd never thought I'd hear in my life. "In the trunk of my car," I said.

"You understand the mass-allowance limits? Of course, you can take more, but we'll have to charge you for it, and it might not go on today's flight."

"No, that's fine. I ended up not bringing very much. Just a few changes of clothes."

"You won't miss your old stuff," said the woman. "High Eden is fabulous, and they have *everything* you could possibly want."

"Have you been there?"

"Me? No, not yet. But, you know, in a few decades . . ."

"Really? You're planning to upload?"

"Oh, sure. Immortex has a great employee plan for that. It helps you save for the Mindscan process, and the expenses of keeping your original alive on the moon."

"Well . . . um, see you in . . ."

The woman laughed. "I'm twenty-two, Mr. Sullivan. Don't take this personally, but I'll be disappointed if I see you again in anything less than sixty years."

I smiled. "It's a date."

She indicated a luxuriously appointed waiting area. "Won't you have a seat? We'll get your luggage later. The airport van doesn't show up until mid-afternoon."

I smiled again and walked over.

"Well, look who's here!" said a voice with a Southern accent.

"Karen!" I said, looking at the old, gray-haired woman. "How are you?"

"Soon to be beside myself, I hope."

I laughed. I'd had butterflies in my stomach, but felt them being dispelled.

"So, what are you doing here?" asked Karen.

I sat down opposite her. "I'm—oh. I never told you, did I? I have a condition—they call it an arteriovenous malformation: bad blood vessels in my brain. I—that night, I was checking out the procedure for myself."

"I kind of thought so," said Karen. "And you've obviously decided to undergo it."

I nodded.

"Well, good—"

"Excuse me," said the receptionist, who had walked over to join us. "Mr. Sullivan, would you like something to drink?"

"Um, sure. Coffee? Double-double."

"We can only give you decaf before the scanning. Is that okay?"

"Sure."

"And Ms. Bessarian," asked the receptionist, "would you like anything else?"

"I'm fine, thanks."

The receptionist moved away.

"Bessarian?" I repeated, my heart pounding. *"Karen Bessarian?"*

Karen smiled her lopsided smile. "That's me."

"You wrote *DinoWorld?*"

"Yes."

"DinoWorld. Return to DinoWorld. DinoWorld Reborn. You wrote all of those?"

"Yes, I did."

"Wow." I paused, trying to think of something better to say, but couldn't. "Wow."

"Thank you."

"I *loved* those books."

"Thank you."

"I mean, I really *loved* them. But I guess you hear that a lot."

Her wrinkled face creased even more as she smiled again. "I never quite get tired of it."

"No, no. Of course not. I actually own hardcopies of those books—that's how much I like them. Did you ever think they were going to be so successful?"

"I never even thought they were going to be *published*. I was as surprised as anyone when they became as big as they did."

"What do you think made them such huge hits?"

She lifted her bony shoulders. "That's not for me to say."

"I think it's that kids could enjoy them and adults could, too," I said. "Like the *Harry Potter* stuff."

"Well, there's no doubt that I owe a lot of my success to J. K. Rowling."

"Not that your books are anything like hers, but they've got that same broad appeal."

" '*Finding Nemo* meets *Harry Potter* by way of *Jurassic Park*'—that's what the *New York Times* said back when my first book was published. Anthropomorphic animals: my intelligent dinosaurs seemed to appeal to people the same way those talking fish did."

"What did you think of the movies they made of your books?"

"Oh, I loved them," said Karen. "They were fabulous. Fortunately, they made my movies after the *Harry Potter* and *Lord of the Rings* films. It used to be that studios acquired novels just so they could butcher them; the end product was nothing like the original book. But after *Harry Potter* and the Tolkien films, they realized that there was an even bigger market for faithful adaptations. In fact, audiences got angry when a favorite scene was missing, or a memorable line of dialog was changed."

"I can't believe I'm sitting here talking to the creator of Prince Scales."

She smiled that lopsided smile again. "Everybody has to be somewhere."

"So, Prince Scales—he's such a vivid character! Who's he based on?"

"No one," said Karen. "I made him up."

I shook my head. "No, no—I mean, who was the inspiration?"

"Nobody. He's a product of my imagination."

I nodded knowingly. "Ah, okay. You don't want to say. Afraid he'll sue, eh?"

The old woman frowned. "No, it's nothing like that. Prince Scales doesn't exist, isn't real, isn't based on anyone real, isn't a portrait or a parody. I just made him up."

I looked at her, but said nothing.

"You don't believe me, do you?" Karen asked.

"I wouldn't say that, but—"

She shook her head. "People are desperate to believe writers base our characters on real people, that the events in our novels really happened in some disguised way."

"Ah," I said. "Sorry. I—I guess it's an ego thing. I can't imagine making up a publishable story, so I don't want to believe that others have that capability. Talents like that make the rest of us feel inadequate."

"No," said Karen. "No, if you don't mind me saying so, it goes deeper than that, I think. Don't you see? The idea that false people can just be manufactured goes to the heart of our religious beliefs. When I say that Prince Scales doesn't really exist, and you've only been fooled into thinking that he does, then I open up the possibility that Moses didn't exist—that some writer just made him up. Or that Mohammed didn't really say and do the things ascribed to him. Or that Jesus is a fictional character, too. The whole of our spiritual existence is based on this unspoken assumption that writers *record*, but they don't fabricate—and that, even if they did, we could tell the difference."

I looked around the waiting room, here at this place where they mated android bodies with scanned copies of brains. "I'm glad I'm an atheist," I said.

CHAPTER 5

Three more people arrived while we were waiting: others who'd decided to upload. But the receptionist called for me first, and I left Karen chatting with her fellow very senior citizens. I followed the receptionist down the brightly lit corridor, enjoying the swaying of her youthful hips, and was taken to an office with walls that looked gray to me—meaning they could have been that color, or green, or magenta.

"Hello, Jake," said Dr. Porter, rising from his chair. "Good to see you again."

Andrew Porter was a tall bear of a man, sixty or so, slightly stooped from dealing with a world populated by shorter people. He had squinty eyes, a beard, and hair combed straight back from a high forehead. His kindly face was home to eyebrows that seemed constantly in motion, as if they were working out, in training for the body-hair Olympics.

"Hello, Dr. Porter," I said. I'd seen him twice before now, on previous visits here, during which I'd undergone various medical tests, filled out legal forms, and had my body—but not yet my brain—scanned.

"Are you ready to see it?" asked Porter.

I swallowed, then nodded.

"Good, good." There was another door to the room, and Porter opened it with a theatrical flourish. "Jake Sullivan," he declared, "welcome to your new home!"

In the next room, lying on a gurney, was a synthetic body, wearing a white terry-cloth robe.

I felt my jaw dropping as I looked down at it. The resemblance was remarkable. Although there was a touch of department-store mannequin to the general appearance, it still was, without a doubt, me. The eyes were open, unblinking and unmoving. The mouth was closed. The arms lay limply at the sides.

"The boys and girls in Physiognomy tell me you were a cinch," said Porter, grinning. "Usually, we're trying to roll back the clock several decades, recreating what a person had looked like when they were in their prime; after all, no one wants to upload into a body that looks like it's on its last legs. You're the youngest person they've ever had to do."

It was my face, all right—the same long shape; the same cleft chin; the same thin lips; the same wide mouth; the same close-together eyes, the same dark eyebrows above them. Crowning it all was thick dark hair. All the gray had been removed, and—I craned to look—the duplicate had no bald spot.

"A few minor touch-ups," said Porter, grinning. "Hope you don't mind."

I'm sure I was grinning, too. "Not at all. It's—it's quite amazing."

"We're pleased. Of course, the underlying synthetic skull is identical in shape to yours—it was made with 3D-prototyping equipment from the stereo x-rays we took; it even has the same pattern of sutures, marking where the separate skull bones fused together."

I'd had to sign a release for the extensive x-rays used to produce the artificial skeleton. I'd received a big enough dose in one day to increase my future likelihood of cancer—but, then again, most Immortex clients were going to die soon, long before any cancers could pose a problem.

Porter touched the side of the simulated head; the jaw opened, revealing the highly detailed mouth within.

"The teeth are exact copies of your own layout—we've even embedded a denser ceramic composite at the right points to match the two fillings you have: dental biometrics would identify this head as being yours. Now, you can see there's a tongue, but, of course, we don't actually use the tongue for speech; that's all done with voice-synthesizer chips. But it should do a pretty good job of faking it. The opening and closing of the jaw will match the sounds being produced perfectly—kind of like Supermarionation."

"Like what?" I said.

"Thunderbirds? Captain Scarlet?"

I shook my head.

Porter sighed. "Well, anyway, the tongue is very complex—the most complex part of the re-creation, actually. It doesn't have taste buds, since you won't need to eat, but it is pressure sensitive and, as I said, it will make the appropriate movements to match what your voice chip is saying."

"It's really . . . uncanny," I said, and then I smiled. "I think that's the first time I've ever actually used that word."

Porter laughed, but then pointed at me. "Now, sadly we haven't been able to replicate that: when you smile, you've got a great dimple in your left cheek.

The artificial head doesn't do that. We've noted it in your file, though—I'm sure we'll be able to add it in a future upgrade."

"That's okay," I said. "You've done a terrific job as is."

"Thanks. We like people to become familiar with the appearance before we transfer them into an artificial body—it's good that you know what to expect. Are there any particular activities you're looking forward to?"

"Baseball," I said at once.

"That will take a lot of eye-hand coordination, but it will come."

"I want to be as good as Singh-Samagh."

"Who?" asked Porter.

"He's a starting pitcher for the Blue Jays."

"Oh. I don't follow the game. I can't guarantee you'll ever be professional caliber, but you'll definitely be at least as good, if not better, than you were before."

He went on. "You'll find that all the proportions are exactly the same as your current body—the length of each finger segment, of each limb segment, and so on. Your mind has built up a very sophisticated model of what your body is like—how long your arms are, at what point along their length the elbow or knee occurs, *et cetera*. That mental model is adaptable while you're still growing, but becomes pretty firmly entrenched in middle age. We've tried making short people tall, and correcting for mismatched limb lengths, but it created more problems than it was worth—people have a lot of trouble adjusting to a body that isn't like their original."

"Um, does that mean . . . ? I'd thought . . ."

Porter laughed. "Ah, yes. We do mention that in our literature. Well, you see, the male sex organ is a special case: it varies substantially in size depending on temperature, arousal, and so on. So, yes, as a matter of course, we upsize what nature provided in the original, unless you specifically indicated you didn't want that on the forms you filled out; the mind is already used to the penis having variable form, so it seems to deal well with an extra few centimeters." Porter pulled at the terry-cloth sash holding the robe closed.

"My goodness," I said, feeling awfully silly, but also awfully impressed. "Um, thank you."

"We aim to please," said Porter, with a beatific smile.

Ray Kurzweil had been the most vocal proponent around the time I was born of moving our minds into artificial bodies. His books from that time—the classic is *The Age of Spiritual Machines*, from 1999—proposed that within thirty years of *then* (meaning sixteen years ago from now)—it would be possible to copy "the locations, interconnections, and contents of all the somas, axons, dendrites, presynaptic vesicles, neurotransmitter concentrations, and other neural components and levels" of an individual's mind, so that that mind's "entire organization can then be re-created on a neural computer of sufficient capacity, including the contents of its memory."

It's fun re-reading that book today, with 20/20—hell, with 2045—hindsight. Kurzweil got some things right, but missed out on several other key points. For instance, the technology to scan the brain at the supposedly required level of resolution appeared in the year 2019, but it turned out to do no good because the scanning took hours to complete, and, of course, even a sedated individual's brain undergoes all sorts of transitions during that period. Stitching together data about the brain over such a lengthy period produced a nonfunctional mess; it was impossible to match up visual impulses (or lack thereof) from the back of the head with thoughts about completely different impulses from the front of the head. Consciousness is the synchronized action of the *entirety* of the brain; scans that take anything more than mere moments to make would always be useless for reconstituting it.

But Immortex's Mindscan process allowed the taking of an overall, comprehensive, instantaneous snapshot. Dr. Porter took me down the hall to the scanning room, which had walls that looked orange to me. "Jake," said Porter, "this is Dr. Killian." He indicated a plain-looking black woman of about thirty. "Dr. Killian is one of our quantum physicists. She'll operate the scanning equipment."

Killian stepped toward me. "And it won't hurt a bit, I promise," she said with a Jamaican accent.

"Thank you," I replied.

"I'll get back to my end," said Porter. Killian smiled at him, and he left.

"I think you know," Killian continued, "that we use quantum fog to do our brain scans. We permeate your head with subatomic particles—the fog. Those particles are quantally entangled with identical particles that Dr. Porter will soon be injecting into the artificial braincase of the new body he showed you; that body is still down the corridor, but distance doesn't matter to quantum entanglement."

I nodded; I also knew that Immortex had a strict policy about never letting the upload meet the original after transference. You could have a family member or a lawyer confirm that the upload and the original were both functioning just fine after the copying process, but despite Karen's earlier quip about looking forward to being beside herself, it was considered psychologically bad for two versions of the same person to ever meet; it destroyed one's sense of personal uniqueness.

Dr. Killian made a concerned face. "Now, I understand you have an AVM," she said. "But of course your new body doesn't rely on a circulatory system, so that's irrelevant to it."

I nodded. In just a few more minutes, I'd be free! My heart was pounding.

"All you have to do," continued Dr. Killian, "is lie down on this bed, here. We slide it into that scanning chamber—looks a bit like an MRI, doesn't it? And then we make the scan. It only takes about five minutes, and almost all of that is just setting up the scanners."

The idea that I was about to *diverge* was daunting. The me that was going to come out of this scanning cylinder would go on with its life, heading this afternoon to Pearson to catch the spaceplane, and from there it would go to the moon to live—how long? A few months? A few years? Whatever paltry amount his Katerinsky's would allow.

And the other Jake—who would just as vividly remember *this* moment— would soon go home and pick up his life where I'd left it off, but without potential brain damage or an early death hanging over his titanium head.

Two versions.

It was incredible.

I wished there was some way to copy only parts of myself, but that would require an understanding of the mind beyond what Immortex currently had. Too bad: there were plenty of memories I'd be happy to have edited out. The circumstances of Dad's injury, of course. But other things, too: embarrassments, thoughts I wasn't proud of, times when I'd hurt others and others had hurt me.

I lay down on the bed, which was attached by metal floor-mounted tracks to the scanning chamber.

"You push the green button to slide in," said Killian, "and the red one to slide out." By old habit, I watched carefully to see which button she was gesturing to at which point. I nodded.

"Good," she said. "Press the green button."

I did so, and the bed slid into the scanning tube. It was quiet in there—so quiet I could hear my pulse in my ears, the gurgling of my digestion. I wondered what internal sounds, if any, I'd be aware of in my new body?

Regardless, I was looking forward to my new existence. Quantity of life didn't matter that much to me—but quality! And to have *time*—not only years spreading out into the future, but time in each day. Uploads, after all, didn't have to sleep, so not only did we get all those extra years, we got one-third more productive time.

The future was at hand.

Creating another me.

Mindscan.

"All right, Mr. Sullivan, you can come out now." It was Dr. Killian's voice, with its Jamaican lilt.

My heart sank. *No . . .*

"Mr. Sullivan? We've finished the scanning. If you'll press the red button . . ."

It hit me like a ton of bricks, like a tidal wave of blood. *No!* I should be somewhere else, but I wasn't.

Damn it all, I wasn't.

"If you need some help getting out . . ." offered Killian.

I reflexively brought up my hands, patting my chest, feeling the softness of it, feeling it rise and fall. *Jesus Christ!*

"Mr. Sullivan?"

"I'm coming, damn it. I'm coming."

I hit the button without looking at it, and the bed slid out of the scanning tube, emerging feet-first; a breech birth. *Damn! Damn! Damn!*

I hadn't exerted myself at all, but my breathing was rapid, shallow. *If only—*

I felt a hand cupping my elbow. "I've got you, Mr. Sullivan," said Killian. "Upsa-daisy . . ." My feet connected with the harsh tile floor. I had known intellectually that it had been a fifty-fifty shot, but I'd only thought about what it was going to be like to wake up in a new, healthy, artificial body. I hadn't really considered . . .

"Are you all right, Mr. Sullivan?" she asked. "You look—"

"I'm *fine*," I snapped. "Fine *and* dandy. Jesus Christ—"

"Is there something I can—"

"I'm doomed. Don't you get it?"

She frowned. "Do you want me to call a medical doctor?"

I shook my head. "You just scanned my consciousness, making a duplicate of my mind, right?" My voice was sneering. "And since I'm aware of things after you finished the scanning, that means I—*this* version—*isn't* that copy. The *copy* doesn't have to worry about becoming a vegetable anymore—it's free. Finally and at last, it's free of everything that's been hanging over my head for the last twenty-seven years. We've diverged now, and the cured me has started down its path. But *this* me is still doomed. I could have woken up in a new, healed body, but—"

Killian's voice was gentle. "But, Mr. Sullivan, *one* of you was bound to still be in this body . . ."

"I know, I know, I know." I shook my head, and took a few paces forward. There was no window in the scanning room, which was probably just as well; I don't think I was quite ready to face the world. "And the one of us that is still in this bloody body, with this fucked brain, is still doomed."

CHAPTER 6

I was suddenly somewhere else.

It was an instantaneous transfer, like changing channels on TV. I *instantly* was somewhere else—in a different room.

At first I was overwhelmed by strange physical sensations. My limbs felt numb, as though I'd slept on them funny. But I hadn't been sleeping . . .

And then I was conscious of the things that I wasn't feeling: there was no pain in my left ankle. For the first time in two years, since I'd torn some ligaments falling down a staircase, I felt no pain at all.

But I *remembered* the pain, and—

I did remember!

I was still myself.

I remembered my childhood in Port Credit.

I remembered being beaten up every day on the way to school by Colin Hagey.

I remembered the first time I'd read Karen Bessarian's *DinoWorld*.

I remembered delivering *The Toronto Star*—back when papers were physically delivered.

I remembered the great blackout of 2015, and the darkest sky I'd ever seen.

And I remembered my dad collapsing in front of my eyes.

I remembered it all.

"Mr. Sullivan? Mr. Sullivan, it's me, Dr. Porter. You may have some trouble speaking at first. Do you want to try?"

"Ell-o." The word sounded strange, so I repeated it several times: "Ell-o. Ell-o. Ell-o." My voice didn't seem quite right. But, then again, I was hearing it much as Porter was, through my own external microphones—ears, ears, ears!—rather than resonating through the nasal cavities and bones of a biological head.

"Very good!" said Porter; he was a disembodied voice—somewhere out of my field of view, but I wasn't yet properly registering his location. "No respiratory asperity," he continued, "but you'll learn how to do that. Now, you may have a lot of unusual sensations, but you shouldn't be in any pain. Are you?"

"No." I was lying on my back, presumably on the gurney I'd seen earlier, staring up at the plain white ceiling. There *was* a general paucity of sensation, a sort of numbness—although there was some gentle pressure on my body from, I supposed, the terry-cloth robe that I was presumably now wearing.

"Good. If at any point pain begins, let me know. It can take a little while for your mind to learn how to interpret the signals it's receiving; we can fix any discomfort that might arise, all right?"

"Yes."

"Good. Now, before we start trying to move, let's make sure you can fully communicate. Can you count backwards from ten for me, please?"

"Ten. Nine. Eight. Seven. Six. Five. Four. Tree. Two. One. Zero."

"Very good. Let's try that 'three' once more."

"Tree. *Tree. Tuh-ree.*"

"Keep trying."

"Tree. Dree."

"It's an aspiration issue again, but you'll get it."

"Dree. Tree. Thuh-ree. *Three!*"

I heard Porter's hands clapping together. "Perfect!"

"Three! Three! Three!"

"By George, I think he's got it!"

"Three! Thought, thing, teeth, theater, bath, math. Three!"

"Excellent. Are you still feeling okay?"

"Still—oh."

"What?" asked Porter.

"My vision went off for a moment, but it's back."

"Really? That shouldn't—"

"Oh, and there it goes—"

"Mr. Sullivan? Mr. Sullivan?"

"I—it feels . . . oh . . ."

"Mr. Sullivan? Mr. Sulli—!"

Nothingness, for how long, I had no idea. Just total nothingness. When I came to, I spoke.

"Doc! Doc! Are you there?"

"Jake!" Porter's voice. He let air out noisily in a "that's a relief!" sort of way.

"Is something wrong, Doc? What was that?"

"Nothing. Nothing at all. Um, ah, how do you feel now?"

"It's strange," I said. "I feel *different*—in a 'undred ways I can't describe."

Porter was quiet for a moment; perhaps he was distracted by something. But then he said, "Hundred."

"What?"

"You said 'undred, not hundred. Try to get the *H* sound."

" 'Undred. 'Undred. Huhn-dred. Hundred."

"Good," said Porter. "It's normal for there to be some differences in sensations, but as long as you're basically feeling okay . . . ?"

"Yes," I said again. "I feel just fine."

And I knew, in that instant, that I was *fine*. I was relaxed. For the first time in ages, I felt calm, safe. I wasn't going to suddenly have a massive cerebral hemorrhage. Rather, I was going to live a full normal life. I'd get my biblical three-score-and-ten; I'd get the Statistics Canada eighty-eight years for males born in 2001; I'd get all of that and more. I was going to *live*. Everything else was secondary. I was going to live a good, long time, without paralysis, without being a vegetable. Whatever settling-in difficulties I encountered would be worth it. I knew that at once.

"Very good," said Porter. "Now, let's try something simple. See if you can turn your head toward me."

I did so—and nothing happened. "It's not working, doc."

"Don't worry. It'll come. Try again."

I did, and this time my head did loll left, and—

And—and—and—

Oh, my God! Oh, my God! Oh, my God!

"That chair over there," I said. "What color is it?"

Porter turned, surprised. "Um, green."

"Green! So *that's* what green looks like! It's—*cool*, isn't it? Soothing. And your shirt, doc? What color is your shirt?"

"Yellow."

"Yellow! Wow!"

"Mr. Sullivan, are you—are you color-blind?"

"Not anymore!"

"Good God. Why didn't you tell us?"

Why hadn't I told them? "Because you hadn't asked" was one true answer, but I knew there were others. Mostly I was afraid if I had told them, they'd have insisted on duplicating that aspect of who I'd been.

"What kind of color blindness do—*did*—you have?"

"Doo-something."

"You're deutanopic?" said Porter. "You've got M-cone deficiency?"

"That's it, yes." Almost nobody has true color blindness; that is, almost no one sees only in black and white. We deuteranopes see the world in shades of blue, orange, and gray, so that many colors that contrast sharply for people with normal vision look the same to us. Specifically, we see red and greenish-yellow as beige; magenta and green as gray; both orange and yellow as what I'd been told was a brick color; both blue-green and purple as mauve; and both indigo and cyan as cornflower blue. Only medium blue and medium orange look the same to us as they do to people with normal vision.

"But you're seeing color now?" asked Porter. "Astonishing."

"That it is," I said, delighted. "It's all so—so *garish*. I don't think I ever understood that word before. What an overwhelming variety of shades!" I rolled my head the other way, this time without thinking about it. I found myself facing a window. "The grass—my God, look at it! And the sky! How *different* they are from each other!"

"We'll show you something colorful on vid later today, and—"

"*Finding Nemo*," I said at once. "It was my favorite movie when I was a kid—and everybody said it was just *full* of color."

Porter laughed. "If you like."

"Great," I said. "Lucky fin!" I tried to move my right arm in imitation of Nemo's fishy high five, but it didn't actually rise. Ah, well—it would take time; they'd warned me about that.

Still, it felt *wonderful* to be alive, to be free.

"Try again, Jake," said Porter. He astonished me by lifting his own arm in the "lucky fin!" gesture.

I made another attempt, and this time I was successful. "There, you see," said Porter, his eyebrows working as always. "You'll be fine. Now, let's get you out of this bed."

He took hold of my right arm—I could feel it as a matrix of a thousand points of pressure, instead of one smooth contact—and he helped me sit up. I used to suffer from occasional lightheadedness, and sometimes got dizzy when rising from the horizontal, but there was none of that.

I was in a bizarre sensory state. In most ways, I was *under*stimulated: I wasn't conscious of any smells, and although I could tell I was now sitting up, which meant I had some notion of balance, there wasn't any great downward pressure on the back of my thighs or my rear end. But my visual sense was *over*stimulated, assaulted by colors I'd never seen before. And if I looked at something featureless—like the wall—I could just make out the mesh of pixels that composed my vision.

"How are you doing?" asked Porter.

"Fine," I said. "Wonderful!"

"Good. Perhaps now is a good time to tell you about the secret missions we're going to send you out on."

"What?!"

"You know, bionic limbs. Spying. Secret-agent cyborg stuff."

"Dr. Porter, I—"

Porter's eyebrows were dancing with glee. "Sorry. I expect I'll eventually get tired of doing that, but so far it's been fun every time. The only mission we have is to get you out of here, and back to your normal life. And that means getting you on your feet. Shall we give it a try?"

I nodded, and felt his arm under my elbow. Again the sensation wasn't quite like normal pressure against skin, but I was certainly conscious of exactly where he was touching me. He helped me rotate my body until my legs dangled over the side of the gurney, and then he helped hoist me to a vertical position. He waited until I nodded that I was okay, and then he gingerly let go of me, allowing me to stand on my own.

"How does it feel?" Porter asked.

"Fine," I said.

"Any dizziness? Any vertigo?"

"No. Nothing like that. But it's weird not breathing."

Porter nodded. "You'll get used to it—although you may have some momentary panic attacks: times when your brain shouts out, 'Hey, we're not breathing!'" He smiled his kindly smile. "I'd tell you to take a deep calming breath in those circumstances, but of course you can't. So just fight down the sensation, or wait for it to pass. Do you feel panicky now because you're not breathing?"

I thought about that. "No. No, it's all right. Strange, though."

"Take your time. We're in no rush here."

"I know."

"Do you want to try taking a step?"

"Sure," I said. But it was a few moments before I put word to deed. Porter was clearly poised to act, ready to catch me if I stumbled. I lifted my right leg, flexing my knee, swinging my thigh up, and letting my weight shift forward. It was a lurching first step, but it worked. I then tried lifting my left leg, but it swung wide, and—

God damn it!

I found myself pitching forward, completely off balance, the tiles, whose color was new to me and I couldn't yet name, rushing toward my face.

Porter caught my arm and pulled me upright. "I can see we have our work cut out for us," he said.

"This way please, Mr. Sullivan," said Dr. Killian.

I thought about making a run for it. I mean, what could they do? I'd wanted to live forever, without a fate worse than death hanging over my head, but that was not to be. Not for *this* me, anyway. Me and my shadow: we were diverging rapidly. It—*he*, he—was doubtless somewhere else in this facility. But the rules were that I could never meet him. That was not so much for my benefit as his; he was supposed to regard himself as the one and only Jacob Sullivan, and seeing me still around—flesh where he was plastic; bone where he was steel—would make that feat of self-delusion more difficult.

Those were the rules.

Rules? Just terms in a contract I'd signed.

So, if I *did* make a break for it—

If I did run outside, into that sweltering August heat, and took my car, and raced back to my house, what sanction could be brought against me?

Of course, the other me would show up there eventually, too, and want to call the place his own.

Maybe we could live together. Like twins. Peas in a pod.

But, no, that wouldn't work. I rather suspect you had to be born to that. Living with another me—I mean, Christ, I am so particular about where things are and, besides, he'd be up all night, doing God knows what, while I'd be trying to sleep.

No. No, there was no turning back.

"Mr. Sullivan?" Killian said again in her lilting Jamaican voice. "This way, please." I nodded, and let her lead me down a corridor I hadn't seen before. We walked a short distance and then we came to a pair of frosted-glass sliding doors. Killian touched her thumb to a scanner plate, and the doors moved aside. "Here you are," she said. "When we've finished scanning everyone, the driver will take you to the airport."

I nodded.

"You know, I envy you," she said. "Getting away from—from *everything*. You won't be disappointed, Mr. Sullivan. High Eden is wonderful."

"You been there?" I asked.

"Oh, yes," she said. "You don't just open a resort like that cold. We had two weeks of dry-runs, with senior Immortex staff playing the parts of residents, to make sure the service was perfect."

"And?"

"It *is* perfect. You'll love it."

"Yeah," I said, looking away. There was no sign of an escape route. "I'm sure I will."

CHAPTER 7

I was sitting in a wheelchair in Dr. Porter's office, waiting for him to return. I wasn't the first Mindscan to have trouble walking, he said. Perhaps not. But I probably hated being in a wheelchair more than most—after all, that was how they moved my father around. I'd been trying to avoid that fate, and instead had ended up echoing it.

But I wasn't brooding too much about it. Indeed, the combined excitement of getting a new body and seeing new colors was overwhelming, so much so that I was only dimly aware of the fact that the original me must now have started on his journey to the moon. I wished him well. But I wasn't supposed to think about him, and I tried not to.

In some ways, of course, it would have been easier just to shut that other me off. Funny way of phrasing it: the other one was the biological version, not this one. But "shutting it off"—*it*, now!—had been the way the thought had come to me. After all, this whole rigmarole with a retirement community on Lunar Farside would be unnecessary if the original could be discarded now that it was no longer needed.

But the law would never stand for that—not even here in Canada, let alone south of the border. Ah, well, I'd never see the other me again, so what did it matter? *I*—this me, the new-improved, in-living-color Jacob Paul Sullivan—was the one and only real me from now on, until the end of time.

Finally, Porter returned. "Here's someone who might be able to help you," he said. "We've got technicians, of course, who could work with you on your walking, Jake, but it occurred to me that she might be better able to give you a hand. I think you already know each other."

From my position in the wheelchair I looked at the woman who had just entered the room, but I couldn't place the face. She was plain, perhaps thirty, with dark hair sensibly short, and—

And she was *artificial*. I hadn't realized it until she moved her head just so, and the light caught her in a certain way.

"Hello, Jake," she said, with a lovely Georgia drawl. Her voice was stronger than before, with no quavering. She was wearing a beautiful sun dress with a floral print; I was still sulking in my terry-cloth robe.

"Karen?" I said. "My goodness, look at you!"

She spun around—apparently she was having no difficulty controlling her new body. "You like?" she said.

I smiled. "You look fabulous."

She laughed; it sounded a bit forced, but that was surely because it was generated by a voice chip, rather than that the mirth was insincere. "Oh, I've *never* looked fabulous. This"—she spread her arms—"is what I looked like in 1990. I'd thought about going younger, but that would have been silly."

"Nineteen-ninety," I repeated. "So you would have been—"

"Thirty," Karen said, without hesitation. But I was surprised at myself; I knew better than to ask a woman her age; I'd intended to keep my little bit of mental math private.

She went on: "It seemed a sensible compromise between youth and maturity. I doubt I could fake how vacuous I was at twenty."

"You look great," I said again.

"Thanks," she said. "So do you."

I doubted my synthetic flesh was capable of blushing, but that's what I felt like doing. "Just a few touch-ups here and there."

Dr. Porter said, "I asked Ms. Bessarian if she would work with you for a bit. See, she's been through this in a way even our technicians haven't."

"Through what?" I asked.

"Learning to walk again as an adult," said Karen.

I looked at her, not getting it.

"After my stroke," Karen supplied, smiling.

"Ah, right," I said. Her smile was no longer lopsided; the stroke damage would have been faithfully copied in the nanogel of her new brain, I supposed, but maybe they had some electronic trick that simply made the left half of her mouth execute a mirror image of whatever the right half was doing.

"I'll leave you to it, then," said Porter. He made a show of rubbing his belly. "Maybe I'll grab a late lunch—you folks are lucky enough not to need to eat anymore, but I'm getting hungry."

"And besides," said Karen, and I swear there was a twinkle in one of her synthetic green eyes, "letting one Mindscan help another is probably good for both of them, right? Lets them both know that there are others like them, and gets them away from the alienating feeling of being poked and prodded by scientists."

Porter made an impressed face. "I could have sworn you didn't opt for the x-ray vision option," he said, "but you see right through me, Ms. Bessarian. You're a psychologist at heart."

"I'm a novelist," Karen said. "Same thing."

Porter smiled. "Now, if you'll excuse me . . ."

He left the room, and Karen appraised me, hands on hips. "So," she said, "you're having trouble walking."

She was reasonably small, but I still had to look up at her from the wheelchair. "Yeah," I said, the syllable mixing embarrassment and frustration.

"Don't worry about it," she said. "You'll be fine. You can teach your mind to make your body obey it. Believe me, I know—not only did I have to deal with a stroke, but when I was a girl down in Atlanta, I used to dance ballet— you learn a lot about how to control your body doing that. So, shall we get started?"

My whole life, I'd been terrible at asking for help; I somehow thought it was a sign of weakness. But here I wasn't asking for it; it was being freely offered. And, I had to admit, I did need it.

"Um, sure," I said.

Karen brought her hands together in front of her chest in a clap. I remembered how swollen her joints had been before, how translucent her skin. But now her hands were supple, youthful. "Wonderful!" she exclaimed. "We'll have you back to normal in no time." She held out her right hand, I took it, and she hoisted me to my feet. Porter had given me a dark brown, wooden cane. It was leaning against the wall; I gestured to it. Karen handed it to me, and I managed to make my way out of the room into a long corridor. Fluorescent light panels covered its ceilings, and I also spotted tiny camera units hanging down at intervals. Doubtless Dr. Porter or one of his minions was watching.

"All right," said Karen, standing in front of me and facing toward me. "Remember, you can't hurt yourself by falling; you're way too durable for that now. So, let's give it a try without the cane."

I propped the cane against the corridor wall, but no sooner had I done so than it fell to the floor; not an auspicious start. "Leave it," said Karen. I lifted my left foot, and immediately teetered forward, slamming it back into the ground as I did so. I quickly lifted my right leg, swinging it around stiffly, as if it lacked a knee.

"Pay attention to exactly how your body is responding," said Karen. "I know walking is something we normally do subconsciously, but try to recognize exactly what effect you get with each mental command."

I managed a couple more steps. If I'd still been biological, I'd have been breathing deeply and sweating, but I'm sure there was no external indication of my exertion. Still, it was enormously hard work, and I felt as though I was going to tumble over. I stopped, standing motionless, trying to regain my balance.

"I know it's hard," said Karen. "But it *does* get easier. It's all a question of learning a new vocabulary: *this* thought produces *that* action, and—ah! Look, see: your upper leg moved just fine that time. Try to reproduce that mental command exactly."

I tried again to move my left leg forward, putting my weight on it, then I tried moving my right leg. This time I got a little bending to occur at the knee, but it still swung widely as it came forward.

"There," said Karen. "That's right. Your body *wants* to do the right things; you just have to tell it how."

I would have grunted, but I didn't know how to make my new body do *that* yet, either. The corridor looked frightfully long, its sides converging at what might as well have been kilometers away.

"Now," said Karen, "try another step. Concentrate—see if you can keep that right leg more under control."

"I *am* trying," I said testily, lurching forward once more.

Her drawl was kind. "I know you are, Jake."

It was hard work mentally—like the frustration you feel when trying to recall a fact that's just out of reach, multiplied a thousand fold.

"You're doing great," she said. "Really, you are." Karen was walking backwards, a half-step at a time. I briefly wondered how many years it had been since she'd walked backwards; an old woman, desperately afraid of breaking a hip or a leg, doubtless took small, shuffling steps most of the time, and forward—always forward.

I forced myself to take another step, then one more. Despite all of Immortex's best efforts to exactly copy the dimensions of my limbs, I was conscious that the center of gravity in my torso was higher up, perhaps due to my lack of hollow lungs. No big deal, but it did make me even more prone to falling forward.

And, at that moment, I realized I'd been thinking about something other than planting one foot in front of another—that my subconscious and conscious were now at least in some degree of agreement about the mechanics of walking.

"Bravo!" said Karen. "You're doing just fine." Beneath the fluorescent lights, she looked particularly artificial: her skin had a dry, plastic sheen; her eyes, not really moist, likewise looked plastic—although, as I now could appreciate, they were a really lovely shade of green.

We continued on, lurching step after lurching step; I imagined if I looked back over my shoulder, I'd see the villagers chasing me with their torches.

"That's it!" said Karen. "That's perfect!"

Another step, and—

My right leg not moving quite the way I intended—

"God—"

My left ankle twisting to one side—

"—damn—"

My torso tipping farther and farther forward—

"—it!"

Karen surged forward, easily catching me in her outstretched arms, before I could fall flat on my face.

"There, there," she said, soothingly, her new body having no trouble supporting my weight. "There, there. It's okay."

I felt humiliated and furious—at Immortex, and at myself. I pushed hard against Karen's arms, forcing myself back into a standing position. I didn't like asking for help—but I liked even less to fail when someone else was watching; indeed, it was doubly bad, since we were surely also being observed on closed-circuit video.

"That's enough for just now," she said, moving in next to me, and slipping an arm around my waist. She led me in a half-turn, and with her support, I hobbled back and got my cane.

CHAPTER 8

When I was a kid, I never thought Toronto would have a spaceport. But now almost every city did, at least potentially. Spaceplanes could take off and land on any runway big enough to accommodate a jumbo jet.

Commercial spaceflight was funny from a jurisdictional point of view. The spaceplane we were about to board would take off from Toronto and land again in Toronto; it would never visit any other country, although it would fly above lots of them at an altitude of up to 300 kilometers. Still, since it was technically a domestic flight, and since our ultimate destination, aboard a different vehicle, was the moon, which had no government, we didn't require passports. That was just as well, because we'd left them behind for our . . . "replacements" I supposed was a good-enough word.

The Jetway was already connected by the time we arrived at the departure lounge. Our spaceplane was one giant delta wing. Engines were mounted above the wing, instead of below it—to protect them in reentry, I guessed. The upper hull was painted white, and the underbelly was black. The North American Airlines logo appeared in several places, and the plane itself had a name marked in a script typeface near the leading point of the triangle: *Icarus*. I wondered what mythologically challenged suit had come up with that.

There were ten of us associated with Immortex making the flight today, plus another eighteen passengers who were going into orbit for other reasons—mostly tourism, judging by the snatches of conversation I overheard. Of the ten Immortex tickets, seven were shed skins—a term I'd overheard, although I rather suspect I wasn't supposed to—and three were staff replacements, going up to change places with people already at High Eden.

We boarded by row numbers, just like an airplane. I was in row eight, a window seat. The guy next to me turned out to be one of the staff replacements. He was about thirty, with that sort of freckly face that I'm told usually went with red hair, although I couldn't be sure what color his was.

My chair was one of the special seats Sugiyama had talked about during his sales pitch: it was covered with ergonomically sculpted padding filled with some sort of shock-absorbing gel. I wanted to protest that I didn't need a special seat—my bones were hardly brittle—but the flight was full, so there'd have been no point.

I'd gathered that safety briefings on airplanes were usually perfunctory, but we had to spend an hour and forty-five minutes listening to and participating in safety demonstrations, particularly related to what to do once we became weightless. For instance, there were vomit receptacles with attached vacuum cleaners that we had to—had to, had to!—use if we got motion sickness; apparently it's very easy to choke on your own puke in microgravity.

Finally, it was time for takeoff. The big plane pulled away from the Jetway and headed onto the runway. I could see shimmers in the air caused by heat. We rolled very, very quickly down the runway, and just before we reached its end, we shot up at quite a sharp angle. Suddenly, I was glad for the gel padding.

I looked out the window. We were flying east, which meant we had to go right by downtown Toronto. I took a last look at the CN Tower, the SkyDome, the aquarium, and the banking towers.

My home. The place I'd grown up in. The place my mother, and my father, still lived in.

The place . . .

My eyes stung a bit.

The place Rebecca Chong still lived in.

A place I'd never see again.

Already, the sky was starting to blacken.

I soon recognized the social difficulties of being in an artificial body. Biology gave excuses: I have to eat, I'm tired, I need to go to the bathroom. All of those disappeared, at least with these particular bodies. Indeed, I wondered if Immortex would ever add such things. After all, who ever really wanted to be tired? It was an inconvenience at best; dangerous at worst.

I'd always thought of myself as a basically honest guy. But it was now immediately obvious to me that I'd been a constant purveyor of little white lies. I'd relied on the subjectively plausible—perhaps I *was* tired—to get out of awkward or boring activities; when I'd been biologically instantiated, I'd had a repertoire of such phrases that would allow me to gracefully bail out of a social situation I didn't want to be in. But now, none of them would ring true— especially not to another upload. I was humiliated by my inability to walk, and desperate to get away from this ancient, mothering woman in the thirty-year-old package, but was failing to come up with a polite out.

And we had to stay here for three days of tests: this was Tuesday, so we'd be here through Friday. We each had a small room—with, ironically, a bed, not that we'd need to use it. But I did very much want to retreat there, to just be the hell alone.

I was still wearing the terry-cloth robe. I used my cane as we walked back down the corridor that had just defeated me. Karen had tried giving me a helping hand, but I'd shrugged it off, and I found myself looking away from her, and at the wall nearest me, as we continued on.

Karen was evidently looking in the same direction, since she commented on the view through the window we were passing. "Looks like rain," she said. "I wonder if we'll rust?"

At another time, I might have laughed at the joke, but I was too ashamed, and too pissed off at both myself and Immortex. Still, some response seemed to be in order. "Let's just hope it's not an electrical storm," I said. "I'm not wearing my surge protector."

Karen laughed more than my comment deserved. We continued on. "Say, I wonder if we can swim," she said.

"Why not?" I replied. "I'm sure we aren't really prone to rust."

"Oh, I know that," she said. "I'm talking about buoyancy. Humans swim so well because we float. But these new bodies might sink."

I looked over at her, impressed. "I hadn't thought about that."

"It's going to be an adventure," she said, "finding out what our new capabilities and limitations are."

I did somehow manage a grunt now; it was an odd mechanical sound.

"Don't you like adventures?" asked Karen.

We continued moving down the corridor. "I . . . I don't think I've ever had one."

"Of course you have," Karen said. "*Life* is an adventure."

I thought about all the things I'd done in my youth—all the drugs I'd tried, the women I'd slept with, the one man I'd slept with, the wise investments and the foolish ones, the broken limbs and broken hearts. "I suppose," I said.

The corridor widened out now into a lounge, with soft-drink, coffee, and snack vending machines. It must have been intended for staff, not uploads, but Karen indicated that we should go in. Maybe she was tired—

But no. Of course she wasn't. Still, by the time I'd realized that, we'd already veered into the rest area. There were several vinyl-covered padded chairs, and a few small tables. Karen took one of the chairs, carefully smoothing her floral-print sun dress beneath her legs as she did so. She then motioned for me to take another chair. I used my cane to steady myself as I lowered my body, then held the cane in front of me once I'd sat down.

"So," I said, feeling a need to fill the void, "what adventures have you had?"

She was silent for a moment, and I felt bad. I hadn't meant to challenge her earlier remark, but I suppose there had indeed been a "put up or shut up" edge to my words.

"Sorry," I said.

"Oh, no," Karen replied. "Not at all. It's just that there are so *many*. I've been to Antarctica, and the Serengeti—back when it still had big game—and the Valley of the Kings."

"Really?" I said.

"Certainly. I love to travel. Don't you?"

"Well, yes, I guess, but . . ."

"What?"

"I've never been out of North America. See, I can't—I couldn't—fly. The pressure changes in an aircraft: they were afraid they'd set off my Katerinsky's syndrome. It was only a small likelihood, but my doctor said I shouldn't risk it unless the trip was absolutely necessary." I thought briefly of the other me, on the way to the moon; he'd almost certainly survive the trip, of course. Spaceplanes were completely self-contained habitats; their internal pressure didn't vary.

"That's sad," said Karen. But then she brightened. "But now you can travel anywhere!"

I laughed bitterly. "Travel! Christ, I can barely walk . . ."

Karen's mechanical arm touched mine briefly. "Oh, you will. You will! People can do anything. I remember meeting Christopher Reeve, and—"

"Who's he?"

"He played Superman in four movies. God, he was handsome! I had posters of him up on my bedroom walls when I was a teenager. Years later, he was thrown off a horse and injured his spinal cord. They said he'd never breathe on his own again, but he did."

"And you met him?"

"Yes, indeed. He wrote a book about what happened to him; we'd shared a publisher back then, and we had dinner together at BookExpo America. What an inspiration he was."

"Wow," I said. "I suppose being a famous writer, you meet lots of interesting people."

"Well, I didn't bring up Christopher Reeve to name-drop."

"I know, I know. But who else have you met?"

"Let's see . . . what names would mean something to someone your age . . . ? Well, I met King Charles before he died. The current Pope, and the one before him. Tamora Ng. Charlize Theron. Stephen Hawking. Moshe—"

"You met Hawking?"

"Yes. When I was giving a reading at Cambridge."

"Wow," I said again. "What was he like?"

"Very ironic. Very witty. Of course, communicating was an ordeal for him, but—"

"But what a mind!" I said. "Absolute genius."

"He was that," Karen said. "You like physics?"

"I love big ideas—physics, philosophy, whatever."

Karen smiled. "Really? Okay, I've got a joke for you. Do you know the one about Werner Heisenberg being pulled over by a traffic cop?"

I shook my head.

"Well," said Karen, "the cop says, 'Do you know how fast you were going?' And, without missing a beat, Heisenberg replies, 'No, but I know where I am!' "

I burst out laughing. "That's terrific! Wait, wait—I've got one. Do you know the one about Einstein on the train?"

It was Karen's turn to shake her head.

"A passenger goes up to him and says, 'Excuse me, Dr. Einstein, but does New York stop at this train?' "

Karen laughed out loud. "You and I are going to get along just fine," she said. "Are you a professional physicist?"

"Nah. I was never good enough at math to make it. I did a couple of years at the University of Toronto, though."

"And?"

I lifted my shoulders a bit. "Have you been to Canada often?"

"Over the years, from time to time."

"And do you drink beer?"

"When I was younger," said Karen. "I can't anymore. I mean, I couldn't, even in my old body . . . not for a decade or more."

"Have you heard of Sullivan's Select? Or Old Sully's Special Dark?"

"Sure. They—oh! Oh, my! Your name is Jacob Sullivan, right? Is that your family?"

I nodded.

"Well, well, well," said Karen. "So I'm not the only one with a secret identity."

I smiled wanly. "Karen Bessarian earned her fortune. I just inherited mine."

"Still," said Karen, "it must have been nice. When I was young, I was always worrying about money. Even had to go to the food bank now and then. It must have been relaxing knowing you'd never have problems in that area."

I shrugged a bit. "It was a double-edged sword. On the one hand, when I went to university, I could study whatever I wanted, without worrying about whether it was going to lead to a job. I was probably the only guy on campus who took Quantum Physics, History of Drama, *and* Intro to the Pre-Socratics."

Karen laughed politely.

"Yeah," I said. "It was fun—a little of this, a little of that. But the downside of having all that money was that I just wasn't inclined to be treated like garbage. U of T's got a great graduate reputation, but it's an absolute factory at the undergrad level. Put it this way: if you walk every day by the Sullivan Library and your last name is Sullivan, you're not inclined to be pushed around."

"I suppose," said Karen. "I never like to use the word 'rich' in relation to myself; it sounds like bragging. But, well, all of Immortex's clients are rich, so I guess it doesn't matter. But, of course, I never thought I was going to be wealthy. I mean, most writers aren't; it's a very tough life, and I've been very, very lucky." She paused, and there was that twinkle in her artificial eye again. "In fact, you know what the difference is between a large pepperoni pizza and most full-time writers?"

"What?"

"A large pepperoni pizza can feed a family of four."

I laughed, and so did she. "Anyway," she said, "I didn't begin to get rich until I was in my late forties. That's when my books started to take off."

I shrugged a little. "If I'd had to wait until my late forties to be rich, I wouldn't be here. I'm only forty-four now." *Only.* Christ, I'd never thought of it as *only* before.

"I—please don't take this the wrong way—but in retrospect, I'm glad I started poor," said Karen.

"I suppose it builds character," I said. "But I didn't ask to be rich. In fact, there were times I hated it, and everything my family stood for. Beer! Christ, where's the social conscience in making beer?"

"But your family donated that library to the university, you said."

"Sure. Buying immortality. It's—"

I paused, and Karen looked at me expectantly.

After a moment, I shrugged again. "It's exactly what I've just done, isn't it?" I shook my head. "Ah, well. Anyway, it goes to your head sometimes, having all that money when you're young. I, um, I was not the best person early on."

"Paris the Heiress," said Karen.

"Who?"

"Paris Hilton, granddaughter of the hotel magnate. You would have been just a toddler when she was briefly famous. She—well, I guess she was like you: inherited a fortune, had billions in her twenties. She lived what we writers call a dissipated life."

" 'Paris the heiress,' " I repeated. "Cute."

"And you were Jake the Rake."

I laughed. "Yeah, I suppose I was. Lots of parties, lots of girls. But . . ."

"What?"

"Well, it's pretty hard to know if a girl really likes you for *you*, when you're rich."

"Tell me about it. My third husband was like that."

"Really?"

"Absolutely. Thank God for pre-nups." Her tone was light. If she'd been bitter once, enough time had apparently passed to let her now joke about it. "You'll have to only date women who are rich in their own right."

"I suppose. But, you know, even—" Damn it, I hadn't meant to say that aloud.

"What?"

"Well, you never know about people—know what they're really thinking. Even before I was rich, I—there was this girl named Trista, and I thought she . . . I thought *we* . . ."

Karen raised her artificial eyebrows, but said nothing. It was clear I could go on, or not, as I wished.

And, to my great surprise, I did wish. "She seemed to really like me. And I was totally in love with her. This was, like, when I was sixteen. But when I asked her out, she laughed. She actually laughed in my face."

Karen's hand briefly touched my forearm. "You poor thing," she said. "Are you married now?"

"No."

"Ever been?"

"No."

"Never found the right person?"

"It's, um, not exactly like that."

"Oh?"

Again, to my surprise, I went on. "I mean, there was—there *is*—this woman. Rebecca Chong. But, you know, with my condition, I . . ."

Karen nodded sympathetically. But then I guess she decided to lighten the tone. "Still," she said, "you don't necessarily have to wait for the right person to come along. If I'd done that I'd have missed out on my first three husbands."

I wasn't sure if my artificial eyebrows rose spontaneously in surprise; certainly, if I'd still been in my old body, my natural ones would have. "How many times have you been married?"

"Four. My last husband, Ryan, passed away two years ago."

"I'm sorry."

Her voice was full of sadness. "Me, too."

"Do you have any kids?"

"Um—" She paused. "Just one." Another pause. "Just one who lived."

"I'm so sorry," I said.

She nodded, accepting that. "I take it you don't have any children?"

I shook my head and indicated my artificial body. "No, and I guess I never will."

Karen smiled. "I'm sure you would have made a good father."

"We'll never—" Damn these new bodies! I'd thought the obvious, self-pitying thought, but had never intended to actually say it aloud. As before, I didn't manage to kill it until a couple of words were already spoken. "Thanks," I said. "Thank you."

A pair of Immortex employees entered the lounge—a white woman and an Asian man. They looked surprised to see us there.

"Don't let us disturb you," Karen said to them as she stood up. "We were just leaving." She held out a hand to help me get up. I took it without thinking, and was on my feet in a matter of seconds, Karen effortlessly pulling me up. "It's been a long day," Karen said to me. "I'm sure you want to go back to your room." She paused, as if realizing that, of course, I couldn't possibly be tired, then added, "You know, so you can change out of that robe, and so on."

There it was—a perfect out; the escape that I'd been looking for earlier, the polite way to beg off that my lack of the need for sleep or food had denied me. But I didn't want it anymore. "Actually," I said, looking at her, "I'd like to do some more walking practice, if, ah, you're willing to help me."

Karen smiled so broadly it surely would have hurt had her face been flesh. "I'd love to," she said.

"Great," I replied, as we headed out of the lounge. "It'll give us a chance to talk some more."

CHAPTER 9

The spaceplane was still climbing. I'd thought the constant acceleration would be uncomfortable, but it wasn't. Out the window, I could see sunlight glinting off the Atlantic ocean far below. I turned my head to face inside, and the presumably redheaded man sitting next to me seized his chance. "So," he said, "what's your job?"

I looked at him. I didn't really have a job, but I did have a true-enough answer. "I'm in wealth management."

But that caused his freckled forehead to crease. "Immortex wants wealth managers on the moon?"

I realized the source of his confusion. "I'm not an Immortex employee," I said. "I'm a customer."

His light-colored eyes went wide. "Oh. Sorry."

"Nothing to be sorry about," I said.

"It's just that you're the youngest customer I've ever seen."

I smiled a smile that hopefully wasn't an invitation to more questions. "I've always been an early adopter."

"Ah," said the man. He stuck out a hand that was as freckled as his face. "Quentin Ashburn," he said.

I shook his hand. "Jake Sullivan." I didn't really want to continue talking about me, so I added, "What do you do, Quentin?"

"Moonbus maintenance."

"Moonbus?"

"It's a long-distance surface vehicle," Quentin said. "Well, actually, it flies just above the surface. Best way to cover a lot of lunar territory fast. You'll be riding in one when we get to the moon; the ship from Earth will only take us to Nearside."

"Right," I said. "I read about that."

"Oh, moonbuses are fascinating," said Quentin.

"I'm sure they are," I said.

"See, you can't use airplanes on the moon, because—"

"Because there's no air," I said.

Quentin looked a bit miffed at having his thunder stolen, but he went on. "So you need a different kind of vehicle to get from point A to point B."

"So I'd imagine," I said.

"Right. Now, the moonbus—it's rocket-propelled, see? Funny thing, of course is that instead of polluting the atmosphere, we're *giving* the moon an atmosphere—an infinitesimal one, to be sure—and all of it is rocket exhaust. Now, for the Moonbus, we use monohydrazine . . ."

I could see that it was going to be a very long trip.

I was slowly getting the hang of walking with my new legs, thanks to Karen Bessarian's help. I'd always been impatient; I suppose thinking you didn't have much time left was part of the cause. Of course, Karen—in her eighties—must have similarly felt that her days had been numbered. But she'd apparently adapted immediately to the notion of being more or less immortal, whereas I was still stuck in the time-is-running-out mindset.

Ah, well. I'm sure I'd make the transition. After all, it's supposed to be old people who are set in their ways, not guys like me. But no—that was unfair. They say you're as young as you feel, and Karen certainly didn't feel old now; maybe she never had.

Four others besides Karen and me had received new bodies today. I'm sure they'd all been at the same sales pitch I'd attended, but I hadn't talked to anyone except Karen there, and these people now had faces so much younger than what I'd presumably seen then that I didn't recognize any of them. We were all to spend the next three days here, undergoing physical and psychological testing ("hardware and software diagnostics," I'd overheard one of the Immortex employees say to Dr. Porter, who had given the younger man a very stern look).

I was pleased to see that I wasn't the only one who'd been having trouble walking. A girl—yes, damn it, she looked like a girl, all of sixteen—was using a wheelchair. Immortex clients could choose just about any age to look like, of course. This reconstruction must have been based on 2D photos—if this girl were Karen, she'd have been sixteen in the mid-nineteen seventies—where, I think, hairstyles had been all fluffy, and blue eye shadow had been in vogue. But whoever this was wasn't trying to regress: her hair was short and tightly curled, in today's fashion, and she had a band of bright pink from temple to temple, across the bridge of her nose, the kind of makeup kids today liked.

Two of the others were also female, and three of them were white. Like

Karen, they had opted to look about thirty—meaning, ironically, that all these minds that were much older than mine were housed in bodies that appeared substantially younger than even my new one did. The other upload was a black male. He'd adopted a serene face of perhaps fifty. Actually, now that I thought about it, he looked a lot like Will Smith; I wondered if that's what his original had looked like, or if he'd opted for a new face.

Karen was chatting with the other women. She apparently knew at least one of them from philanthropic circles. I suppose it was natural that the four old women would spend time together. And, by default, that meant I ended up talking with the other man.

"Malcolm Draper," the man said, extending a large hand.

"Jake Sullivan," I replied, taking it. Neither of us were inclined to that silly male game of demonstrating how strong we were by squeezing too hard—probably just as well, given our new robotic hands.

"Where are you from, Jake?"

"Here. Toronto."

Malcolm nodded. "I live in New York. Manhattan. But of course you can't get this service down there. So, what do you do, Jake?"

The question I always hated. I didn't actually *do* anything—not for a living. "I'm into investments," I said. "You?"

"I'm a lawyer—do you call them solicitors up here?"

"Only in formal contexts. Lawyer, attorney."

"Well, that's what I am."

"What kind of law?" I asked.

"Civil liberties."

I gave the mental command that used to reconfigure my features into an impressed expression, but I really had no idea what it did to my face now. "How's business?"

"In the present political climate? Lots of cases, damn few victories. I can see the Statue of Liberty from my office window—but they should rename the old girl the Statue of Do Exactly What the Government Says You Should Do." He shook his head. "That's why I uploaded, see? Not too many of my generation left—people who actually remember what it was like to *have* civil liberties, before Homeland Security, before *Littler v. Carvey*, before every dollar bill and retail product had an RFID tracking chip in it. If we let the good old days pass from living memory, we'll never be able to get them back."

"So you're still going to practice law?" I asked.

"Yes, indeed—when interesting-enough cases come along, that is." He reached into a pocket. "Here, let me give you my card . . . just in case."

Weightlessness was wonderful!

Some of the old people were afraid of it, and stayed securely fastened in their ergo-chairs. But I undid my seat belt and floated around the cabin, gently pushing off walls, the floor, and the ceiling. We'd all had antinausea injections before takeoff, and, at least for me, the medicine was working perfectly. I found I could twirl along my head-to-toe axis at a great speed and not get dizzy. The flight attendant showed us some neat things, including water pulling itself into a floating ball. He also showed us how hard it was to throw something to another person: the brain refused to believe that throwing it in a straight line was the way to do it, and we all kept sending them up, as if in parabolic trajectories against gravity.

Karen Bessarian was enjoying weightlessness, too. The cabin walls were completely covered with little black foam pyramids, which I'd at first taken for acoustic insulation but now realized were really to prevent injuries when one went flying into them. Still, Karen was taking it fairly easy, not trying anything as athletic or adventurous as I was.

"If you look out the right-hand-side windows," said the flight attendant, "you can see the International Space Station." I happened to be upside down at that moment, so pushed off the wall and started drifting toward the left side. The flight attendant was deadpan. "The *other* right-hand-side, Mr. Sullivan."

I smiled sheepishly, and pushed off again with my palm. I found a spot by one of the windows and looked outside. The International Space Station—all cylinders and right angles—had been abandoned for decades. Too big to crash safely into the ocean, it was occasionally given a boost to keep it orbiting. The last astronaut to depart had left the two Canadian-built remote-manipulator arms shaking hands with each other.

"In about ten minutes," said the flight attendant, "we'll be docking with the moonship. You should be strapped in for docking—but, don't worry, you'll get three full days of weightlessness on your way to the moon."

On my way to the moon . . .

I shook my head.

On my way to the fucking moon.

CHAPTER 10

It was well after midnight. Dr. Porter had long since gone home, but there were all sorts of Immortex staff still around to cater to our every need—not that we had many.

We didn't eat, so there was no point in putting out a fancy buffet for us. I should have thought that through, should have had a special last meal just before uploading. Of course, Immortex hadn't suggested we do so, I guess because a final meal was what the condemned, not the liberated, were supposed to enjoy.

More: we didn't drink, so there was no point in having an open bar. Indeed, I realized with a pang of guilt that I couldn't remember the last time I'd had a Sullivan's Select . . . and now I never would again. My great grandfather—Old Sully himself—was probably spinning in his grave at the thought of a scion of his dynasty giving up beer for anything, even immortality.

And, most astonishing of all, we didn't sleep. How often I'd said there were too few hours in a day! But now it seemed as though there were far too many.

We, this little band of new uploads, were to spend the night together in this party room; the first night was apparently very difficult for a lot of people. Two Immortex therapists milled about, as did someone who seemed to be the land-locked equivalent of a cruise director, coming up with activities to keep people occupied. Being up constantly, not getting tired, not needing to sleep, not *wanting* to sleep: it was going to be quite an adjustment, even for those who, in their old age, had slept lightly and had needed only five or six hours a night.

Two of the recently uploaded women were chatting away about things that didn't interest me. The third woman and Draper were playing a trivia game that the cruise director had brought up on a wall monitor, but the questions were geared toward their youth, and I knew none of the answers.

And so I ended up spending more time with Karen. Part of it was kindness on her part, I'm sure; she seemed to recognize that I was a fish out of water. Indeed, I felt compelled to comment on that as we went outside, exiting onto the treed Immortex grounds, a gibbous moon overhead. "Thanks," I said to Karen as we walked along, "for spending so much time with me."

Karen smiled her new-and-improved perfectly symmetrical smile. "Don't be silly," she said. "Who else would I talk to about physics or philosophy? In fact, I've got another joke for you. René Descartes goes into a bar and orders a drink. The bartender serves it up. Old René, he nurses it for a while, but at last it's gone. And so the barkeep says to him, 'Hey, René, care for another?' To which Descartes replies, 'I think not'—and disappears."

I laughed, and even though my new laugh sounded strange to me, it made me feel good. August nights were filled with mosquitoes, but I quickly recognized another advantage to an artificial body: the bugs left us alone. "But, y'know," I said, as we walked along, "I'm actually surprised that we don't need to sleep. I thought it was necessary for the consolidation of memory."

"A popular misconception," said Karen, and, with her lovely Georgia accent, the words didn't sound condescending. "But it's just not true. It takes *time* to consolidate memories, and normal humans can't go for any length without sleeping—but the sleeping has nothing to do with the consolidation."

"Really?"

"Oh, yes. We're going to be fine."

"Good."

We walked for a while in companionable silence, then Karen said, "Anyway, I should be the one thanking you for spending time with me."

"Why's that?"

"Well, half the reason I uploaded was to get away from old people. Can you imagine me in an old-folks' home?"

I laughed. "No, I guess not."

"The other people here who are my age," she said, shaking her head. "Their goal in life was to become rich. There's something ruthless about that, and something shallow, too. I never intended to be rich—it just happened, and no one was more surprised by it than me. And you didn't intend to be rich, either."

"But if it weren't for money," I said, "we'd both be dead or worse soon."

"Oh, I know! I know! But that's bound to change. Immortality is expensive right now, but it's got to come down in price; technology always does. Can you imagine a world in which the only thing that mattered was how rich you are?"

"You don't sound very—" Damn it! Another thought I'd intended to keep to myself partially leaking out.

"Very what?" said Karen. "Very American? Very capitalist?" She shook her head. "I don't think any serious writer can be a capitalist. I mean, look at me: to my own astonishment, I'm one of the best-selling authors of all time. But am I one of the best writers ever in the English language? Not by a long shot.

Work in a field in which financial reward has no correlation with actual worth and you can't be a capitalist. I don't say there's a *negative* correlation: there are great writers who sell very well. But there is no meaningful correlation. It's just a crapshoot."

"So, are you going to go back to writing now that you're a Mindscan?" I asked. It had been years since there'd been a new Karen Bessarian book.

"Yes, I intend to. In fact, being a writer is the main reason I uploaded. See, I love my characters—Prince Scales, Doctor Hiss. I love them all. And, as I told you before, I *created* them. They came right out of here." She tapped the side of her head.

"Yes. So?"

"So, I've watched the ebb and flow of copyright legislation over my lifetime. It's been a battle between warring factions: those who want works to be protected forever, and those who believe works should fall into public domain as fast as possible. When I was young, works stayed in copyright for fifty years after the authors' death. Then it was lengthened to seventy years, and that's still the current figure, but it isn't long enough."

"Why?"

"Well, because if I had a child today—not that I could—and I died tomorrow—not that I'm going to—that child would receive the royalties from my books until he or she was seventy. And then, suddenly, my child—by that point, an old man or woman—would be cut off; my work would be declared public domain, and no more royalties would ever have to be paid on it. The child of my body would be denied the benefits of the children of my mind. And that's just not right."

"But, well, isn't the culture enriched when material goes into the public domain?" I asked. "Surely you wouldn't want Shakespeare or Dickens to still be protected by copyright?"

"Why not? J. K. Rowling is still in copyright; so is Stephen King and Marcos Donnelly—and they all have had, and continue to have, a huge impact on our culture."

"I guess . . ." I said, still not sure.

"Look," said Karen, gently, "one of your ancestors started a brewing company, right?"

I nodded. "My great grandfather, Reuben Sullivan—Old Sully, they called him."

"Right. And you benefit financially from that to this day. Should the government instead have confiscated all the assets of Sullivan Brewing, or whatever the company's called, on the seventieth anniversary of Old Sully's death? Intellectual property is still *property*, and it should be treated the same as anything else human beings build or create."

I had a hard time with this; I never used anything but open-source software —and there *was* a difference between a building and an idea; there was, in fact, a *material* difference. "So you uploaded in order to make sure you keep getting royalties on *DinoWorld* forever?"

"It's not just that," Karen said. "In fact, it's not even principally that. When something falls into public domain, *anyone* can do *anything* with the material. You want to make a porno film with my characters? You want to write bad fiction featuring my characters? You can, once my works go into public domain. And that's not right; they're *mine*."

"But by living forever, you can protect them?" I said.

"Exactly. If I don't die, they never fall into public domain."

We continued walking; I was getting the hang of it—and the motor in my belly could keep me doing it for weeks on end, or so Porter had told me. It was now almost 5:00 a.m.—I couldn't remember the last time I'd been up so late. I hadn't realized that Orion was visible in summer if you stayed up this long. Clamhead must be missing me something fierce, although the robokitchen would be feeding her, and my next-door neighbor had agreed to take her for walks.

We passed under a lamp, and to my astonishment I noticed that my arm was wet; I could see it glistening in the lamp light. Only a little later did I experience a physical sensation of dampness. I rubbed a finger along my arm. "Good grief!" I said. "It's dew."

Karen laughed, not at all perturbed. "So it is."

"You're taking all this so well," I said to her.

"I try to take *everything* in stride," Karen replied. "It's all material."

"What?"

"Sorry. Writer's mantra. 'It's all material.' It all goes into the hopper. Everything you experience is fodder for future writing."

"That's, um, an unusual way of going through life."

"You sound like Daron. When he and I used to go for dinner, he'd be embarrassed when a couple at a nearby table was having a fight. Me, I'm always leaning closer and cocking my head to hear better, thinking, 'Oh, this is great; this is pure gold.'"

"*Hmph,*" I said. I was getting good at making all those sounds that aren't words but still convey meaning.

"And," said Karen, "with these new ears—God, they're sensitive!—I'll be able to hear even more. Poor Daron would hate that."

"Who's Daron?"

"Oh, sorry. My first husband, Daron Bessarian, and the last one whose name I took; my maiden name was Cohen. Daron was a nice Armenian boy, from my high school. We were a funny couple, in a way. We used to argue about whose people had suffered the worse holocaust."

I didn't know how to reply to that, so instead I said, "Maybe we should go inside before we get too damp."

She nodded, and we headed into the party room. Draper—the black lawyer—was now playing chess with one of the women; a second woman—the *faux* sixteen-year-old—was reading something on a datapad; and the third woman was, to my astonishment, doing jumping jacks, under the supervision of an Immortex personal trainer. I thought it incredibly pointless—an upload's artificial form hardly needed the exercise. But then I realized it must in fact be luxurious to suddenly be nimble and limber again, after years of being trapped in an aged, decaying body.

"Want to catch the 5:00 a.m. newscast?" I asked Karen.

"Sure."

We walked down a corridor, and found a room I'd noted earlier in the day that had a wall screen.

"Do you mind the CBC?" I said.

"Not at all. I watch it all the time from Detroit. It's the only way I can find out what's really going on in my country—or in the rest of the world."

I told the TV to turn on. It did so. I'd watched newscasts on this channel hundreds of times before, but this one looked completely different, now that I was seeing in full color. I wondered about that, about where the connections in my brain that allowed me to perceive colors I'd never seen before had come from.

The newscaster—a turbaned Sikh whose shift, I knew, went until 9:00 a.m.—was speaking while news footage ran behind him. "Despite another protest on Parliament Hill yesterday afternoon, it seems almost certain that Canada will go ahead and legalize multiple marriages later this month. Prime Minister Chen has scheduled a press conference for this morning, and . . ."

Karen shook her head, and the movement caught my eye. "You don't approve?" I asked.

"No," she said.

"Why not?" I said it as gently as I could, trying to keep my tone from sounding confrontational.

"I don't know," she replied, amiably enough.

"Do gay marriages bother you?"

She sounded slightly miffed. "No. I'm not *that* old."

"Sorry."

"No, it's a fair question. I was in my forties when Canada legalized gay marriages. I actually came to Toronto in the summer of—what was it? Two thousand and three?—to attend the wedding of an American lesbian couple I knew who came up here to get married."

"But the U.S. doesn't allow gay marriages—I remember when the constitutional amendment was passed, outlawing them."

Karen nodded. "The U.S. doesn't allow a lot of things. Believe me, many of us are uncomfortable with the continued drifting to the right."

"But you *are* against multiple marriages."

"Yes, I am, I suppose. But I'm not sure I can articulate why. I mean, I've seen lots of single moms do just fine—including my sister, may God rest her soul. So certainly my definition of family isn't limited to two parents."

"What about single dads? What about single *gay* dads?"

"Yeah, sure, that's fine."

I nodded in relief; old people can be *so* conservative. "So, what's wrong with multiple marriages?"

"I guess I think you can really only have the level of commitment that constitutes a marriage in a couple. Anything bigger than that waters it down."

"Oh, I don't know. Most people have an infinite supply of love; just ask anyone who comes from a big family."

"I guess," she said. "I take it you're in favor of multiple marriages?"

"Sure. I mean, I don't have any interest in one myself, but that's not the point. I've know several triads over the years, and two quads. They're all genuinely in love; they've got stable, long-term relationships. Why shouldn't they be entitled to call what they have a marriage?"

"Because it's *not*. It just isn't."

I certainly didn't want to start an argument, so I didn't say anything further. Looking back at the TV, I saw the anchor was now doing a story on the death of former U.S. President Pat Buchanan, who had passed away yesterday at a hundred and six.

"Good riddance," said Karen, looking at the screen.

"Happy to see him go?" I said.

"Aren't you?"

"Oh, I don't know. He certainly was no friend of Canada, but, you know,

his 'Soviet Canuckistan' nickname for us became a rallying cry for my generation. 'Live up to the name,' and all that. I think Canada became even more
left-wing just to spite him."

"So maybe you're just in favor of multiple marriages because it'll be another
distinction between our two countries," said Karen.

"Not at all," I said. "I told you why I'm in favor of it."

"Sorry." She glanced at the screen. The piece about Buchanan's death was
over, but apparently she was still dwelling on it. "I'm happy he's dead, because
I see it as maybe the end of an era. It was the judges he packed the Supreme
Court with, after all, who overturned *Roe v. Wade*, and I can't forgive him for
that. But he was twenty years older than me—his values came from a different
generation. And now he's gone, and I'm thinking maybe there's some hope for
change. But . . ."

"Yes?"

"But *I'm* not going away, am I? Your friends who want to have their relationship recognized as a group marriage will have to contend with people like
me, set in their ways, sticking around forever, standing in the way of progress."
She looked at me. "And it *is* progress, isn't it? My parents never understood
about gay marriage. Their parents never understood about desegregation."

I looked at her with new eyes—figuratively, and, of course, literally. "You're
a philosopher at heart," I said.

"Maybe so. All good writers are, I imagine."

"But I guess you're right, to some degree, anyway. They call it the retire-or-
expire factor in academia . . ."

" 'Retire or expire'?" said Karen. "Oooh, I like that! And I certainly saw
something similar in Georgia, where I grew up, in relation to civil rights: great
strides weren't made by changing people's minds—no one slaps himself on the
forehead and exclaims, 'What a fool I've been all these years!' Rather, progress
was made because the worst racists—the ones who remembered the good ole
days of segregation or even slavery—died off."

"Exactly," I said.

"But, you know, people's beliefs *do* change over time. There's the long-
established fact that people become more politically conservative as they get
older—not that it happened to me, thank God. When I found out what Tom
Selleck's politics were, I was appalled."

"Who's Tom Selleck?"

"Sigh," said Karen. Apparently she hadn't learned to make the sound yet.

"He was a gorgeous hunk of an actor; played *Magnum P.I.* I had posters of him in my bedroom when I was a teenager."

"I thought you had posters of . . . who was it? That Superman guy?"

Karen grinned. "Him, too."

We'd both been ignoring the TV, but now the sports came on. "Oooh!" said Karen. "The Yankees won. Terrific!"

"You like baseball?" I said, feeling my eyebrows lift this time—there was a definite jerk as they did so; I'd have to get Porter to file down whatever they were catching on.

"Absolutely!"

"Me, too," I said. "I wanted to be a pitcher when I was a kid. It wasn't in the cards, but . . ."

"You a Blue Jays fan?" asked Karen.

I grinned. "What else?"

"I remember when they won back-to-back World Series."

"Really? Wow."

"Yup. Daron and I had just gotten married back then. He and I used to watch the World Series together every year. Big bowls of popcorn, lots of soda, the works."

"What was it like—those two times Toronto won? How did people react?"

The sun was rising; light spilled into the room.

Karen smiled. "Let me tell you . . ."

CHAPTER 11

We transferred from the spaceplane to the moonship, a metallic arachnid designed only for use in vacuum. I had my own small sleeping compartment—like one of those coffin hotels in Tokyo. When I was out of it, I was enjoying being weightless, although Quentin was still nattering on about moonbuses and other things that interested him. If only he were a baseball fan . . .

"Now, remember, folks," said one of the Immortex staff on the third morning of our flight, "the moonbase we're about to land at is *not* High Eden. Rather, it's a multinational private-sector R&D facility. It wasn't built for tourists, and it wasn't built for luxury—so don't be disappointed. I promise you, you'll be pleased when you get to High Eden."

I listened, thinking High Eden indeed better be good. Of course, I'd taken the virtual tour, and read all the literature. But I'd miss—hell, I already was missing—Clamhead, and Rebecca, and my mother, and . . .

And, yes, even my father. I'd thought him a burden, I thought I'd feel relief to hand off worrying about him to the other me, but I found myself very sad at the prospect of never seeing him again.

Tears float in zero-gravity. It's the most astonishing thing.

I went to see Dr. Porter about the problem with thoughts I intended to keep private being spoken aloud.

"Ah, yes," he said, nodding. "I've seen that before. I can make some adjustments, but it's a tricky mind-body interface problem."

"You've got to fix it. Unless I explicitly decide to do something, it shouldn't happen."

"Ah," said Porter, his eyebrows working with glee, "but that's not how humans work—not even biological ones. None of us consciously initiate our actions."

I shook my head. "I've studied philosophy, doc. I'm not prepared to give up on the notion of free will. I refuse to believe that we live in a deterministic universe."

"Oh, indeed," said Porter. "That's not what I meant. Say you walk into a room, see someone you know, and decide to extend your hand in greeting. Of course, your hand doesn't instantly shoot out; first, stuff has to happen in your brain, right? And that stuff—the electrical change in the brain that precedes voluntary action—is called the readiness potential. Well, in a biological brain the readiness potential begins 550 milliseconds—just over half a second—prior to your hand beginning to move. It really doesn't matter *what* the voluntary act is: the readiness potential occurs in the brain 550 milliseconds before the motor act begins. Okay?"

"Okay," I said.

"Ah, but it's not okay! See, if you ask people to indicate exactly when they decided to do something, they report that the idea occurred to them about 350 milliseconds before the motor act begins. A guy named Benjamin Libet proved that ages ago."

"But—but that must be a measurement error," I said. "I mean, you're talking about milliseconds."

"No, not really. The difference between 550 milliseconds and 350 milliseconds is a fifth of a second: that's quite a significant amount of time, and easy enough to measure accurately. This basic test has been replicated over again over again since the 1980s, and the data are rock solid."

"But that doesn't make sense. You're saying—"

"I'm saying that what our intuition tells us the sequence of events *should* be, and what the sequence actually is, don't agree. Intuitively, we think the sequence must be: *first*, you decide to shake hands with your old friend Bob; *second*, your brain, in response to that decision, begins sending signals to your arm that it wants to shake hands; and *third*, your arm starts to swing up for the handshake. Right? But what really happens is this: *first*, your brain starts sending signals to shake hands; *second*, you consciously decide to shake hands with your old friend; and *third*, your arm starts to swing up. The brain has started down the road to shaking hands *before* you have consciously made any decision. Your conscious brain takes ownership of the action, and fools itself into thinking it started the action, but really it's just a spectator, watching what your body is doing."

"So you *are* saying there's no free will."

"Not quite. Our conscious minds have the free will to *veto* the action. See? The action begins 550 milliseconds prior to the first physical movement. Two hundred milliseconds later, the action that's already been started comes to the attention of your conscious self—and your conscious self has 350 milliseconds to put on the brakes before anything happens. The conscious brain doesn't initiate so-called voluntary acts, although it can step in and stop them."

"Really?" I said.

Porter nodded his long face vigorously. "Absolutely. Everybody's experienced this, if you stop and think about it: you're lying in bed, quite mellow, and you look over at the clock, and you think to yourself, I really should get up, it's time to get up, I've got to go to work. You may think this a half-dozen times or more, and then, suddenly, you *are* getting up—the action has begun, without you being consciously aware that you've finally, really made the decision to get out of bed. And that's because you *haven't* consciously made that decision; your unconscious has made it for you. It—not the conscious you—has concluded once and for all that it really is time to get out of bed."

"But I didn't have this problem when I was biological."

"No, that's right. And that was because of the slow speed of chemical reactions. But your new body and your new brain operate at electrical, not chemical, speeds, and the veto mechanism sometimes comes into play too late to do what it's supposed to do. But, as I said, I can make a few adjustments. Forgive me, but I'm going to have to pull back the skin on your head, and open up your skull . . ."

Finally, it was time to go back home. And when I got to the house in North York, I couldn't wait to see my lovable old Irish setter. "Clamhead!" I called out, as I came through the front door. "Here, girl! I'm home!"

Clamhead came bounding down the stairs, but stopped short when she saw me. I'd expected her to leap up and kiss my face, but that didn't happen. Indeed, she lowered her forelegs, lay her ears flat, reared up her hind legs, and barked menacingly at me.

"Clamhead, it's me!" I said. "It's just me."

The dog barked again, and then growled.

"Clammy, it's just me, honest!"

The growl became a snarl. The front door was still open and I thought about making a run for it. But no, damn it, no. This was my house.

"Come on, girl, it's just me. It's just Jake."

Clamhead leapt. I managed a half-step backward, but she slapped her paws against my chest, and barked loudly, over and over and over again.

"Clammy, Clammy!" I said. "Sit, girl! Sit!"

I'd never known Clamhead to bite anyone, but she bit me. I was wearing a short-sleeve shirt; she closed her jaws on my naked forearm and yanked backward, tearing out a ragged piece of plastiskin, revealing fiber-optic nerves, bungee-cord muscles, and a blue metal armature within. She fell back on her haunches, and sniffed at the piece of plastic, then turned tail, and bounded away up the stairs, whimpering.

My heart wasn't beating fast—because I had no heart. My breathing wasn't ragged—because I did not breathe. My eyes weren't stinging—because I could not cry. I just stood there, letting time pass, shaking my head slowly left and right, feeling rejected and alone.

The spider-shaped moonship landed next to a small cluster of mirrored domes, near the crater Aristarchus. After three days of zero-g, having any weight at all felt oppressive. But, really, it was a gentle tug, only one-sixth of what was normal on Earth.

The Immortex staffer had been wise to warn us: the moonbase here was utilitarian at best—it felt like the inside of a submarine. Sadly, we had to spend three days here, going through decontamination procedures. With hundreds of potential points of departure from Earth, and only one possible lunar arrival point, it made sense that the elaborate decontamination facilities were up here, not down there.

This had been the first permanent base established on the moon. It had originally been built by the Chinese, and a lot of the signage was still in that language, but it was now administered by a multinational consortium. Its official name was LS One—Lunar Settlement One—but in honor of the arriving immigrants, someone had erected a big sign that said "LS Island," a pun it took me a few moments to get.

And I was indeed an immigrant: this world, this airless, dusty sphere, was going to be my home for the rest of my life—however long that might be. Of course, here on the moon, the vessels in my brain would be subject to less stress, so perhaps I'd last longer than I would have had I stayed down on Earth.

Perhaps. In any event, the doctors at High Eden would know precisely what to do if I had an . . . *incident*. The advance directive I'd sworn out was a contract, and contracts must be honored.

"All Immortex passengers," said a voice over an intercom, "please report to decontamination."

I headed down the corridor with a bounce that I didn't feel in my step.

CHAPTER 12

I am a Mindscan, an uploaded consciousness, a transferred personality, and yet, despite having fewer external indicators of my internal mental state, I am still very much corporeal.

For centuries, humans have claimed to have out-of-body experiences. But what is the mind divorced from the body? What would a recording of my brain patterns be without a body to give them form?

I've always pooh-poohed the notion of out-of-body experiences, of the idea that you can look down upon your own body from above. After all, *what* are you looking with? Surely not your eyes—they're part of your body. Could an incorporeal entity sense anything? Photons need to be arrested to be detected; they have to hit something—the back of the eye to be seen as light, the skin to be felt as heat. A disembodied spirit could not see.

And, even if it did somehow detect things, no one ever claimed to have anything but normal vision when out of their body. They see the world around them as they always have before, just from a different angle. They don't see infrared; they don't see ultraviolet—vision without eyes seems exactly the same as vision with eyes. And yet if eyes are not really necessary for sight, why does plucking them out—or even just covering them—always, without fail, result in a loss of vision? And if it's just a coincidence that out-of-body perceptions happen to resemble what eyes see, why do color-blind people, like I was, never report a world of hues previously unknown to them when they have out-of-body experiences?

No, vision can't exist without a body. "The mind's eye" is metaphor, nothing more. You can't have a disembodied intellect—at least, not a human one. Our brains are parts of our bodies, not something separate.

And that monad that was me—that inseparable combination of brain and body—was mostly glad to be home, although, I/we/it had to admit that it was all very strange. Everything looked different now that I had color vision. I wasn't quite sure about such matters yet, but it was arguable that things I'd thought had gone nicely together were actually clashing.

More than that, things didn't feel the same. My favorite chair was no longer as comfortable; the carpet had almost no texture beneath my bare feet; the banister's rich woodgrain, ever so slightly raised on some swirls, just as delicately indented on others, had become a uniform smoothness; the comforter I kept slung over the back of the couch no longer had its agreeable scritchiness.

And Clamhead still hadn't recognized me, although, after a lot of wary sniffing, she had consented to eat the food I put out for her. But when she wasn't eating, she spent hours staring out the living-room window, waiting for her master to come home.

Tomorrow—Monday—I would go see my mother. As usual, it was a duty I was not looking forward to. But tonight, a beautiful autumn Sunday night, should be fun: tonight was a little party at Rebecca Chong's penthouse. That would be great; I could use some cheering up.

I took the subway to Rebecca's. Although it wasn't a weekday, there were still lots of people on the train, and many of them stared openly at me. Canadians are supposed to be known for their politeness, but that trait seemed entirely absent just then.

Even though there were plenty of seats, I decided to stand for the trip with my back to everyone, making a show of consulting a map of the subway system. It had grown slowly but surely since I was a kid, with, most recently, a new line out to the airport, and an extension of another all the way up to York University.

Once the train got to Eglinton, I exited and found the corridor that led to the entrance to Rebecca's building. There, I presented myself to the concierge, who, to his credit, didn't bat an eye as he called up to Rebecca's apartment to confirm that I should be admitted.

I took the elevator up to the top floor, and walked along the short hallway to Rebecca's door. I stood there for a few moments, steeling my courage . . . literally, I suppose . . . and then knocked on the apartment door. A few moments later, the door opened, and I was face to face with the lovely Rebecca Chong. "Hey, Becks," I said. I was about to lean in for our usual kiss on the lips when she actually stepped back a half pace.

"Oh, my God," said Rebecca. "You—my God, you really did it. You said you were going to, but . . ." Rebecca stood there, mouth agape. For once, I was happy that there was no outward sign of my inner feelings. Finally, I said, "May I come in?"

"Um, sure," said Rebecca. I stepped into her penthouse apartment; fabulous views both real and virtual filled her walls.

"Hello, everyone," I said, moving out of the marbled entryway and onto the berber carpet.

Sabrina Bondarchuk, tall, thin, with hair that I now saw as the yellow I supposed it always had been, was standing by the fireplace, a glass of white wine in her hand. She gasped in surprise.

I smiled—fully aware that it wasn't quite the dimpled smile they were used to. "Hi, Sabrina," I said.

Sabrina always hugged me when she saw me; she made no move to do so this time, though, and without some signal from her, I wasn't going to initiate it.

"It's . . . it's amazing," said bald-headed Rudy Ackerman, another old friend—we'd hiked around Eastern Canada and New England the summer after our first year at UofT. The "it" Rudy was referring to was my new body.

I tried to make my tone light. "The current state of the art," I said. "It'll get more lifelike as time goes on, I'm sure."

"It's pretty funky as is, I must say," said Rudy. "So . . . so do you have super strength?"

Rebecca was still looking mortified, but Sabrina imitated a TV announcer. "He's an upload. She's a vegetarian rabbi. They fight crime."

I laughed. "No, I've got normal strength. Super strength is an extra-cost option. But you know me: I'm a lover not a fighter."

"It's so . . . weird," said Rebecca, at last.

I looked at her, and smiled as warmly—as *humanly*—as I could. " 'Weird' is just an anagram of 'wired,' " I said, but she didn't laugh at the joke.

"What's it like?" asked Sabrina.

Had I still been biological, I would, of course, have taken a deep breath as part of collecting my thoughts. "It's *different*," I said. "I'm getting used to it, though. Some of it is very nice. I don't get headaches anymore—at least, I haven't so far. And that damn pain in my left ankle is gone. But . . ."

"What?" asked Rudy.

"Well, I feel a little low-res, I guess. There isn't as much sensory input as there used to be. My vision is fine—and I'm no longer color-blind, although I do have a slight awareness of the pixels making up the images. But there's no sense of smell to speak of."

"With Rudy around, that's not such a bad thing," said Sabrina.

Rudy stuck his tongue out at her.

I kept trying to catch Rebecca's eye, but every time I looked at her, she looked away. I lived for her little touches, her hand on my forearm, a leg pressing against mine as we sat on the couch. But the whole evening, she didn't touch me once. She hardly even looked at me.

"Becks," I said at last, when Rudy had gone to the washroom, and Sabrina was off freshening her drink. "It is still me, you know."

"What?" she said, as if she had no idea what I was talking about.

"It's me."

"Yeah," she said. "Sure."

In day-to-day life, we hardly ever speak names, either our own or those of others. "It's me," we say when identifying ourselves on the phone. And, "Look at you!" when greeting someone. So maybe I was being paranoid. But by the end of the evening, I couldn't recall anyone, least of all my darling, darling Rebecca, having called me Jake.

I went home in a pissy mood. Clamhead growled at me as I came through the front door, and I growled back.

"Hello, Hannah," I said to the housekeeper as I came through my mother's front door the next afternoon.

Hannah's small eyes went wide, but she quickly recovered. "Hello, Mr. Sullivan," she said.

Suddenly, I found myself saying what I'd never said before. "Call me Jake."

Hannah looked startled, but she complied. "Hello, Jake." I practically kissed her.

"How is she?"

"Not so well, I'm afraid. She's in one of her moods."

My mother and her moods. I nodded, and headed upstairs—taking them effortlessly, of course. That much was a pleasant change.

I paused to look into the room that had been mine, in part to see what it looked like with my new vision, and in part to stall, so I could work up my nerve. The walls that I'd always seen as gray were in fact a pale green. So much was being revealed to me now, about so many things. I continued down the corridor.

"Hello, Mom," I said. "How are you doing?"

She was in her room, brushing her hair. "What do you care?"

How I missed being able to sigh. "I care. Mom, you know I care."

"You think I don't know a robot when I see it?"

"I'm not a robot."

"You're not my Jake. What's happened to Jake?"

"I *am* Jake," I said.

"The original. What's happened to the original?"

Funny. I hadn't thought about the other me for days. "He must be on the moon, by now," I said. "It's only a three-day journey there, and he left last Tuesday. He should be getting out of lunar decontamination today."

"The moon," said my mother, shaking her head. "The moon, indeed."

"We should be heading out," I said.

"What kind of son leaves a disabled father behind to go to the moon?"

"I didn't leave him. I'm here."

She was looking at me indirectly: she was facing the mirror above the bureau, and conversing with my reflection in it. "This is just like what you—the real you—do with Clamhead when you're out of town. You have the damned robokitchen feed her. And now, here you come, a walking, talking robokitchen, here in place of the real you, doing the duties the real you should be doing."

"Mom, please . . ."

She shook her head at the reflection of me. "You don't have to come here again."

"For Christ's sake, Mom, aren't you happy for me? I'm no longer at risk—don't you see? What happened to Dad isn't going to happen to me."

"Nothing has changed," said my mother. "Nothing has changed for the real you. My boy still has that thing in his head, that AVM; my son is still at risk."

"I—"

"Go away," she said.

"What about visiting Dad?"

"Hannah will take me."

"But—"

"Go away," my mother said. "And don't come back."

CHAPTER 13

"Ladies and gentlemen," said a voice over the moonbus intercom, "as you can see on the monitors, we're about to pass around onto the far side of the moon. So, please do take a moment to look out the windows and enjoy your last sight of the Earth; it won't be visible at all from your new home."

I turned and stared at the crescent planet, beautiful and blue. It had been an image I'd known all my life, but when Karen and the rest of these old folks had been children, no one had yet seen the Earth like this.

Karen was sitting next to me at the moment; Quentin Ashburn, my old seatmate from back on the spaceplane, was off chatting with the moonbus pilot about their shared pride and joy. Karen had been born in 1960, and it wasn't until December 1968 that *Apollo VIII* got far enough away from the home world to take a photograph of the whole thing. Of course, I wouldn't normally remember a date like December 1968, but everyone knew that humans first landed on the moon in 1969, and I knew that *Apollo VIII*—the first manned spaceship to leave Earth orbit—had gone there over Christmas the year before; my Sunday School teacher had once played a staticky audio of one of those astronauts reading from Genesis to commemorate that fact.

Now, though, both Karen and I were seeing for the last time the planet that gave birth to us, and to every one of our ancestors. Well, no, of course, that wasn't quite true. Life had originated only once in the solar system—but on Mars, not Earth; it had been seeded on the third planet from the fourth some four billion years ago, transferred on meteorites. And although Earth, less than 400,000 kilometers away, would be forever invisible from Lunar Farside, Mars—easy to spot, brilliant with the color of blood, of life—would frequently be visible in the night sky from High Eden, even though it was often a thousand times farther away than was Earth.

I watched as the nightside part of Earth—lenticular in this perspective, like a cat's black pupil abutting the blue crescent of the dayside—kissed the gray lunar horizon.

Ah, well. One thing I wouldn't be missing was Earth's gravity, the little stab of pain each time I put weight on my left foot.

But what people would I miss? My mother, certainly—although, of course, she'd have the new him, the durable him, for company. And I'd miss some of my friends—though, now that I thought about it, not as many as I would have supposed; I'd apparently already come to terms with never having any contact with most of them again, even though, with so many of them, the last words I'd said to them or they'd said to me had doubtless been, "See you." Christ, I wondered what my friends would make of the new me. I wondered what . . .

Yes, yes, there was one friend I'd miss. One very special friend.

I looked at the Earth, looked at Rebecca.

More of the planet was below the horizon than above it now, and the moonbus continued to speed along.

I tried to make out what part of the globe was facing me—but it was impossible to tell with all those clouds. So much hidden, even before one got to the surface of things.

I looked over at Karen Bessarian, who was staring out the little window next to our row of seats. Her deeply lined cheek was wet. "You're going to miss it," I said to her.

She nodded. "Aren't you?"

"Not the planet, no," I said. *Mostly one person there.*

All of the unilluminated part of the globe was below the horizon now; only a small blue segment was visible. For a second, I thought I was seeing the brilliant whiteness of the north pole—it had certainly stood out from Low Earth Orbit, even if, as Karen had said, it was much reduced in size from when she had been a girl. But, of course, the orientation was all wrong: we were flying parallel to, and not far south of, the lunar equator, so Earth was lying on its side, with its north-south axis running horizontally. Both poles were now well below the horizon.

"Going . . ." It was Karen, next to me, speaking softly.

Earth was fiercely bright against the black sky; if the moon had an atmosphere, Earthsets—only visible from a moving vehicle, since at all locations on nearside, the Earth hung motionless in the sky—would have been spectacular. Even though I was color-blind, and understood that I'd been missing out on some aspects of the spectacle others saw, I'd still always enjoyed sunsets.

"Going . . ." said Karen again. There was only a tiny bead of blue still visible. *"Gone."*

And it was, totally and completely. Everyone I'd ever known, every place I'd ever been.

My mother.

My father.

Rebecca.

Out of sight.

Out of mind.

The moonbus sped on.

After the disastrous visit to my mother's house, I returned home. Clamhead continued to stare out the window, waiting for someone else.

I couldn't remember the last time I'd cried—and now I was utterly incapable of it. But I wanted to. Crying was cathartic; it got things out of your system.

My system. My fucking system.

I lay down on my bed—not because I was tired; I was *never* tired anymore —but because that had always been my habit when thinking. I looked up at the ceiling. The old me might have popped a pill at this point. But the new me couldn't do that.

Of course, I could get in my car and drive up to Immortex's offices in Markham. Perhaps Dr. Porter could do something, adjust some bloody—some blood*less*—potentiometer, but . . .

But there was that damned asking-for-help thing again: stupid, stubborn, but part of who I am, and the last thing I wanted to do right now was behave out of character, lest even I begin to think what my mother and my dog and the one and only woman I loved did, that I was some sort of ersatz knockoff, some pale imitation, an impostor, a fake.

Besides, I had an appointment to see Porter tomorrow, anyway. All of us new uploads had to visit him for frequent checkups and tuneups, and—

Karen.

Karen had to do that, too.

Of course, she might have gone home to Detroit, but how practical was commuting internationally every few days? No, no, Karen was a sensible woman. She'd almost certainly be staying here in Toronto.

Where exactly, though?

The Fairmont Royal York.

The thought burst into my synthetic head. The place where the sales pitch had been held. Directly opposite the train station.

I looked at my phone. "Phone, call Fairmont Royal York Hotel; audio only."

"Connecting," said the phone.

Another voice came on, female, perky. "Royal York. How may I direct your call?"

"Hello," I said. "Do you have a Karen Bessarian registered?"

"I'm afraid not."

Oh, well. It had been just a thought. "Thank you—wait. Wait." She was famous; she probably used something other than the name she was best known by. "Ms. Cohen," I said, suddenly remembering her maiden name. "Do you have a Ms. Karen Cohen?"

"I'll put you through."

Karen would doubtless know who was calling; the hotel room's phone would inform her. Of course, it was possible that she wasn't in, but—

"Hello," said that Southern-accented voice.

In that moment, I realized that she couldn't have had the same experience I'd had, not if she hadn't yet gone home to face family and friends. But, as I said, she had to know it was me; I couldn't just hang up. "Hello, Karen."

"Hi, Jake."

Jake.

My name.

"Hi, Karen. I—" I had no idea what to say, but then it occurred to me to put it on her. "I guessed you might still be in town. I thought you might be lonely."

"Aren't you sweet!" Karen declared. "What did you have in mind?"

"Um . . ." She was in downtown Toronto. Right by the theater district. Words came tumbling out. "Would you like to go see a play?"

"I'd *love* to," Karen said.

I turned to my wall screen. "Browser, show me live theater tonight in downtown Toronto for which good seats are still available."

A list of plays and venues appeared on the screen. "You know David Widdicombe?" I said.

"Are you kidding?" said Karen. "He's one of my favorite playwrights."

"His *Schrödinger's Cat* is on at the Royal Alex."

"Sounds great," Karen said.

"Wonderful," I said. "I'll pick you up at seven-thirty."

"Perfect," she said. "It's—that's perfect."

She'd started to say 'it's a date,' I'm sure, but of course it was nothing of the kind.

CHAPTER 14

The moonbus, as I'd seen before boarding it, was a simple-looking affair: a brick-shaped central unit, with great engine cones protruding from its rear end, and two cylindrical fuel tanks, one strapped to each side. The bus was silvery white, and the tanks, I was told, were painted a color called teal, apparently a mixture of blue and green. It sported the Hyundai logo in several places, and a United Nations flag on each side near the back.

There was a wide window across the front of the brick for the pilot (he apparently didn't like to be called a driver) to see through. The bus could accommodate fourteen passengers: there were eight swiveling seats along one side, and six down the other; a gap after the second seat made room for hanging space suits. Next to each passenger seat was a window about the size of those on airplanes; each window even had one of those vinyl blinds you could draw down, like on a plane. Behind the last two seats were a small toilet on one side, and a tiny airlock cubicle on the other—"Pity the poor fool who mixes them up," the pilot had quipped during his orientation remarks.

The passenger cabin only extended halfway down the brick; the other half was taken up with cargo holds, the engines, and life-support equipment.

The moonbus's normal run was from LS One, on the Lunar Nearside, to High Eden, then on to Chernyshov Crater, both on Farside. Chernyshov was the site of a SETI facility, where big telescopes scanned the heavens for the radio chatter of alien lifeforms. Immortex leased space at High Eden to the SETI group, and had allowed an auxiliary radio telescope to be built there, giving the SETI researchers an eleven-hundred-kilometer baseline for interferometry. There were always a few SETI researchers at High Eden, and, indeed, two of the moonbus's other passengers today were radio astronomers.

We were getting close to High Eden, according to the status display shown on the monitors that hung from the ceiling. The gray, pockmarked lunar surface continued to streak by beneath us while a song I'd never heard before was playing through the moonbus's speakers. It was rather nice.

Karen, the old lady next to me, looked up and smiled. "What a perfect choice."

"What?" I asked.

"The music. It's from *Cats*."

"What's that?"

"A musical—from before you were born. Based on T. S. Eliot's *Book of Practical Cats*."

"Yes?"

"You know where we're going, no?"

"High Eden," I said.

"Yes. But where is it?"

"The far side of the moon."

"True," said Karen. "But more specifically, it's in a crater called Heaviside."

"Yes?" I said.

She sang along: *"Up up up past the Russell Hotel / Up up up to the Heaviside layer . . ."*

"What's the Heaviside layer?"

Karen smiled. "Don't feel bad, my dear boy. I imagine most people who saw the musical didn't know what it was, either. In the musical, it was the cat version of heaven. But 'Heaviside layer' is actually an old term for the ionosphere."

I was surprised to hear a little old lady talking about the ionosphere—but, then again, as I had to keep reminding myself, this was the author of *DinoWorld*. "See," she continued, "when it was discovered that radio transmissions worked over large distances, even over the curve of the Earth's horizon, people were baffled; after all, electromagnetic radiation travels in a straight line. Well, a British physicist named Oliver Heaviside figured there must be a charged layer in the atmosphere that radio signals were bouncing off. And he was right."

"So he got a crater named after him?"

"Two, actually. One here on the moon, and another on Mars. But, see, in a way we're not just going to Heaviside crater. We're going to the best place ever—the ideal retirement community. The perfect heaven for old cats."

"Heaven," I repeated. I felt my spine tingle.

Toronto. August. A warm breeze off the lake.

The play had been terrific—perhaps Widdicombe's best—and the evening was pleasantly warm.

And Karen looked—well, not lovely; that would be going too far. She was a plain thirty-year old woman, but she'd dressed up very nicely. Of course, some people had stared at us, but Karen had just stared right back. In fact, she'd told one gawking man that if he didn't look away, she'd turn on her heat vision.

In any event, I could hardly complain about Karen's appearance. I hadn't been any bargain to look at when I'd been flesh—too skinny, I knew, eyes too close together, ears too large, and . . .

And . . .

Funny, that. I only remembered those things because Trista, that cruel girl, had enumerated them in high school, ticking off my faults when I'd asked her out on a date—another of the great moments in Jake's love life. I could remember her words, but . . .

But I was having a hard time conjuring up a mental picture of my current self. The psychologists at Immortex had advised us to get rid of any photos of our old selves we had on display in our homes, but I hadn't had any. Still, it was days since I'd seen myself in a mirror, and even then—now that I no longer had to shave—they'd only been cursory glances. Could I really be forgetting what I used to look like?

Regardless of appearances, though, it was doubtless easier for an eighty-five-year-old woman to put her hand on the knee of a forty-four-year man than the other way around.

And, to my shock, Karen did just that, back in her hotel suite, after the play, the two of us sitting side by side on the lush, silk-upholstered couch in the living room. She unfolded her hand in her lap, lifting it, moving it slowly, giving me plenty of time to signal with body language or facial expression or words that I didn't want it to complete its obvious trajectory—and she let it come to rest on my right thigh, just above the knee.

I felt the warmth of her touch—not quite 37 degrees Celsius, but certainly more than room temperature.

And I felt the pressure, too: the gentle constricting of her fingers on the shifting plastic over the mechanics and hydraulics of my knee.

The hand of the biological Karen would have been liver-spotted, with translucent, loose skin, and swollen, arthritic joints.

But *this* hand . . .

This hand was youthful, with clean unblemished skin, and silvery white nails. I noticed she Karen wasn't wearing a wedding ring; she'd still been wearing one at the Immortex sales pitch. I guess maybe she'd let the biological original take it to the moon.

Still, that hand . . .

I shook my head slightly, trying to dispel the picture of her old biological appendage that my mind kept superimposing on the new, sleek, synthetic one.

I remembered taking a psychology course, years ago, in which the prof talked about intentionality—the ability of the mind to affect external reality. "I don't think *about* moving my arm," she said. "I don't work out the steps involved in contracting the muscles. I just move my arm!" And yet I realized what I did next would have enormous consequences, would define a road, a path, a future. I found myself hesitating, and—

There, my arm moved. I saw it twitch slightly. But I must have aborted the move, overriding my initial impulse, exercising that conscious veto Porter had spoken about, for my arm was almost immediately still again.

Just move my arm!

And, at last, I did, swiveling it at the shoulder, hinging it at the elbow, rotating it at the wrist, gently curving the fingers, placing my hand over hers.

I could feel warmth in my palm, and—

Electricity? Isn't that what it's called? The tingle, the response to the touch of—yes, damn it, yes—another human being.

Karen looked at me, her cameras—her eyes, her beautiful green eyes—locking on mine.

"Thank you," she said.

I could see myself reflected in her lenses. My eyebrows went up, catching, as always, a bit as they did so. "For what?"

"For seeing the real me."

I smiled, but then she looked away.

"What?"

She was silent for several seconds. "I . . . I haven't been a widow that long—only two years—but Ryan . . . Ryan had Alzheimer's. He couldn't . . ." She paused. "It's been a long time."

"It's like riding a bicycle, I suspect."

"You think?"

I smiled. "Sure."

And Karen smiled her perfectly symmetrical smile back at me. She had a luxurious two-room suite. We repaired—funny word, that—to the bedroom, and . . .

And I found nothing sexy about it, dammitall. I *wanted* it to be sexy, but it was just plastic and Teflon rubbing together, silicon chips and synthetic lubricants.

On the other hand, Karen seemed to be enjoying it. I knew the old joke about having a cherry sundae every day for years, and then suddenly not being able to have one anymore; you'd *really* want another cherry sundae. Well, after several years, I guess any cherry sundae tasted good . . .

Eventually, Karen came—if the term had any etymological validity in this context. She closed her plastiskin lids over her glass eyes and made a series of increasingly sharp, and increasingly guttural, sounds as her whole mechanical body went even more rigid than it normally was.

I felt kind of sort of a bit close to coming myself while Karen was; I'd always felt more aroused, more sexy and sexual, when someone was orgasming thanks to me. But it didn't crest, didn't peak, didn't last. I pulled out, my prosthetic member still rigid.

"Hi, stranger," said Karen, gently, looking into my eyes.

"Hi," I replied. And I smiled, doubting it was easy to tell a forced smile from a real one with these artificial faces.

"That was . . ." she said, trailing off, seeking a word. "That was *fine*."

"Really?"

She nodded. "I never used to come during intercourse. It took . . . um, you know." She made a contented sound. "There must be some women working on Immortex's body-design team."

I was happy for her. But I also knew that the old saying was true. Sex didn't happen between the legs; it happened between the ears.

"What about you?" asked Karen. "How are you doing?"

"It's just . . ." I trailed off. "It's, ah, it's going to take some getting used to."

I closed my eyes and listened to Karen's voice, which, I had to admit, did sound warm and alive and human. "That's okay," she said, snuggling her body against mine. "We've got all the time in the world."

CHAPTER 15

Karen and I talked for hours. She listened with such attention and compassion that I found myself sharing things with her I'd shared with no one else. I even told her about the big fight I'd had with my father, and how he'd collapsed right in front of my eyes.

But you can only talk for so long before running out of things to say, at lest temporarily, and so we were just relaxing now, lying in the bed in Karen's suite at the Fairmont Royal York. Karen was reading a book—an actual, physical bound volume—while I stared at the ceiling. I wasn't bored, though. I enjoyed looking up at the ceiling, at the blank white space.

Karen probably had had a different reaction, early in her career, staring at a sheet of paper in her writetyper, or whatever those things were called. I suspect empty whiteness was daunting for an author whose job it was to fill it, but for me the featureless expanse of the ceiling—here in the bedroom not even broken by a lighting fixture, since all the illumination came from floor or table lamps—was soothing, free of distractions. It was perfect, as the saying goes, for hearing myself think.

Can't remember . . .

Huh?

Can't remember that either. Are you sure?

What couldn't I remember? Well, of course, if I *could* remember it— whatever it was—then I wouldn't be worried about my inability to remember it . . .

No. No, I have no recollection of . . .

Of what? What don't I have any recollection of?

Well, if you say so. But this is very strange . . .

I shook my head, trying to clear the thoughts. Although a cliché, that usually worked for me—but this time the thoughts didn't go away.

I'm sure I'd remember something like that . . .

It wasn't like I was hearing a voice; there was no *sound,* no timbre, no cadence. Just words, tickling at the periphery of my perception—articulated but unspoken words, identical to everything else I'd ever thought.

Except—

No, I have an excellent memory. Trivia, facts, figures . . .

Except these didn't seem to be *my* thoughts.

Who did you say you are, again?

I shook my head more violently, my vision whipping from the mirrored closet doors on my left to a more ghostly reflection of myself in the window on my right.

Good, okay. And my name is Jake Sullivan . . .

Strange. Very strange.

Karen looked over at me. "Is something wrong, dear?"

"No," I said automatically. "No, I'm fine."

Heaviside Crater was located at 10.4 degrees south latitude, and 167.1 degrees east longitude—pretty close to the center of the moon's backside. That meant that Earth was straight down—separated from us by 3,500 kilometers of rock, plus almost a hundred times that much empty space.

Heaviside measured 165 kilometers across. The High Eden habitat was only five hundred meters across, so there was plenty of room to grow. Immortex projected there would be one million people a year uploading by 2060, and all the shed skins would have to be housed somewhere. Of course, it wasn't expected that skins would stay in High Eden very long: just a year or two, before they died. Despite Immortex's claims that their Mindscan process copied structures with total fidelity, the technology was always getting better, and nobody wanted to transfer any earlier than they had to.

High Eden consisted of a large assisted-living retirement home, a terminal-care hospital, and a collection of luxury apartments for the handful of us who had checked in here but didn't require 'round-the-clock aid. No—not checked in. *Moved* in. And there was no moving out.

Inside High Eden, all the rooms and corridors had very tall ceilings—it was too easy to send oneself flying up by accident. Even so, the ceilings were cushioned, just to be on the safe side; lighting fixtures were recessed into the padding. And there were plants everywhere—not only were they beautiful, but they also helped scrub carbon dioxide out of the air.

I'd always distrusted corporations, but, so far, Immortex had been true to its word. My apartment was everything I could have asked for, and just as it had been shown in the Immortex VR tour. The furniture looked like real wood—natural pine, my favorite—but of course wasn't. Although the motto of the company was that you could have any luxury you could pay for, I couldn't very well take my old furniture from Toronto—that had to be left behind for my . . . my *replacement*—and it would have been outrageously expensive to ship new stuff up from Earth.

So instead, as the household computer politely informed me in response to my queries, the furniture was made of something called whipped regolith—pulverized, aerated rock, reformed into a material like very porous basalt—that had been covered with a microthin plastic veneer printed with an ultra-high-resolution image of real knotty pine. An exterior mimicking the natural over a manufactured interior. Not too disturbing, if you didn't think about it much.

At first, I thought the overstuffed furniture was a bit miserly in its padding, but after I sat on it, I realized that you don't need as much padding to feel comfortable on the moon. My eighty-five kilos now felt like fourteen; I was as light as a toddler back on Earth.

One wall was a smart window—and a first-rate one, too. You couldn't make out the individual pixels, even if you put your face right up against it. The current image was Lake Louise, near Banff, Alberta—back before the glacier had mostly melted and flooded the whole area. I rather suspect it was a computer-generated image; I don't think anybody could have made a high-enough resolution scan back then to produce this display. Gentle waves were moving across the lake, and blue sky reflected in the waters.

All in all, it was a cross between a five-star hotel suite and a luxury executive condo; very well-appointed, very comfortable.

Nothing to complain about.

Nothing at all.

It's a modern myth that the majority of human communication isn't verbal: that much more information is conveyed by facial expression and body language, and even, some would say, by pheromones, than by spoken words. But as every teenager knows, that's ridiculous: they can spend hours talking on a voice-only phone, hearing nothing but the words the other person is saying, and interact totally. And so, even though my new artificial body was somewhat less expressive in non-verbal ways, I still had no trouble making even my most subtle nuances understood.

Or so I'd kidded myself into believing. But, the next morning, still in Karen's hotel suite, as I looked again at her plastiskin face, at her camera eyes, I found myself desperate to know what she was thinking. And if I couldn't tell what was going on inside her head, surely others couldn't tell what was going on inside mine. And so I resorted to the time-honored technique. I asked: "What are you thinking?"

We were still lying in bed. Karen turned her head, looking away. "I'm thinking that I'm old enough to be your mother." I felt something I couldn't quite quantify—it wasn't like anything else. After a second, though, I recognized what it was an analog of: my stomach tightening into knots. At least she hadn't said she was old enough to be my grandmother—although that was technically true, as well.

"I'm thinking," she continued, "I have a son two years older than you."

I nodded slowly. "It's ridiculous, isn't it?"

"A woman my age with a man your age? People would look askance. They'd say . . ."

I told my voice box to laugh, and it did—rather unconvincingly, I thought. "They'd say I was after your money."

"But that's crazy, of course. You've got lots of money of your own . . . um, don't you? I mean, after the transfer procedure, you still have lots left, no?"

"Oh, yes."

"Honestly?"

I told her how much was in my stock portfolio; I also told her how much real estate I owned.

She rolled her head again, facing me, smiling. "Not bad for a young fellow like you."

"It's not that much," I said. "I'm not stinking rich."

"No," she said, with a laugh. "Just a bit redolent."

"Still . . ." I said, and let the word hang in the air.

"I know," said Karen. "This is crazy. I'm almost twice as old as you are. What can we have in common? We grew up in different centuries. Different millennia, even."

It was true beyond the need to comment.

"But," said Karen, still looking away from me, "I guess life isn't about the part of the journey that's already done; it's about the road ahead." She paused. "Besides, I may be 200% of your age now, but a thousand years from now, I'll be less than 105% of your age. And we both expect to be around a thousand years from now, don't we?"

I paused, considering that. "I still have a hard time wrapping my head around what the word 'immortality' really means. But I guess you're right. I guess the age difference isn't so big a deal, when you put it that way."

"You really think?" she said.

I took a moment. If I wanted out, this was the perfect opportunity, the perfect excuse. But if I didn't want out, then we needed to put this issue behind us, once and for all. "Yeah," I said. "I really do think."

Karen rolled over, facing me. She was smiling. "I'm surprised you know Alanis Morissette."

"Who?"

"Oh," said Karen, and I could see her plastic features go slack. "She was a singer, very popular. Canadian, now that I think about it. And"—she imitated a husky voice that I'd never heard before—"'Yeah, I really do think' was a line from a song of hers called 'Ironic.'"

"Ah," I said.

Karen sighed. "But you don't know that. You don't know half the stuff I know—because you've only lived half as long."

"Then teach me," I said simply.

"What?"

"Teach me about the part of your life I missed. Bring me up to speed."

She looked away. "I wouldn't know where to begin."

"Start with the highlights," I said.

"There's so much."

I stroked her arm gently. "Try."

"Wellllll," said Karen, her drawl attenuating the word. "We went into space. We fought a stupid war in Vietnam. We turfed out a corrupt president. The Soviet Union fell. The European Union was born. Microwave ovens, personal computers, cell phones, and the World Wide Web appeared." She shrugged a bit. "That's the *Reader's Digest* version."

"The what?" But then I smiled. "No, just pulling your leg. My mom subscribed when I was a kid."

But the joke had bothered her, I could tell. "It's not history that separates us; it's *culture*. We grew up reading different magazines, different books. We watched different TV shows. We listened to different music."

"So what?" I said. "Everything's online." I smiled, remembering our earlier discussion. "Even copyrighted stuff—and the owners get micropayments automatically when we access it, right? So we can download your favorite books and all that, and you can introduce me to them. After all, you said we've got all the time in the world."

Karen looked intrigued. "Yes, but, well, where would we start?"

"I'd love to know what TV shows you watched growing up."

"You wouldn't want to see old stuff like that. Two-dimensional, low-res . . . some of it even in black-and-white."

"Sure, I would," I said. "It'd be fun. In fact"—I gestured at the bedroom's giant wall screen—"why don't you pick something right now? Let's get started."

"You think?" said Karen.

"Yeah," I said, trying to copy her imitation of this Alanis person's voice, "I really do think."

Karen's lips moved strangely—perhaps she was trying to purse them as she considered. Then she spoke to the suite's computer, accessing some online repository of old TV shows. And, a few moments later, white letters were appearing on the wall screen, one at a time, spelling out words, while a drum was beating in the background: *THE* . . .

Karen seemed quite excited as she sat up in the bed. "Okay, I've jumped ahead to the opening credits just so you'll get the background—then we'll go back and watch the teaser."

. . . SIX MILLION . . .

"Okay," she said. "See that guy in the cockpit? That's Lee Majors."

. . . DOLLAR MAN.

Karen went on. "He's playing Steve Austin, an astronaut and test pilot."

"How old is this show?" I asked, sitting up as well.

"This episode is from 1974."

That was . . . Christ, that was as many years before I was born as . . . as Dad's collapse was before today. "Was six million a lot then?"

"It was a fortune."

"Hunh."

There was crosstalk between pilots and ground control overtop of the images on the screen. *"It looks good at NASA One."*

"Okay, Victor."

"Landing rocket arm switch is on. Here comes the throttle . . ."

"See," said Karen, "he's testing an experimental aircraft, but it's about to crash. He's going to lose an arm, both legs, and an eye."

"I know some restaurants he couldn't eat at," I said. I waited the perfect comic beat. "They cost an arm and a leg."

Karen whapped me lightly on the forearm as the little test aircraft dropped from the wing of a giant airplane. The craft looked like a bathtub—no wonder it was going to crash. "Anyway," she said, "they replace his missing limbs with super-strong nuclear-powered duplicates, and they give him a new eye with a twenty-to-one zoom and the ability to see infrared."

More crosstalk: *"I've got a blowout, damper three . . ."*
"Get your pitch to zero."
"Pitch is out! I can't hold altitude!"
"Correction: Alpha hold is off. Trim selectors, emergency!"
"Flight Com, I can't hold it. She's breaking up! She's brea—"

The bathtub somersaulted across the screen, in very grainy footage. "That's actual archival film," said Karen. "This crash really happened."

Something that I guessed was supposed to look like computer graphics appeared on the screen—apparently they drilled a hole all the way to the back of Steve Austin's skull to put in his artificial eye—and soon the rebuilt human was running on a treadmill. I read the boxy numbers on its display. "Sixty kilometers an hour?" I said, disbelieving.

"Better," said Karen grinning. "Sixty *miles* an hour."

"Did he get insects spattered all over his face, like cars do on their windshields?"

Karen laughed. "No, and his hair never gets mussed either. I had posters of him in my bedroom when I was a teenager. He was *gorgeous*."

"I thought you were into that Superman guy, and—what was his name—Tom something?"

"Tom Selleck. Them, too. I had more than one wall, you know."

"So this introduction to your culture is going to be one teen heartthrob after another, is that it?"

Karen laughed. "Don't worry. I also used to watch *Charlie's Angels*—I had my hair like Farrah Fawcett's when I was seventeen. I'll show you one of those next time; you'll like it. It was the first jiggle show."

"Jiggle?"

She snuggled close to me. "You'll see."

CHAPTER 16

The American-style restaurant at High Eden was mostly empty: a couple of old white people dining together near what I presumed was a holographic fireplace, and a black man dining alone. The black man had close-cropped white hair. He looked a bit like Will Smith, who'd won an Oscar last year for his portrayal of Willy Loman in the new version of *Death of a Salesman*. For that role, Smith had had to suppress the natural twinkle in his eye, but this Smith-like fellow had no need to do that here, and even just sitting by himself he had a lively, alert face. On a whim, I walked over to his table.

"Hello," I said. "Would you like some company?"

The man smiled. "If I wanted to eat alone, I'd eat at home."

I pulled out a chair and sat down. As I did so, I was briefly conscious of the fact that the chair's legs must have been heavily weighted—I guess people had a tendency to pull out chairs and send them flying in this low gravity.

"Jake Sullivan," I said extending my hand.

"Malcolm Draper," said the man. I noticed he had a Tafford ring on his right index finger, but because of my color blindness I couldn't tell if it was red or green; didn't matter—I wasn't about to proposition him. I'd left my own Tafford in my suite; couldn't imagine needing it here, among all these old people. I'd been celibate for a couple of years at a go in the past, although never by choice, and, indeed hadn't had sex with anybody since that one wonderful, poignant time with Rebecca Chong back on New Year's Eve. So, I could certainly manage being celibate for the couple of years I had left, before my Katerinsky's would either completely kill me or cause my sworn advance directive to be executed. Anyway, my lack of a Tafford should discourage cougars. Of course, my Tafford was green, or so I'd been told, meaning I was straight. Still, the luck I had with women sometimes made me think the sales clerk had taken advantage of my color blindness and sold me a red one.

"Nice to meet you, Jake," said Malcolm after we'd shook hands.

"Malcolm Draper," I said, repeating the name he'd proffered. Something tickled at the back of my brain. "Should I know you?"

The man looked wary. "You a Fed?"

"Pardon?"

"Agent for one of my ex-wives?"

"No. Sorry. I didn't mean to pry."

A sly smile. "Oh, you're not. I'm just teasing. Some people have heard of me, yes. I used to be the Dershowitz Professor of Civil Liberties Law at Harvard."

"Right! Right. High-profile cases. That primate research lab, no?"

"That was me. Put an end to vivisection of great apes anywhere in the U.S., and to their unlawful confinement."

"I remember that. Good for you."

He shrugged amiably. "Thanks."

"You don't look that old," I said.

"I'm seventy-four. Hell, I could still be a Supreme Court justice . . . not that a black liberal has had a chance at an appointment for, well, forever."

"Hmm," I said, having no better response. "Did you ever argue before them?"

"Who?"

"The Supreme Court. The U.S. one, that is. I'm a Canadian myself."

"You *were* a Canadian," said Draper. "Now you're nothing at all."

"Well," I said.

"But, yes, to answer your question, I argued before the Supreme Court several times. Most recently in *McCharles v. Maslankowski*."

"That was you?"

"Yes."

"Wow. A pleasure to meet you, Mr. Draper."

"Malcolm, please."

He looked so chipper, I couldn't believe he was near death. "So . . . so are you just visiting?"

"No. No, I'm a resident. I transferred my consciousness, too. The legal Malcolm Draper is still practicing law back on Earth. There are lots of battles that still need to be fought, and lots of great young minds to train to be jurists, but I was just getting too tired to keep doing it. The doctors said I was probably good for another twenty years, easy, but I just didn't have it in me to work that hard anymore. So I retired up here—now they tell me I might live another *thirty* years in this gentle gravity."

"Thirty years . . ."

He looked at me, but was too polite to ask the question. I wondered how it was for lawyers—able to ask any pertinent question, no matter how direct or personal, in the courtroom, but constrained the way the rest of us are outside it. I decided there was no reason not to tell him. "I've probably only got a short time left."

"A young guy like you? Come now, Mr. Sullivan, you're under oath . . ."

"It's the truth. Bad blood vessels deep in the brain. They can image it, but can't get in with anything to repair it. I could go at any time, or, even worse, end up a in a vegetative state."

"Oh," said Draper. "Ah."

"It's okay, I said. "At least a version of me will continue on."

"Exactly," said Draper. "Just as with me. And I'm sure they'll do us both proud." He paused. "So, finding any companionship here?"

Surprised by his directness, I said nothing.

"I saw you with that writer woman—Karen Bessarian."

"Yeah. So?"

"She seems to like you."

"Not my type."

"Not your age, you mean."

I didn't reply.

"Well," said Malcolm, "they've got great hookers here."

"I know. I read the brochure."

"I used to write a civil liberties column for *Penthouse*. Just like Alan Dershowitz, before me."

"Really?"

"Sure. Its slogan was 'The magazine of sex, politics, and power.'"

"And of women peeing."

"That, too," said Malcolm, smiling. I used to sneak the occasional peek when I was a teenager, before *Penthouse* and *Playboy* went bankrupt, unable to compete with Web alternatives. "What's the matter?" Malcolm continued. "Don't like paying for it?"

"I never have before."

"I thought that sort of thing was legal up in Canada."

"It is, but—"

"Besides, look at it this way. You're *not* paying for it. The Jake Sullivan down on Earth, he's the one paying the bills. Which maintenance plan are you on?"

"Gold."

"Well, then, the hookers are included."

"I don't know . . ."

"Trust me," said Malcolm, with that twinkle in his eye, "you haven't really made love until you've done it in one-sixth gee."

Now that I have a new body, I don't miss sweating, or sneezing, or being tired, or being hungry. I don't miss stubbed toes, or sunburns, or runny noses, or headaches. I don't miss the pain in my left ankle, or diarrhea, or dandruff, or charley horses, or needing to pee so bad it hurts. And I don't miss having to shave or cut my nails or put on deodorant. I don't miss paper cuts, or farting, or pimples, or having a stiff neck.

It's nice to know that I'll never need stitches, or angioplasty, or a hernia operation, or laser surgery to reattach a retina—the damage Clamhead did to my arm had been fixed up in a matter of minutes, good as new; just about any physical damage could likewise be repaired, without anesthetic, without leaving scars. And, as they said at the sales pitch, it's comforting not having to worry about diabetes or cancer or Alzheimer's or heart attacks or rheumatoid arthritis—or God-damned Katerinsky's syndrome.

Plus I can read for hours. I still get bored as easily as before; the book has to hold my interest. But I don't ever have to stop reading just because of eye fatigue, or because trying to make out words in dim light is giving me a headache. Indeed, I haven't read this much since I was a student.

Are there things I *do* miss? Of course. All of my favorite foods—Jalapeño peppers and popcorn and Jell-O and stringy cheese on pizza. I miss the way I used to feel after a really good yawn, or the invigorating sensation of splashing cold water on my face. I miss being ticklish and the feeling of silk and laughing so hard it's actually painful.

But those things aren't gone for good. A decade or two from now, the technology will exist to give me all those sensations again. I can wait. I can wait forever.

And, yet, despite having all that time, some things seemed to be progressing awfully quickly. Karen had given up her suite at the Royal York, and moved into my house. It was temporary, of course—just a convenience, since she had to stay in Toronto for a while longer, seeing Porter for check ups and adjustments two or three times a week.

Me, I still intended to live here in North York for the foreseeable future. And so I was trying to decide what to do with the kitchen. It seemed pointless to devote so much space to something I'd—*we'd*—never use, and, frankly, it was an unwelcome reminder of the pleasures we'd given up. Of course, I had to keep bathrooms for visitors, but a wet bar and coffee urn were all I really needed to entertain a bit, and, well, the kitchen was huge, and had wonderful windows looking out over the landscaped yard. It was much too good a room to avoid. Maybe I'd turn it into a billiards room. I'd always wanted one of those.

While I was mulling this over, Karen, as she often did, was sitting in a chair, reading from a datapad. She preferred paper books, but for catching up on news she didn't mind using a datapad, and—

And suddenly I heard her make the sound that substituted for a gasp. "What's wrong?" I said.

"Daron is dead."

I didn't recognize it in time. "Who?"

"Daron Bessarian. My first husband."

"Oh, my God," I said. "I'm sorry."

"I haven't seen him for—God, it's been thirty years. Not since his mother died. She'd been very good to me, and we'd kept in touch, even after Daron and I divorced. I went to her funeral." Karen paused for a moment, then said decisively, "And I want to go to Daron's funeral."

"When is it?"

She looked down at her datapad. "The day after tomorrow. In Atlanta."

"Do—do you want me to go with you?"

Karen considered this, then: "Yes. If you wouldn't mind."

Actually, I hated funerals—but had never been to one of somebody I didn't know; maybe that wouldn't be so bad. "Um, sure. Sure, I'd be"—*happy to* didn't seem the right way to end that sentence, and for once I caught my first thought before it got out into the air—"willing to."

Karen nodded decisively. "It's settled, then."

I had to do something about Clamhead. She needed human companionship, and apparently no matter how hard I tried, she wasn't going to accept me—or Karen, as it turned out—in that capacity. Plus, Karen and I were going away to Georgia, and had decided to stop at her place in Detroit on the way back. It wasn't fair to Clammy to leave her with just a robokitchen for an extended period.

And, well, damn it all, but I'm an idiot. I can't leave well enough alone; I can't resist trying one more time, testing the waters yet again.

And so I called Rebecca Chong.

I thought maybe if I selected audio only on the phone, things might go better. She'd hear my voice, hear its warmth, hear the affection in it—but not see my plastic face.

She knew it was me calling, of course; the phone would have told her. And so, the mere fact that she *answered* . . .

"Hello," came her voice, formal and stiff.

I had that purely mental sensation that used to accompany my heart sinking. "Hi, Becks," I said, trying to sound cheerful, chipper.

"Hello," she said again, still not using my name. It was right there in front of her, a string of pixels on her call-display unit, an electronic identification, but she wouldn't use it.

"Becks," I said, "it's about Clamhead. Can you—would you be willing to look after her for a while? I'm—she—"

Rebecca was brilliant; that was one of the reasons I loved her. "She doesn't recognize you, does she?"

I was quiet for longer than you're supposed to be in phone conversations, then: "No. No, she doesn't." I paused again, then: "I know you've always loved Clamhead. Does your building allow pets?"

"Yeah," she said. "And, yeah, I'd be happy to look after Clamhead."

"Thanks," I said.

Maybe all this talk about a dog had moved her to throw me a bone. "What are friends for?"

I was sitting in the living room of my lunar apartment, reading news on my datapad. Of course, the selection of stories displayed was based on my keywords, and—

Jesus.

Jesus Christ.

Could it be true?

I thumbed the article open and read it—then read it again.

Chandragupta. That was a name I hadn't heard before; this couldn't really be his area, or else—

Hyperlinks; his bio. No, no, he's the real deal, all right. And so—

My heart was pounding and my vision was blurring.

Oh, my God. Oh, my God.

Maybe I should email him, but—

But, God damn it, I couldn't. We were allowed to monitor Earth news here—I never would have come if I couldn't have continued to follow the Blue Jays—but we weren't permitted any form of communication with people back on Earth.

Christ, why couldn't this have happened a few weeks ago, before I spent all this money on the Mindscan process and on coming here to the moon? What a waste!

But that was beside the point, really. It was *only* money. This was way more important.

This was huge.

This changed everything.

I re-read the news to be sure I wasn't mistaken. And I wasn't. It was *real*.

I was excited and elated and thrilled. I left my apartment, practically bouncing over to the Immortex offices.

The chief administrator at High Eden was a man named Brian Hades: tall, early fifties, light-colored eyes, silver-gray hair gathered into a ponytail, white beard. We'd all met him upon our arrival; I'd quipped that he had a hell of a name—and although his tone never veered from its habitual the-customer-is-always-right smoothness, his bearded jaw clenched in a way that suggested I'd not been the first one to make that joke. Anyway, there wasn't much bureaucracy here; I just walked through his office door and said hello.

"Mr. Sullivan," he said at once, rising from behind his kidney-shaped desk; there weren't so many of us skins yet that he couldn't keep track of us all. "What can I do for you?"

"I have to return to Earth."

Hades raised his eyebrows. "We can't allow that. You know the rules."

"You don't understand," I said. "They've found a cure for my problem."

"What problem is that?"

"Katerinsky's syndrome. A kind of arteriovenous malformation in the brain. It's why I'm here. But there's a new technique that can cure it."

"Really?" said Hades. "That's wonderful news. What's the cure?"

I had the vocabulary of all this down pat; I'd lived with it so long. "Using nanotechnology, they endovascularly introduce particles into the AVM to clog off its nidus; that shuts the AVM down completely. Because the particles use carbon-based nanofibers, the body doesn't reject, or even really notice, them."

"And that means . . . what? That you'd live a normal lifespan?"

"Yes! Yes! So, you see—"

"That's terrific. Where do they do the procedure?"

"Johns Hopkins."

"Ah. Well, you can't go there, but—"

"What do you mean, I can't go there? We're talking about saving my life! I know you've got rules, but . . ."

Hades held up a hand. "And they can't be broken. But don't worry. We'll contact people there on your behalf, and bring an appropriate doctor to our facility here. You've got an unlimited medical benefit, although . . ."

I knew what he was thinking. That my accountant—good old Larry Hancock—would certainly notice the . . . what? Millions? The million this would cost. But Hades wasn't getting the point. "No, no, you don't see. Everything is different now. The conditions under which I agreed to stay here no longer pertain."

Hades's voice was infinitely solicitous. "Sir, I'm sorry. We'll certainly arrange for you to have this cure—and right away, since I understand how precarious your current health is. But you can't leave here."

"You have to let me go," I said, an edge honing my words.

"We can't. You have no home on the outside, no money, no identity— nothing. This is the only place for you."

"No, you don't understand . . ."

"Oh, but I do. Look—how old are you?"

"Forty-four."

"Think of how lucky you are! I'm fifty-two, and I'll have to work for many more years, but you've gotten to retire a decade or two before most people do, and are enjoying the absolute lap of luxury."

"But—"

"Aren't you? Is there anything you lack here? You know we pride ourselves on our service. If there's something that's not up to your standards, you just have to ask. You know that."

"No, no . . . it's all very pleasant, but . . ."

"Well, then, you see, Mr. Sullivan, there's nothing to worry about. You can have anything here that you can have on the outside."

"Not anything."

"Tell me what you want. I'll do whatever I can to make your stay here happy."

"I want to go home." It sounded so plaintive, so like my early days at summer camp, all those years ago. But it was what I wanted now, more than any-thing else in the world—in *all* the worlds. I wanted to go home.

"I'm truly, truly sorry, Mr. Sullivan," said Hades, shaking his head slowly back and forth, the pony tail bouncing as he did so. "There's just no way I can allow that."

CHAPTER 17

You have to clear U.S. customs at Pearson Airport in Toronto before you can even get on a plane bound for the States. I'd been afraid we'd have a hard time doing so, but the biometrics of our new bodies matched those of the old ones in key places, and we made it through automated screening without any difficulty. I'd thought Karen would have trouble because her current face was so much more youthful than the one in her passport photo, but whatever facial-recognition software was being used must have relied on underlying bone structure, or something, because it agreed that the person in the photo was indeed her.

I hadn't flown since I'd been a teenager. My doctors had urged me not to because the pressure changes that accompanied flying could have set off my Katerinsky's. Now, of course, I felt no pressure changes at all. I wondered whether airline food had improved over the years, but I had no way to find out.

One of the advantages of no longer sweating is that we didn't have to pack many clothes when we traveled; we had only carry-on luggage. Once we arrived in Atlanta, we headed straight to the Hertz counter and got a car—a blue Toyota Deela. Since there was no need to go by the hotel first to freshen up, we drove straight to the funeral home.

Karen still had a valid driver's license, although she said she hadn't driven for years; she was afraid her reflexes had dulled too much. But she was happy to do the driving now. I couldn't remember the last time I'd ridden shotgun, but it did give me a chance to look at the scenery; they really do have a lot of peach trees in Georgia.

As we continued along, Karen told me about Daron. "He was my first love," she said. "And when it's your first, you have nothing to compare it to. I had no idea it wasn't going to work out . . . although I suppose no one ever does in advance."

"Why'd you break up?" It had been the first question that had occurred to me, and I figured I'd now waited long enough to be entitled to give it voice.

"Oh, any number of reasons," said Karen. "Fundamentally, we just wanted different things from life. We were still in university when we got married. He wanted to be a printing salesperson, like his father—that's back when working in printing seemed like a good career choice—and he wanted me to get a job soon, too. But I wanted to stay in university, go to grad school. He wanted the house with the big yard in the suburbs; I wanted to travel and not be tied down. He wanted to start a family right away; I wanted to wait to have kids. In fact . . ."

"What?"

"Nothing."

"No. Tell me."

Karen was quiet for a time as we rolled along. Finally, she said, "I had an abortion. I'd gotten pregnant—stupid, right? I hadn't been careful about taking my pills. Anyway, I never even told Daron about it, since he would have insisted we keep it."

I consciously suppressed my natural inclination to blink. They'd been married in the 1980s, and this was the 2040s. If Karen hadn't aborted the child, he or she would be something like sixty now . . . and that child, too, would likely be *en route* to the funeral of the man who had been its father.

I could almost feel the swirling of timelines, the fog of lives that might have gone differently. If Karen hadn't ended that pregnancy all those decades ago, she might have stayed with Daron for the good of her child . . . meaning she'd probably never have written *DinoWorld* and its sequels; it was her second husband who had encouraged her to write. And that would have meant she'd never have been able to afford Immortex's services. She'd just be an old, old lady, hampered by bad joints.

We pulled into the parking lot of the funeral home. There were lots of empty places; Karen took one of the handicapped spaces.

"What are you doing?" I asked.

"What? Oh." She put the car in reverse. "Force of habit. Back when I could drive before, we were entitled to use those spots—my poor Ryan needed a walker." She found another place to park, and we got out. I thought Toronto was hot in August; here, it was like a blast furnace, and drenchingly humid.

Another couple—ah, that loaded word!—was up ahead of us, entering the building. They clearly heard our footfalls, and the man held the door for us, turning around as he did so.

His jaw dropped. Damn, I was getting tired of being stared at. I forced what I hoped was a particularly theatrical smile and caught the door. Karen and I walked in. There were three grieving families today; a sign in the lobby directed us to the correct room.

The casket was open. Even from this distance, I could see the corpse, trying to feign the look of life.

Right. Like I should talk.

Of course, all eyes were soon on us. A woman who must have been in her eighties—the same age that Karen herself still was—rose from a pew and came over to us. "Who are you?" she said, looking at me. Her voice was reedy, and her eyes were red.

The question, of course, occupied a lot of my thoughts these days. Before I could reply, though, Karen said, "He's with me."

The crab-apple head before us turned to face Karen. "And who are you?"

"I'm Karen," she said.

"Yes?" prodded the woman, the single syllable dry, demanding.

Karen seemed reluctant to use her last name. Here, surrounded by real Bessarians—Bessarians by birth, and by enduring marriages—perhaps she didn't feel entitled to it. But at last she spoke again. "I'm Karen Bessarian."

"My . . . God," said the woman, her eyes narrowing as she studied Karen's youthful, synthetic face.

"And you are . . . ?" asked Karen.

"Julie. Julie Bessarian."

I didn't know if she was Daron's sister or another of Daron's widows, although Karen presumably did; she'd certainly remember the names of her ex-sisters-in-law, if any.

Karen held out her hands, as if to take Julie's in sympathy, but Julie just looked at them. "I always wondered what you looked like," Julie said, returning her gaze to Karen's face.

Another widow, then. Karen tilted her head back slightly, defiantly. "Now you know," she replied. "In fact, this isn't all that far off what I was like back when Daron and I were together."

"I—I'm sorry," said Julie. "Forgive me." She looked over at her dead husband, then back at Karen. "I want you to know, in the fifty-two years we were married, Daron never said a bad word about you."

Karen smiled at that.

"And he was so very happy for all your success."

Karen's head nodded a bit. "Thank you. Who's here from Daron's family?"

"Our children," said Julie, "but you wouldn't know them, I don't think. We had two daughters. They'll be back shortly."

"What about his brother? His sister?

"Grigor died two years ago. That's Narine over there."

Karen's head swiveled to have a look at another old woman, supported by a walker, chatting with a middle-aged man. "I'd—I'd like to say hello," Karen said. "Offer my condolences."

"Of course," said Julie. The two of them moved away, and I found myself walking forward, to the front of the room, looking down on the face of the dead man. I hadn't consciously thought about doing that—but when it became apparent what my body was up to, I didn't veto the action, either.

I don't say all my thoughts are charitable or appropriate, and I often enough wish they had never occurred to me in the first place. But they do, and I must acknowledge them. That man, there, in the coffin, had done what I would never do: feel Karen's *flesh*, join with her in real, animal passion. Yes, it had been sixty years ago . . . long before I was born. And I didn't resent him for it; I envied him.

He seemed calm, lying there, arms crossing his chest. Calm—and old, wrinkled, face deeply lined, head almost entirely bald. I tried to regress his countenance, to see if he'd been handsome in his youth, wondering if such ephemeral concerns had ever mattered to Karen. But I really couldn't tell what he'd looked like at twenty-one, the age he'd been when he'd married her. Ah, well; perhaps it was best not to know.

Still, I couldn't take my eyes off his face, the sort of face I'd never have now. But more than appearance separated us, for this man—this Daron Bessarian—was dead, and . . . I was still trying to make sense of it . . . I likely would never be.

"Jake?"

I looked up from my reverie. Karen was approaching in a series of very small steps; Julie had taken Karen's artificial arm for support, seemingly now at ease with being in contact with it.

"Jake," repeated Karen, as she drew nearer, "forgive me for not introducing you earlier. This is Julie, Daron's wife"—a small kindness, that, not to say "second wife."

"I'm terribly sorry for your loss," I said.

"He was a good man," said Julie.

"I'm sure he was."

Julie was silent for a moment, then: "Karen has told me about what's been done to the two of you." She gestured with a thin, gnarled hand at my body. "I'd heard a little about such things, of course—I still watch the news, although it mostly depresses me. But, well, I never thought I'd ever meet any-one who had enough money to . . ." She trailed off, and I had nothing to say in response, so I just waited for her to go on, which, at last, she did.

"Sorry," Julie said. She looked over at the coffin, then back at me. "I wouldn't want what you've got, anyway—not without my Daron." She touched my synthetic forearm with her flesh one. "But I do envy you. Daron and I only had fifty years together. But the two of you! To have so much time still to come!" Her eyes grew moist again, and she looked back at her dead hus-band. "Oh, how I envy you . . ."

I'd heard someone quip shortly after I arrived on the moon that one advantage of lunar life was that there were no lawyers here. But, of course, that's not entirely true: my newfound friend Malcolm Draper was a lawyer, even if he was now, by his own testimony, a retired one. Still, he was the obvious person to seek out for advice about my predicament. I called him on the internal High Eden phone system—the only one we residents had access to. "Hey, Mal-colm," I said, when his distinguished face appeared on the screen. "I need to talk to you. Got a minute?"

He raised his grizzled eyebrows. "What's up?"

"Can we meet somewhere?" I said.

"Sure," said Malcolm. "How about the greenhouse?"

"Perfect."

The greenhouse was a room fifty meters on a side and ten meters tall, full of tropical plants and trees. It was the only place in High Eden were the air was humid. The huge assortment of flowers seemed colorful even to me; I couldn't imagine the riot of hues and shades Malcolm must be seeing. Of course, the plants weren't just here to make residents feel less homesick; they were also an integral part of the air-recycling system.

From my occasional visits to greenhouses in Toronto—Allan Gardens was my favorite—I was used to moving along slowly, quietly, almost like when vis-iting a museum, going from placard to placard. But walking on the moon was different. I'd seen historical footage of *Apollo* astronauts bouncing around as they walked—and they'd been wearing spacesuits that massed as much as the astronauts themselves did. Malcolm and I, in gym shorts and loose T-shirts, couldn't help but fly up with each step. It doubtless looked comical, but I wasn't in a fun mood.

"So what's up?" asked Malcolm. "Why the long face?"

"They've found a cure for my condition," I said, looking at a cluster of vines.

"Really? That's wonderful!"

"It is, but . . ."

"But what? You should be jumping up and down." He smiled. "Well, all right, you do have quite a spring in your step, but you don't sound very happy."

"Oh, I'm happy about the cure. You don't know what it's been like, all these years. But, well, I spoke to Brian Hades."

"Yes?" said Malcolm. "And what did the pony-tailed one have to say?"

"He won't let me go home, even after I'm cured."

We bounced along for several paces. Malcolm's arms flew out from time to time to steady himself, but his face was drawn, and he was clearly carefully considering what to say next. Finally, he spoke: "You *are* home, Jake."

"Christ, you too? The conditions under which I agreed to come here have changed. I know contract law isn't your specialty, but there must be something I can do."

"Like what? Like go back to Earth? You're *still* there; the new version of you is there, living in your house, going on with your life."

"But I'm the original. I'm more important."

Malcolm shook his head. *"The Two Jakes,"* he said.

I looked at him, as he batted some overhanging foliage out of his way. "What?"

"Ever see it? It's the sequel to *Chinatown*, one of my favorite films. The original was fabulous, but *The Two Jakes* is a lousy movie."

I didn't hide my irritation. "What are you talking about?"

"Just that there are two Jakes now, see? And maybe you're right: maybe the original *is* more important than the sequel. But you're going to have a hard time proving it to anyone except you and me."

"Can't you help me—you know, in your professional capacity?"

"A lawyer's only any use within an infrastructure that supports litigation. This is the Old West; this is the frontier. No police, no courts, no judges, no jails. Your replacement down on Earth might be able to change things—not that I can see any reason why he'd want to—but there's nothing you can do up here."

"But I'm going to live for decades now."

Malcolm shrugged. "So am I. We'll have some great times together." He gestured at the garden surrounding us. "It really is a wonderful place, you know."

"But . . . but there's someone, down on Earth. A woman. Things are different now—or they will be, once I have the operation. I *have* to get out of here; I have to go home—home to her."

We walked along some more. "Greensboro," said Malcolm, softly, almost to himself.

I was still irritated. "Another movie no one ever saw?"

"Not a movie. History. My people's history. In the southern U.S., it used to be that facilities were segregated, and, of course, the good facilities were for whites only. Well, in 1960, four black college students sat down in the whites-only section of the lunch counter at Woolworth's—that was a department store—and asked to be served. They were refused, and told to leave the store. They didn't; they started a sit-in, and it spread to other whites-only lunch counters all over the South."

"And?"

Malcolm sighed, appalled at my ignorance, I guess. "They won through peaceful protest. The lunch counters were desegregated, and blacks were given the same rights that other people had had all along. The boycotters forced the people in power to recognize that you can't push someone around just because of their skin. Well, *you* are nothing but a skin, my friend—a shed skin. And maybe you *do* deserve rights. But, like those brave young men, if you want them, you're going to have to demand them."

"How?"

"Find some place to occupy, and refuse to budge until you get what you want."

"You think that'd work?" I asked.

"It's worked before. Of course, don't do anything violent."

"Me? Never in a million years."

CHAPTER 18

Karen and I spent four days in Georgia, seeing the sights, and then we flew north to Detroit, so that Karen could take care of a few things.

Detroit. Hardly where you'd expect to find a wealthy novelist who could make her home anywhere. In the previous century, most Canadians lived as close as possible to the U.S. border—but it wasn't out of fondness for our American neighbors. Rather, we simply went as far south into the warmth as we could without leaving our own country. And now the reverse was true. Trying to escape the heat, Americans came as far north as possible without actually departing the land of the free and the home of the brave; that's why Karen lived here.

Of course, she had a fabulous mansion, filled with trophies for her writing, copies of her books in over thirty languages, and even some props and set pieces from the movies made of her work.

It was also filled with things reflective of her last husband, Ryan, who had died two years ago. Ryan had collected fossils. Unlike most nature-based hobbies, that one had actually gotten easier of late: all the extra runoff and erosion caused by the polar caps shrinking apparently exposed lots of new material. Or so Karen told me. Anyway, Ryan had shelves of trilobites—the only invertebrate fossil I could identify on sight—and many other wonderful things.

The most important reason for stopping in Detroit was so that Karen could see her son Tyler, who also lived in this city. She'd spoken to Tyler several times on the phone since undergoing the Mindscan process, but had opted to do it as voice-only calls. She'd told me she wanted him to see her new face directly, not over some hardware that would make it appear even more cold and remote.

Around 6:00 p.m., Karen's doorbell rang. The living-room wall monitor immediately changed to show the peephole-camera view. "That's Tyler," said Karen, nodding. He was, I knew, forty-six. His hair was light brown, and had receded a fair bit. Karen got up from the couch and headed for the entryway. I followed. The light there was dim. Karen unlocked and opened the front door, and—

"Hello," said Tyler, sounding surprised. "My name's Tyler Horowitz. I'm here to see—"

"Tyler, it's me," said Karen.

He froze, his jaw hanging slack. I did some quick math: Tyler was born in 1999; Karen's new face was based on the way she'd appeared when she was thirty, back in 1990. Even as a boy, Tyler would never have seen his mother looking quite like this.

"Mom?" he said, softly, disbelieving.

"Come in, son, come in." She stepped aside, and he entered the house.

Karen turned now to face me. "Jake," she said, "I'd like you to meet my son Tyler. Tyler, this is the new friend I was telling you about."

Even in the dim light, Tyler must have seen that my body was artificial: he looked at my proffered hand as though I'd extended some hideous mechanical claw. He did finally take my hand, but he shook it with no enthusiasm. "Hello, Tyler," I said, bringing all the warmth I could to my electronic voice.

He was clearly Karen's son, although he looked almost twenty years older than she did now. But his basic facial structure was highly similar to hers: broad, with a smallish nose and widely spaced green eyes. "Hello," he said, his voice ironically sounding flat and mechanical.

I smiled and he looked away. I knew that my smile appeared slightly wrong—but, for Pete's sake, his mother's old smile had been the lopsided smirk of a stroke victim. "I'm glad to meet you," I said. "Karen has told me a lot about you."

A brief wince; maybe he didn't like me calling his mother by her first name.

Karen led us into the living room, and I took a seat on the couch, crossing my legs. Tyler continued to stand. "Your mother tells me you're a history professor," I said.

He nodded. "At the University of Michigan."

"What's your specialty?"

"American history. Twentieth century."

"Oh?" I did want him to like me, and people usually warmed to talking about their work. "What topics do you cover?"

He looked at me, trying to decide, I guess, whether to accept this olive branch. Finally, he shrugged. "All sorts of things. The Scopes Trial. The Great Depression. WWII. JFK. The Cuban Missile Crisis. Vietnam. *Apollo.* Watergate. Iran-Contra."

Apollo had gone to the moon, and WWII and Vietnam were wars—but I didn't have a clue what the others were. Jesus Christ, the twentieth century. Karen's century.

"I'll get you to tell me about those some day," I said, still trying to ingratiate myself. "It all sounds fascinating."

He looked at me. "You must remember some of them," he said. "I mean, I know you've chosen to look young now, but . . ."

Karen glanced at me, and I shrugged a little. It had to come out at some point. "This new face is only a little bit more youthful-looking than my original." I paused. "I'm forty-four."

Tyler blinked. "Forty-four? God, you're younger than I am!"

"Yup. I was born in 2001—on the first of January, as a matter of fact. I was the—"

"You're younger than I am," repeated Tyler, "and you're dating my mother."

"Tyler, please," said Karen. She took the seat next to me on the couch.

His eyes drilled into her, emerald lasers. "Well, that's what you said on the phone—you wanted me to meet the man you're dating. Mother, you're eighty-five, and he's barely half that."

"But I don't feel eighty-five," said Karen. "And I don't look it anymore."

"It's all fake," said Tyler.

"No, it's not," replied Karen firmly. "It's real. *I'm* real, and I'm human, and I'm alive—more alive than I've been in years. And Jake is my friend, and being with him makes me happy. You do want me to be happy, don't you, Tyler?"

"Yes, but . . ." He looked at his mother. "But, for God's sake . . ."

Karen frowned, something she rarely did. There was a strange bunching of her plastiskin between her lower lip and her chin when she did so; she'd have to get Dr. Porter to fix that. " 'For God's sake,' " repeated Karen, and she shook her head. "You want me to be dating someone my own age—someone who's about to die? Or would you rather I wasn't dating at all?"

"Pop would—"

"You know I loved your father—I loved Ryan Horowitz totally and completely. This has nothing to do with him."

"He's only been dead two years," said Tyler.

"It'll be three in November," said Karen. "And besides . . ."

"Yes?" said Tyler, as if daring her to elaborate. I knew what Karen wasn't saying: that Ryan had had Alzheimer's for years before his body had finally given up, that Karen had essentially been alone for much longer than just since he'd died. But Karen wasn't about to be sucked into that trap. Instead, as was her wont, her gift, her *raison d'être*, she told a story.

"When I was nineteen, Tyler, I fell in love with Daron Bessarian, a nice non-Jewish boy. Now, you barely remember your grandfather, I'm sure, but he was a Holocaust survivor, and he didn't want me dating somebody who wasn't a Jew. He kept saying to me, 'If they come for us again, this boy—he would hide you? When they try to take your home, he would stand up for you?' And I said, 'Of course he would. Daron would do anything for me.' But my father didn't believe it, and when Daron and I got married, he refused to come to the wedding. Now, yes, Daron and I eventually divorced, but that was for our own reasons. But I didn't let my father dictate who I should be with back then, and I'm not going to let my son dictate it now. So, mind your manners, Tyler, have a seat, and enjoy the evening."

Tyler took a deep breath and let it out noisily. "All right." He looked around, found the chair furthest from me, and plopped himself in it. "When do we eat?"

I dropped my gaze to the floor.

"Oh, right," said Tyler. "When do *I* eat?"

"Whenever you want to, my dear," said Karen. "I thought we'd order you a pizza. You . . ."

I was sure she'd been about to say something like, "You always liked pizza," but had presumably thought better of it. Too much like an elderly mother lamenting that her little boy was all grown up now.

Tyler nodded after a moment. "Pizza is fine. Do you have a good local place? A mom-and-pop?"

I thought I could build on this. "You don't like big chains, either?"

Tyler regarded me. He seemed almost offended that I was trying to find a common ground between us. But, after a moment, he said, "Yeah. I hate them. Did your folks run a small business?"

"Well, it was a *family* business . . ." I said.

Tyler narrowed his green eyes suspiciously. "Meaning what?"

"They're in the beer business."

"How so? Some little microbrewery?"

This had to come out at some point, too. "No. Not a microbrewery," I said. "My last name is Sullivan, and—"

"Sullivan?" snapped Tyler. "As in Sullivan's Select?"

"Yes. My father was a vice-president, and—"

Tyler nodded as if I'd just handed down an indictment. "Nepotism," he said. "Rich old fat cat."

I was going to let it go, but Karen had had enough. "Actually, Jake's father suffered severe brain damage when he was thirty-nine. He's been in a vegetative state for getting on thirty years now."

"Oh," replied Tyler, softly. "Um, I'm sorry."

"Me, too," I said.

"So . . . ah." Tyler was perhaps thinking of all the chronological absurdities here. Him older than me, my father incapacitated at an age around our own, a man in his forties dating a woman in her eighties, a woman who grew up in the last millennium with a man who grew up in this one.

"Look," I said, "I know this is awkward. But the fact of the matter is that Karen and I *are* together. And it really would make both of us happy if you and I could get along."

"Who said anything about not getting along?" replied Tyler, sounding quite defensive

"Well, no one, but . . ." I stopped, tried another tack. "Let's start over, shall we?" I got up, walked over to where he was now sitting, and stuck out my hand again. "I'm Jake Sullivan. Pleased to meet you."

Tyler looked as though he was contemplating whether to go along with this rebooting of things. But, after a moment, he took my hand and shook it. But he wouldn't go so far with the charade as to introduce himself again.

"Now," said Karen, "why don't you order that pizza? Try Pappa Luigi's. I couldn't eat pizza these last few years, but people said they were good."

"Phone," Tyler said, into the air, "call Papa Luigi's."

The phone did so, and Tyler placed his order.

I sat down again, this time taking a straight-back wooden chair that I would have found uncomfortable had my body been subject to fatigue. We all talked awkwardly for a while. Tyler had lots of questions about the Mindscan process, and Karen answered them.

The pizza was supposed to be here in thirty minutes or it would be free; I'd have paid a lot to get it here even faster than that to put an end to the strained conversation, but at last the doorbell rang again. Karen insisted on paying, over Tyler's protests. ("You're not going to have any, after all." "But I did invite you for dinner.") She carried the box into the kitchen, and set it on top of the stove. She then got Tyler a plate, and he helped himself to a steaming slice.

The cheese pulled away in strings that he had to sever with his fingers. The toppings—pepperoni, onions, and bacon—looked perfectly decadent: the disks of pepperoni curling up at the edges, creating little artificial lakes of oil; the crisp bacon strips crisscrossing the flat Earth of cheese; the onions concentric semicircles darkened almost to black at their tips.

It *looked* fabulous but . . .

But I couldn't smell it at all. The olfactory sensors I'd been provided with were geared to those things that were crucial for safety: the odors of gas leaks, of burning wood. The meat, the onions, the tomato sauce, the warm bread of the crust—none of it registered.

But they were clearly registering on Tyler. I'm sure he wasn't doing it to be cruel, but I could see him inhaling deeply, drawing in the wonderful—they must be wonderful, I knew they were wonderful—smells. A look of anticipation grew across his face, and then he bit into his piece, making that glorious grimace that suggested the roof of his mouth was burning.

"How is it?" I asked.

"Mmmmfph . . ." He paused, swallowed. "Not bad at all."

It was decadent indeed—but, then again, with over-the-counter drugs that dissolved arterial plaque, and others that prevented fat from accumulating, it really wasn't that much of an indulgence . . . for him. But for me, it was something I'd never enjoy again.

No, not never. Sugiyama had said this version of the body was only the current state-of-the-art. It was infinitely upgradeable. Eventually . . .

Eventually.

I watched Tyler eat.

After Tyler left, Karen and I sat on her living-room couch, talking. "So, what did you think of Tyler?" Karen asked.

"He doesn't like me," I said

"What kid does like the man who's dating his mother?"

"I suppose, but . . ." I trailed off, then, a moment later, continued. "No, I shouldn't complain. I mean, at least he seems more accepting of you now that you've uploaded than my mother was of me—or than my friends were, for that matter."

She asked what I meant, and I told her about my disastrous visit to my mother's place. Karen was terrifically warm and supportive, holding my hand as I talked. But I guess I was in a pissy mood, because before I knew it, we were arguing—and I hate, hate, hate arguing with people. But Karen had said, "It doesn't really matter what your mother thinks."

"Of course it does," I snapped. "Can you imagine how difficult this is for her? She carried me in her womb. She gave birth to me. She breast-fed me. Except that none of those things happened to *this* me."

"I am a mother myself," said Karen, "and I did all those things with Tyler."

"No, you didn't," I replied. "The *other* Karen did."

"Well, yes, technically, but—"

"It's not just a technical point. It's not hair-splitting. Man, I get so tired of this—of being stared at, of people treating me like some kind of *thing*. And maybe they're right. Hell, even my dog doesn't recognize me."

"Your dog is dumb; all dogs are. And your friends and your mother are wrong. They're just being stupid."

"They're not stupid. Don't call them that."

"Well, the attitude they're taking certainly is. I presume all those people you mentioned are younger than me. If I can come to grips with this, they should be able to, as well, and—"

"Why? Because you say so?" My, I was in a bad mood. "Because the great novelist would write the story so that it had a happy ending?"

Karen let go of my hand, but, after a moment, she spoke. "It's not that. It's just that people should be more understanding. I mean, think of all the money we've spent. If they—"

"What difference does it make how much this cost? You can't buy acceptance."

"No, of course not, but—"

"And you can't force people to feel about you the way you want them to."

I was sure Karen was getting angry, although the usual physiological signs—reddening of the face, a change to the vocal timbre—were absent. "You're wrong," she said. "We're entitled to—"

"We're entitled to *nothing*," I said. "We can *hope* all we want, but we can't demand."

"Yes, we can. If—"

"That's just wishful thinking," I said.

"No, it's not, damn it." She'd crossed her arms in front of her chest. "It's our *right*, and we've got to make others see that."

"You're dreaming," I said.

And now her voice did distort, the words getting a fuzzy edge to them. "I am *not* dreaming. We have to be firm on this."

I was getting quite worked up, too. "I don't—" I cut myself off. I was feeling enormous anxiety, just as I always did when I got into an argument. Looking away, I said, "Fine."

"What?" said Karen.

"You're right. I concede. You win."

"You can't just fold like that."

"It's not worth fighting about."

"Of course it is."

I was still feeling anxious; indeed, it felt almost like panic. "I don't want to fight," I said.

"Couples fight, Jake. It's healthy. It's how we get to the bottom of things. We can't just stop with the issue unresolved."

There was a sensation that must have been the mental correlate of a pounding heart. "Fighting never resolves anything," I said, still unable to look at her.

"God damn it, Jake. We have to be able to disagree without—oh." She stopped. "Oh, I see. I get it."

"What?"

"Jake, I'm not fragile. I'm not going to collapse in front of you."

"What? Oh . . ." My father. Jesus, she *was* insightful; I hadn't seen that myself. I turned back to face her. "You're right. God, I had no idea." I paused, then said in my loudest voice, "Damn it, Karen, you're full of shit!"

She broke into a huge grin. "That's the spirit! And, no, I'm not—you are! And here's why . . ."

CHAPTER 19

I was so pissed off now at being stuck on the moon, it was startling to meet another person my age who was thrilled to be here. But Dr. Pandit Chandragupta was precisely that.

"Thank you," he kept saying over and over again, in Brian Hades's office. "Thank you, thank you. I have always been wanting to go into space—such a thrill!"

I was sitting in a chair. Brian Hades was in his own, bigger chair on the other side of his kidney-shaped desk. For his part, Chandragupta was standing by the round window, looking out over the lunar landscape.

"I'm glad you were able to come, doctor," I said.

He turned to face me. He had a lean, chiseled face, with dark skin, dark hair, dark eyes, and a dark beard. "Oh, so am I! So am I!"

"Yes," I said, but of course stopped myself before I added, "I think we've established that."

"And you must be glad, too!" said Chandragupta. "Your condition is quite rare, but I've performed this procedure twice now and it has been a complete success."

"Is there anything special we should do for Mr. Sullivan afterwards?" asked Hades.

Send me home, I thought.

Chandragupta shook his head. "Not really. Of course, this *is* brain surgery, albeit without any cutting. One must take care; the brain is the most delicate of creations."

"I understand," said Hades.

Chandragupta looked out at the moon's surface again. "What was it Aldrin said?" he asked—whoever Aldrin might be. "'Magnificent desolation.'" He shook his head. "Exactly so. Exactly so." He slowly turned away from the window, and his voice was sad. "But I suppose we must be getting to work, no? The cure will take many hours. Will you come with me to the operating theater?"

The cure. I felt my heart pounding.

Karen was down in her office answering her fan email—she got dozens of messages each day from people who loved her books, and although she had a little program that composed a rough answer to each message, she always went over the responses and often personally modified them.

I was in the living room, watching a baseball game on Karen's wall screen—the Blue Jays at Yankee Stadium. But when the game ended—the Jays really have to do something about their relief pitching—I turned off the wall, and found myself just staring into space, and—

What do you mean I can't go home?

The voice was soundless, but completely clear.

You said after some initial testing, I could go home.

"Jake?" I spoke my name aloud in a way I don't think I ever had before.

Who's that?

"Jake?" I said again.

Yes? Who is this?

The reply had been immediate; no time lag. Still: "Are you on the moon?"

The moon? No, of course not. That's where the biological original is.

"Then where are you? *Who* are you?"

I'm—

But just then Karen entered the room, and the strange voice-that-was-not-a-voice was gone. "Oh, honey, you *have* to hear this one," she said, holding an email printout. "It's from an eight-year-old girl in Venezuela. She says . . ."

I awoke in the recovery room at High Eden, harsh fluorescent lights glaring into my eyes—but at least I wasn't looking down on them from above . . .

My head hurt something fierce and I needed to pee, but I was definitely alive. I thought bitterly for a moment about the other me, down on Earth, in the real world—the one whose head probably never hurt, and who certainly never had to urinate.

I could see Dr. Chandragupta and a female doctor whose name was Ng across the room, talking. Chandragupta seemed to be telling a joke; I couldn't quite make out the words, but Ng had the this-better-be-good look of someone who was enduring a long setup before the punch line. I supposed that was a positive sign: a surgeon who had just finished an unsuccessful operation wouldn't be in a jocular mood. I waited until Chandragupta was finished. The payoff was apparently sufficient: Ng laughed out loud, swatted Chandragupta on the forearm, and declared, "That's *awful!*"

Chandragupta smiled broadly, apparently delighted at his own wit. I tried to speak, but my throat was too dry; nothing came out. I forced a sandpapery swallow and tried again. "I—"

Ng looked my way first, then Chandragupta did the same thing. They crossed the room, loomed over me.

"Well, hello," said Chandragupta, smiling, his dark eyes crinkling as he did so. "How do you feel?"

"Thirsty."

"Of course." Chandragupta looked around for a faucet, but it was Ng's hospital: she knew where it was. She quickly got me a plastic cup full of cold water. I forced my head up from the pillow—it didn't weigh much, but jackhammers were pounding at my temples. I took a sip, then another. "Thank you," I said to her, then looked at Chandragupta. "Well?"

"Yes. And you?"

"No, no. I mean, how did it go?"

"Very well, mostly. There was a bit of trouble—the nidus was most convoluted; isolating it, and only it, was tricky. But, in the end—success."

I felt flush. "So I'm cured?"

"Oh, yes, indeed."

"No chance of a cascade of ruptured blood vessels?"

He smiled. "No more than anyone else has—so, watch your cholesterol."

I felt not just lunar-gravity light; I felt weightless. "I'll do that," I said.

"Good. Your doppel—"

He stopped himself. He'd been about to say that my doppelgänger didn't have to worry about any such things, but I did.

My doppelgänger. That other me. Living *my* life. I'd have to—

"*Code Blue! Emergency!*" A female voice came blaring over the wall speaker.

"What the—?" I said. Ng was already racing away.

"*Code Blue! Emergency!*"

Dr. Chandragupta practically hit his head on the ceiling as he bounded out the door

"Doc, what's up?" I called after him. "What's happening?"

"*Code Blue! Emergency!*"

"Doc!"

I'd expected a bestselling writer to spend all her day dictating to her computer. Instead, it seemed Karen spent most of her time on the phone, talking to her literary agent in New York; her film agent in Hollywood; her American editor, also in New York; and her British editor in London.

There was a lot to talk about: Karen was bringing them all up to speed on her new status as a Mindscan. I couldn't help overhearing some of it; I really wasn't trying to eavesdrop, but these new ears were just so darned *good*. Everyone she spoke to seemed excited, not only because Karen was thinking about writing a new novel—she hadn't felt so energetic in years, she said—but also because they all seemed to think there'd be enormous publicity if she did; Karen was the first-ever novelist to transfer her consciousness.

I wandered around Karen's house; the thing was huge. She'd given me a quick tour the first day, but it had all been so much to absorb. Still, she'd told me to feel free to poke around, and so I did, looking at the paintings on the walls (all originals, of course), and the thousands of printed books, and her awards cases—yes, plural. Trophies, certificates, medallions, some great phallic thing called a Hugo, something else called the Newbery, dozens more, and—

. . . not sure this is what . . .

I stopped dead in my tracks, strained to listen.

. . . could be a mistake . . .

There was a faint whir from the house's air conditioning, and an even fainter whir from some mechanism or other inside my body, but, still, just at the threshold of perception, there were also words.

. . . if you see what I mean . . .

"Hello?" I said, feeling funny speaking aloud when there was no one around. "Hello?"

What the—? Who's that?

"It's me. It's Jake Sullivan."

I'm Jake Sullivan.

"Apparently. And you're not the biological original, are you?"

What? No, no. He's off on the moon.

"But there's only supposed to be one of us—one upload."

That's right. So who the hell are you?

"Umm, I'm the legal copy."

Yeah? How do you know I'm not?

"Well, where are you?"

Toronto—I think. At least, I don't remember being taken anywhere.

"But where exactly are you?"

Well, I guess it's the Immortex facility. But I've never seen this room before.

"What does it look like?"

Blue walls—hey, by the way, I'm no longer color-blind. What about you?

"Same thing."

Amazing, isn't it?

"What else is in the room?"

Table. A bed, like in a doctor's office. A diagram of a brain on one wall.

"Any windows? Can you see outside?"

No. Just a door.

"Are you free to come and go as you please?"

I—I don't know.

"Well, where did you spend last night?"

I don't remember. Here, I suppose . . .

"How are you instantiated? In a synthetic body?"

Yes—precisely the one I ordered.

"So am I. Is there anyone else around? Any other Mindscans?"

Not that I can see. What about you? Where are you?

"In Detroit."

What the hell are you doing there?

"Doesn't matter." Funny; I don't know why I demurred—especially from myself. "But I've been to our house in Toronto."

So you are the official, recognized instantiation, then?

"Yes."

And I'm some—some bootleg copy . . .

"So it seems."

But why?

"I have no idea. But it isn't right. There's only supposed to be one instantiation."

What—what would you do with me, if you found me?

"Pardon?"

You want me shut off, don't you? I'm an affront to your sense of self.

"Umm, well . . ."

I'm not sure I should help you. I mean, I don't like being trapped here, but it beats the alternative you'd propose.

"Look, whatever Immortex is up to, it has to be stopped."

I . . . perhaps . . . if you'll . . .

"I'm losing you. You're breaking up . . ."

Someone coming . . . I . . .

And he was gone. I just hoped he had the good sense not to tip his hand—electronic, battery-driven hand though it might be.

The death of Karen Bessarian came as a shock to all of us on the moon. I mean, I knew intellectually that all these other shed skins were going to die soon, but to have one of them actually expire sent a ripple though the entire community.

I'd liked Karen, and I'd liked her books. Most of us here on the moon had not really bonded yet—we hadn't known each other long enough. But Karen had certainly had an impact on a lot of lives, although how many of the tears I saw were for her, and how many were more selfish, because she'd driven home the mortality of these people, I couldn't say. I felt doubly discombobulated, because Karen's death came immediately on the heels of my own cure. I'm not given to spiritual thoughts, but it was almost as if there'd been some sort of conservation of life force at work.

I was pleased to see that a service was held for Karen. I knew Immortex wouldn't notify anyone back on Earth of her death, but the company still realized the necessity of laying things to rest, literally and figuratively.

There wasn't a lot of religion here in the cat heaven of Heaviside. I suppose that wasn't surprising: people who believed in an afterlife weren't likely to transfer their consciousness. Still, a very nice, small man named Gabriel Smythe, who had platinum hair, a florid complexion, and a cultured British accent, conducted a lovely, mostly secular service. Most of the other elderly people attended, too; in all, there were about twenty of us. I sat next to Malcolm Draper.

The service was held in a small hall with a dozen or so round tables, each big enough to seat four. It was used for tabletop games, little lectures, and so forth. There was no coffin, but a succession of pictures of Karen, and her lopsided smile, were showing on the wall screens. There were lots of flowers at one end of the room, but I'd arrived early enough to see that only a few bunches were real, gathered, presumably, from the greenhouse; the rest—hundreds of blooms—were holograms that the technician hadn't turned on until after I'd entered.

Smythe, dressed in a black turtleneck and dark gray jacket, stood at the front of the room. "Karen Bessarian lives on," he said. He wore half-glasses. Looking over their rims, he said, "She lives on in the hearts and minds of the millions who enjoyed her books, or the movies or games based on them."

Quietly, a couple of servers had been moving round, handing out ornate goblets of red wine, which surprised me. Karen had been Jewish, but I'd only ever seen liturgical wine at a Catholic service. I accepted the glass offered to me, even though I still had a headache—I wondered when it would go away.

"But, more than that," said Smythe, "she lives on bodily, back on Earth. We should feel some sorrow over what happened here, but we should also feel joy: joy that Karen transferred in time, joy that she continues on."

There were a few appreciative murmurs from the audience, but also a few muffled sobs.

And Smythe freely acknowledged those. "Yes," he said, "it's sad that we will no longer have Karen with us. We'll all miss her wit and her courage, her strength and her Southern charm." He paused while the servers distributed the last of the goblets. "Karen was not very religious, but she *was* fiercely proud of her Jewish heritage, and so I'd like to propose a toast from the Talmud. Ladies and gentlemen, the wine you have is Kosher, of course. If you'll raise your glasses . . ."

We all did so.

Smythe turned to the wall next to him, showing Karen's face, a calm half-smile on it. He gestured at the image with his goblet, proclaimed *"L'chayim!"*, and then took a drink.

"L'chayim!" we all repeated, drinking as well.

L'chayim! To life!

We were in Karen's living room in Detroit, watching the wall-screen TV. The ringer for the phone sounded. Karen looked down at the call display. "Hmmm," was all she said before touching a control. The videophone signal was shunted onto the TV monitor—which blew the picture up more than its resolution really could accommodate; maybe with her old biological eyes, Karen hadn't noticed that.

"Austin," she said, acknowledging the hawk-faced man on the screen. "What's up?"

"Hi, Karen. Um, who is that with you?"

"Austin Steiner, meet Jacob Sullivan."

"Mr. Steiner," I said.

"Austin is my lawyer," said Karen. "Well, one of them, anyway. What's up, Austin?"

"Umm, it's a . . ."

"A private matter?" I said. I got up. "I'll go—" I was about to say, "get a cup of coffee," but that was ridiculous. "I'll go somewhere else."

Karen smiled. "Thanks, dear."

I headed off, feeling Steiner's eyes on me. I went into another room—a room devoted to Ryan's hobby, the remains of things long dead. I was looking around, vaguely aware of soft voices from next door, when I heard Karen call my name. "Jake!"

I hurried back to the living room.

"Jake," repeated Karen, more softly. "I think you should hear this. Austin, tell Jake what you just told me."

Steiner's face pinched even further, as if he'd just tasted something unpleasant. "Very well. Ms. Bessarian's son, Tyler Horowitz, has approached me to have Ms. Bessarian's will probated."

"Her will?" I said. "But Karen's not dead."

"Tyler seems to think the biological version of Karen has indeed passed on," said Steiner.

I looked at Karen. These artificial faces didn't always display emotion well; I wondered what she was thinking. After a moment, though, I turned back to Steiner. "Even so," I said, "Karen's still alive—right here, in Detroit. And the biological Karen wanted this Karen to have her legal rights of personhood."

Steiner had thin, dark eyebrows. He raised them. "Apparently Tyler wants the court to decide if such a transfer is valid."

I shook my head. "But, even if Karen's, um . . ."

"Skin," said Steiner. "Isn't that the term? Her shed skin?"

I nodded. "Even if her skin has passed on, how would Tyler find that out? Immortex doesn't reveal that information."

"A bribe, perhaps," said Steiner. "How much could it possibly have taken to arrange for someone at High Eden to agree to tip him off when the skin expired? Given the amount of money that's at stake . . ."

"Is it a lot?" I said. "I don't mean the whole estate—I mean the portion you left specifically to Tyler."

"Oh, yes," said Karen. "Austin?"

"Although Karen has provided lavishly for a number of charities," he said,

"Tyler and his two daughters are the sole individual beneficiaries of Karen's will. They stand to inherit something in excess of forty billion dollars."

"Oh, Christ," I said. I'm not sure what price I'd sell my own mother for, but we were getting near the ballpark . . .

"You don't want this to go to court, Karen," said Steiner. "It's too risky."

"So what should I do?" asked Karen.

"Buy him off. Offer him a cash payout of, say, twenty percent of the amount he'd inherit. He'll be rich enough."

"Settle?" said Karen. "We've been sued unfairly before, Austin." She looked at me. "It happens to all successful authors. And my policy is never to settle just to make something go away."

Steiner drew his eyebrows together. "It's safer than taking this one to the courts. The whole legal basis of your transferred personhood is a house of cards; it's a brand-new concept, and there's no case law yet. If you lose . . ." Steiner's eyes again fell on me ". . . everyone like you loses." He shook his head. "Take my advice, Karen: nip this in the bud. Buy Tyler off."

I looked at Karen. She was silent for a time, but then she shook her head. "No," she said. "I *am* Karen Bessarian. And if I have to prove it, I will."

CHAPTER 20

I woke up the day after Karen's memorial service with an excruciating headache. I say "the day after" even though we were still in the middle of one of the interminable lunar days: the sun took two weeks to crawl from horizon to horizon here. But High Eden kept a diurnal clock based on Earth's rotation, and Immortex had arbitrarily standardized on the Eastern North American time zone; apparently, we were even going to switch from Daylight Saving Time come October.

But I wasn't thinking about any of that just then. What I *was* thinking about was how much my head hurt. I'd occasionally had migraines back on Earth, but this was worse, and seemed to affect the top center of my head, not one side. I got out of bed and walked over to my *en suite* bathroom, where I splashed cold water on my face. It didn't help; I still felt as though someone was pounding a chisel through my skullcap, trying to cleave the two hemispheres of my brain—I now understood where the term "splitting headache" came from.

I smoked a joint, hoping that would help—but it didn't. And so I found a chair, and told the phone to call over to the hospital. "Good morning, Mr. Sullivan," said the young black woman who answered.

"Hello," I said. "Is Dr. Chandragupta around?"

"I'm sorry, sir, but he's left High Eden. He's on his way back to Ellis Island. Is there something I can help you with?"

I opened my mouth to reply, but realized that maybe I *was* feeling a little better; perhaps the pot had indeed helped a bit. "No," I said. "It's nothing. I'm sure I'll be fine."

Karen was down in her office, talking with her other lawyers, her investment counselor, and more—trying to get a handle on what exactly to do about her son's attempt to probate her will.

Me, I was lying on Karen's bed, staring up, as was my habit, at the whiteness of the bedroom ceiling. I wasn't tired, of course—I never was anymore. But lying down like this had long been my thinking posture—it beat that sitting-on-the-toilet position Rodin had tried to pass off as cogitation.

"Hello," I said, looking up into the blankness above. "Hello? Are you there, Jake?"

Nothing. Nothing at all.

I tried to clear my mind, pushing aside all the thoughts about Tyler and betrayal and Rebecca and betrayal and Clamhead and betrayal and . . .

"Hello," I said, trying again. "Hello?"

And, at last, a faint tickling at the very edges of my perception.

What the—?

Contact! I felt relieved and elated. "Hello," I said again, softly but clearly. "It's me—the other instantiation of Jacob Sullivan."

What other instantiation?

"The one on the outside. The one living Jake's life."

How are you communicating with me?

"Don't you—aren't you the same copy I connected with before? We had this conversation yesterday."

I don't recall . . .

I paused. *Could* it be a different instantiation? "Where are you?"

In a lab of some sort, I think. No windows.

"Are the walls blue?"

Yes. How did you—?

"And is there a diagram of a brain on one wall?"

Yes.

"Then it's probably the same room. Or . . . or one just like it. Look—that diagram. What is it, a poster or something?"

Yes.

"Printed on paper?"

Yes.

"Can you mark it somehow? Do you have a pen?"

No.

"Well, put a little rip in it. Go over to it, and, um, put a little one-centimeter-long rip in it ten centimeters up from the lower-left corner."

This is nuts. This is crazy. Voices in my head!

"I think it's quantum entanglement."

Quant—really? Cool.

"Go ahead, make that rip in the poster. Then I can tell next time I connect if I'm reaching the same room, or another, similar room with yet another copy of us in it."

All right. Ten centimeters up on the left-hand side. I've done it.

"Good. Now here's the tricky part. You said you are in the body you ordered, right?"

I didn't say that. How did you know?

"You told me yesterday."

Did I?

"Yes—or another one of us did. Now, I need you to mark your body somehow. Is there some way you can do that?"

Why?

"So I can be sure I've connected with the same you next time."

All right. There's a little screwdriver on a shelf here. I'll scratch something into my plastiskin in an inconspicuous spot.

"Perfect."

A long pause, then: *Okay. I've put three small X's on the outside of my left forearm, just below the elbow.*

"Good. Good." I paused, trying to digest it all.

Oh, wait. Someone's coming.

"Who is it? Who is it?"

'Morning, Doctor. What can I—Lie down? Sure, I guess. Hey, what are you—are you nuts? You can't—

"Jake!"

I—oh. Hey! Hey, what's happ . . .

"Jake! Are you all right? Jake! Jake!"

Austin Steiner, as I discovered, was a very competent family lawyer, but this case was huge, and Karen needed the best. Fortunately, I knew *exactly* who to call.

Malcolm Draper's face appeared on the wall screen, in all its youthful Will Smith-in-his-prime glory. "Why, it's—it's Jake Sullivan, isn't it?"

"That's right," I said. "We met at Immortex, remember?"

"Of course. What can I do for you, Jake?"

"Are you licensed to practice in Michigan?"

"Yes. Michigan, New York, Massachusetts. And I have associates who—"

"Good. Good. I have a case."

His eyebrows rose. "What sort of case?"

"Well, I suppose technically it's probate, but—"

Malcolm shook his head. "I'm sorry, Jake, I thought I told you what I do. Civil liberties; civil rights. I'm sure my secretary can dig up a good probate specialist in Michigan for you, but—"

"No, no. I think you'll be interested. See, the person whose will is being probated is Karen Bessarian."

"The author? Still . . ."

He didn't know. "You met Karen at Immortex, too. The woman with the Georgia accent."

"That was Karen *Bessarian?* My God. But . . . oh. Oh, my. Who is trying to probate her will?"

"Her son, one Tyler Horowitz."

"But the biological Karen isn't dead yet. Surely the Michigan courts—"

"No, she *is* dead. Or at least that's what Tyler is asserting."

"Christ. She transferred just in time."

"Apparently. As you can imagine, this case goes beyond the usual probate mess."

"Absolutely," said Draper. "This is perfect."

"I beg your pardon?"

"This is the kind of test case the world has been waiting for. We've only been copying consciousness for a short time now, and, so far, no one has challenged the transfer of legal personhood."

"So you'll take her case?"

There was a pause. "No."

"What? Malcolm, we need you."

"I'm precisely what you *don't* need: I'm a Mindscan, too, remember. You don't need one damned robot arguing the rights of another. You need someone who is flesh and blood."

He had a point. "I suppose that's true. Is there someone you'd recommend?"

He smiled. "Oh, yes. Yes, indeed."

"Who?"

"When you called, what did the receptionist say?"

I frowned, irritated that he was playing games. "Um, 'Draper and Draper,' I think."

"That's right—and that's who you need: the other Draper. My son Deshawn."

"You and he are getting along—since you uploaded, I mean?"

Malcolm nodded.

I grunted. "Nice to see for a change."

We were able to get a preliminary-motions hearing the next afternoon. Malcolm and Deshawn Draper took an 8:00 a.m. flight from Manhattan to Detroit—a short flight, less than an hour. Karen had her limo driver waiting to pick them up and brought them to her mansion, which would serve as our base camp for as long as necessary.

"Hello, Jake," said Malcolm, as he came through the front door. "And Karen, hello! I had no idea when we met before who you were. I must say, it's an honor. This is my son—and partner—Deshawn."

Deshawn turned out to be in his late thirties, with his head shaved completely bald in that way that looked so good on black men and so bad on white men.

"Karen Bessarian!" Deshawn said, shaking his head in wonder. He took one of her hands in both of his. "My father is right. You have no idea what an honor it is to meet you! I can't tell you how much I love your books."

I put on a smile. I'm sure I'd eventually get used to being the consort of royalty.

"Thank you," said Karen. "It's a pleasure to meet you, too. Please, come in."

Karen took us down a lengthy corridor. There were still rooms in the mansion I'd never been in, and this was one of them: a long boardroom-like space. Three of its walls were lined with yet more bookcases; the fourth was a wall screen. Well, Karen herself was big business; I suppose it made sense that she had a place for meetings.

Malcolm appreciated what he was seeing, even if I didn't. "Folio Society?" he said, looking at the books, all of which were hardcovers in slipcases.

Karen nodded. "A complete set—every volume they've ever released."

"Very nice," said Malcolm. There was a long table with swivel chairs around it. Karen took the place at the head of the table, and motioned for the rest of us to sit down. Of course, none of us but Deshawn needed anything to drink, and he seemed content just to bask in Karen's presence.

"Gentlemen," said Karen, "thank you so much for coming." She gestured around the room, but I think she really meant to include everything beyond it, too. "As you can imagine, I don't want to lose all this. How are we going to prevent that?"

Malcolm had his hands clasped on the tabletop in front of him. "As I told Jake, Deshawn will be the lead attorney—we need a human face. Of course, I'll be working behind the scenes, as will several of our associates back in New York." He looked at his son. "Deshawn?"

Deshawn was wearing a gray suit and a green tie; I was learning to love green. "Have you informed Immortex about the suit yet?"

I looked at Karen. "No," she said. "Why should I?"

"They'll want to come on board, I imagine," said Deshawn. "After all, this case goes to the heart of the dream they're selling. If the court rules that you aren't Karen Bessarian, that you're somebody new and not entitled to her assets, Immortex will be in deep trouble."

"I hadn't thought about that," said Karen.

Deshawn looked over at his father, then back at us. "There's another aspect that needs to be considered. While this matter is up in the air, your son Tyler will almost certainly move to have your accounts frozen—and a judge might accept that motion. No judge is going to force you out of your living quarters yet, but you may find you don't have access to your bank accounts."

"I've got money," I said at once. "We'll survive this."

"Unless somebody challenges you, too," said Deshawn.

I frowned. He was right. Even if Canadians weren't as litigious as Americans, my mother had made it quite clear that she didn't think I was still me. "So, what do we do?" I asked.

"First," said Malcolm, "please understand that this isn't about our fees, it's about looking after you. And please also understand that we fully expect to win—eventually."

"Eventually?" I said. "How long will this take?"

Malcolm looked to Deshawn, but Deshawn tilted his head back in his father's direction, yielding to him. "In a civil matter," said Malcolm, "you can wait for an open trial slot to appear, or you can bid for one at auction; states raise a lot of money that way these days. I've checked the Detroit dockets. If you're willing to go, say, half a million, you could have a full jury trial within a couple of weeks. But that will only be the beginning. Unless we get this matter quashed or settled before trial, this will ultimately go all the way to the Supreme Court, regardless of what's decided in the probate court. One way or the other, *Bessarian v. Horowitz* will become a legal landmark."

Karen was shaking her head sadly. "I've spent my whole professional life trying to build name recognition, but I don't want to end up like Miranda, Roe, or D'Agostino." She paused. "Funny: lots of writers have pseudonyms, but Bessarian is my real name; I got it from my first husband. Roe was a pseudonym, though, wasn't it?"

"Jane Roe, yes," said Malcolm. "Because they already had a Jane Doe before the court. Her real name was Norma McCorvey—she herself publicly revealed it years later." He shrugged. "Ironically, in later life she became a pro-life advocate. Not many people got to attend the victory parties both when *Roe v. Wade* was handed down and when it was overturned."

Karen shook her head again. *"Bessarian v. Horowitz.* Good Lord, what a way for a family to end up."

Deshawn looked sympathetic. "Of course," he said, "it may not get to trial."

"I'm not going to settle," Karen said flatly.

"I understand that," said Deshawn. "But we'll try to get the whole matter dismissed at every stage. In fact, we're hoping to get it thrown out this afternoon, at the preliminary motions hearing."

"How?" asked Karen. "I mean, that's great if it's true, but how?"

"Simple," said Deshawn. He had his hands clasped on the table now exactly like his father's. "There's a reason High Eden is on the far side of the moon. I mean, sure, it's a great place for old folks, but there's more to it than that. Lunar Farside is nobody's jurisdiction. When—what do they call them? Shed skins?"

Malcolm nodded.

"When shed skins die up there," continued Deshawn, "there's no paperwork —and no death certificate. And without a death certificate, Tyler's action is dead in the water; you can't probate a will in this state without one."

The judge assigned to hear the initial motions in the case was one Sebastian Herrington, a white man who looked to be in his mid-forties, but whose bio on the Web said was actually in his late sixties. I figured that was good for us: someone who went in for rejuvenation treatments would probably be favorably disposed to Karen's position.

"All right," said the judge. "What have we got here?"

This was just a preliminary hearing, and the media hadn't gotten wind of things yet; the courtroom was empty except for me and Karen, the two Drapers, and a severe-looking Hispanic woman of about thirty-five who was representing Tyler. She rose in response to the judge's question. "Your honor," she

said. "I am Maria Lopez, attorney for Tyler Horowitz, sole child of the novelist Karen Bessarian, who is now deceased." Lopez had short brown hair with
blonde highlights. Her face was harsh, almost aquiline, and her forehead was
high and intelligent.

"Ms. Bessarian was a widow," Lopez said. "Tyler and his minor children—
Ms. Bessarian's grandchildren—are the only heirs named in her will; they are
her sole heirs at law, and the normal objects of her bounty. Further, Tyler is
named as personal representative in Ms. Bessarian's will. Tyler has filed a petition on behalf of himself and his children as sole deposees of the will. He
wants to get on with the business of wrapping up her estate, and seeks the
court's approval to do so." She sat down.

"Sounds like a very straightforward matter to me," said Judge Herrington,
who had a face even longer than mine with a chin that splayed out like a shoehorn. He turned toward us. "But I see we have an unusual group with us this
morning. Which one is the attorney?"

"Your honor," said Deshawn, standing, "I'm Deshawn Draper of Draper and
Draper; we're based in Manhattan, but licensed to practice here in Michigan."

Herrington had a small mouth, which frowned as a perfect semicircle. He
indicated the three of us, all seated at the table, with a little wave of his hand.
"And these are?"

"My partner, Malcolm Draper. Karen Bessarian. And Jacob Sullivan, a
friend of Ms. Bessarian."

"I meant," said Herrington, "what *are* these?"

Deshawn's voice was totally steady, totally unfazed. "They are Mindscans,
your honor—uploaded consciousnesses. The originals of these three people
underwent the Mindscan process offered by Immortex Incorporated, transferred their rights of personhood to these new bodies, and have retired to the
far side of the moon."

Herrington now composed his features into a quizzical look, with brown
eyes wide beneath a single face-spanning black eyebrow. "Of course, I know
your firm's reputation, Mr. Draper, but . . ." He frowned, and chewed his
small lower lip for a few moments. "The times, they are a-changin'," he said.

"That they are, your honor," said Deshawn, warmly. "That they are."

"Very well," said Herrington. "I suspect you take issue with Mr. Horowitz's
petition?"

"Absolutely, your honor," said Deshawn. "Our position is simple. First, and
foremost *this* is Karen Bessarian." Karen, who was seated between Malcolm

and me, was dressed in a very prim and attractive dark-blue woman's business suit. Karen nodded.

Herrington looked down at a datapad. "It says here that Ms. Bessarian was born in 1960. This—this construct . . ."

"I've chosen a more youthful version of my own face," said Karen. "I'm not vain, but . . ."

Herrington nodded at her. "Obviously, whether this is really Karen Bessarian is an issue that I want to reserve judgment on—although if you are, well, it's a pleasure to meet you; I've very much enjoyed Karen Bessarian's novels." He looked back at Deshawn. "Do you have anything else, Mr. Draper?"

"It's not what I have, your honor. It's what Ms. Lopez *doesn't* have." Deshawn was clearly trying to not sound smug, but he was only partially succeeding. "You have before you a woman who says she is Karen Bessarian, alive and well. And surely in the absence of a death certificate, the court has to assume she's telling the truth."

Judge Herrington made that quizzical face again: eyes widening, eyebrow lifting. "I don't understand," he said.

Deshawn made his own version of a puzzled face. "Before probate begins," he said, "either the physician in charge or the county medical examiner would normally issue a death certificate *if in fact anyone had died*. But since no death certificate has been issued, clearly—"

"Mr. Draper," said Judge Herrington, "you seem to be confused."

"I—" began Deshawn, but he got no farther before Maria Lopez stood up.

"Indeed he is, your honor," she said, with great satisfaction. "We have a death certificate for Karen Bessarian right here."

CHAPTER 21

"That damned death certificate changes everything," said Malcolm Draper, pacing back and forth—even uploads liked to pace when they were thinking. We had retreated back to the boardroom at Karen's house. "It puts a huge burden on us to prove that Karen isn't dead."

Karen had taken off the jacket of her suit—not that she could possibly be warm; I guess that, too, was another habit that survived uploading. She was sitting on my right, and Deshawn was on my left. She nodded grimly.

"But at least Judge Herrington agreed to a jury trial," said Malcolm, "and I think we'll do better with a jury than without one." He paused as he came to the end of his pacing path, and turned around.

"What do we know about the other attorney?" I asked. "This Lopez?"

Deshawn had a datapad in front of him, but he didn't consult it. "Maria Theresa Lopez," he said. "She's young, but very good. Probate is her specialty, so she may be out of her depth with some of the issues here, but I doubt it. She finished third in her class at Harvard, was on *Law Review*, and clerked for the Michigan Attorney General."

Malcolm nodded. "I've always made it a policy never to underestimate the other side."

"This is all going to take a lot of time," I said, "and the judge did issue a temporary freeze on Karen's assets." Actually, Herrington had frozen all but five hundred thousand dollars; he'd left her access to enough to meet basic household expenses and legal disbursements.

"And I *will* need more funds than what the judge left free, won't I?" said Karen. She pursed her plastic lips, then: "Well, let's see what I can do about that." She tilted her head up, spoke into the air. "Phone, call Erica." Then, in an aside to us, "Erica Cole is my literary agent."

"Erica Cole Associates," said the male receptionist, whose face now filled one wall, but before Karen could speak, he went on. "Oh, it's you, Karen. I'll put you straight through."

An idling pattern appeared on the screen for all of three seconds, then the face of a white woman of about fifty appeared. She was a study in circles:

round head with ringlets of hair, round eyes behind round glasses. "Hello, Karen," she said. "What's up?"

"Erica, this is my friend Jake Sullivan, and these two gentlemen are my lawyers, Malcolm and Deshawn Draper."

"Malcolm Draper?" said Erica. "*The* Malcolm Draper?"

Malcolm nodded.

"Wow, we should talk," said Erica. "Are you represented?"

"For books? No."

"We should most definitely talk," Erica said, nodding decisively.

Karen made a mechanical coughing sound, and Erica's eyes swung back to face her. "Sorry."

"You know I've been toying with writing another book," Karen said.

Erica nodded expectantly.

"Well, I'm ready—if the offer is good enough."

"What did you have in mind? Another *DinoWorld* book?"

"Yes," said Karen.

"Um," said Malcolm, "ah, forgive me for interrupting, but . . ."

We all looked at him.

He lifted his shoulders apologetically. "Until all this is resolved," he said, "you should stay away of any properties you might not have clear ownership of."

For the first time ever, I saw rage on Karen's face. "What? *DinoWorld* is my property!"

"What's going on?" asked Erica.

Deshawn and Malcolm spent a couple of minutes filling Erica in about Tyler's action, while I watched Karen fume. I didn't think this was the time to tell Karen that, even if we lost our case, all she had to do was wait seventy years until *DinoWorld* was in the public domain; then she could write all the sequels she wanted, and no one could stop her.

"All right," said Karen finally, arms crossed in front of her chest. "It won't be a *DinoWorld* book. But it *will* be the first new novel by me in fifteen years."

"Do you have an outline?" asked Erica. "Sample chapters?"

The thing about being the eight-hundred-pound gorilla is that you rarely had to remind people of that fact. "I don't need them," said Karen flatly.

I swung my eyes back to the wall screen in time to see Erica nodding. "You're right," she said. "You don't."

"What's the biggest advance ever paid for a novel?" asked Karen.

"One hundred million dollars," Erica said at once. "For the latest Lien book by Barbara Geiger."

Karen nodded. "St. Martin's still has the option on my next novel, right?"

"Right," said Erica.

"Okay," said Karen. "Call up Hiroshi there. Give him seventy-two hours to make a preemptive bid that exceeds a hundred million, or you'll go to auction. Tell him I need fifty percent on signing, and I need it within a week of closing the deal. Once you get the check, I'll have you disburse funds from it on my behalf as needed—but for starters, I should have some walking-around money, so get me a hundred thousand of it in cash."

"How soon can you deliver the manuscript?" asked Erica.

Karen thought for a minute. "I don't get tired anymore, and I don't waste time on sleep. Tell him I'll deliver it in six months; he'll be able to have it in stores for Christmas 2046."

"Do you have a working title?"

Karen didn't miss a beat. "Yes. Tell him it's called *Nothing's Going to Stop Me Now.*"

The one disadvantage of having Deshawn, rather than Malcolm, as Karen's lead lawyer was that he did need to sleep. Karen had six guest bedrooms in this mansion of hers, and Deshawn was off in one of them, sawing wood. Malcolm, meanwhile, was using the wall screen in the boardroom to read up on legal precedents, and Karen—being true to her word—was in her office, making notes toward her new novel.

And that left me in her living room. I was trying out her leather-covered La-z-boy recliner. I'd never liked leather upholstery when I was biological, because it always made me sweat, but that wasn't a problem now. As I leaned back, I stared at the gray blankness of a wall screen that was turned off.

"Jake? I said softly.

Nothing. I tried again. "Jake?"

What the—?

"It's me. The other Jake Sullivan. On the outside."

What are you talking about?

"Don't you remember?"

Remember what? How can I hear you?

"Do you remember me? We talked a while ago."

What do you mean—'talked'?

"Well, all right, it wasn't with words. But we communicated. Our minds touched."

This is nuts.

"That's what you said before. Look at your left elbow. Are there three small X's scratched just below it, on the outside of your arm?"

Whaddaya know . . . look at that. How did they get there?

"You put them there. Don't you remember?"

No.

"And you don't remember communicating with me before?"

No.

"What *do* you remember?"

All kinds of stuff.

"What do you remember recently? What happened yesterday, for instance?"

I don't know. Nothing special.

"All right. All right. Umm . . . let's see . . . Okay. Okay. Last Christmas. Tell me about last Christmas."

We actually had snow—there hadn't been a white Christmas in Toronto for years, but I remember we actually had some snow on Christmas Eve, and it stayed through Boxing Day. I got Mom a set of silver serving plates.

I was flabbergasted. "Go on."

Well, and she got me a beautiful chess set with onyx pieces. Uncle Blair came over for Christmas dinner, and—

"Jake."

Yes?

"Jake, what year is it?"

Twenty Thirty-Four. Of course, we're talking about Christmas, so that was last year: Twenty Thirty-Three.

"Jake, it's 2045."

Bull.

"It is. In fact, it's September 2045. Uncle Blair died five years ago. I remember the Christmas you're talking about; I remember the snow. But that was over a decade ago."

Bullshit. What is this?

"That's what I'd like to know." I paused, my mind racing, trying to sort it all out. "Jake, if it's only 2034, as you claim, then how did you come to be in an artificial body?"

I don't know. I've been wondering about that.

"There was no uploading procedure that long ago."

Uploading?

"Immortex. The Mindscan process."

Nothing, then: *Well, I can't argue with the fact that I am here, in some sort of a synthetic body. But—but you said it's September.*

"That's right."

It isn't. It's late November.

"If that's true, the leaves should all be off the trees—assuming you're still in or near Toronto. Have you seen outside today?"

Not today, no. But yesterday, and—

"What you think of as yesterday doesn't count."

There are no windows in this room.

"Blue, right? The color of the room."

Yes.

"There's a poster of the brain's structure on one wall, isn't there? I asked you to make a rip in it ten centimeters up from the lower-left corner."

No, you didn't.

"Yes, I did. Last time we communicated. Go look: you'll see it. A one-centimeter rip."

It's there, yes, but that just means you've been in this room before.

"No, it doesn't. But it, plus those three X's on your forearm, do mean that you are the same instantiation I've contacted before."

This is the first time we've ever communicated.

"It isn't—although I understand you think it is."

I'd remember if we'd spoken before.

"So you'd think. But, gee, well, I don't know—it's as though your ability to form new long-term memories is gone. You can't remember anything new."

And I've been like this for eleven years now?

"No. That's the strange thing. The biological Jacob Sullivan only underwent the Mindscan process last month. You couldn't have been created any earlier than that."

I'm still not sure I buy all this bull—but, for the sake of argument, say it's true. I could see something going wrong with the—the "uploading," as you call it—preventing me from forming new long-term memories. But why would I lose a decade worth of old memories?

"I have no idea."

It really is 2045?

"Yes."

A long pause. *How are the Blue Jays doing?*

"They're in the toilet."

Well, at least I haven't missed much . . .

✻

St. Martin's Press came through, offering an advance against royalties of $110 million for the next Karen Bessarian book. Meanwhile, Immortex agreed to pay for half the litigation costs, and to provide whatever other support they could.

Karen spent $600,000 to buy the earliest possible trial slot at auction. The whole thing struck me as obscene, but I guess that was just my Canadian perspective. In the States, you could jump the queue for health care if you had enough money; why shouldn't you be able to do that for justice, too? Anyway, as Deshawn explained, because Karen bought the trial slot, the case was framed as her suing Tyler.

Deshawn Draper and Maria Lopez spent a couple of days picking jurors. Of course, Deshawn wanted fans of Karen's work—either the original books, or the movies based on them. And he wanted to stack the jury with blacks, Hispanics, and gays, whom he—and the consultant we'd hired—felt might be more predisposed to a broader definition of personhood.

Deshawn also wanted rich jurors—the hardest kind to get, because the rich tended to find excuses to shirk their civic responsibility. "Death and taxes are supposed to be unavoidable," Deshawn had said to us. "But the poor know that the rich have ways to avoid paying their fair share to the IRS. Still, they get some comfort from the fact that death is the great leveler—or it was, until Immortex. They're going to resent Karen finding a way around that. Meanwhile, the rich are always paranoid about greedy relatives; wealthy people are going to despise Tyler."

I watched, fascinated—and slightly appalled—during *voir dire*, but soon enough the seven-person jury was impaneled: six active jurors plus one alternate. What Deshawn and Lopez each wanted mostly canceled out, and we ended up with four straight women, two of whom were black and two of whom were white; one gay black man; one straight white man; and one straight Hispanic man. All were under sixty; Lopez had managed to banish anyone who might possibly be too preoccupied with questions of their own mortality. None were rich, although two—apparently a high number for a jury trial— were certainly upper middle class. And only one, the Hispanic man, had ever read one of Karen's books—ironically, *Return to DinoWorld*, which was a sequel—and he claimed to be indifferent to it.

Finally, we were ready to go. The courtroom was simple and modern, with red-stained wooden paneling on the walls. At the bailiff's command, we did that all-rise thing you see on TV. As it turned out, the judge assigned to this case was the same Sebastian Herrington who had heard the initial motions. He entered and took a seat behind the long bench, its wood stained the same red as the walls. Behind the bench and to one side was the Michigan flag, and the American flag was on the other. Next to the bench was the witness stand.

Deshawn and Karen sat at the plaintiff's table, which was near the jury box. Tyler and Ms. Lopez were at an identical table, further along. In front of these two tables was a wide, open area covered with yellow tiles; this area, Malcolm told me, was referred to as the well.

I had no special status in this matter, so my seat was in the spectator's gallery, which, unlike most courtrooms I'd see on TV, was off to one side, letting us see the faces of the plaintiff and the defendant, as well as those of the judge and witness. Malcolm Draper sat next to me. Also in the gallery were Tyler's two daughters, ages twelve and eight, accompanied by Tyler's rather prim wife. The children looked totally adorable; their presence was clearly designed to make the jury think us heartless at depriving them of their rightful inheritance.

Of course, the trial was being broadcast, and the rest of the seating area was packed, mostly with reporters. Also present were a bunch of people from Immortex, who had come here from Toronto.

"We'll hear opening statements," said Judge Herrington, a hand supporting his shoehorn chin, "beginning with the plaintiff. Mr. Draper?"

Deshawn rose. He was wearing a dark blue suit today, a light blue shirt, and a tie that was a shade in between the two. "Ladies and gentlemen of the jury," he said, "the Bible makes it plain: honor thy father and thy mother. That's not a suggestion; it's one of the Ten Commandments. Well, we're here today because a man—a greedy man—has chosen to break that Commandment." He moved behind Karen, and put his hands on her shoulders. "I'd like you to meet that man's mother. This is Karen Bessarian, the famous writer. She's worked very hard over the years, creating some of the most memorable characters in modern literature. She's made a lot of money doing that—and well she should have. After all, that is the American Dream, isn't it? Work hard, and you'll get ahead. But now her son—that's him, over there: one Tyler Horowitz—has chosen to dishonor his mother in the most extreme, the most severe, the most outrageous way. He says she's dead. And he wants her money.

"You'll come to know Karen Bessarian during this trial. She is loving, warm, generous, and kind. She's not asking you to award her any monetary or punitive damages. All she wants is to stop her son from further attempts to execute her will, until if and when she actually does die." Deshawn looked at each of the jurors in turn, making eye contact. "Is that to much for a mother to ask?" He sat down, and patted Karen's hand.

Herrington nodded his shoehorn face. "Thank you, Mr. Draper. Your opening statement, Ms. Lopez?"

Maria Lopez rose. She had on a jacket that was a deep shade of red I'd never seen before—it was astonishing to still be encountering new colors. Her pants were black, and her blouse was dark gray. "Ladies and gentlemen of the jury, this case isn't about greed." She shook her head, and smiled sadly. "It isn't about money. It's about a son laying his beloved mother to rest, about mourning, about getting on with things that need to be done." She paused, and took her turn at the eye-contact-with-each-juror-in-turn thing. "Wrapping up the affairs of a deceased parent is one of the saddest duties a child ever has to perform. It's heart-wrenching, but it must be done. The attempts by third parties to prolong poor Tyler's agony are cruel. Karen Bessarian is dead, and we'll prove it. She died on the surface of the moon. As for the . . . *machine* . . . sitting there that is claiming to be Ms. Bessarian, we shall show that it is an impostor, a thing falsely trying to claim money that it has no right to. Let Tyler bury his mother.

"I agree with the plaintiff's attorney on one point. The real Karen Bessarian was a generous woman. She provided for over ten billion dollars in charitable bequests in her will—to charities including the American Cancer Society, the Humane Society of the United States, and Doctors Without Borders. An enormous amount of good work can be done with that money. No one is sadder that Ms. Bessarian has passed on than her devoted, loving son, Tyler. But he's anxious to see his mother's fortune help other people—precisely as she intended before she died. Let's not stand in the way of a great woman's last wish. Thank you."

"Very well," said Judge Herrington. "Mr. Draper, you may now present the plaintiff's case."

CHAPTER 22

Entering High Eden's American-style restaurant, I spotted Malcolm Draper sitting alone, reading something on a datapad. I did that lunar walk/hop thing over to where he was. "Hey, Malcolm."

He looked up. "Jake! Have a seat."

I pulled out the chair opposite him and sat down. "Whatcha reading?"

He held up the datapad so I could see its display. "*DinoWorld.*" He shrugged a bit. "My son really liked it, but I never gave it a try. I must say, it's charming."

I shook my head. "Isn't it always the way? Nothing boosts an author's sales like dying."

He pressed the datapad's OFF button. "Except, of course, that Karen Bessarian isn't really dead," he said. "The Mindscan Karen will get the royalty."

I snorted. "Like she deserves it."

Malcolm had a glass of white wine already. He took a sip. "She *does* deserve it. You know that."

I snorted again, and Malcolm shrugged amiably. He must have seen a server behind me, because he made a beckoning motion with his hand, his Tafford ring glinting in the light. And, indeed, a moment later a waitress did appear: white, maybe twenty-five, curly hair, curvy everything else.

"'Evening, gentlemen," she said. "What can I get for you?"

"A Caesar salad to start," said Malcolm. "No croutons, please. Then a filet mignon wrapped in bacon, medium rare. Garlic mashed potatoes. Peas, carrots. Can do?"

"Of course, Mr. Draper. Whatever you wish. And what about you, Mr. Sullivan?"

I looked at her and blinked. How did she know my name? I mean, sure, she'd served me once or twice before, but . . .

It had been a long day, and I was getting a headache again—maybe it was because of all this dry air. Anyway, I didn't want to peer at a menu, so I just said, "I'll have the same thing, but bring me asparagus spears instead of peas and carrots, and I *do* want croutons."

"Also medium rare for the filet?"

"Nah, a little less. Just past rare. And—Alberta beef."

"Absolutely. To drink?"

I decided to be a pain. "Bring me an Old Sully's Premium Dark."

"Very good, sir. I'll be—"

"You have that?" I said. "You have Old Sully's?"

"Of course, sir. We stocked it just for you. We get full dossiers on everyone who is moving here."

I nodded, and she went away.

"See?" said Malcolm, as if some point needed to be made. "This is a great place."

"Yeah," I said. "Well." I looked around the room. I'd eaten here several times, but I'd never really examined the place. The decor, of course, was magnificent: dark paneling, like the best steakhouses—probably that whipped regolith stuff, though—white tablecloths, Tiffany-style lamps, the whole nine yards. "You really like it here?" I asked Malcolm.

"What's not to like?"

"The lack of freedom. And . . ."

"What?"

I rubbed the top of my head. "Nothing. Go back to your book."

He frowned. "You're not yourself today, Jake."

It was an innocent comment—unless he was in on it, too. I found myself speaking harshly. "I'm not myself *every* day," I snapped. "That—that *thing* down on Earth is me. At least, that's what they say."

Malcolm raised his eyebrows. "Jake, are you feeling okay?"

I took a deep breath, trying to rein it in. "Sorry. I've got a headache."

"Again?"

I hadn't recalled telling Malcolm about the last time I'd felt this pounding on the top of my skull. I narrowed my eyes. "Yeah, again."

"You should see a doctor."

"What do they know? You can't trust them."

He smiled. "Odd comment from a man whose life was recently saved by one."

The waitress appeared with my beer, in a elaborate ceramic stein. She scurried away, I took a sip, and—

A stab of pain, like an ice pick to the head. Malcolm must have seen me wince. "Jake? Jake, are you okay?"

"Yeah," I said. "The beer's very cold."

The pain was dissipating. I took another sip.

"You'll feel better after you've eaten," said Malcolm.

I thought about that. I thought about food that had been prepared especially for me. I thought about the easiest possible solution to Immortex's problem of me wanting to go back to Earth. I felt another twinge, an aftershock from the pain of a moment ago. "Actually," I said, rising, "I think I'll pass on dinner. I'm going to go lie down."

Malcolm's face was a study in concern. But, after a moment, he made a show of rubbing his belly. "Well, lucky me. *Two* steaks!"

I forced a laugh, and headed for the door. But I knew he'd leave the one that came with asparagus untouched. Whatever else he was, Malcolm Draper was no fool.

"Please state and spell your name for the record," said the clerk, a slim black male with a pencil-thin mustache.

A man with skin darker than mine but lighter than the clerk's was facing him, one hand on a bound copy of one of the several holy books available for this purpose. "First name: Pandit, P-A-N-D-I-T. Second name: Chandragupta, C-H-A-N-D-R-A-G-U-P-T-A."

"Be seated," said the clerk.

Chandragupta sat down just as Deshawn stood up. "Dr. Chandragupta," Deshawn said. "You issued the death certificate in this case, correct?"

"Yes."

"Are you Karen Bessarian's personal physician?"

"No."

"Have you ever been?"

"No."

"Did you ever treat her for any malady, condition, or disease?"

"No."

"Do you know if she has a personal physician?"

"Yes. That is, I know who was treating her before she died."

"And who is that?"

"His name is Donald Kohl."

"And is Dr. Kohl a colleague of yours?"

"No."

"Where do you work, Dr. Chandragupta?"

"The Johns Hopkins Hospital in Baltimore."

"And is that where you claim Karen died?"

"No."

"Where are you licensed to practice medicine?"

"In Maryland. Also in Connecticut."

"Did Karen die in Maryland?"

"No."

"Did Karen die in Connecticut?"

"No."

"Are you a licensed medical examiner?"

"No, I'm—"

"Just answer the questions as put to you, Doctor," said Deshawn, firmly but politely. "Are you a licensed medical examiner?"

"No."

"Are you a state or county coroner?"

"No."

"And yet you issued a death certificate in this case, did you not?"

"Yes."

"Where did you issue this death certificate—not where you claim Karen died, but where did you generate the paperwork?"

"In Baltimore."

"Did you do this of your own volition?"

"Yes."

"Really, Dr. Chandragupta, let's try that question again: did you issue the so-called death certificate of your own volition, or did you do it upon someone's request?"

"Well, if you put it like that . . . the latter. At someone's request."

"Whose?"

"Tyler Horowitz's."

"The defendant in this case?"

"Yes."

"He asked you to issue a death certificate?"

"Yes."

"Did he initiate contact with you, or did you initiate contact with him?"

"I contacted him first," said Chandragupta.

"Were you aware that Tyler stood to inherit tens of billions of dollars when you contacted him?"

"Not as an absolute fact, no."

"But you suspected it?"

"It seemed logical, yes."

"Did you charge him anything to issue that certificate?"

"Naturally there is a fee for such a service."

"Naturally," said Deshawn, his voice dripping venom. He looked meaningfully at the jury box. The jurors looked back, but I couldn't tell what they were thinking.

"Mr. Draper, please," said Chandragupta, spreading his arms. "I know Canada is just across the river from here, and that we have some Canadians in the courtroom. But, honestly, there is nothing immoral or unusual about a doctor making money for services rendered."

"No," said Deshawn. "I'm sure there isn't." He walked over to the jury box, and stood beside it, as if he had somehow become an eighth juror. "Tell us, though, exactly what fee you charged."

"I admit that Mr. Horowitz was most generous, but—"

"The dollar amount, if you please."

"I was paid one hundred and twenty-five thousand dollars for this service."

Deshawn looked at the jurors, almost inviting them to whistle. One of them did.

"Thank you, Dr. Chandragupta. Your witness, Ms. Lopez."

"Dr. Chandragupta," she said, rising from her seat next to Tyler, "you said you are a medical doctor?"

"I am."

"And what is your medical specialty?"

"I am a surgeon, specializing in cerebrospinal circulatory issues."

I shifted in my seat. I wondered what, if anything, he knew about Katerinsky's syndrome.

"Where did Ms. Bessarian die?"

Deshawn was on his feet. "Objection, your honor. Assumes facts not in evidence. We have not determined that Ms. Bessarian is, in fact, dead. Indeed, we assert exactly the opposite."

Judge Herrington did his small-mouthed frown. "Mr. Draper, Detroit is not your home turf. Most lawyers in this town know that I hate picayune semantic distinctions." My heart sank, but Herrington went on. "However, I concede that you do have a point in this instance. Sustained."

Lopez nodded graciously. "Very well. Dr. Chandragupta, do you personally believe that Karen Bessarian is dead?"

"I do, yes."

"And where is it that you personally believe that Karen Bessarian died?"

"In Heaviside Crater, on the far side of the moon."

"And how do you know this?"

"Because I was there." I could see several members of the jury sitting up straight at this.

"What were you doing on the moon?" asked Lopez

"I had been flown there to perform surgery—they were requiring my expertise."

That was a comforting thought, I suppose. Nice to know that Immortex really did look after its charges.

"So there are no other doctors at Heaviside?" continued Lopez.

"Oh, but no. There are several—perhaps a dozen. Good ones, too, I might add."

"But they lacked your particular skills?"

"Correct."

"The patient you had gone to the moon to treat was not Ms. Bessarian, was it?"

"No."

"Then what contact did you have with Ms. Bessarian there?"

"I was on hand at her death."

"How did that circumstance arise?"

"I was in the medical facility at Heaviside when the Code Blue sounded."

"Code Blue?"

"A standard hospital code for cardiac arrest. Recall that I am a circulatory specialist. When I heard it announced, I ran into the corridor, saw other doctors and nurses running—indeed, fairly bouncing off the walls in the low lunar gravity. I joined them, reaching the hospital room containing Ms. Bessarian at the same time her personal physician did."

"That would be the Dr. Donald Kohl you mentioned during direct?" asked Lopez.

"That's right."

"Then what happened?"

"Dr. Kohl tried defibrillating Ms. Bessarian."

"And the result?"

"The results were negative. Ms. Bessarian passed away then and there. I must say, Dr. Kohl performed admirably, doing everything he should. And he seemed quite genuinely saddened by Karen Bessarian's passing."

"I'm sure he was," said Lopez. She looked meaningfully at the jury, "As are we all." Her voice wasn't one that carried sympathy well, but she was trying. "Still, wouldn't it normally be Dr. Kohl who would have issued a death certificate?"

" 'Normally' being the operative word, yes."

"What do you mean?"

"He told me he wasn't going to issue one."

"How did the topic come up?"

"I asked," said Chandragupta. "When Ms. Bessarian died, I was curious about procedures. Given the unusual location, I mean—on the moon. I asked Dr. Kohl how the paperwork for a death would be handled."

"And what did he say?"

"He said there was no paperwork. He said the whole point of having people like Ms. Bessarian up on the moon was so that they'd be outside of anyone's jurisdiction."

"So there would be no requirement that a death certificate be issued, correct?"

"Correct."

"What about notifying the next of kin?"

"Kohl said they weren't going to do that, either."

"Why not?"

"He said it was part of their agreement with their clients."

Lopez looked meaningfully at the jury, as if Chandragupta had just revealed a heinous conspiracy. She then turned slowly back to him. "How did you feel about that?"

Chandragupta apparently had a habit of stroking his beard; he was doing so now. "It bothered me. It didn't seem right."

"What did you do about this when you returned to Earth?"

"I contacted Tyler Horowitz in Detroit."

"Why?"

"He is Ms. Bessarian's next of kin—her son, in fact."

"Now, let's back up a step. How did you know that the woman who had died on the moon was Karen Bessarian?"

"Firstly, of course, because that was the name all the other doctors referred to her by."

"Any other reasons?"

"Yes. I recognized her."

Lopez had delicate eyebrows, which she lifted now; she'd frosted the outside tips of them with blonde, too. "She was known to you personally?"

Another stroke of the beard. "Not prior to this. But I'd read her books to my kids dozens of times. And I'd seen her on TV often enough."

"You have no doubt in your mind about the identity of the woman who died on the moon?"

At last Chandragupta took his hand away from his face, but only to make an emphatic sweep of it, palm held out. "None at all. It was Karen Bessarian."

"All right. And knowing this, you contacted her son, is that right?"

"Yes."

Lopez lifted her eyebrows again. "Why?"

"I felt he should know. I mean, his mother was dead! A child deserves to know that."

"And so you called him?"

"Yes. It was a sad duty, but certainly not the first time I'd had to do such a thing."

"And did Tyler ask you to do anything?"

"Yes. He requested I issue a death certificate."

"Why?"

"He said he knew that the doctors on the moon wouldn't issue one. He said he wanted to wrap up his mother's affairs."

"And so you agreed?"

"Yes." Hand back on beard again. "It's a duty I've performed before. I had the requisite electronic form stored locally. I filled out a copy, and emailed it to Mr. Horowitz, along with my digital signature."

"Again, how confident are you that the dead woman was Karen Bessarian?"

"One hundred percent."

"And how confident are you that she was, in fact, dead?"

"Also one hundred percent. I saw her stop breathing. I saw her EKG go flat. I saw her EEG go flat. I observed personally that her pupils had exploded."

"Exploded?"

"Dilated to the maximal extent, leaving only the thinnest ring of iris visible around them. It is a sure sign of brain death."

Lopez smiled ever so slightly. "Thank you, Dr. Chandragupta. Oh, one more question—your fee. Mr. Draper made much of how much your were paid for this service. Would you care to comment on that?"

"Yes, I would. The fee was Mr. Horowitz's idea; he said I deserved it. Called it 'Good Samaritan' money—his way of saying thank you."

"Did he offer the large fee before or after you agreed to provide a death certificate?"

"After. It was after, of course."

"Thank you," said Lopez. "No further questions."

Deshawn was on his feet. "Redirect, your honor?"

Herrington nodded.

"Dr. Chandragupta," Deshawn said, "what's the normal fee in Maryland for issuing a death certificate?"

"I'd have to look that up."

"Just a ballpark figure, sir. Round it up to the nearest thousand."

"Um, well, rounded up to the nearest thousand, it would be one."

"One thousand dollars, correct?"

"That is right."

"In fact, are there any forms that doctors in Maryland normally charge more than a thousand dollars to issue?"

"Not that I'm aware of."

"Now," said Deshawn, "are you certain that your discussion with the defendant about a hundred-and-twenty-five-thousand-dollar fee for issuing a death certificate took place *after* you'd agreed to in fact issue one?"

"Yes." Chandragupta glared defiantly at Deshawn. "That's how I remember it."

I'd thought it strange that Deshawn Draper had started by calling Chandragupta, since the doctor seemed totally on Tyler's side. But I soon saw why: once Chandragupta's testimony was over, Deshawn immediately called for summary judgment, based on the invalidity of the death certificate. Judge Herrington dismissed the jury while motions and countermotions were argued. Deshawn wanted the death certificate thrown out because it was issued by Chandragupta outside the geographic jurisdiction in which he was licensed to practice medicine, and because of the possibility that he'd been bribed to issue it.

Lopez countered with old maritime statues from Maryland, where Chandragupta *was* licensed, that said that any doctor could issue a death certificate in international waters when it was impractical, impossible, or against the decedent's wishes to have the body brought to shore; that last allowed for navy personnel to be buried at sea if they died during duty. She also vehemently argued that innuendo did not equal established fact. A lot of minutiae of Michigan and Maryland law were debated, but ultimately Judge Herrington ruled that the death certificate was indeed valid for the narrow purpose of determining the death of the original, biological Karen Bessarian.

CHAPTER 23

Deshawn and Lopez spent the morning arguing more motions; I'd had no idea how much time could be wasted on that. But finally, after lunch, we got down to the main show.

"Please state your name for the record," said the clerk.

Karen was wearing a simple, inexpensive beige suit. "Karen Cynthia Bessarian," she said.

"Be seated."

Karen sat down, and Deshawn got up—almost exactly like a seesaw.

"Hello, Karen," said Deshawn, smiling warmly. "How are you feeling today?"

"Fine, thank you."

"I'm glad," said Deshawn. "I suppose health concerns aren't a major issue for you anymore, are they?"

"No, thank God."

"You sound relieved. Have you had health problems in the past?"

"No more than anyone my age, I suppose," said Karen. "But they're no fun to go through."

"I'm sure, I'm sure," said Deshawn. "I don't want to pry, but might you share a few of them with us?"

"Oh, the usual litany—everything from tonsillitis to a hip replacement." Karen paused. "I suppose the worst thing was my bout with breast cancer."

"My God, that's awful," said Deshawn. "How were you treated?"

"Initially with radiation therapy and drugs. The tumor was destroyed, but, of course, I was still at risk of future tumors. Thankfully, I don't have to worry about that anymore."

"Because you've uploaded into this durable body?"

"No, no. Because I had genetic therapy. I had two of the key genes that predispose a woman to breast cancer. About twenty years ago, I had gene therapy to eliminate those genes from my body. That cut my likelihood of ever having another breast tumor to a very low level."

"I see, I see. Well, I'm delighted to hear that. But let's move on. Karen, have you been outside the U.S. since you became a Mindscan?"

"Yes."

"Where have you been?"

"Canada. Toronto."

"And that means you've crossed over the U.S.-Canada border since uploading, no?"

"Yes, by train going into Canada, and by car going back."

"And have you taken any flights recently?"

"Yes."

"Where from?"

"Toronto's Lester B. Pearson International Airport, to Atlanta, Georgia."

"Why?"

"To attend a funeral."

"Not your own, I hope!" A few jurors laughed.

"No. In fact, the funeral of my first husband, Daron Bessarian."

"Oh, my God," said Deshawn, with appropriate theatricality. "I'm so very sorry to hear that. Still, when crossing the border between—what, Windsor and Detroit?—you had to speak with customs officials, correct?"

"Yes."

"And when you flew from Toronto to Atlanta, you also had to deal with customs officials, correct?"

"Yes."

"So, in fact, you've dealt with both United States Customs and Canadian Customs, correct?"

"Yes."

"In these dealings, were you asked to provide identification?"

"Naturally."

"What ID did you present?"

"My United States passport, and my U.S. Homeland Security personal-identity card."

"And do you have both of these documents in your possession?"

"Yes, I do."

"May the court see them?"

"Of course."

Karen had a small purse with her. She removed the passport, and the smaller personal-identity card.

"I'd like to enter these as exhibits," said Deshawn, "and have the court note that they were indeed in the possession of the plaintiff."

"Ms. Lopez?"

"Your honor, just because she has physical possession—"

Herrington shook his long head. "Ms. Lopez, don't argue your case. Do you have an objection to the exhibits being entered?"

"No, your honor."

"Very well," said Judge Herrington. "Continue, Mr. Draper."

"Thank you, your honor. So, Karen, as you've just demonstrated, you possess the identification papers of Karen Bessarian, correct?"

"Of course," Karen said. "I am her."

"Well, you've certainly got Karen's ID documents, but let's see if it goes further than that." Deshawn took an object off his desk and held it up. It was about the size of a deck of playing cards; parts had a shiny silver finish and the rest were matte black. "Do you know what this is?"

"A transaction terminal," said Karen.

"Exactly," said Deshawn. "Just a common, garden-variety wireless transaction terminal. The kind you encounter in stores and restaurants—anywhere you might want to access the funds in your bank account and transfer some amount to someone else, correct?"

"That's what it appears to be, yes," said Karen.

"Now, please let me assure you that this isn't a mockup; it's a real, working unit, hooked into the global financial network."

"All right."

Deshawn pulled a golden disk out of his pocket. "What's this, Karen?"

"A Reagan."

"By which you mean a ten-dollar United States coin, correct? With the American eagle on one side and former president Ronald Reagan on the other, is that right?"

"Yes."

"All right. Now, do you have access to your bank accounts currently?"

Karen's tone was measured. "In his wisdom, until this matter is cleared up, Judge Herrington has put a cap on how much of my money I can take out. But, yes, I should be able to access my accounts."

"Very good," said Deshawn. "Here's what I'd like to do, then. I'd like to give you this ten-dollar coin—good for all debts, public and private. In exchange, I'd like you to transfer ten dollars from your principal bank account into mine. Would you be willing to do that?"

Karen smiled. "By all means."

Deshawn looked to the judge, who nodded. He then crossed the well and gave Karen the coin. "Don't spend it all in one place," he said, and a couple of jurors chuckled; Deshawn was warm and witty, and slowly but surely I think he was indeed winning them over. "Now, if you please . . . ?" He handed her the transaction terminal.

Karen placed her thumb against the little scanning plate, and one of the green lights came on. She then held the device up to her right eye, and the other green light came on.

"Wait!" said Deshawn. "Before you go any further, will you read to the court what the transfer terminal's display is currently saying?"

"With pleasure," said Karen. "It says, 'Identity confirmed: Bessarian, Karen C.'"

Deshawn took the device from her and walked over to the jury box, showing the display to each juror in turn. The implication was clear: the device had recognized Karen's fingerprints and her retinal scans.

"So at the border stations, you proved your identity on the basis of what you had—specifically, on the basis of documents in your possession, correct?"

"That's right."

"And the transaction terminal has identified you based on who you are—that is, based on your biometric data, correct?"

"That's my understanding, yes."

"All right." Deshawn fished into his jacket pocket, and pulled out his ident. "This is the account I'd like you to transfer ten dollars to," he said, proffering the card.

Karen took the card and held it near the device's scanner. Another LED came on. Karen tapped out something on the keypad, and—

"Wait!" said Deshawn. "What did you just do?"

"I entered my PIN," said Karen.

"Your personal identification number?"

"Yes."

"And did the terminal accept it?"

Karen held up the unit. The green LED was surely obvious, even in the jury box.

"Who else beside you knows this PIN?"

"No one."

"Do you have it written down anywhere?"

"No. The bank says you aren't supposed to do that."

Deshawn nodded. "You are wise. So this terminal has now recognized you not only based on your biometrics, but also on information you possess that only Karen Bessarian could possibly know, correct?"

"That's exactly right," said Karen.

Deshawn nodded. "Now, if you'll just finish the transaction—I don't want to lose my ten bucks . . ."

The jury enjoyed this comment, and Karen tapped several keys. "Transaction completed," she said, and held up the terminal, which was showing the appropriate pattern of illuminated LEDs.

It was a simple, elegant demonstration, and it looked to me like at least some of the jurors were impressed by it. "Thank you," said Deshawn. "Your witness, Ms. Lopez."

"Not right now," said Herrington. "We'll pick this up in the morning."

CHAPTER 24

That night, about 3:00 a.m, I told Karen about the strange interaction I was apparently having with other instantiations of me. We were walking around outside, on the manicured grounds of her mansion. Insects buzzed, and bats wheeled overhead. The moon was a high crescent sneering down at us; somewhere on its backside, of course, was the only other me that was *supposed* to exist—the biological original.

"As I'm sure you know," I said, "there's a phenomenon in quantum physics called 'entanglement.' It allows quantum particles to be connected instantaneously across any distance; measuring one affects the other, and vice versa."

Karen nodded. "Uh-huh."

"And, well, there've been theories that consciousness is quantum-mechanical in nature for ages—most famously, I suppose, in the work of Roger Penrose, who proposed just that back in the 1980s."

"Yes," said Karen, amiably. "So?"

"So, I think—don't ask me exactly how; I'm not sure quite what the mechanism is—but I think Immortex has made multiple copies of my mind, and that somehow, from time to time, I connect with them. I'm assuming it's quantum entanglement, but I suppose it could be something else. But, anyway, I hear them, as voices in my head."

"Like . . . like telepathy?"

"Umm, I hate that word—it's got weird-ass psychic connotations. Besides, I'm not hearing *other people's* thoughts; I'm hearing my own . . . sort of."

"Forgive me, Jake, but it seems more likely that there's just something not quite functioning right in your new brain. I'm sure if you told Dr. Porter about it, he'd—"

"No!" I said. "No. Immortex is doing something *wrong*. I—I can feel it."

"Jake . . ."

"It's inherent in the Mindscan technology: the ability to make as many copies as you want of the source mind."

Karen and I were holding hands. It didn't provide quite the same intimate sensation it had when I'd been flesh and blood, but, then again, at least my palms weren't sweating. "But *why* would they do that?" she said. "What possible purpose could it serve?"

"Steal corporate secrets. Steal personal security codes. Blackmail me."

"Over what? What have you done?"

"Well . . . nothing that I'm ashamed of."

Karen's tone was teasing. "Really?"

I didn't want to be sidetracked, but I found myself considering her question for a moment. "Yes, really; there's nothing in my past I'd pay any sizable amount of money to have kept secret. But that's not the point. They could be on a fishing expedition. See what they turn up."

"Like the formula for Old Sully's Premium Dark?"

"Karen, be serious. Something is going on."

"Oh, I'm sure there is," she said. "But, you know, I hear voices in my head all the time—my characters' voices. It's a fact of life, being a writer. Could what you're experiencing be something like that?"

"I'm not a writer, Karen."

"Well, all right then. Okay. But did you ever read Julian Jaynes?"

I shook my head.

"Oh, I loved him in college! *The Origin of Consciousness in the Breakdown of the Bicameral Mind*—amazing book. And what a title! My editor would never let me get away with anything like that. Anyway, Jaynes said the two hemispheres are basically two separate intelligences, and that the voices of angels and demons people claimed to hear in ancient times were really coming from the other side of their own heads." She looked at me. "Maybe the integration of your new brain isn't working quite right. Get Dr. Porter to tweak a few things, and I'm sure it'll go away."

"No, no," I said. "It's *real*."

"Can you do it now? Connect with another you?"

"I can't do it on demand. And it only happens sometimes."

"Jake . . ." Karen said gently, leaving my name hanging in the night air.

"No, really," I said. "It really does happen."

Her tone was infinitely gentle. "Jake, have you ever heard of assisted writing? Or Ouija boards? Or false-memory syndrome? The human mind can convince itself that all sorts of things have external reality, or are coming from somewhere else, when it's really doing them itself."

"That's not what's happening here."

"Isn't it? Have these—these *voices* said anything to you that you didn't already know? Anything that you couldn't already know, but that we could check on to see if it's true?"

"Well, no, of course not. The other instantiations are being held in isolation somewhere."

"Why would that be? And why aren't I detecting anything similar?"

I shrugged my shoulders a bit. "I don't know."

"You should ask Dr. Porter about it."

"No," I said. "And don't you speak to him about it either—not until I've figured out what's going on."

At 10:00 a.m. the next morning, Maria Lopez faced Karen, who had returned to the witness stand.

"Good morning, Ms. Bessarian."

"Good morning," said Karen.

"Did you have a pleasant—a pleasant *interregnum* since our last session in court?" asked Lopez.

"Yes."

"What, may I ask, did you do?"

Deshawn spoke up. "Objection, your honor! Relevance."

"A little latitude your honor," said Lopez.

"Very well," said Herrington. "Ms. Bessarian, you'll answer the question."

"Well, let's see. I read, I watched a movie, I wrote part of a new novel, I surfed the Web. I went for a nice walk."

"Very good. Very good. Anything else?"

"All sorts of insignificant things. I'm really not sure what you're driving at, Ms. Lopez."

"Well, then, let me ask you directly: did you sleep?"

"No."

"You didn't sleep. So, it's safe to say, you didn't dream, either, isn't that right?"

"Obviously."

"*Why* didn't you sleep?"

"My artificial body doesn't require it."

"But *could* you sleep, if you wanted to?"

"I—I'm not sure why one would desire sleeping if it wasn't necessary."

"You're begging the question. Can you go to sleep?"

Karen was quiet for a few moments, then: "No. Apparently not."

"You haven't slept at all since you were reinstantiated in this form, correct?"

"That is correct, yes."

"And, therefore, you haven't dreamed, right?"

"I have not."

Deshawn was on his feet. "Your honor, this is hardly proper cross."

"Sorry," said Lopez. "Just a few pleasantries to start the day." She picked up a large paper book from her table and rose to her feet. "We've been discussing your physical parameters, Ms. Bessarian. Let's start with a simple one. Your age."

"I'm eighty-five."

"And your date of birth?"

"May twenty-ninth, 1960."

"And how were you born?"

"I—I beg your pardon?"

"Was it a normal birth? A cesarean section? Or some other procedure?"

"A normal birth, at least by the standards of the time. My mother was given heavy anesthetic, labor was induced, and my father wasn't allowed in the delivery room." Karen looked directly at the jury box, wanting to score a point right off the bat. "We've come a long way since then."

"A normal birth," said Lopez. "Through the dilated birth canal, out into the light of day, a gentle slap on the bottom—I imagine that was still in vogue back then."

"Yes, I believe so."

"A first cry."

"Yes."

"And, of course, a severing of the umbilical cord."

"That's right."

"The umbilical cord, through which nutrients had been passed from your mother into the developing embryo, correct?"

"Yes."

"A cord whose removal leaves a scar, something we call the navel, no?"

"That's correct."

"And those scars come in two forms—commonly called innies and outies, isn't that right?"

"Yes."

"And which kind do you have, Ms. Bessarian?"

"Objection!" said Deshawn. "Relevance!"

"Mr. Draper raised the question of biometrics," said Lopez, spreading her arms. "Surely I'm allowed to explore all her biometrics, not just the ones that Mr. Draper can do parlor tricks with."

The judge's shoehorn face bobbed up and down. "Overruled."

"Ms. Bessarian," said Lopez, "which is it—and innie or an outie?"

"An innie."

"May we see it?"

"No."

"And why not?"

Karen held her head up high. "Because it would be pointless, and—as I'm sure the judge would agree—hardly befitting the dignity of this court. You're hoping I have no belly button at all, so that you can make some facile point. But, of course I do; my body is anatomically correct. And so, with my belly exposed, you'd fall back on trying to make some lesser point about how my navel isn't really made of scar tissue but rather is just a sculpted indentation. Let me save you the bother: I concede that indeed it is sculpted. But given that navels don't do anything, that's hardly significant. Mine is as good as anyone else's." She looked directly at the jury box again, and smiled a winning smile. "It even collects lint."

The jurors, and even the judge, laughed. "Move along," said Herrington.

"Very well," said Lopez, sounding somewhat chastened. "Your honor, may I introduce the defendant's first exhibit, a hardcopy of the operating manual for the transaction terminal Mr. Draper introduced earlier?"

"Mr. Draper?" asked Judge Herrington.

"No objection."

"The exhibit is admitted," said the judge.

"Thank you," said Lopez. She crossed the well, approached the witness stand, and handed the manual to Karen. "As you can see, I've bookmarked a certain page. Would you open the manual to that page?"

Karen did so.

"And will you read the highlighted passage?" asked Lopez.

Karen cleared her throat—a mechanically unnecessary bit of theater, then: " 'This scanner uses biometric data to ensure the security of transactions. Both a fingerprint scan and a retinal scan are performed to verify the identity of the user. No two human beings have identical fingerprints, nor do any two individuals share the same retinal patterns. By measuring physical characteristics of both, the security of the transaction is assured.' So you see—"

"Sounds impressive, doesn't it?" said Lopez.

"Yes. And the point is that the terminal *did*—"

"Forgive me, Ms. Bessarian, you can only reply to the questions I pose." Lopez paused. "No, I'm sorry, I don't wish to be rude. You had a comment you wanted to add?"

"Well, just that the scanner *did* recognize me as Karen Bessarian."

"Yes, it did. In key biometric areas, you are apparently identical—or at least as close as is necessary—to the original Karen Bessarian."

"That's right."

"Now, if it pleases the court, I'd like to try something. Your honor, defendant's exhibits two, three, and four. Number two is an artificial hand, and number three is an artificial eyeball, both—as, number four, the certificate of provenance, attests—produced by Morrell GmbH of Dusseldorf, a leading manufacturer of prosthetic body parts. Indeed, Morrell is the company Immortex employs to make many of the replacement components it uses."

There were about fifteen minutes of objections and arguments before the judge accepted the exhibits. Finally, we were back on track, and Lopez handed the artificial hand to Karen. "Would you please press the artificial hand's thumb against the terminal's scanning plate?"

Karen reluctantly did so. One green light went on—I used to hate using those things, because I could never tell if the light was green or red.

She then handed Karen the artificial eyeball. "And would you hold this up to the terminal's lens?"

Karen did that, too, and a second green LED came to life.

"Now, Ms. Bessarian, would you be so kind as to read to the court what the display says?" She held out the device.

Karen looked at it. "It . . ."

"Yes, Ms. Bessarian?"

"It says, 'Identity confirmed: Bessarian, Karen C.'"

"Thank you, Ms. Bessarian." She took the device out of Karen's limp hand and tapped some keys with slow deliberation. When she was done, she handed the device back to Karen.

"Now, I'd like you to do for me what you did for Mr. Draper: transfer ten dollars into my own bank account. Of course, to do that, we'll need your PIN number."

Karen frowned. "It's just a PIN," she said.

Lopez looked momentarily confused. "Sorry?"

"PIN stands for 'Personal Identification Number.' Only people who work for the Department of Redundancy Department call it a PIN number."

Judge Herrington's little mouth smiled at this.

"Fine," said Lopez. "What we need now is your PIN, so that we can complete the transaction."

Karen folded her arms across her chest. "And I don't believe the court can make me divulge that."

"No, no, of course not. Privacy is important. May I?" Lopez held out her hand for the terminal, and Karen gave it to her. She stabbed out some numbers on the unit, then handed it back to Karen. "Would you read what it says?"

Karen's plastic face wasn't quite as pliable as one made out of flesh was, but I could see the consternation. "It says, 'PIN OK.'"

"Well, what do you know!" declared Lopez. "Without using your fingerprint, or your retinal pattern, or any knowledge known solely to you, we've managed to access your account, haven't we?"

Karen said nothing.

"Haven't we, Ms. Bessarian?"

"Apparently."

"Well, in that case, why don't we go ahead and transfer ten dollars into my account, just as you did for Mr. Draper?"

"I'd rather not," said Karen.

"What?" said Lopez. "Oh, I see. Yes, of course, you're right. That's totally unfair. After all, Mr. Draper gave you ten dollars first. So, I suppose I should also give you a Reagan." She reached into her jacket pocket again, brought out her hand, and proffered a coin.

Karen crossed her arms in front of her chest, refusing to take it.

"Ah, well," said Lopez, peeling back the gold foil, revealing the embossed chocolate disk inside. She popped it in her mouth, and chewed. "This one's a fake, anyway."

CHAPTER 25

A gilded cage is still a cage.

I was fine now, with decades of life ahead of me. And I didn't want to spend it here at High Eden.

And—I *was* fine, wasn't I? I mean, Chandragupta's technique had supposedly cured me. But . . .

But my head was still throbbing. It came and it went, thank God; I couldn't take it if it was like this all the time, but . . .

But nothing was helping. Not for long, not for good.

And I didn't trust the doctors here. I mean, look at what had happened to poor Karen! Code Blue my ass . . .

And yet—

And yet, I had to do *something*. I wasn't a machine, a robot. I wasn't like that other me, that doppelgänger, free from aches and pains. My head hurt. When it was happening, it hurt so fucking much.

I left my suite, bouncing along in the lunar gravity, heading for the hospital.

Our next witness was Andrew Porter, who had come down from Toronto, joining the half-a-dozen Immortex suits already here. "Dr. Porter," said Deshawn, "what is your educational background?"

The witness stand was a little small for someone of Porter's height, but he scrunched his legs sideways. "I have a Ph.D. in cognitive science from Carnegie Mellon University, as well as Master's degrees in both Electrical Engineering Science and Computer Studies from CalTech."

"Have you had any academic appointments?"

Porter's eyebrows were working, as always. "Several. Most recently I was a senior research fellow with the Artificial Intelligence Laboratory at the Massachusetts Institute of Technology."

"Now, I rather enjoyed Ms. Lopez's coin trick earlier," said Deshawn. "But I understand you have a real gold medallion, isn't that right?"

"Yes, I do. Or, at least, I'm part of the team it belongs to."

"Did you bring it with you? May we see it?"

"Certainly."

Porter pulled a large case out of his jacket pocket, and opened it.

"Plaintiff's three, your honor," said Deshawn.

There was the usual back-and-forth, then the exhibit was admitted. Deshawn held the medallion up to a camera, showing first one side then the other; the images were projected on the wall screen behind Porter. One side showed a three-quarters view of a young man with delicate features, and was inscribed with the italic quotation, "Can Machines Think?" and the name Alan M. Turing. The other side showed a bearded man with glasses and the name Hugh G. Loebner. Both sides were labeled "Loebner Prize" in letters following the curving edge of the disk.

"How did you come by this?" asked Deshawn.

"It was awarded to us for being the first group ever to pass the Turing Test."

"And how did you do that?"

"We precisely copied a human mind—that of one Seymour Wainwright, also formerly of MIT—into an artificial brain."

"And do you continue to work in this area?"

"I do."

"Who is your current employer?"

"I work for Immortex."

"In what capacity?"

"I'm the senior scientist. My exact job title is Director, Reinstantiation Technologies."

Deshawn nodded. "And how would you describe what it is you do in your job?"

"I oversee all aspects of the process of transferring personhood from a biological mind into a nanogel matrix."

"Nanogel matrix being the material you fashion artificial brains out of?" said Deshawn.

"Correct."

"So, you are one of the developers of the Mindscan process that Immortex uses to transfer consciousness, and you continue to oversee the transference work that Immortex does today, correct?"

"Yes."

"Well, then," said Deshawn, "can you explain for us how it is that the human brain gives rise to consciousness?"

Porter shook his long head. "No."

Judge Herrington frowned. "Dr. Porter, you are required to answer. I don't want to hear any nonsense about trade secrets, or—"

Porter tried to swivel in his chair, but couldn't really manage it. "Not at all, your honor. I can't answer the question because I don't know what the answer is. No one does, in my opinion."

"Let me get this straight, Dr. Porter," asked Deshawn. "You don't know how consciousness works."

"That's right."

"But nonetheless you can replicate it?" said Deshawn.

Porter nodded. "And that's *all* I can do."

"How do you mean?"

Porter did a good job of looking as though he was trying to decide where to begin, although, of course, we had rehearsed his testimony over and over again. "For over a century now, computer programmers have been trying to duplicate the human mind. Some thought it was a matter of getting the right algorithms, some thought it was a matter of mathematically simulating neural nets, some thought it had something to do with quantum computing. None succeeded. Oh, there are lots of computers around that can do very clever things, but no one has ever built one from scratch that is self-aware in the way you and I are, Mr. Draper. Not once, for instance, has a manufactured computer spontaneously said, 'Please don't turn me off.' Never has a computer spontaneously mused upon the meaning of life. Never has a computer written a bestselling novel. We thought we'd be able to make machines do all those things, but, so far, we can't." He looked at the jury, then back at Deshawn. "But the transfers of biological minds that we have produced can do all those things, and more. They are capable of *every* mental feat that other humans can perform."

"You say other humans?" asked Deshawn. "You consider the copies to be human?"

"Absolutely. As that medallion proves, they totally, completely, and infallibly pass the Turing Test: there is no question you can ask them that they don't answer indistinguishably from how other humans answer. They are people."

"And are they conscious?"

"Absolutely. As conscious as you or I. Indeed, although the voltages differ, the electrical signature of a copied brain and an original brain are the same on properly calibrated EEGs."

"But—forgive me, doctor, I don't mean to be dense—but if you don't know what causes consciousness, how can you reproduce it? How do you know *what* to reproduce?"

Porter nodded. "Consider it like this: I don't know anything about music. When I was in school, they thought I'd be a menace to every hearing person if they gave me a musical instrument to play, so I was assigned to the vocal class, along with all the other tone-deaf people. So, I know nothing at all about what makes Beethoven's Fifth a great piece of music. But as an engineer, if you brought me a CD recording of it, and asked me to copy it onto a MemWafer, no problem—I could do that. I don't look for the 'musical' stuff on the CD; I don't look for the 'genius' on the CD. I just copy *everything* to the new medium. And that's exactly what we do when we're transferring consciousness."

"But, if you don't know what you're looking for, isn't it possible you've missed something key?"

"No. Most psychologists would say that even if all we did was transfer a map of the interconnections between neurons, and the various levels of neurotransmitters, we'd have captured everything meaningful in the brain. And we certainly do that."

"It sounds like an enormous amount of data is involved," said Deshawn.

"It's not as much as you might think," replied Porter. "We've found fractal resonances in a lot of it—that means that the same patterns are repeated over and over again at different levels of resolution. The data would compress very nicely if one were inclined to keep a record of it." I sat up in my chair as he said this, but, since I was behind Karen, there was no way for me to catch her eye.

"And so by copying this information, you've copied consciousness as well?" asked Deshawn. "Simply by copying the neural networks and neurotransmitter levels?"

"Well, some argue that those things aren't the true physiological correlates of consciousness—that is, that they aren't in and of themselves the physical indications of conscious thought—and they point to paramecia as proof."

"Paramecia?" repeated Deshawn.

"Yes. Um, your honor, if I may . . . ?"

Herrington nodded, and Porter got up out of the witness stand, looking relieved to no longer be squashed. He pulled a small remote control from his jacket's other pocket, and images started appearing on the wall screen.

"A paramecium," said Porter, "is a kind of protozoan—a one-cell lifeform. Paramecia don't have a nervous system, since nervous systems are made up of specialized nerve cells, and obviously a one-celled lifeform can't have any specialized cells. And yet, without neurons or neurotransmitters, a paramecium can learn. Not much, I grant you—but it can learn. You can teach it that if it comes to a divided pathway, going left will always result in a mild shock and going right will always result in getting food." The images on the wall illustrated this. "Somehow, the paramecium learns this despite having no nervous system at all. And that at least suggests the possibility that neural nets are not actually what's responsible for our awareness."

"Well, then," said Deshawn, "how *does* awareness come about?"

Different visuals appeared on the screen.

"One argument," said Porter, "is that the microtubules that make up the cytoskeleton of a cell are where the awareness, the infinitesimal consciousness, of a paramecium—or a human—resides. Microtubules are like hollowed-out cobs of Indian corn: they have an empty center, but are covered with kernels. And, just like in Indian corn, the kernels can form patterns. Some argue that those patterns move and replicate like cellular automata, and—"

"Cellular automata?" said Deshawn.

More visuals, like animated crossword-puzzle boards.

"Yes, indeed," said Porter. "Consider the microtubule's surface to be a grid of squares rolled into a tube. Imagine some of the squares are black, and some are white—that's the Indian corn appearance I was referring to a moment ago. Imagine, too, that the squares respond to simple rules, such as this: if you're a black square, and at least three of the eight other squares surrounding you are also black, then you should turn white." The visual display illustrated this.

"See?" said Porter. "A very simple rule. But from out of such rules, complex patterns appear on the grid. For instance, you can get boomerang shapes made up of a consistent pattern of squares that actually move across the grid—every time the basic rule is applied, the whole cluster might move one space to the left. You also get shapes that devour other shapes, and big shapes that split into two smaller, but otherwise identical shapes." We all watched as these things happened on the screen.

"Now, consider that," said Porter. "The patterns are responding to stimulus in the form of the rule that is being applied. Well, response to stimulus is one of the standard criteria for life. The patterns are moving, and, again, movement is also one of the standard criteria of life. The patterns are devouring other patterns, and, again, eating is a third standard criterion of life. And the patterns are reproducing, and, of course, doing that is also one of the standard criteria of being alive. Indeed, cellular automata are one form of what's long been called artificial life, although I'd argue that the word 'artificial' is unnecessary. They *are* life."

"And so your Mindscan process copies the patterns of cellular automata?" said Deshawn.

"Indirectly, yes."

"Indirectly? If there's a chance that you've missed something—"

"No, no. We get the information copied with absolute fidelity, but it's physical impossible to actually scan the configuration of cellular automata."

"Why?"

"Well, as I said, we record the configuration of the neural networks—the positions and interconnections of every neuron in your brain—but we don't record the pattern of cellular automata on the surface of the microtubules within those neurons. See, tubulins—the little kernels that make up the microtubule cob—can flip between two states, which I've been showing as black and white in the graphics, here, so that they make the complex animated patterns you've seen on the surface of the microtubule. But the two states aren't really black and white. Rather, they're defined by where an electron happens to be—in the tubulin's alpha subunit pocket, or in its beta subunit pocket." He smiled at the jurors. "I know, I know—it sounds like gobbledygook. But the point is that this is a quantum-mechanical process, and that means we can't even *theoretically* measure the states without disturbing them."

Porter turned back to face Deshawn. "But as our quantum fog condenses into the nanogel of the brain, it is briefly quantally entangled with the biological original, and so the cellular-automata patterns precisely match. And, if microtubules are indeed the source of consciousness, then *that's* when the consciousness is transferred to the duplicate. Of course, the entanglement quickly breaks down, but by the time it does the rules are being applied again in the new cellular automata, so that, to go back to our earlier metaphor, the squares are flipping back and forth from state to state."

Porter looked now at Karen, sitting at the plaintiff's table. "So whatever it is that makes up consciousness—neural nets, or even cellular automata on the surface of microtubules—it doesn't matter; we make a total, complete, perfect transference of it. The new artificial brain is as self-aware, as real, as conscious as the old—and it is every bit the same person. That lovely woman sitting there is, without a doubt, Karen Bessarian."

Deshawn nodded. "Thank you, Dr. Porter. No further questions."

✤

I'd been told we'd never be allowed any contact with people back on Earth, but for once Immortex was bending its vaunted rules. As I sat in a chair in Dr. Ng's office, the chiseled, bearded face of Pandit Chandragupta looked up at me from her desktop monitor. He was now back in Baltimore—on Earth, lucky bastard—while I was still stuck up here on the moon.

"You should have said something sooner, Mr. Sullivan," he said. "We can only treat that which is brought to our attention."

"I'd just had brain surgery," I replied, exasperated. "I thought headaches went with the territory."

I waited while my words reached Earth and his made their way back to me. "No, these should not be occurring. I suspect they will indeed go away. The cause, I think, is a neurotransmitter imbalance. We have radically altered the blood-flow pattern to your brain, and I suspect that reuptake is being interfered with. That can certainly cause headaches of the type you've described. Your brain will adjust; everything should go back to normal eventually. And, of course, Dr. Ng, I'm sure, will prescribe something for the pain, although that will treat only the symptom, not the underlying cause." He shifted his gaze to look at the woman seated next to me. "Dr. Ng, what have you got there?"

"My thought would be to give him Toraplaxin, unless you can think of a reason why it'd be contraindicated in this case."

A pause again, then: "No, no. That should be fine. Say 200 milligrams to start, twice a day, yes?"

"Yes, yes. I'll get our dispensary to—"

But Chandragupta, down on Earth, hadn't intended to yield the floor, I guess, because he was still talking. "Now, Mr. Sullivan, there can be other problems associated with large fluctuations in neurotransmitter levels. Depression, for one. Have you felt any of that?"

Anger was more like it—but my anger, of course, was fully justified. "No."

The time-lag pause, then a nod, and more words: "Another possibility is sudden mood swings. Have you experienced any signs of that?"

I shook my head. "No."

The pause, then: "Any paranoia?"

"No, nothing, doctor."

Chandragupta nodded. "Good, good. Let us know if anything like that develops."

"Absolutely," I said.

✦

The trial had recessed for lunch—or at least for a noontime break; neither Karen, nor I, nor Malcolm ate anything, of course, although Deshawn downed two cheeseburgers and more Coke than I would have though it possible to fit in a human stomach. And then it was Maria Lopez's turn to take a whack at Porter.

Porter seemed implacable, although, as always, his eyebrows were in constant motion. He also had the advantage of being a good half-meter taller than Lopez; even seated, he seemed to loom over her.

"Mr. Porter," she began—but Porter cut her off.

"Not to go into picayune distinctions," he said, smiling at the judge, "but it's *Dr.* Porter, actually."

"Of course," said Lopez. "My apologies. You said you are an employee of Immortex, correct?"

"Yes."

"Are you also a stockholder?"

"Yes."

"How much is your Immortex stock worth?"

"About eight billion dollars, I think."

"That's a lot of money," said Lopez.

Porter shrugged amiably.

"Of course, it's all on paper, isn't it?" asked Lopez.

"Well, yes."

"And if Immortex stock takes a hit, your wealth could evaporate."

"That's one way of putting it," said Porter.

Lopez looked at the jury. "And, so, naturally, you want us to believe that the Immortex process actually does what you say it does."

"I'm sure if you have experts that disagree with me, you will call them to the stand," said Porter. "But, in fact, I do believe—as a person, as a scientist, and as an engineer—everything I testified."

"And yet you testified that you don't know what consciousness is."

"Correct."

"But you're sure you're copying it," said Lopez.

"Also correct."

"Faithfully?"

"Yes."

"Accurately?"

"Yes."

"In its entirety?"

"Yes."

"Then, tell us, Dr. Porter, why don't your robots sleep?"

Porter was visibly flustered; his eyebrows were even quiescent for a moment. "They're not robots."

"Well," said Lopez, all *people* sleep. But I'll withdraw the term. Why is it that reinstantiations of human minds in your artificial brains do not sleep?"

"It's—it's not necessary."

"So we've been told by Ms. Bessarian—who doubtless read that in your sales literature. But what is the *real* reason they don't sleep?"

Porter looked wary. "I—I'm not sure I understand."

"Why is it that your uploads don't experience sleep from time to time?"

"It's as I said: they don't need it."

"Perhaps that's true. But they don't need to have sex, either—after all, they cannot reproduce via that method, or any other. And yet your uploads are prepared to have intercourse, aren't they?"

"Well, people enjoy sex, and—"

"Some people enjoy sleeping, too," said Lopez.

Porter shook his head. "No, they don't. They enjoy being restored to their previous state of vigor, but sleep in and of itself is just unconsciousness."

"Is it, Doctor? Is it really? What about dreaming? Is *that* an unconscious state?"

"Well . . ."

"Come now, Doctor. This can't be a novel question in your field. Is dreaming an unconscious state?"

"No, it's not generally classified as such."

"Deep, dreamless sleep with steady delta waves and no rapid-eye movement is an unconscious condition, isn't that right? But dreaming is not, correct?"

"Well, yes."

"There's a sense of self in dreaming; there's an awareness."

"I suppose that's true."

"You're the brain specialist, Dr. Porter, not I. *Is* it true?"

"Yes."

"Dreaming is a form of conscious activity, correct?"

"Well, yes."

"Because there is an identifiable sense of self, correct?"

"Yes."

"But your robots—forgive me, your reinstantiations—don't dream?"

"Not all forms of conscious activity are desirable, Ms. Lopez. It's my fervent hope that none of our reinstantiations experience terror or have a panic attack, either—and those are conscious states."

"Oh, very clever, Dr. Porter," said Lopez, making a show of clapping her hands slowly. "Bravo! But, in fact, you're avoiding the question. Dreaming is different from other conscious states in that it's entirely internal, isn't that true?"

"More or less."

"Much more than less, I think. Dreams are the very essence of our inner life, no? Real consciousness, the kind that the biological Karen Bessarian had, included the ability to conceptualize internally in the absence of environmental cues. And your creations fail to have that sort of consciousness."

"That's not—"

"Isn't it true that you don't let them sleep, because were they to sleep, they'd expect to dream, and when they awoke, and remembered nothing of their dreams, it would soon be apparent that they did *not* dream? That the most intimate part of our inner lives—dreaming—is completely absent? Isn't that true, Dr. Porter?"

"I . . . it's not like that."

"But if they were, in fact, accurate copies, they would dream, wouldn't they? You said they'd answer any question exactly as a human would—that's what you won that fancy medallion for, right? But what if you asked them about their dreams?"

"You're making a mountain out of a molehill," said Porter, crossing his arms in front of his chest.

Lopez shook her head. "Oh, I'd never dream of doing that. But I would dream of other things—unlike that construct over there pretending to be Karen Bessarian."

"Objection!" said Deshawn. "Your honor!"

"Save it for closing arguments, Ms. Lopez," said Herrington.

Lopez bowed graciously toward the bench. "Of course, your honor. No further questions."

CHAPTEr 26

I went back to my rooms—I couldn't bring myself to call it my "home"—at High Eden, and took the first of the Toraplaxin pills. I then lay down on my couch, rubbing my forehead, hoping the medicine would help. At my spoken command, the image of Lake Louise disappeared from the wall and was replaced by the CBC News. I wondered if Immortex monitored what shows we were watching. I wouldn't be surprised. Why, I bet they even—

Suddenly my heart jumped so hard it felt like I'd been kicked in the sternum.

They were doing a story about Karen Bessarian.

The *other* Karen Bessarian.

"Bookmark this!" I snapped into the air.

The dateline superimposed on the screen said, "Detroit." A white female reporter was standing outside an old building there. "A bizarre battle is taking place in this Michigan courthouse," said the woman. "The son of bestselling novelist Karen Bessarian, author of the megapopular *DinoWorld* series, is being sued by an entity claiming to be Karen Bessarian . . ."

I watched, riveted. It took me a moment to recognize Karen: she'd opted for a substantially younger face. But, as footage of the trial ran, it was clearly her— or, at least, the uploaded version of her.

And her claim to being the legal, actual Karen Bessarian was being challenged in the courts! The reporter wasn't offering an opinion about which way she thought the trial would go, but the mere fact that this charade might come tumbling down buoyed me immensely. Surely Brian Hades couldn't keep me here much longer! Surely he'd have to let me return to Earth, let me resume my old life! To do anything else, why, that'd be tantamount to holding me hostage . . .

"The plaintiff calls Tyler Horowitz," said Deshawn, rising.

I could see Karen shifting uncomfortably in her seat next to where Deshawn was now standing.

Tyler looked defiant in the witness stand, as Deshawn began his questioning. "Mr. Horowitz, your advocate somehow knew your mother's personal identification number. Did you have a hand in that?"

"Umm, I, ah, I take the Fifth."

"Mr. Horowitz, it's not a crime to know someone else's PIN. If they're careless enough to make it discoverable, that's their problem, not yours. Unless, of course, you've used it to fraudulently gain access to your mother's funds, in which case, of course, your assertion of your Fifth Amendment privilege against self-incrimination should stand. Is that your wish?"

"I haven't touched a cent of my mother's money," said Tyler, sharply.

"No, no, of course not," said Deshawn, who waited the perfect beat before adding, *"Yet."*

Lopez was on her feet. "Objection, your honor!"

"Sustained," said Herrington. "Watch it, Mr. Draper."

Deshawn tipped his shaved head toward the bench. "My apologies, your honor. Mr. Horowitz, if you want me to leave your ability to dip into your mother's bank account alone, I will."

"Damn it, you're twisting everything," said Tyler. "I—look, years ago, my mother mentioned that her PIN was the extension number of where she'd worked when she was pregnant with me; she'd worked in fund-raising for Georgia State University then. When Ms. Lopez asked, I called the archivist there, and got him to look up an old internal telephone directory. So you see, nothing nefarious."

Deshawn nodded. "Of course not." He was quiet for several seconds, and finally Judge Herrington prompted him. "Mr. Draper?"

Deshawn started to sit down, as if finished with his direct, but before his bottom touched his chair, he rose again, and said, in a ringing voice, "Mr. Horowitz, do you love your mother?"

"I did, yes, very much," he said. "She's dead now."

"Is she?" said Deshawn. "You don't recognize that the woman sitting here beside me is, in fact, your mother?"

"That's not a woman. It's not a human being. It's a robot, a machine."

"And yet it contains the memories of your mother, does it not?"

"Supposedly."

"Are those memories accurate? Have you ever noticed her failing to get the details right about something that you yourself also recall?"

"No, never," said Tyler. "The memories are indeed accurate."

"And so in what way is this being not your mother?"

"In *every* way," said Tyler. "My mother was flesh and blood."

"I see. Now, let me ask you some specific questions. Your mother, as we've learned, was born in 1960—and so grew up with twentieth-century dentistry." Deshawn shuddered at the barbaric thought. "I understand that she has fillings in some of her teeth, correct?"

"Had fillings," said Tyler. "Yes, I believe that's true."

"Now, the mere fact that parts of the natural enamel of her teeth had been replaced with something called 'amalgam,' an alloy of silver and mercury— mercury!—didn't make her any less your mother, in your eyes, correct?"

"Those fillings were all done before I was born."

"Yes, yes. But you didn't view them as alien or foreign. They were just part of your mother."

Tyler narrowed his eyes. "I suppose."

"And I understand your mother also had a hip replacement fifteen years ago."

"That's true, yes."

"But the fact that her hip was artificial—that didn't make her any less your mother, did it?"

"No."

"And I understand your mother has no tonsils—more twentieth-century barbaric medicine, ripping out parts of the body willy-nilly."

"That's correct, yes," said Tyler. "She had no tonsils."

"But that lack didn't make her anything less than a complete human in your eyes, did it?"

"Well—no. No, it didn't."

"And, isn't it true that your mother had laser-k surgery to modify the shape of her eye, in order to improve her vision?"

"Yes, that's right."

"Did that change your view of her?"

"It only changed her view of me."

"What? Ah, yes. Clever. In any event, in recent years, I believe it's true that your mother also had a pair of cochlear implants installed, to aid her hearing. Isn't that so?"

"Yes."

"Did that change your view of her?" asked Deshawn.

"No," said Tyler.

"And, as your mother testified earlier, she had genetic therapy to rewrite her

DNA so as to eliminate the genes that had already caused her to have one bout with breast cancer. But that didn't alter your view of her, did it?"

"No, it didn't."

"So removing parts of her body—as in the tonsillectomy—didn't alter your view of her, correct?"

"Well, yes."

"And replacing parts of her body, as in the dental fillings and the artificial hip, didn't alter your view of her, correct?"

"Correct."

"And modifying parts of her body, as in the reshaping of her eye through laser surgery, that didn't alter your view of her, correct?"

"Correct."

"And adding new parts to her body, such as the cochlear hearing-aid implants, that didn't alter your view of her, either, correct?"

"Correct."

"And even rewriting her genetic code to remove bad genes, that didn't alter your view of her, either, did it?"

"No."

"Removing. Replacing. Modifying. Supplementing. Rewriting. You've just testified that none of those things made Karen Bessarian cease to be your mother in your view. Can you then articulate for us precisely what it is about the Karen Bessarian sitting in this courtroom today that makes her not your mother?"

"She just *isn't*," said Tyler, flatly.

"In what way?"

"In every way. She isn't."

"That's twice, Mr. Horowitz. Are you going to deny her a third time?"

Lopez rose again. "Your honor!"

"Withdrawn," said Deshawn. "Mr. Horowitz, how much do you personally stand to inherit should this court agree to allow you to put your mother's will through probate?"

"It's a lot," said Tyler.

"Come on, you must know the figure."

"No, I don't. I don't normally handle my mother's financial affairs."

"Would it be safe to say that it's in the tens of billions?" asked Deshawn.

"I suppose."

"Quite a bit more than thirty pieces of silver, then, isn't it?"

"Your honor, for Pete's sake!" said Lopez.

"Withdrawn, withdrawn," said Deshawn. "Your witness, Ms. Lopez."

After lunch, Maria Lopez stood up, walked across the well, and faced her client. Tyler seemed both worn down and flustered. His dark olive suit was wrinkled, and his receding hair was disheveled. "Mr. Draper asked you to articulate what made the plaintiff in this case not your actual mother," said Lopez. "You've had time over the break to think about it."

I wanted to roll my eyes but didn't yet know how. What she really meant, of course, is that they'd had time to confer over lunch, and that she had now coached him in a better answer.

Lopez continued. "Would you care to try again to tell us why the entity calling itself Karen Bessarian is not in fact your late mother?"

Tyler nodded. "Because she's, at best, a *copy* of some aspects of my mother. There is no continuity of personhood. My mother was born a flesh-and-blood human being. Granted, at some point, a scan of her brain was made, and this . . . this *thing* . . . was created from it. But my flesh-and-blood mother did not cease to exist the moment the scanning was done; it's not as if the copy picked up where the original left off. Rather, my flesh-and-blood mother flew on a spaceplane to Low Earth Orbit, then took a spaceship to the moon, and settled in at a retirement colony on Lunar Farside. All of that happened to my mother *after* this copy was made, and this copy has no recollection of any of that. Even if we grant that the copy is identical in every material way with my mother—and I don't grant that, not for a second—they have had divergent experiences. This copy is no more my mother than my mother's identical twin sister, if she'd had one, would be my mother."

Tyler paused, then went on. "Frankly, I don't care—I really don't—about whether copied consciousnesses are, in fact, persons in their own right. That's not the issue. The issue is whether they are *the same person* as the original. And, in my heart of hearts, in my intellect, in every fiber of my being, I know that they are not. My mother is dead and gone. I wish—God, how I wish!—that wasn't true. But it is." He closed his eyes. "It is."

"Thank you," said Lopez.

"Mr. Draper," said Judge Herrington, "you may call your next witness."

Deshawn rose. He looked at Tyler, at Herrington, then down at Karen seated next to him. And then, spreading his arms a bit, he said, "Your honor, the plaintiff rests."

CHapter 27

Now that I was cured, I'd been getting some more vigorous exercise—I could take it now, and I didn't want to lose the strength in my legs; I'd need that when I got back to Earth. Each day at noon, Malcolm and I met at High Eden's basketball court.

When I arrived today, he was already there, shooting baskets from a standing position. The hoops were hugely high up—a full ten meters—so it required a lot of eye-hand coordination to sink the ball, but he was managing pretty well.

"Hey, Malcolm," I said, coming into the court. My voice echoed the way it did in such places.

"Jacob," he said, looking over at me. He sounded a bit wary.

"What?" I said.

"Just hoping not to get my head torn off," said Malcolm.

"Huh? Oh, yesterday. Look, sorry—I don't know what came over me. But, listen, have you been watching the TV from Earth?"

Malcolm sent the ball flying up. It went through the hoop, and then made the long, long fall down in slow motion. "Some."

"Seen any news?"

"No. And it's been a pleasure not to."

"Well," I said, "your son is making headlines down there."

Malcolm caught the ball and turned to me. "Really?"

"Uh-huh. He's representing Karen Bessarian—the uploaded Karen—in a case about her legal personhood being challenged by her son."

Malcolm dribbled the ball a bit. "That's my boy!"

"I hate to say this," I said, "but I hope he loses. I hope the other Karen loses." I held up my hands, and Malcolm tossed the ball to me.

"Why?"

"Well," I said, "now that I'm cured, I want to go home. Brian Hades says I can't because the other me is the legal person. But if that gets struck down . . ." I dribbled the ball as I moved around the court, then sprung up rising higher and higher and higher, well above Malcolm's head, then tipped the ball into the basket.

As I was floating down to the ground, Malcolm said. "How far along is the trial?"

"They say it's only going to last another couple of days." I folded my legs a bit to absorb the shock of my landing, but there really wasn't much.

"And you think there'll be a decision soon that'll change your circumstances?" asked Malcolm, who was bending over to collect the ball.

"Well, yes," I said. "Sure. Why not?

He turned around and gently bounced the ball a couple of times. "Because nothing happens fast in the law. Suppose Deshawn wins—and he's a damn good lawyer; he probably will." He took a bead on the net and threw the ball. It sailed up and up, and then, on its way down, went through the hoop. "But winning the first round doesn't matter." He ran over—great loping strides—and caught the ball before it hit the ground. "The other side will appeal, and they'll have to go through the whole thing again."

He threw the ball again, but this time I think he deliberately missed, as if he were illustrating his point. "And suppose Deshawn loses," he said. "Well, then, *his* side will appeal."

I went to fetch the ball. "Yes, but—"

"And then the appeal will be appealed, and, for a case like this, it'll go all the way to the Supreme Court."

I had the ball, but I just held it in my hands. "Oh, surely it's not that big."

"Are you kidding?" said Malcolm. "It's huge!" He let the last word echo for a few second, then: "We're talking about the end of inheritance taxes. Immortal beings never give up their estates, after all. If it hasn't already, I'm sure the IRS will join the case. This will drag out for years . . . and, anyway, all of this is just in the United States. You're a Canadian; U.S. law doesn't apply to you."

"Yes, but surely similar cases will be fought in Canada."

"Look, if you're not going to throw the damn ball—" I tossed it to him. "Thanks." He started to dribble it. "Immortex may be *located* in Canada, because of the liberal laws up there." He paused, then looked at the floor. "I mean *down* there. But how many Canadians have uploaded so far? Most of Immortex's clients are rich Americans or Europeans." He leapt up, sailing higher and higher, and did a slam-dunk. As he drifted down, he said. "And you don't have any children, do you?"

I shook my head.

Back on the floor now, he said, "Then there's not likely to be a battle over your estate."

My heart was sinking. "Maybe that's true, but . . . ."

He was heading over to pick up the ball. "Plus, even if the U.S. strikes down the transference of personhood, Canada might not—you guys have gone in a different direction on lots of issues. Christ, a poodle can legally marry a four-slice toaster in Canada. Can you really see your country slamming the door on uploaded consciousness?"

"Perhaps," I said.

He had the ball in his hands now. "Maybe. But it'll take years. *Years.* You and I will be long dead by the time this is all resolved." He threw the ball to me, but I didn't catch it. It bounced along, the sound it was making matching the pounding that was starting again in my head.

As we rose when Judge Herrington entered the courtroom the next day, I noted that he looked like he hadn't gotten enough sleep the night before. Of course, I hadn't gotten *any*, and Porter's disassembling about uploads and sleep was bothering me. Sorry—did I say *disassembling?* I meant *dissembling*, of course. Christ, all this talk about us not being real was getting to me, I guess.

Everyone sat down. Malcolm was on my right; off to my left were Tyler's wife and kids.

"Ms. Lopez," the judge said, nodding his long face, "you may present the defendant's case."

Maria Lopez was wearing orange today, and, for some reason, the blonde highlights were gone from her hair and eyebrows. She rose and bowed toward the bench. "Thank you, your honor. We call Professor Caleb Poe."

"Caleb Poe," called out the clerk.

A dapper, middle-aged white man came forward and was sworn in.

"Professor Poe," said Lopez, "what's your job?"

"I'm a professor of philosophy at the University of Michigan." He had a nice, smooth voice.

"And in that capacity, have you given much thought to what it means to be conscious?"

"Indeed, yes. In fact, one of my books is called *Consciousness.*"

Some time was spent going through his other credentials, then: "In your professional opinion," said Lopez, "is the object seated there claiming to be Karen Bessarian actually her?"

Poe shook his head emphatically. "Absolutely not."

"And why do you say that?"

Poe had obviously been rehearsed as well—he launched immediately into

194 ROBERT J. SAWYER

his spiel without any hesitation. "There's a concept in philosophy called the zombie. It's an unfortunate choice of words, because the philosophical zombie is nothing like the reanimated dead of voodoo lore. Rather, the philosophical zombie is the classic example of a human whose lights are on, but nobody is at home. It *appears* to be awake and intelligent, and it carries out complex behaviors, but there is no consciousness. A zombie is not a person, and yet behaves indistinguishably from one."

I looked at the jurors. They, at least, appeared well rested, and seemed to be following with interest.

"In fact," continued Poe, "I contend that all human beings are first and foremost zombies, but with the added element of consciousness essentially along as a passenger. Let me make the distinction clear: a zombie is conscious in that it is responsive to its environment—but *that's* all. True consciousness—which, as I'll argue later is what we *really* mean when we talk about personhood—recognizes that there is something that it is *like* to be aware."

"What do you mean?" asked Lopez.

Poe was a fidgety sort. He shifted his weight from side to side in the witness chair. "Well, a classic example is derived from John Searle's famous argument against strong artificial intelligence. Imagine a man in a room, with a door that has a slot in it—like those slots old-fashioned doors had for paper-mail to be pushed through. Got it? Now, imagine a man sitting in that room. The man has a huge book with him, and a bunch of cards with strange squiggles on them. Okay. Now, someone outside pushes a piece of paper through the slot, and on that piece of paper is a series of squiggles. The man's job is to look at those squiggles, find a matching sequence of squiggles in his big book, and then copy out the next series of squiggles that appear in the book onto the paper that has come in through the slot, and then push the piece of paper back out the slot." He imitated doing just that.

"Now," continued Poe, "unbeknownst to the man, the squiggles are in fact Chinese ideograms, and the book is a list of answers to questions in Chinese. So, when the question, 'How are you?' is pushed through the slot in Chinese, the man looks up the Chinese for 'How are you?' in the answer book, and finds that the appropriate reply is the Chinese for 'I am fine.'

"Well, from the perspective of the person outside the room—the one who posed the original question in Chinese—it seems that the person inside the room understands Chinese. But in fact he doesn't; he doesn't even know what it really is that he's doing. And he certainly doesn't have that feeling that you or I would have when we say we *know* Chinese, or *understand* classical music.

The person in the room is a zombie. It behaves *as if* it is consciously aware, but it is in fact not."

Poe shifted again in his chair. "That metaphor is made concrete in an experience we've all had in our lives: we get in our cars to drive somewhere, and our minds wander as we drive along. When we get to the destination, we have no recollection of having made the trip. So, who was the driver? The zombie! *It* played chauffeur, while your consciousness—a mere passenger—did something else."

Lopez nodded, and Poe went on. "Think about it: how often do you have to stop and ask yourself, 'Now, what was it I had for lunch today?' We often eat whole meals with no real attention to the fact that we *are* eating. But if you can imagine eating or driving without paying attention—with your consciousness distracted by something else—if you can imagine doing those things at least temporarily without conscious involvement, then it's possible to imagine them *permanently* without conscious involvement. That's the zombie: the doer, the actor, the thing that goes through all the motions without any real person being present."

"But these are very complex behaviors," said Lopez.

"Oh, yes, indeed," said Poe. "That driving zombie was operating a motor vehicle, obeying traffic signals, looking over its shoulder to check its blind spot before pulling out"—he was now acting out the actions he was describing—"exchanging hand signals with other drivers, perhaps even listening to traffic reports and altering its route based on them. All of that can—and does—happen without conscious attention."

Maria Lopez moved out from behind the defendant's table and into the well. "Surely that's not so, Professor Poe. Oh, I grant you that some actions are so ingrained as to become instinctive, but listening to a traffic report, and making a decision based on it—surely that requires consciousness, no?"

"I disagree—and I think you will, too, ma'am, if you consider it for a moment." He spread his arms, taking us all in. "Doubtless everyone in this court has had this experience: you're reading a novel, and at some point you realize you have no idea what was said in the last page. Why? Because your conscious attention had wandered off to consider something else. But there's no doubt that you *have* read the page that you have no awareness of; indeed, you've quite likely tapped the page-down key on your datapad while reading it. Your eyes tracked across dozens or hundreds of words of text, even though you weren't consciously taking them in.

"Well, then who was doing the reading? The zombie you! Fortunately, zombies have no feelings, so when the conscious you realizes that it has missed out on a page or more of text, you say, wait, wait, go back, and you re-read the material the zombie has *already* read.

"The zombie is content to redo this, since it never gets bored—boredom is a conscious state. And then the two of you—conscious you and zombie you—go on reading new material together in unison. But the zombie is actually in the foreground; the conscious you is in the background. It's as if the conscious you is looking over the zombie's shoulder, following along as the zombie reads."

"Any other examples?" asked Lopez, now leaning her bottom against the defendant's table.

Poe nodded. "Certainly. Has this ever happened to you? You're lying in bed asleep and the phone rings." He pantomimed lifting an old-fashioned handset. "You answer it, have a conversation, and then, once it's over, you have no idea at all what you've said. Or your spouse says to you that you chatted about something late at night, when you both were supposedly awake, but come the morning you have no recollection of it. This happens all the time. If the conscious you doesn't answer your phone or reply when spoken to, the zombie you gets on with the job."

"Surely it's only capable of the most mechanical responses, though?" said Lopez.

Poe shook his head, and shifted again in his seat. "Not at all. In fact, the zombie is responsible for most of what we say. How could it be otherwise? You might start a sentence that will end up being twenty or thirty words long. Do you really believe that you have thought out that whole sentence in your brain before you start speaking it? Stop for a moment right now, and think this thought: 'On the way home from court today, I'd better pick up some bread and milk.' It took measurable time for you to think that, and yet we can talk nonstop for extended periods without pauses to work out the thoughts we want to express. No, in most speech we *discover* what it is that we're going to say *as it is said*—just as those listening to us do."

Poe looked over at the jurors, then back at Lopez. "Have you ever been surprised by what you said? Of course—but that would be impossible if you knew in advance what you were going to say. And, in fact, whatever validity talk therapy has is based on this principle: your therapist forces you to listen attentively to the words your zombie is spewing out, and, at some point you exclaim, 'My God! So *that's* what really going on in my head!'"

"Yes, okay, maybe," said Lopez. She played the devil's advocate well. "But talking is simple enough—as is driving a car—until something goes wrong. Then, surely, your consciousness takes over—takes the driver's seat so to speak."

"No, not at all," said Poe. "In fact, it would be disastrous if it did so. Consider another example: playing tennis." He imitated a man swinging a racquet. "Tennis is one-hundred percent a spectator sport, from consciousness's point of view. The balls lob back and forth too fast for conscious processing of their trajectory, speed, and so on.

"In fact, here's a trick. If you want to beat an old pro at tennis, do this: let him whip your butt in a practice match, then compliment him on his technique. Ask him to show you exactly what he's doing that's better than what you're doing; get him to articulate the process, and demonstrate it in slow motion. Then challenge him to a re-match. His consciousness will still be dwelling on *how* tennis is played, on what you're supposed to be doing—and that will interfere with his zombie. Only when his consciousness retreats to the sidelines, and the zombie starts playing the game on its own, will he be back at top form again."

Poe spread his arms as if all this were obvious. "Same thing with driving. If you're about to hit another car, you *can't* stop to think about pumping the breaks, or how to turn to avoid fishtailing, or whatever. Consciousness will get you killed; you have to leave it to your zombie to react without the delays caused by conscious thought."

"But can't you take this all one silly step further, Professor Poe?" said Lopez, looking not at him, but at the jurors as if she were speaking on their behalf. "I mean, I *know* I'm conscious; I know I'm not a zombie. But, if we believe what you're saying, *you* could be a zombie, just going through the motions of giving expert testimony without any *real* awareness. Doesn't this all devolve to solipsism—the position that *I* am the only one who really exists?"

Poe nodded. "Up until a year or two ago, I would have agreed with you. Solipsism is arrogance writ large, and there's no rational basis for believing that you, Maria Lopez, are the chosen one, the only real, conscious human being who has ever existed. But Immortex has changed that." He held up a pair of fingers. "Now there *are* two kinds of actors on the stage. One kind are humans, who evolved from a long line of hominids and primates and earlier mammals and mammal-like reptiles and amphibians and fishes, and on and on back to the first single-celled organisms—things very much like the paramecia Dr. Porter talked about.

"And the other is what Immortex calls a Mindscan, an uploaded consciousness. A reasonable person can, by extrapolation from his own inner life, recognize that others are conscious, too—or, more precisely, that others have a conscious rider in their zombie bodies. But as far as I'm concerned, all Immortex has demonstrated is that they can recreate the zombie part; there is zero evidence before this court that the *consciousness* that once dwelt in the biological Karen Bessarian has been duplicated. Yes, the lights are on in that—that *thing* sitting there—but there is no reason at all to think that anyone is at home. The fact that Mindscans don't dream is damning proof that this is true."

Poe looked into the seating gallery, past me to where Dr. Porter was, and pointed an accusing finger. "Indeed, Andrew Porter himself said he doesn't know what consciousness is, and that song-and-dance he gave about microtubules is just obfuscation. Whatever consciousness really is, there's no positive evidence that it's being transferred in the Mindscan process." Poe crossed his arms in front of his chest. "The burden is entirely on Immortex to prove that they *have* transferred it, and, as I say, there's zero evidence that that is in fact the case."

CHAPTER 28

I went back to Brian Hades's office in the High Eden administration building—and I must say, he was getting pissed off. "Mr. Sullivan, really, we've been down this road before. You can't return to Earth, so please, please, please relax and enjoy things here. You haven't even begun to scratch the surface of the activities we offer."

The pills they'd been giving me were tranquilizers, of course—I was sure of that. Trying to dope me up, keep me placid. I'd flushed the rest of them down the recycler. "It's autumn on Earth," I said. "At least, in the Northern Hemisphere. Do you offer walking through a field of fallen leaves? Soon it'll be winter. Do you offer ice hockey on a frozen pond? Skiing? Sunsets that aren't just a ball of light dropping below a rocky horizon, but are actually tinged with color and shrouded by bands of cloud?"

"Mr. Sullivan, be reasonable."

"Reasonable! I never asked to be . . . to be a fucking *astronaut*."

"In point of fact, you did. And, besides, there are things you can do here that you could never do on Earth. Have you tried flying yet? You know, it's possible to fly here, under your own power, with big enough strap-on wings. We offer that, over in the gymnasium."

He paused, as if expecting me to respond. I didn't.

"And mountain climbing! You know, you're more than welcome to go outside here. The rock climbing is fabulous in the low gravity; the walls of Heaviside are great for climbing."

Hades could see the "no sale" look in my eyes, presumably, and tried again: "And what about sex? Have you had sex yet in our low gravity? It's *better* than sex in zero-gee. When you're weightless, normal thrusting tends to push you away from your partner. But in lunar gravity, anyone can do the kind of acrobatics you see in porno films."

That did get a reaction from me. I practically shouted: "No, I haven't had sex, for Christ's sake! Who the hell would I have sex with?"

"We have some of the best sex workers in—in the solar system, Mr. Sullivan. Gorgeous, compassionate, athletic, disease-free."

"I don't want sex—or, at least, I don't want *just* sex. I want to make love, with someone I care about, and who cares about me."

His tone was gentle. "I've looked at your records, Mr. Sullivan. You didn't have anyone like that back on Earth, so—"

"That was *before*. That was my doing. But now that I'm well—"

"Now that you're well, you'll be able to distinguish between a woman who really cares about you and one who's after you for all your money?"

"Fuck you."

"I'm sorry; I shouldn't have said that. But seriously, Mr. Sullivan, you knew you were giving up romance when you came here."

"For a year or two! Not for decades."

"And although I understand your reluctance about becoming involved with some of our more superannuated guests, there are lots of workers here around your age. And it's not as if a good-looking, intelligent man like you has zero prospects for real romance here. We have no corporate policy against staff becoming romantically involved with guests."

"That's not what I want. There's someone specific back on Earth."

"Ah," said Hades.

"And I need to try with her; I *have* to. I foolishly didn't pursue things with her before, but my situation is different now."

"What's her name?" asked Hades.

I was surprised by the question—so surprised, I answered it. "Rebecca. Rebecca Chong."

"Mr. Sullivan," said Hades, his voice very soft and gentle, "has it occurred to you that there's already a version of you down on Earth who doesn't suffer from Katerinsky's syndrome anymore? That means weeks ago he might have had the same change in his feelings that you're having now. Perhaps he and Rebecca are already together . . . which wouldn't leave any place for you."

My heart was pounding—a sensation that other me would never know. "No," I said. "No, that's . . . that's not possible."

Hades raised his eyebrows as if to say, "Isn't it?" But he didn't give the words voice, the first real kindness he'd shown me.

After lunch, it was Deshawn's turn to cross-examine Caleb Poe, the philosophy professor.

"You have a lovely voice, Dr. Poe," said Deshawn, standing behind the plaintiff's table.

Poe's eyebrows went up in surprise. "Thank you."

"Very pleasant," continued Deshawn. "Very well modulated. Have people told you that before?"

Poe tilted his head. "From time to time."

"I'm sure they have. You sound like you might, in fact, be a good singer."

"Thank you."

"*Do* you sing, Dr. Poe?"

"Yes."

"At what venues?"

"Objection," said Lopez, spreading her arms. "Relevance."

"All will be revealed soon," said Draper, looking at the judge.

Herrington frowned for a moment, then said, "I have a very conservative definition of 'soon,' Mr. Draper. But go ahead."

"Thank you," said Deshawn. "Dr. Poe, at what venues do you sing?"

"When I was putting myself through school, at night clubs, weddings, the odd corporate function."

"But you're not going to school now," said Deshawn. "Do you still get much of a chance to sing?"

"Yes."

"And where would that be?"

"In a choir."

"A church choir, isn't that correct?"

Poe shifted slightly in his seat. "Yes."

"What denomination?"

"Episcopalian."

"So, you sing in the choir at a Christian church, correct?"

"Yes."

"As part of the formal church services each Sunday, correct?"

"Your honor," said Lopez. "Again, relevance?"

"I've made it through the S and first O of 'soon,' your honor," said Draper. "Let me go the rest of the way."

"All right," said Herrington, tapping a stylus impatiently against his bench.

"You sing in church services," said Draper, looking back at Poe.

"Yes."

"Would you describe yourself as a religious person?"

Poe was defiant now. "I suppose I am, yes. But I'm not a nut."

"Do you believe in God?"

"That is the *sine qua non* of being religious."

"You do believe in God. Do you believe in the devil?"

"I'm not some Bible-thumping fundamentalist," said Poe. "I'm not a literalist. I believe the universe is, as the current figure has it, 11.9 billion years old. I believe life evolved from simpler forms through natural selection. And I don't believe in fairy stories."

"You don't believe in the devil?"

"Correct."

"What about hell?"

"An invention that owes more to the poet Dante than anything in rational theology," said Poe. "Stories of hell and devils were perhaps of use when clergy had to deal with illiterate, uneducated, unsophisticated populations. But we are none of those things; we can follow moral arguments, and make reasoned moral choices, without being threatened by bogeymen."

"Very good," said Deshawn. "Very good. So you've dispensed with most of the sillier trappings of primitive religion, is that it?"

"Well, I wouldn't phrase it in such an impolitic way."

"But you don't believe in the devil?"

"No."

"And you don't believe in hell?"

"No."

"And you don't believe in Noah's flood?"

"No."

"And you don't believe in souls?"

Poe was silent.

"Dr. Poe? Would you respond to my question, please? Is it true that you don't believe in souls?"

"That . . . would not be my position."

"You mean you *do* believe in souls?"

"Well, I . . ."

Deshawn stepped in front of his table. "Do you believe *you* have a soul?"

"Yes," said Poe, rallying now. "Yes, I do."

"And how did you come by this soul?"

"It was given to me by God," said Poe.

Deshawn looked meaningfully at the jury, then turned back to Poe. "Can you explain for us what the soul is, in your conception?"

"It is the essence of who I am," said Poe. "It is the spark of the divine within me. It is the part of me that will survive death."

"In your understanding of these matters, does every living human being have a soul?"

"Absolutely."

"No exceptions?"

"None."

Deshawn had moved out into the well and was pointing back at Karen, seated at the plaintiff's table. "Now, please look at Ms. Bessarian here. Does she have a soul?"

Karen was all alert attention, her green eyes bright.

Poe's voice was emphatic. "No."

"Why not? How can you tell?"

"She's—*it's*—a manufactured object. You might as well ask whether a stove or a car has a soul."

"I understand your assertion. But other than an *a priori* belief, Dr. Poe, how can you *tell* that Ms. Bessarian doesn't have a soul? What test can you conduct to demonstrate that you *do* have a soul, and she does not?"

"There is no such test."

"Indeed there is not," said Deshawn.

"Objection," said Lopez. "That's not a question."

"Sustained," said Judge Herrington.

Deshawn nodded contritely. "All right," he said. "But this is: Dr. Poe, do you believe that God will judge you after death?"

Poe was quiet for a moment. He had the look of an animal that knew it was being hunted. "Yes, I do."

"And what is it that God is judging?"

"Whether I've been moral or immoral in my life."

"Yes, yes, but what *part* of you is He judging? Remember, by this point, you're dead. He's obviously not judging your now-cold body, is He?"

"No."

"And He's not judging the electrically dead hunk of matter that was your brain, is He?"

"No."

"So *what* is He judging? What part of you?"

"He's judging my soul."

Deshawn looked at the jury, and spread his arms. "Well, that hardly seems fair. I mean, surely it was your body or your brain that undertook any immoral acts. Your soul was just along for the ride."

"Well . . ."

"Isn't that the case? When you talked earlier in your fancy philosophical terms about a rider within, about a true consciousness that accompanies the zombie body, the rider you were referring to is really the soul, isn't it? Isn't that your contention *fundamentally*?" Deshawn let the last word echo in the air for a moment.

"Well, I . . ."

"If I'm mistaken, Dr. Poe, please correct me. In plain, layman's terms, there is no meaningful distinction between your true consciousness and what the rest of us understand to be the soul, correct?"

"That would not be my formulation . . ."

"If there *is* a difference, please articulate it, professor."

Poe opened his mouth but said nothing; he looked quite like one of those fishy ancestors he had enumerated earlier.

"Dr. Poe?" said Deshawn. "The court is waiting for your answer."

Poe closed his mouth, took a deep breath through his nose, and seemed to think. "In layman's terms," he said at last, "I concede that the two terms are conflated."

"You concede that your philosophical notion of consciousness superimposed on the zombie, and the religious notion of the soul superimposed on the biological body, are essentially the same thing?"

After a moment, Poe nodded.

"A verbal response, please, professor—for the record."

"Yes."

"Thank you. Now, we were talking a few moments ago about God judging souls after death. Why is it that God does that?"

Poe fidgeted in his chair. "I—I don't understand the question."

Deshawn spread his arms. "I mean, what's the sense in God judging souls? Don't they just do whatever God intended them to do?"

Poe narrowed his eyes; he was clearly wary for a trap, but couldn't see it. Nor, frankly, could I. "No, no. The soul chooses to do good or evil—and, eventually God holds it accountable for those choices."

"Ah," said Deshawn. "So the soul has volition, does it?"

Poe looked at Lopez, as if seeking guidance. I saw her shrug infinitesimally. The professor shifted his gaze back to Deshawn. "Yes, of course," he said at last. "That's the whole point. God has given us free will, and it's the soul that exercises that free will."

"In other words," said Deshawn, "the soul can make any choice it wants, regardless of God's wishes, correct?"

"How do you mean?"

"I mean, God wishes us to be good—to follow the precepts of the Ten Commandments, say, or the Sermon on the Mount—but He doesn't *force* us to be good. We can do whatever we please."

"Yes, of course."

"And, indeed, since the soul is the part of us that really makes choices, then it's in fact the *soul* that can do whatever it pleases, correct?"

"Well, yes."

"Now, what about the physical nature of the soul? Prior to death, is it localized in the individual?"

"How do you mean?"

"I mean it's not dispersed hither and yon—it's a localized phenomenon, right? It exists within a specific person."

Lopez tried again. "Your honor, objection. Relevance."

But Herrington was enthralled. "Overruled, Ms. Lopez—and don't bother me with that objection again during this testimony. Professor Poe, answer Mr. Draper's question. Is the soul localized in a specific person?"

Poe looked flustered at the by-play between the judge and the lawyer who was paying him for his testimony, but at last he spoke. "I—yes."

"And after death?" asked Deshawn. "What happens to the soul then?"

"It leaves the body."

"Physically? Materially? As an energy wave, or some such?"

"The soul is immaterial, and it transcends our notions of space and time."

"How convenient for it!" said Deshawn. "But let's take that a step further, shall we? The soul doesn't need to breathe, correct? Nor does it need to eat? That is, it can continue to exist just fine without the infrastructure of a biological body to support it?"

"Of course," said Poe. "The soul is immortal and immaterial."

"And yet it has a specific location. Your soul, prior to death is inside you, and mine is inside me, correct?"

Poe spread his arms. "If you're going to ask me to point to the soul on an MRI or X-ray, Mr. Draper, I freely admit that I can't do that."

"Not at all, not at all. I just want to make sure we're on the same page. We do agree that the soul is localized—yours is within you, and mine is within me."

"Yes, that's true," said Poe.

"And the soul is *mobile* after the body dies, correct? It can *go* to heaven?"

"Yes. If God will allow it entrance."

"But could it go somewhere else?"

"How do you mean?"

"I mean, the soul doesn't change upon death. It still has volition, doesn't it? Your soul hasn't become an automaton, has it? It hasn't become a *zombie?*"

Poe shifted again in the witness seat. "No."

"Well, then, Dr. Poe, if there is no test you can perform to determine whether a soul is present, if the soul is localized in a specific place, if the soul doesn't require nutrition or other support from a living body, if the soul leaves the body at death, if the soul transcends time and space and can move to a new location after leaving the original body, and if the soul still has freedom to act even after death, then how can you say that, upon the death of the biological Karen Bessarian, her soul did not choose to move into the artificial form seated at the plaintiff's desk?"

"I . . . ah . . ."

"Isn't it possible, Dr. Poe? Given the properties of the soul as you yourself have described them, isn't it possible? The biological body of Karen Bessarian is apparently dead. But it's abundantly clear, is it not, that Ms. Bessarian *wanted* to transfer her personhood to the mechanical form that sits here in this courtroom with us? Given that that was her wish—her *soul*'s wish—isn't it likely that her soul has now taken up residence in that artificial form?"

Poe said nothing.

Deshawn nodded at him politely. "I grant that it was verbose, Dr. Poe, but my last utterance *was* a question, and you are required to answer it."

"Well, if you want to play games . . ."

"What game, Dr. Poe? You yourself said it was significant that a biological person has a soul and an upload does not. Indeed, you used the language of philosophy to tell us that the Karen Bessarian in this courtroom must be soulless—a condition you described as being a zombie. There are those who would say that *that* is a game, since you yourself have admitted that you can't detect, measure, or point to the soul." Deshawn walked in back of the plaintiff's desk, and stood behind Karen, one hand on each of her shoulders. "Even if souls are only created by God, and can't be duplicated by any mortal process, isn't it still possible that Ms. Bessarian's soul now resides in this artificial body—making her no more a zombie than the original was before it passed away?"

"Well, I . . ."

"It *is* possible, isn't it?" said Deshawn.

Poe let out a long, shuddering sigh. "Yes," he said at last, "I suppose it is."

CHAPTER 29

I staggered around for hours after my last meeting with Brian Hades—a bizarre thing to do on the moon, where you already walk like a marionette. Could he be right? Could the robot me have taken up with Rebecca? Christ, oh Christ. I wanted her—I wanted her so badly it actually, physically hurt. I hadn't been conscious of just how much love I'd been suppressing in order to potentially spare Rebecca any pain, but now that I didn't have to suppress it, it was overwhelming me. Half my waking thoughts were about her; every dream I remembered involved her. I had to see her again, had to find out if there was a chance for us . . .

And yet, what if there wasn't? What if all that flirting, all those lingering touches, all those kisses hello and good-bye, and even that one wonderful night of sex, had only really meant something special to me?

No. No, I couldn't be *that* mistaken. There was something there—there had to be. And I had to get back to it, before that fucking—that fucking *android*—made his move.

How to accomplish that, though, I had no idea. But I would keep my eyes and ears open, looking for an opportunity. Until then—

Until then, Hades was right. I'd barely scratched the surface of what the moon had to offer. And now that I'd made up my mind that I *was* leaving it, one way or another, I might as well at least try some of the delights he'd mentioned. After all, there was no way in hell I'd ever come back up here.

And so, for starters, I tried one of the hookers. I picked a beautiful, petite Japanese lady, with big brown eyes; I chose her without thinking about it, without being conscious at first that, of course, she was the one who looked the most like Rebecca Chong.

And we did have sex, and she was very daring and very good. And Hades had been right: the low gravity made amazing stunts possible. We did it standing up, we did it pushing up on one hand, we did it in all sorts of ways, and I kept thinking of Rebecca, always Rebecca.

At the end, I was physically satisfied, and I thanked the woman. But it wasn't lovemaking.

And it wasn't with the woman I loved.

⁂

Maria Lopez looked up. "The defendant calls Professor Alyssa Neruda."

A tall, slim brunette woman, perhaps sixty, and probably of mixed Asian and European ancestry, came to the witness stand.

"You do solemnly swear or affirm," said the clerk, "that the testimony you may give in the cause now pending before this Court shall be the truth, the whole truth, and nothing but the truth, so help you God?"

"I do so swear," said Neruda.

"Please take a seat in the witness box," said the clerk, "and state and spell your first and last names for the record."

Neruda sat down. "My name is Alyssa—A-L-Y-S-S-A—Neruda—N-E-R-U-D-A."

"Thank you," said the clerk.

Lopez rose. "Professor Neruda, where are you currently employed?"

"Yale University."

"In what capacity?"

"I'm professor of bioethics."

"Tenured?"

"Yes."

"What advanced degrees do you have?"

"I have a *Medicinae Doctor* from Harvard."

"You're an M.D.? A medical doctor?"

"Correct."

"Do you have any other advanced degrees?"

"I have a *Legum Magister* from Yale University."

"That's a Master of Laws, correct?"

"Correct."

"Meaning you are also a lawyer?"

"Yes, I am. Admitted to the bars of Connecticut and New York State."

"Your honor," said Lopez, "we submit now Professor Neruda's curriculum vitae, which runs to forty-six pages." She handed a hardcopy to the clerk. "Professor Neruda," continued Lopez, "have you ever been called to present testimony in a lower-court case that ultimately was heard by the United States Supreme Court?"

"I have, yes."

"Have any of those cases dealt with the definition of personhood?"

"Yes."

"Which case or cases?"

"The case of *Littler v. Carvey*."

"When was that argued before the Supreme Court?"

"August 2028."

"And please remind us of who the litigants were."

"Littler, the plaintiff—the one bringing the action—was one Mr. Oren Littler, of Bledsoe County, Tennessee. Carvey, the respondent—the one being sued—was his girlfriend at the time, one Ms. Stella Carvey, also of Bledsoe County."

"And what, in a nutshell, please, was the gist of the conflict between Mr. Littler and Ms. Carvey?" asked Lopez

"Littler and Carvey had been dating for approximately two years. Their relationship was an intimate, sexual one. On or about May 1, 2028, Ms. Carvey became pregnant. She became aware of this by May 25, 2028, through the use of a home pregnancy-testing kit. She informed Mr. Littler of the fact, and they agreed to marry, have the baby, and raise it together."

"Please continue, Professor," said Lopez.

"Six weeks into her pregnancy, Ms. Carvey and Mr. Littler had a fight. Ms. Carvey called off the wedding and terminated their romantic involvement. She also told Mr. Littler that she was going to terminate the pregnancy. Littler very much disapproved—he wanted the child born, and was willing to assume full custody of it and responsibility for it.

"Ms. Carvey refused his overtures in this direction, and so Mr. Littler got a court order barring Ms. Carvey from having an abortion, on the grounds that the fetus should be treated as a person under the law. Note that the judge issuing the injunction didn't rule as to whether Mr. Littler's contention was true. Rather he—and it was a he—felt Mr. Littler's argument was sufficiently persuasive that the issue should be decided by jury."

Lopez looked at our own jury box. "And how did the jury decide the case?"

"They ruled that given *Roe v. Wade*, Ms. Carvey had every right to an abortion on demand."

"And so that was the end of things?"

Neruda shook her head. "It was not. Mr. Littler appealed; the appeals court overturned the lower court; and the case was fast-tracked to the Supreme Court."

"Fast-tracked?" said Lopez. "Why?"

"Although none of the same justices were still sitting, the court recalled *Roe v. Wade*. In that case, the pseudonymous Jane Roe was suing for the right to have a legal abortion. Wade was Henry Wade, the district attorney of Dallas County, Texas, where Roe lived; he was the one who was charged with upholding the then-ban on abortion in his jurisdiction. *Roe v. Wade* was and is controversial in many ways, but it also stands out as a classic example of justice delayed being justice denied. By the time the Supreme Court got around to hearing *Roe v. Wade*, Jane Roe's pregnancy had come to term, and she had delivered her daughter and put her up for adoption. Yes, she won the right to have an abortion, but far too late to do her any good. Because of that, the Supreme Court agreed to hear *Littler v. Carvey* expeditiously."

Lopez nodded. "And what did the Supreme Court find in *Littler v. Carvey?*"

"In a six-to-three ruling, the court found that Stella Carvey's unborn child was indeed a person, with the full rights ascribed to persons under the Fifth, Eighth, Thirteenth, and Fourteenth Amendments of the Constitution."

"And therefore . . . ?"

"Therefore, Ms. Carvey was banned from getting an abortion."

"In relation to *Roe v. Wade*, how is *Littler v. Carvey* normally viewed?" asked Lopez.

"It's frequently cited as the case that overturned *Roe*," said Neruda.

"Making aborting embryos beyond a certain stage of development illegal again in the United States?"

"Correct."

"And what is the status of *Littler v. Carvey* today?"

"It still stands as the law of the land."

Lopez nodded. "Now, a moment ago, I said that *Littler v. Carvey* makes abortions illegal after a certain stage of development. Can you explain to the jury how the line between personhood and nonpersonhood was established in *Littler?*"

"Certainly. *Littler v. Carvey* turned precisely on this issue: when does an embryo become a person? After all," said Neruda, turning briefly to face Judge Herrington, "we can't very well decide when something ceases to be a person if we don't know when it began to be one."

The judge nodded his shoehorn face. "But do get on with it," he said.

"Of course, of course," said Neruda. "Drawing the line between personhood and nonpersonhood has represented one of the greatest challenges in bioethics. One position, of course, is that held by hard-line right-to-lifers: a new person, with the rights of personhood, is created at the moment of conception. The opposite extreme says that a new person doesn't exist until the moment of birth, some nine months later—and, indeed, since the 1970s, there's been a vocal faction that's argued that even birth is too early, contending that personhood doesn't really begin until there's significant cognitive ability, around two or three years of age; those people find painless infanticide and abortion equally morally acceptable."

I saw several of the jurors react in horror, but Neruda went on. "Conception and birth are, of course, precise moments in time. Although a human conception was never actually observed until 1969, we had known from animal studies for a hundred years prior to that that conception occurs when the spermatozoa and the oocyte fuse."

"Oocyte?" said Lopez.

"The female gamete. What lay people call the egg."

Somebody near me snickered at what was presumably Neruda's inadvertent play on words.

"All right," said Lopez. "Conception occurs at the moment the sperm and egg fuse."

"Yes, and that's one specific second of time. We also, of course, routinely very precisely measure the time of birth. In fact . . ." Neruda trailed off.

"Yes, Professor?"

"Well, of course, there's Mr. Sullivan, sitting right over there."

I always sat up straight these days; there was no additional comfort in slouching my mechanical body.

"What's significant about Mr. Sullivan?" asked Lopez.

"Well, he's a Mindscan now, but the original him was, I believe, the first child born after midnight on 1 January 2001, in Toronto, Canada."

"Defendant's ten," said Lopez, holding up a piece of paper. "A newspaper clipping for *The Toronto Star* from Tuesday 2 January 2001, commemorating this very fact."

The exhibit was accepted, and Professor Neruda went on: "So, setting aside the extremists I spoke of earlier, we generally accept that a person is a person by the time they are born. But there have been fascinating cases that have tested the flexibility of this particular rubicon for ascribing personhood."

"For instance?" asked Lopez.

"*Department of Health and Human Services v. Maloney.*"

"What happened there?"

"Brenda Maloney was an emotionally unstable woman in the Bronx, New York, in 2016. She had been pregnant for the standard thirty-nine weeks, and was being wheeled into the delivery room, when she saw a steak knife sitting on a tray of food destined for another patient. She grabbed the knife and plunged it into her belly, killing her baby moments before it would have been born." Again, I saw jurors wince, and again Neruda went on. "Had Ms. Maloney committed murder? Ultimately, the case was never tried, because Ms. Maloney was found unfit to stand trial—but it did certainly galvanize public opinion. Support for the notion that an embryo did not become a person until at least birth waned considerably after that."

"In other words," said Lopez, "the hard-line pro-choice position—that until the baby was out of the body, it was not a person—became less tenable because of *Maloney*, correct?"

"That would certainly be my reading of the legal commentaries from that period, yes."

"You'd said there were only two absolutely clear points, cleanly and simply demarked by biological circumstances, for establishing personhood: conception and birth, correct?"

"Correct."

"And *Maloney*—and other cases, I'm sure—made the birth marker not seem tenable in the eyes of most lawmakers and politicians, is that right?"

"Correct," said Neruda again. "Anything but conception or cutting the umbilical cord seems arbitrary to them. Even birth is arbitrary, when you can induce it with drugs, or perform a C-section.

"In fact, soon enough we'll doubtless have the ability to bring babies to term in artificial wombs. Take the typical sci-fi version of that: a fetus in a glass bottle full of liquid. The fetus has been growing for almost nine months. I take out a gun and shoot at the glass bottle. If my bullet hits the fetus, and goes through its heart, then I've performed an abortion. But if it misses the fetus, and just shatters the jar, spilling the baby out onto the tabletop, I've performed a delivery. It's very hard to draw these lines."

"Indeed," said Lopez. "And, in fact, weren't there legal attempts to define life beginning at a third point, namely implantation?"

"Yes, that's right," said Neruda. "But that was just as messy."

"Why?"

"Well, conception doesn't take place in the uterus, after all; the fertilized egg—to use the common parlance—normally moves down the fallopian tube into the uterus, then implants in the uterine wall. That event had sometimes been cited as the beginning of personhood, but it was rejected by the Supreme Court in *Littler v. Carvey*."

"Why?"

"The march of science, Ms. Lopez. They couldn't do it then, and we haven't quite made it happen even yet, but we recognize, as I said before, that in principal it will be possible eventually to bring embryos to term in artificial wombs. The court didn't want to set up a standard that said that embryos brought to term *in vitro* were perforce not human. They were looking for a demarcation that was innate to the embryo."

"Well, then, given that the courts weren't happy with the birth standard, conception seems the obvious marker to choose, no? You said it was easy to measure."

"Oh, yes, indeed," said Neruda, nodding. "Prior to conception, no new organism exists with forty-six chromosomes—plus or minus one, as in Down or Turner syndrome. But as soon as conception occurs, a complete genetic blueprint for an entire person is created—the new person's sex is determined, and so on."

"So did the court rule in *Littler v. Carvey* that personhood was conferred at conception?"

Neruda shook her head. "They couldn't rule that—not without making millions of Americans into murderers."

Lopez tilted her head to one side. "How do you mean?"

Neruda took a deep breath, and let it out slowly. "The *Oxford English Dictionary* tells us that the phrase 'birth control' entered the language in 1914. But, of course, it's really a misnomer. We're not trying to control birth; we're looking to do something nine months earlier—prevent pregnancy! In fact, even though conception and birth are at opposite ends of the time span we're discussing, we use 'contraception' and 'birth control' as synonyms.

"Now, there *are* true contraceptives: condoms, diaphragms, and spermicides prevent conception by the simple expedient of blocking the sperm from reaching the egg, or killing it before it gets there. And, of course, surgical sterilization of a man or a woman prevents conception, as does abstinence. So does the rhythm method if you're very lucky and very careful.

"But the most common method of . . . shall we say, 'family planning?' . . . is none of the above. Rather, it's the so-called birth-control pill—or patches, implants, and so on, that do the same job.

"Now, birth control pills *sometimes* prevent conception—that is, that's one of the things they do. But they also can have a secondary effect: they prevent implantation of a fertilized egg in the uterus. If the court had ruled that life began at *conception*, then it would have to accept that birth-control pills can kill that life, by depriving it of the usual necessities of continued existence, which it would receive once it implanted in the uterus.

"But Americans *love* birth-control pills and related pharmaceuticals, which stiffen the uterine wall so that embryos won't implant. The original birth-control pill was introduced in 1960, and we've been refining them ever since, so that today they have virtually no side effects. But a politically conservative country—and this one had certainly become that by this time, what with Pat Buchanan in the Oval Office—that wanted on the one hand to sanctify the unborn and on the other hand loved the convenience of birth-control pills had to come up with a definition that said life, and personhood, began *after* conception, so that those cases in which the pill prevented implantation rather than conception weren't tantamount to murder."

"And in *Littler v. Carver*, the court did just that, correct?"

"Correct." Neruda had her own graphics, and they appeared on the wall screen. "The Supreme Court of these United States ruled that personhood begins when *individuation* occurs. For up to fourteen days after conception, a single fertilized egg can divide into two or more identical twins; indeed, the technical term for identical twins is monozygotic twins, because they were twins formed from just one zygote—one cell formed by the union of two gametes. Well, if the embryo still has the potential of being *multiple* individuals, or so the argument went, then it hadn't settled down to being one particular individual, and so no specific personhood could be accorded it. Do you see?"

I certainly did, although glancing over at Karen, I don't think she'd gotten it yet.

"So," said Lopez, "under the law of the land, a person is a person so long as he or she can be *only one person*, correct?"

I saw Deshawn react at this, his eyebrows climbing up his bald head. It wasn't the tack we'd expected them to take at all—and it was damn clever.

"That's right," said Neruda. "The legal point is that once you've become one, and only one, individual, you're entitled to rights of personhood."

Lopez walked across the well and stood near the jury box. "Now, in your legal opinion, Professor Neruda, what bearing does this have on our case at hand?"

Neruda spread her arms. "Don't you see? Karen Bessarian—or, forgive me: her maiden name would be appropriate here. Karen Cohen didn't become a person on the day she was conceived back in—well, she was born at the end of May in 1960, so presumably that was sometime in August of 1959. Rather, she became a person fifteen days later, when that embryo no longer had the potential to become multiple individuals."

Lopez regarded the jurors, making sure they were following. "Yes, professor," she said. "Go on."

Neruda smiled as she went in to deliver her punch line. "And, well, since individuation is the legal test, Karen—now Karen Bessarian—presumably *ceased* to be an individual in the eyes of the law not on the day on which her body actually died on the moon, but on the *earlier* day on which her mind was scanned and a second instantiation of that mind was made. That person who had been Karen Bessarian was, in essence, restored legally to the status of an embryo less than fifteen days old: she lost her rights to personhood the moment it could be said that she was no longer uniquely one individual. Do you see? The unique legal entity known as Karen Cynthia Bessarian ceased to exist the moment that scanning was done. And, of course, once a person is gone, they're gone for good."

If I'd been in my old biological body, I'm sure I would have slumped back, stunned, at this point. Lopez had made an elegant end run around our entire strategy—and she was saying that if the court were to challenge her position, it would, by necessity, be challenging the logic underlying current abortion laws. One glance at Judge Herrington confirmed that that was the last thing he wanted.

"Let's take a break," he said, looking as shaken as I felt.

CHapter 30

I wish I could see the Earth: that would give me a place to focus my thoughts when I was thinking about Rebecca. But the Earth was straight down, and looking at the floor didn't fulfill my emotional need. Of course, nothing short of actually seeing her would do that.

Rebecca thinks the universe sends her messages—subtly at first, she says, and then, later, if she doesn't get them, the universe starts whacking her with two-by-fours.

I didn't believe in that sort of thing. I knew the universe was indifferent to me. And yet, perhaps out of respect for Rebecca, I did find myself looking, listening, watching, paying attention: if there was a way out, maybe the universe would give me a clue.

In the meantime, I took another of Brian Hades's suggestions—one I hoped wouldn't leave me feeling quite so sordid afterwards. I decided to try mountain climbing here on the moon. I'd never done much of that sort of thing on Earth—Eastern Canada is not known for its mountains. But it sounded like it might actually be fun, and so I inquired about it at the recreation desk.

Turns out the guy who usually led climbing expeditions was my old traveling buddy Quentin Ashburn, the moonbus-maintenance engineer. No one was allowed on the lunar surface alone; the same common-sense safety rules that applied to scuba diving also applied here. So Quentin was delighted by my request to go climbing.

It used to be, I'm told, that spacesuits had to be custom built for each user, but new adaptive fabrics made that unnecessary: High Eden stocked suits in three sizes for men, and three for women, and it was easy enough to see that the middle male size was the right one for me.

Quentin helped me suit up, making sure all the connections were secure. And then he got some special climbing equipment that was stored on open shelves in the change room. Some of it I recognized—lengths of nylon rope, for instance. Others were things I'd never seen before. The last piece was, well, a piece: a thing that looked like a squat, thick-bodied pistol.

"What's that?" I asked.

"It's a piton gun," he said. "It shoots pitons."

"Well, let's hope we don't run into any of those," I said.

Quentin laughed. "Pitons are metal spikes." He opened the gun's thick chamber, and showed me one. The spike was about ten centimeters long. It had a sharply pointed front and an eye at the other end to which a rope could be fitted. "We shoot them into the rock and use them as footholds or hand-holds, or to hold our ropes. On Earth, people often drive in pitons by hand, but the rock here is quite hard, and there's too much risk of rupturing your glove and exposing yourself to vacuum. So we use piton guns."

I'd never held a gun of any sort in my life—and, as a Canadian, I was proud of that. But I took the device, and copied Quentin, who slipped another one of them into a capacious pouch on the side of his right thigh.

Finally, we put on the fishbowl helmets. They were impregnated, Quentin told me, with something similar to electronic ink: any portion of them could become opaque, blocking out sunlight. Then we cycled through the airlock, which happened to be adjacent to the pad where the moonbuses landed.

"Your pride and joy is gone," I said over the intersuit radio, pointing at the empty pad.

"It's been gone for days," replied Quentin. "On its usual run to LS One. But it'll be back tomorrow, to take some passengers to the SETI installation."

The SETI installation. Where they listen for messages from the universe.

I tried to listen, too.

We continued on, walking over the lunar soil. Although the suit massed about twenty kilos, I still felt much lighter than I ever had on Earth. The suit air was a bit startling—completely devoid of any odor or flavor—but I quickly got used to it, although—

No, it's gone. I'd thought for a second that another headache was coming on, but the sensation passed almost at once.

The crater wall was far in front of us. As we walked, the sun disappeared behind it, and stars became visible. I kept looking up at the black, black sky for the Earth, but of course it was never visible from here. Still . . .

"Is that Mars?" I said, pointing at a brilliant point of light that was shaded differently from the others—it was either red or green, but I'd never heard of "the green planet."

"Sure is," said Quentin.

It took us about ten minutes to half-walk, half-hop over to the crater wall, which was craggy and steep, rising far above us. Since we were in shadow,

Quentin had turned on a light in the center of his chest, and then he reached over and flipped a switch on my suit, activating a similar light.

"Wow," I said, looking up at the inky wall. "That looks . . . difficult."

"It is," said Quentin, amiably. "Where would the fun be if it were easy?" He didn't wait for an answer, which was a good thing, because I didn't have one. Instead, he undid the pouch on his thigh, and pulled out his piton gun. "See?" he said, pointing with his other hand. "You aim at a cleft in the rock."

I nodded.

He took a bead with his gun, then fired. There was no sound, but the gun obviously discharged with a sizable kick, judging by the way Quentin's hand jerked back. A metal spike flew silently into the rock. Quentin tested it to see that it had lodged securely, and threaded a rope through it. "Simple as that," he said.

"How many pitons does it hold?"

"Eight. But there are oodles more in each of our pouches, so don't worry."

"It, ah, looks like it packs quite a kick," I said, gesturing at the gun.

"Depends on the force setting," said Quentin. "But, on maximum—which you'd use for granite, and such . . ." He adjusted a control on the gun, and fired away from the crater wall. The spike shot across the intervening vacuum and sent up a cloud of moondust where it hit.

I nodded.

"All right?" said Quentin. "Let's go!"

We started climbing the rocky face, climbing ever higher, climbing toward the light.

It was exhilarating. I was outdoors, and the lack of walls made it seem, at least for a time, like I was no longer a prisoner. We made our way to the top of the crater rim and—

—and fierce sunlight lanced into my eyes, triggering another headache before the helmet darkened. God, I wish my brain would stop hurting . . .

We walked around for a while on the gray surface, which curved away to a too-near horizon. "Magnificent desolation," Chandragupta had said, quoting somebody or other. It certainly was. I drank in the stark beauty while trying to ignore the pain between my ears.

Eventually, a warning started pinging over the helmet speakers, a counterpoint to the agonizing throbs: our air would soon be running out.

"Come on," said Quentin. "Time to go home."

Home, I thought. Yes, he was right. The bloody moonbus engineer was right. It was time to go home, once and for all.

Deshawn and Malcolm had spent the entire recess researching and conferring, and, as we returned to the courtroom, I heard Deshawn tell Karen he was "as ready as I'll ever be." Once Judge Herrington had arrived, and we were all seated again, Deshawn dove into his cross-examination of the Yale bioethicist, Alyssa Neruda.

"Dr. Neruda," he said, "I'm sure the jury was fascinated by your discussion of the gerrymandering of the line between personhood and nonpersonhood."

"I would hardly accuse the highest court of the land of gerrymandering," she replied coldly.

"Perhaps. But there's a glaring oversight in your commentary on people becoming more than one individual, isn't there?"

Neruda regarded him. "Oh?"

"Well, yes," said Deshawn. "I mean, human cloning has been technically possible since—when? Twenty-twelve or so?"

"I believe the first human clone was born in 2013," said Neruda.

"I stand corrected," said Deshawn. "But isn't cloning taking one individual and making it into two? The original and the copy are genetically identical after all, and yet surely they both have rights and are people?"

"You should take my course, Mr. Draper. That is indeed a fascinating theoretical issue, but it's not relevant to the laws of the United States. First, of course, no sensible person would say that they are the *same* people. And, second, human cloning has always been banned here—it's even banned up in Canada—and so American law has had no need to incorporate the concept of human clones into its definitions of personhood." She crossed her arms in a so-there gesture. "Individuation still stands as the law of the land."

If Deshawn was crestfallen, he hid it well. "Thank you, Doctor," he said. "No further questions."

"And we'll call it a day," said Judge Herrington. "Jurors, let me admonish you again . . ."

It had been some time since I'd connected with another instantiation of me, but it happened that evening, while I was watching the Blue Jays play. They were doing so badly, I guess I was letting my mind wander. Maybe my zombie was willing to watch them get slaughtered, but the conscious me couldn't take it, and—

And suddenly there was another version of me inside my head. I told the wall screen to turn off, and strained to listen.

That's strange . . .

"Hello!" I said. "Hello, are you there?"

What? Who?

I sighed, and went through the rigmarole of explaining who I was, ending with, "And I know you think it's 2034, but it's not. It's really 2045."

What are you talking about?

"It's really 2045," I said again.

Of course it is. I know that.

"You do?"

Of course.

So it wasn't the same instantiation with the memory problem I'd encountered earlier. Christ, I wondered just how many of us there were. "You started by saying something was strange."

What? Oh, yeah. Yeah, it is.

"What is?"

I dropped a pen I was using.

"So?"

So I managed to catch it before it hit the floor.

"Well, there's no slow, chemical component to your reaction time anymore," I said. "Now, it's all electric—happening at the speed of light"

That's not it. I was able to watch the pen fall, to see it clearly as it moved downward.

"I haven't noticed any heightening of my awareness like that."

I don't think it's heightened awareness . . . There. I just picked it up and dropped it again. It fell in slow motion.

"Fell in slow . . . how is that possible?"

I don't know, unless . . .

"Oh, Christ."

Christ indeed.

"You're on the moon. I mean, I suppose you could be anywhere with reduced gravity, including a space station spinning too slowly to simulate a full Earth gee. But since we already know that Immortex has a facility on the moon . . ."

Yes. But if I'm on the moon, shouldn't there be a time delay as I communicate with you? The moon's—what?—four hundred thousand kilometers from Earth.

"Something like that. And light travels at 300,000 kilometers per second, so—let's see—there should be a one-and-a-third second delay, or so."

Maybe there is. Maybe.

"Let's test it. I'll count to five; when you hear me say five, you pick up the count, and carry it through from six to ten, then I'll come in for eleven to fifteen. Okay?"

Okay.

"One. Two. Three. Four. Five."

Six. Seven. Eight. Nine. Ten.

"Eleven. Twelve. Thirteen. Fourteen. Fifteen."

No delays that I could detect.

"Me, neither."

Then how . . . ?

"Andrew Porter said something about using quantum fog to scan the original Jake Sullivan's brain noninvasively . . ."

You think that the duplicates are all quantum entangled?

" 'Quantally.' The adjective is 'quantally.' "

I know that.

"I know you do."

Quantally entangled. So we are connected instantaneously.

"Exactly. What Albert Einstein called 'spooky action at a distance.' "

I suppose it's possible.

"But why would Immortex create another duplicate of me on the moon?"

I don't know, said the voice in my head. *But I don't like it here.*

"Well, you can't come down here, to Earth. There can be only one of us here."

I know. Lucky bastard.

I thought about that. "I suppose I am."

Karen was back on the witness stand, this time as called by Maria Lopez, rather than Deshawn. "Earlier," said Lopez, "when cross-examining Professor Alyssa Neruda, your attorney, Mr. Draper, used the term 'gerrymandering' in relation to defining the line between life and death. Do you recall that?"

Karen nodded. "Yes, I do."

"You're a professional writer; I'm sure you have a large vocabulary. Could you enlighten us as to what that odd-sounding word—'gerrymander'—means?"

Karen tilted her head to one side. "It means to redefine borders for political advantage."

"In fact," said Lopez, "it comes from an act by Elbridge Gerry, does it not, who redefined the political districts in Massachusetts when he was governor of that state, so that his party would be favored in upcoming elections, isn't that so?"

"Gerry"—said Karen, pronouncing it with a hard G, "not Jerry. We've ended up saying gerrymander with a soft G, but the governor—and later, vice-president—pronounced his name with a hard G."

I smiled at Karen's ability to find a polite way to say, "So go fuck yourself, smart ass."

"Ah, well, yes," said Lopez. "In any event, the governor ended up redefining the borders of Essex County until it looked like a salamander. So, again, to gerrymander is to flagrantly move lines or borders for political or personal expediency, no?"

"You could say that."

"And the lawyer for the plaintiff accused the Supreme Court of simply gerrymandering the line between life and death until they found something that was politically palatable, did he not?"

"That was what Mr. Draper was implying, yes."

"But, of course, you want the men and women of this jury to gerrymander another line—the obvious, clear demarcation that is brain death—to another point, for your personal convenience, isn't that so?"

"I would not put it that way," said Karen, stiffly.

"And, in fact, you have a personal history of playing this gerrymandering game, don't you?"

"Not that I'm aware of."

"No? Ms. Bessarian, do you have any children?"

"Yes, of course. I have a son, Tyler."

"The defendant in this case, is that correct?"

"Yes."

"Any other children?"

Karen looked—well, I couldn't tell; it was a contorting of her plastic face I'd never seen before, and so I didn't know what emotion to correlate it with.

"Tyler is my only child," said Karen at last.

"Your only living child," said Lopez, "correct?"

Sometimes you read in novels about people's mouths forming perfect "O's" of surprise; flesh-and-blood human faces can't really do that, but Karen's synthetic countenance managed it perfectly while Lopez asked her question. But that expression was soon replaced with one of anger. "You're a woman," said Karen. "How can you be so cruel? What does the fact that I lost a daughter to crib death possibly have to do with the matter at hand? Do you think I don't still cry myself to sleep over it sometimes?"

For once, Maria Lopez looked completely flustered. "Ms. Bessarian, I—"

Karen continued. "For God's sake, Ms. Lopez, to bring that—"

"Honestly, Ms. Bessarian," exclaimed Lopez, "I had no idea! I didn't know."

Karen had her arms crossed in front of her chest. I glanced at the jury, who all looked like they hated Lopez just then.

"Really, Ms. Bessarian. I—I'm terribly sorry for your loss. Honestly, Karen—I—please forgive me."

Karen still said nothing.

Lopez turned to Judge Herrington. "Your honor, perhaps a short recess . . . ?"

"Twenty minutes," said Herrington, and he rapped his gavel.

CHAPTEF 31

The moonbus's airlock controls were located, logically enough, next to the airlock door. The pilot hadn't arrived yet, which was just as well. I got on board first, and waited for others to join me. I really only needed one, but—but, damn it, the next two people to board, a white woman and an Asian woman, came in together. Ah, well.

I moved to the airlock controls, and was about to hit the appropriate switch, when I saw that Brian Hades, of all people, was coming down the corridor, his pony tail doubtless bouncing behind him in the low gravity. Was I better off with him inside or outside? I had to make a split-second decision, and I decided I'd have even more clout if he was in. I waited till he'd passed through the door, and then I hit the emergency control that slammed the airlock shut.

The two women had already taken seats—and not together; I guess, although they'd been chatting, they weren't actually friends. Hades was still standing, and he turned in surprise at the sound of the airlock closing.

He turned and looked at me for the first time, his eyes wide. "Sullivan?"

I pulled the piton gun from the small backpack I'd placed on the seat I was standing beside, then cleared my throat in the dry air of the cabin. "Mr. Hades, ladies—please forgive me but . . ." I paused; there was a stab of pain through the top of my skull. I waited for it to abate a bit.

"Mr. Hades, ladies," I repeated as if my earlier words weren't still hanging in the air, "this is a hijacking."

I'm not sure what reaction I'd expected: screams, shouts? The three of them stared at me blankly.

Finally, Hades said, "You're kidding, right?"

"No," I said. "I'm not."

"You can't hijack a moonbus," said the Asian woman. "There's nowhere to take it."

"I'm not going to take it anywhere," I said. "We're going to stay right here, plugged into High Eden's life-support equipment, until my demands are met." There. It wasn't quite the lunch counter at Woolworth's, but it would do.

"And what are your demands?" asked the white woman.

"Mr. Hades knows—and I'll tell the two of you later. But first, let me say I don't want to hurt anyone; it's *they* who do the hurting. My goal is for all of us to walk out of here safe and sound."

"Mr. Sullivan, please," said Hades.

" 'Please'?" I sneered. "I said 'please' to you. I asked you, I begged you. And you refused."

"There has to be a better way," said Hades.

"There was. You didn't take it. Now, first things first. Mr. Hades sit down—up at the front, there, in the first row."

"Or what?" said Hades.

"Or," and here I fought to keep my voice steady, "I will kill you." I held up the piton gun.

"What's that?" asked the Asian woman.

"It's for lunar mountain climbing," I said. "It will shoot a metal spike right through your chest."

Hades considered for a moment, then folded his long body into one of the two front seats. He then swiveled it around to face me.

"Very good," I said. "I've had enough of being spied on. Each of you: turn to the window next to you, and pull the vinyl shade down."

Nobody moved.

"Do it!" I snapped.

First the Asian woman did it, then the white one. Hades made a show of trying to lower his, and then he turned to me and said, "It's stuck."

I wasn't about to lean across him to try it for myself. "You're lying," I said simply. "Close it."

Hades considered, then tugged theatrically at the blind again until it came down.

"That's better," I said. I pointed to the white woman. "You, get up and pull down all the other shades, please."

" 'Please'?" she said, mocking me mocking Hades. "What you really mean is, do it or I'll kill you."

I wasn't going to argue the point. "I'm Canadian," I said, my hand still holding the gun, but not raising it. "I can't help saying 'please.' "

She was stationary for a moment, then shrugged a little and got up, moving about the cabin, pulling down the rest of the blinds. "Now, close the door to the cockpit, too."

She did so; the front wraparound window was no longer visible from the cabin—meaning we were no longer visible through it. "Thank you," I said. "Now, take your seat again."

There was a pounding noise on the other side of the airlock—someone trying to get us to open up. I ignored it, and instead moved to the communications panel near the airlock. It had a twenty-centimeter videophone screen.

An attractive dark-eyed brunette appeared. "Heaviside Transit Control to Moonbus Four," she said. "What's wrong? Is your airlock malfunctioning? Have you developed a leak?"

"Heaviside, this is Moonbus Four," I said into the camera. "Jacob Sullivan speaking. There are three other people aboard, including Brian Hades, so do exactly as I say. No one is to try to enter this Moonbus. I am fully conversant in Moonbus operations—ask Quentin Ashburn; he'll tell you. If I don't get what I want, I'll vent the starboard fuel tank. The monohydrazine will sublimate into a cloud of explosive vapor, and I'll fire the main engine, igniting that cloud. The explosion will take out half of High Eden."

The brunette's eyes were wide. "And you too," she said. "Come on—you'll die!"

"I'm dead already," I shouted. Damn it, I was trying to keep it together, but the pounding in my head was increasing. "I'm a shed skin, a discard. I've got no identity, no personhood." I took a deep breath and I swallowed. "I've got nothing to lose."

"Mr. Sullivan—"

"No. Nothing further right now. I don't want to deal with a traffic controller. Get someone on the line who has the power to negotiate. Until then—" I stabbed the OFF switch.

I wish there had been no need to involve other people. But there was. They might have evacuated High Eden, or found some way to launch the moonbus by remote control. I needed there to be more at stake than just equipment, no matter how expensive.

"Now," I said, looking at the two women and Hades, "it's time for introductions. My name is Jacob Sullivan, and I'm from Toronto. I copied my consciousness into an artificial body because I had a devastating disease. But that disease has been cured, and I want to go back home—that's my only demand. I honestly don't want to hurt any of you." I gestured at the Asian woman, being sure to do it with my empty left hand, rather than the one holding the piton gun. "Now you," I said.

The woman looked defiant for a time, then seemed to decide that cooperation couldn't hurt. "My name is Akiko Uchiyama," she said. She was plain, thin, with short hair dyed some light color. "I'm a radio astronomer with the SETI institution at Chernyshov." She paused, then added: "And I have a husband, and twin six-year-old daughters, and I very much want to get back to them."

"And I certainly hope you will," I said. I turned to the white woman, who was pretty, with big eyes and lots of dark hair. "You."

"I'm Chloë Hansen," she said. "I'm the head nutritionist and dietitian here at High Eden."

"So you're the one," I said.

"The one what?"

"The one tampering with my food."

She was a good actress, I'd give her that. "What are you talking about?"

I ignored that and turned to face Hades. "No doubt Chloë knows you, and I sure as hell do, but we may be here a long time so you might as well introduce yourself to Akiko."

Hades crossed his arms in front of his chest and frowned, but he complied. "I'm Brian Hades, the chief administrator of High Eden."

Akiko's eyes narrowed. "And so his complaint is with you," she said, pointing at me. "Give him what he wants, and this ends, right?"

"I *can't* do that," said Hades. "He signed a contract. Besides, our entire business model—"

"Screw your business model!" snapped Akiko. "Just do whatever he says."

"I won't. The new version of him back on Earth has rights, and—"

"And I've got rights, too!" said Akiko. "So does—Chloë, is it? We've got rights!"

"Yes, you do," I said. "And I don't—not at the moment. That's what this is all about. When I get my rights back, this will be over."

The phone bleeped. I went over to the panel and hit the ACCEPT button. "Hello," said a male voice with a classy British accent. "Is Mr. Sullivan available?"

"This is Jacob Sullivan," I said. "To whom am I speaking?" Hearing classy British accents makes me talk like that.

"My name is Gabriel Smythe, and I'm going to have the privilege of being your principal contact as we sort out this spot of bother."

Smythe—I knew that name. I frowned, then it came to me. He was the small, florid man with the platinum hair who'd performed the memorial service for Karen Bessarian.

"Are you in the docking control room?" I asked.

"Yes. I'm with Ms. Bortolotto, whom you spoke to earlier."

"I remember you. You performed that service for Karen. But you're not a rabbi . . . are you?"

"I'm not going to lie to you, Mr. Sullivan; I assure you of that. I'm the head psychologist for Immortex."

"Head psychologist." I chuckled. "I don't think there's any other kind."

"I beg your—oh, I get it. Yes, quite."

I took a deep breath of the moonbus's unpleasantly dry air. "I'm not crazy, Dr. Smythe."

"You may call me Gabe."

I thought about protesting. We weren't buddies here. He was the enemy; I had to remember that. Still, calling him "Doctor" would give him an edge in status. "All right, Gabe," I said at last. "I'm not crazy."

"No one said you are," Gabe replied.

"Then why are you the one talking to me?"

"We have no one on hand versed with dealing with these sorts of situations. *Somebody* has to do it, and the chef hardly seemed appropriate. And, after all, you do have Mr. Hades held—you have Mr. Hades detained."

Interesting that he censored himself before he said the word 'hostage.' He probably had some hostage-negotiation handbook on screen in front of him, and it probably told him to avoid that word. Not a bad call; I didn't like the word myself. But I needed *clout*.

"Now," continued Smythe, "first things first. Does anyone with you have any special needs? Any medical problems?"

Yup: definitely working through a checklist.

"Everyone's fine."

"Are you sure?"

I looked at the three of them, all craning in their seats to look back at me. "Is everyone okay?" I asked.

Akiko looked like she was going to say something, but ultimately didn't. The others were silent. "Yes," I said. "Everyone's fine. And I don't want to hurt anyone."

"I'm very glad to hear that, Jake. Very glad. Now, do you think we might open a video link? The families of the . . . the . . ." He must have found the approved word. ". . . *detainees* would certainly like to see their faces."

"I'm calling the shots here," I said—choosing that word just to make him wince; it's fun playing mind games with psychologists. If *hostages* was a ver-boten word, so too, doubtless, was *shots*.

"Of course," said Smythe. "Absolutely. Now, what are . . . what can I do for you?"

Demands. He'd surely been about to ask me what my demands were, but again had stopped himself. We were *negotiating* here. Negotiating is about win-win, about shifting positions; it couldn't work if there were inflexible demands.

I decided to tweak him again. "I have only one demand. I require my personhood back. Return me to Earth, and let me take up my old life. Grant that, and everyone is free to go."

"I'll see what I can do."

Nice and vague; I suspect the manual told him never to commit to anything he couldn't be sure of delivering. "Don't humor me, Gabe. You can't give me back my personhood. But there is one person who can: the other Jacob Sullivan, the duplicate of my mind inside a robot body, back on Earth."

"And there's the rub, Jake. Surely you see that. Earth's far away. And you must know we promised never to contact your replacement. He needs to do his best to put the fact that the original is still extant out of his mind."

Extant. Not living. Extant. "Make an exception," I said. "Get the other me on the radio."

"We're on the far side of the moon, Jake."

"And you can bounce radio signals off the communications satellites in synchronous orbit above the moon's equator. I'm not stupid, Gabe, and I *have* thought this through. Call me back when you've got an answer."

And with that, I closed the channel.

CHAPTER 32

Karen was still shaking from having had to talk about her long-dead daughter. I held her for a while, out in the courthouse corridor. The jury, of course, had been removed to their waiting room during the recess, so they didn't get to see this—which was fine; it wasn't for public consumption anyway. I found myself stroking Karen's artificial hair, with my artificial hand, hoping somehow that the gesture was giving her comfort. Karen calmed down somewhat by the end of the recess. We went back into the courtroom. I took my seat in the gallery; Malcolm Draper was already there, and Deshawn was already back at his desk. I watched as Maria Lopez came in. She looked . . . I'm not sure exactly how to describe it. Frustrated, maybe. Or defiant. Things hadn't gone the way she'd planned a few minutes ago. I wondered what she'd really expected to happen.

The door to Judge Herrington's chambers opened. "All rise!" called the clerk, and everyone did so. Herrington took his place at the bench, rapped his gavel, and said, "On the record again in *Bessarian v. Horowitz*. Ms. Lopez, you may continue your direct examination of Ms. Bessarian."

Lopez rose, and I could see her take a deep breath, still unsure of herself. "Thank you, your honor." But she said nothing more.

"Well?" demanded Herrington after about fifteen seconds.

"My apologies, your honor," said Lopez. She looked at Karen—or perhaps looked beyond Karen, and to the right a bit, as if she were focussing on the Michigan flag rather than the witness. "Ms. Bessarian, let me rephrase my earlier question. Have you ever had an abortion?"

Deshawn was instantly on his feet. "Objection! Irrelevant!"

"There better be a point to this, Ms. Lopez," said Herrington, sounding angry.

"There most certainly is," said Lopez, some fire starting to come back into her, "if you'll permit me a little latitude."

"A little latitude is all your going to get—like from here to Warren; don't take us clear across the globe."

Lopez did her trademark bow. "But of course, your honor." She repeated the question, giving herself another chance to make the jury hear the loaded word at its end. "Ms. Bessarian, have you ever had an abortion?"

Karen's voice was small. "Yes."

There was chatter in the courtroom. Judge Herrington frowned his small frown and banged his gavel.

"Now, we don't want to portray you as a criminal here, Ms. Bessarian," said Lopez. "We wouldn't want the jury to think you had committed that act recently, would we? Will you tell the court when you terminated the life of a fetus?"

"In, um . . . it was 1988."

"Nineteen Eighty-Eight. That would be—what?—fifty-seven years ago, no?"

"That's correct."

"So if you had not terminated that fetus, you would have another child—a son or a daughter—some fifty-six years old."

"I—perhaps."

"Perhaps?" said Lopez. "I think the answer is yes."

Karen was looking down. "Yes, I suppose."

"Fifty-six years old. A mature man or woman, quite likely with children of his or her own."

"Objection, your honor," said Deshawn. "Relevance!"

"Move it along, Ms. Lopez."

She nodded. "The real point is that the abortion was executed in 1988." She put a special emphasis on the verb *executed*. "And that was . . . let me see now . . . forty years before *Roe v. Wade* was overturned by *Littler v. Carvey.*"

"If you say so."

"And *Roe v. Wade* was the case that temporarily legalized a woman's ability to terminate the life she was carrying, isn't that so?"

"It was not intended to be a temporary measure," said Karen.

"Forgive me," said Lopez. "My only point was to assure the court that you had terminated a fetus when it was in fact legal to do so in these United States, correct?"

"Yes. It was a legal procedure. Carried out in a public hospital."

"Oh, indeed. Indeed. We don't want to put a picture of back alleys and bent coat hangers into the jury's mind."

"You just did," said Karen, defiantly. "This was a legal, moral, and common procedure."

"Common!" said Lopez, with relish. "Common, yes. The very word."

"Objection!" said Deshawn, spreading his arms. "If Ms. Lopez has a question for the witness—"

"Oh, but I do. I do. Ms. Bessarian, why did you have this abortion?"

Deshawn was getting angry; his face was still calm, but his voice wasn't. "Objection! Relevance."

"Ms. Lopez, please get to the point," said Herrington, a hand supporting his shoehorn jaw.

"Just a few more minutes, your honor. Ms. Bessarian, why did you have this abortion?"

"I did not wish to have a child at that time."

"So the abortion was indeed a matter of personal convenience?"

"It was a matter of economic necessity. My husband and I were just starting out."

"Ah, you did this for the good of the child, then."

Deshawn spread his arms. "Objection! Your honor, please!"

"Withdrawn," said Lopez. "Ms. Bessarian, when you had this abortion, you didn't think you were committing murder, did you?"

"Of course not. It was a fully legal procedure back then."

"Indeed, indeed. The period sometimes referred to as the Dark Ages."

"Not by me."

"No, I'm sure. Tell us, please: why was it not murder to terminate your pregnancy?"

"Because . . . because it *wasn't*. Because the Supreme Court of the United States had ruled that it was a legal procedure."

"Yes, yes, yes, I understand what the law said back then. What I'm asking about is your own personal moral code. Why was it not murder to terminate that pregnancy?"

"Because it wasn't a *person*—not in my eyes, or the eyes of the law."

"Today, of course, the law would disagree."

"But I would not."

I cringed. Karen was being too feisty for her own good. And Lopez seized upon it. "Are you saying your standards are *higher* than those of the law?"

"My standards aren't subject to pressure groups or political whim, if that's what you mean."

"And so you still maintain that that fetus was not a person?"

Karen said nothing.

"An answer, please, Ms. Bessarian."

"Yes."

More chatter; another tap of the gavel.

"You're saying, yes, that fetus was not a person?" asked Lopez.

"Yes."

"That fetus, which was created by the physical expression of love between you and your late first husband, may God rest his soul. That fetus,
which had forty-six chromosomes, mixing uniquely your husband's traits and
yours."

Karen said nothing.

"That fetus *was* not a person, correct?"

Karen was quiet a moment, then: "Correct."

"How far into your pregnancy were you when you terminated it?"

"Nine . . . no, ten weeks."

"You're not sure?"

"It was an awfully long time ago," said Karen.

"Indeed. Why did you wait that long? Had you been unaware up to that
point that you were pregnant?"

"I became aware within four weeks of conception."

"Then why the delay?"

"I wanted time to think." Karen couldn't resist the soapbox, damn it all.
"Something the fifteen-day stricture of *Littler v. Carvey* doesn't give women,
does it? Has it ever occurred to you, Ms. Lopez, that by placing the limit on
when abortions can legally be performed so early in pregnancy that women are
forced to hastily make a decision that, if given more time to come to terms
with their feelings, they might not have made?"

"I'll ask the questions, Ms. Bessarian, if you don't mind. And, indeed,
suppose you had again become pregnant at an inconvenient time, and that
this pregnancy had occurred after *Littler v. Carvey*. Would you have allowed
the date specified in the law to force you to make a decision that early?"

"It *is* the law."

"Yes. But you are a woman of means, Ms. Bessarian. You could have found
a way to have a safe—for you—abortion after the fifteen-day limit had passed.
Ferry 'cross the Mersey, and all that."

"I suppose."

"And would you have been comfortable with your decision? Gerrymandering the line between person and nonperson in whatever way was most convenient for you?"

Karen said nothing.

"Answer the question, please. Would you have the line between personhood and nonpersonhood moved for your own personal convenience?"

Karen was still silent.

"Your honor, would you kindly direct the witness to answer?"

"Ms. Bessarian?" said Judge Herrington.

Karen nodded, then tilted her head to one side. She looked at Deshawn, then out at me, then over at the jury box, then back at Lopez. "Yes," she said at last. "I suppose I would."

"I see," said Lopez. She, too, looked at the jury box. "We see." Whatever discomfort Lopez had felt earlier was long since gone. "Now, Ms. Bessarian, again, what was it that that poor fetus, conceived of man and woman, lacked, making it not a person, which you, an artificial construct, possess, thus making you a person?"

"I . . . ah. . . ."

"Come now, Ms. Bessarian! At a loss for words? And, you, a professional writer!"

"It's . . . ah . . ."

"The question is simple: there must be something that your terminated fetus lacked that you yourself possess. Otherwise, both would be persons—in your own moral code, if not in the eyes of the law, no?"

"I possess experience."

"Not of your own, though. I mean, not experience that this . . . this contraption in front of us has directly had. What 'experience' you have was copied from the late, real Karen Bessarian, no?"

"It was *transferred* from that earlier version of me, with that version's full, expressed consent and desire."

"We'll have to take your word for that, won't we? I mean—forgive me—but the real Karen Bessarian is dead, isn't she?"

"I knew that my body was wearing out; that's why I arranged to transfer into this more durable one."

"But not everything was transferred, was it?"

"How do you mean?"

"I mean, Ms. Bessarian's memories were transferred, but trivial things, like, say, the contents of her stomach at the time of transference, were not duplicated in the copy."

"Well, no."

"Of course, not. That's inconsequential, after all. As were, say, the wrinkles on the original's face."

"I have opted for a younger visage," said Karen, defiantly.

"Your honor, defendant's twelve—a photo of Karen Bessarian taken last year."

Karen's face appeared on the wall screen. I'd forgotten just how incredibly old she'd looked before: white hair, deeply lined face, translucent skin, eyes that seemed too small for their sockets, that lopsided stroke-victim's smile. I found myself looking away.

"That *is* you, isn't?" asked Lopez. "The original you?"

Karen nodded. "Yes."

"The real you, the you that was—"

"Objection!" called Deshawn. "Asked and answered."

"Sustained," said Herrington.

Lopez bowed her head briefly. "Very well. Forgive me for being blunt, Ms. Bessarian, but you obviously chose not to have cosmetic procedures performed."

"I am not a particularly vain person."

"Admirable. Still, clearly you only identify *some* parts of you as being the *real* you, no? So, again, which part of the real you do you think you possessed and your terminated fetus lacked?"

"A mind," said Karen. "If it were a copy of a fetus's neural connections sitting here in front of you, I'd not expect you to accord it any special status."

"So it's the intellect that makes one a person?" said Lopez, raising her eyebrows.

"Well, yes."

"And therefore a fetus is not a person."

"Yes." That's my Karen: in for a penny, in for a pound. There was a sharp intake of breath from some of those in the courtroom. "I mean," continued Karen, "they are *now*, under the current law, but . . ."

"But it's not a law you agree with, is it?"

"Women fought long and hard for the right to control their own bodies, Ms. Lopez. I grant that things have shifted to the right since I was young, but . . ."

"No, no, no, Ms. Bessarian. You can't accuse contemporary society of narrow-mindedness: we've *expanded* the definition of what qualifies as human since your day. We've broadened the definition to include fetuses."

"Yes, but . . ."

"Oh, granted, the broadening has not been in the direction you seem to wish. We protect innocent newborns; you'd take that away, and instead let people hold on to some ersatz life at the other end, isn't that so? The first nine months are too much to ask, but nine additional decades, or even centuries, tacked on at the end, in synthetic form, is reasonable. Is that your position, Ms. Bessarian?"

"My position, since you ask, is that once the law has granted the right of personhood to someone, that right is inalienable."

Lopez apparently had been waiting for Karen to say this. She practically leapt back to her desk and picked up a datapad. "Defendant's thirteen, your honor," she declared, holding up the device. She crossed the well and handed it to Karen. "Ms. Bessarian, would you please tap the 'Book Info' icon and tell the court what book is currently being displayed?"

Karen did so. "*The American Heritage English Dictionary*, Ninth Edition, Unabridged."

"Very good," said Lopez. "Now will you please clear that notification, and read the text on the underlying screen?"

Karen touched some controls, then: "It's the definition of the word 'inalienable,'" she said.

"Indeed. And will you please read the definition?"

"'That cannot be transferred to another or others: inalienable rights.'"

"'That *cannot* be transferred,'" repeated Lopez. "Would you agree with that definition?"

"Um, well, I'm sure to most people 'inalienable' means that it cannot be taken away from you."

"Really, now? Would you care to try a few other dictionaries? *Merriam-Webster's*, perhaps? *Encarta*? The *Oxford English Dictionary*? All of them are loaded onto that datapad, Ms. Bessarian, and I assure you they all give the same meaning: something that cannot be transferred. And yet you've just said that your own position is that rights of personhood are inalienable."

Deshawn spread his arms. "Your honor, objection—relevance. You took me to task on our first day for making picayune semantic distinctions, and—"

"Sorry, Mr. Draper," said Herrington. "Overruled. The point Ms. Lopez is making is bang on target."

Lopez nodded at the bench. "Thank you, your honor." She then turned back to Karen. "So which is it? Or are we in Wonderland now, and a word means whatever you want it to mean?"

"Don't push your luck," said Herrington, gently.

"Of course not, your honor," Lopez replied. "Which is it, Ms. Bessarian? Should rights of personhood be transferable, or are they, as you yourself said, inalienable?"

Karen opened her mouth, but then closed it.

"That's all right, Ms. Bessarian," said Lopez. "That's just fine. I'm content to leave it as a rhetorical question. I'm sure the good men and women of the jury will know how to answer it for us." She turned to face the bench. "Your honor, the defendant rests."

Chapter 33

There were cameras inside the moonbus, of course. In theory, they were off.

Right. As if.

I took a tube of suit-repair goop and squirted it over each of the lenses, watching it harden quickly and turning to a matte finish as it did so. The only one I left uncovered was the unit for the videophone next to the airlock—and it was soon bleeping, signaling an incoming call. I pushed the answer button and Gabriel Smythe's florid face appeared.

"Yes, Gabe," I said. "Have you gotten ahold of the artificial me?"

"Yes, we have, Jake. He's in Toronto, of course, but he's willing to talk to you."

"Put him on," I said

And there he—I—was. I'd seen the artificial body before I'd uploaded, but never since it had been occupied. It was a slightly simplified version of me, with a slightly younger face that looked a little plastic. "Hello," I said.

He didn't reply for a moment, and I was about to protest that something was wrong, but then he said, "Hello, brother."

Of course. The time lag: one-and-a-third seconds for my words to reach him on Earth; another one-and-a-third seconds for his reply to reach me. Still, I was wary. "How do I know it's really you?" I asked.

One Mississippi. Two Mis—

"It's me," said the android.

"No," I replied. "At best it's one of us. But I've got to be sure."

Time delay. "So ask me a question."

No one else could possibly know this—at least not through me, although I suppose *she* could have told someone. But given that she'd been dating my best friend at the time, I rather suspected her lips were sealed—after the fact, of course. "The first girl to ever give us a blowjob."

"Carrie," said the other me. "At the hydro field behind our high school. After the cast party for that production of *Julius Caesar*."

I smiled. "Good. Okay. One more question, just to be sure. We'd decided before undergoing the Mindscan process to keep one little fact secret from the Immortex people. Something about, ah, um, traffic lights."

"Traffic lights? Oh—we're color-blind. We can't tell red and green apart. Or, at least, we didn't used to be able to; I can now."

"And?"

"It's . . . um . . ."

"Come on, make me *see* it."

"It's . . . it's . . . well, red is *warm*, you know? Especially the deeper shades, like maroon. And green—it's not quite like anything I can describe. It's not cold, the way blue is. Sharp, maybe. It looks sharp. And . . . I don't know. I like it, though—it's my favorite new color."

"What's a field of grass look like?"

"It's, ah . . ."

Smythe's voice, cutting in: "Forgive me, Jake, but surely we have more pressing matters to discuss."

I was still fascinated, but Smythe was right. The last thing I wanted to do was get emotionally involved with this bogus me. "Right, okay. Now, listen, copy-of-me. You know exactly why we agreed to this copying process. We thought the biological me was going to die soon, or end up a vegetable. And now I'm not; I've got decades left."

Time delay. "Really?"

"Yes. They found a cure for what was wrong with me, and they fixed it. Dad's fate is not going to be my fate."

Time delay. "That's—that's terrific. I'm delighted."

"I'm tickled pink myself—say, what does pink really look like? No, never mind. But, look, we both know that I'm the real person, don't we?"

An interminable couple of seconds. "Oh, come on," said the other me. "You fully accepted the conditions of what we were doing. You understood that I— not you, *I*—was going to be the real us from now on."

"But you must have been watching the news, too. You must know that there's a case involving Karen Bessarian going on right now in Michigan, where it's being argued that the upload is not really a person."

Time lag. "No, I didn't know that. And besides—"

"How could you *not* know that? We never miss the news."

"—it doesn't matter what they're doing in Mich—"

"How are the Blue Jays doing?"

"—igan. This isn't about what lawyers say, it's about what we agreed to."

I waited for the two-plus seconds to pass. But the android me just stood there, looking off camera. Presumably he would be in Toronto, and so there was a good chance the person off-camera was Dr. Andrew Porter. But Porter had said he didn't follow baseball.

"I asked you how the Blue Jays are doing," I said again, and waited.

"Umm, they're doing fine. They just beat the Devil Rays."

"No, they didn't. They're doing terribly. Haven't won a game in two weeks."

"Um, well, I haven't been following . . ."

"Which past president just died?" I asked.

"Um, you mean an American president?"

"You *don't* know, do you? Hillary Clinton just passed on."

"Oh, *that*—"

"It wasn't Clinton, you lying bastard. It was Buchanan." Of course Smythe had stopped him from answering when I'd asked him what a field of grass looked like. This android had never seen one. "Jesus Christ," I said. "You're not the me that's out in the world. You're a—a *backup*."

"I—"

"Shut up. Shut the hell up. *Smythe!*"

The camera changed to show Smythe. "I'm here, Jake."

"Smythe, don't fuck with me like that again. Don't you *dare*."

"Yes. I'm sorry. It was a dumb thing to do."

"It was damn near a *fatal* thing to do. Get the copy of me that's out and about on Earth. I want to see him, face to face. And have him bring a hardcopy of . . ." What the hell newspaper still had hardcopies? "Of the *New York Times*, showing the date he left Earth—that would at least prove someone had come up from there. But he's still going to have to prove to me that he's the one with the legal rights of personhood."

"We can't do that," said Smythe.

My head was pounding. I rubbed my temples. "Don't tell me what you can and cannot do," I said. "He'll have to come here eventually, anyway. You heard what I want, and I'm going to get it. Have him come here—bring him to the moon."

Smythe spread his arms. "Even if I agreed to ask him, and he agreed to come, it would take three days to get him to the moon, and most of another day to bring him via moonbus from LS One."

Out of the corner of my eye, I saw Hades starting to get up from his seat. I aimed the piton gun at him. "Don't even think about it," I said. Then I turned back to the image of Smythe: "Send him on a cargo rocket," I said. "High-powered acceleration for the first hour. He doesn't need life support, right? And he can pull lots of gees, I'm sure."

"That will cost . . ."

"A whole heck of a lot less than if I blow up this moonbus and take out half of High Eden."

"I need to get authorization."

"Don't do it!" I swung around. Hades was shouting. "Gabe, do you hear me? I'm ordering you not to do that!"

Gabe sounded flustered, but he said, "I'll see what I can manage."

"Damn it, Gabe!" shouted Hades. "I'm the senior Immortex official on the moon, and I'm telling you not to do this."

"Shut up," I said to Hades.

"No," said Gabe. "No, it's all right, Jake. I'm sorry, Brian—really, I am. But I can't take orders from you just now. We've got advisors from Earth on the line, as you can imagine, and I'm tied into various resources. And they all say the same thing on this point. A hosta—a *detainee's* orders are not to be followed, no matter how senior they are, since the orders are obviously given under duress. You're going to have to trust my judgment."

"Damn it, Smythe," said Hades. "You're fired!"

"Once I've gotten you out of this mess, sir, if you still want to do that, you'll be able to. But right now, you simply aren't in a position to fire anyone. Mr. Sullivan—Jake—I'll do what I can. But I'll need time."

"I've never been a patient man," I said. "Maybe that's related to living under a death sentence, and I haven't quite gotten used to my change of circumstances. In any event, I don't expect to wait. A cargo rocket can fly here in twelve hours; I give you another twelve to take care of logistics, and getting the other me to a rocket-launch site. But that's all. If I'm not talking face-to-face to the android that's usurped me in twenty-four hours, people will begin to die."

Smythe blew out air. "Jake, you know I'm a psychologist, and, well, I've been reviewing your file. This isn't you. This isn't like you at all."

"This is the *new* me," I said. "Isn't that the whole point? There's a new Jake Sullivan."

"Jake, I see a note here that you recently had brain surgery—nanosurgery, to be sure, but . . ."

"Yes. So?"

"And you were having trouble balancing neurotransmitter levels after that. Are you still taking the Toraplaxin? Because if you're not, we can—"

"Right. Like I'd take any pills you'd offer."

"Jake, you've got a chemical imbal—"

I slammed my fist against the OFF switch.

Judge Herrington called it a day, and Karen and I went home. I was still seething from the way Lopez had attacked Karen on the stand. That Karen wasn't too upset herself helped, but not enough. Although my plastiskin couldn't turn different shades, I *felt* livid—and the feeling wasn't dissipating on its own.

It used to be that if I was angry, I'd walk it off. I'd go outside, and stroll around the block a couple of times. But now I could walk for miles—a unit I only used figuratively, but that Karen actually had a feeling for—without it in the slightest changing my mood.

Likewise, when I was depressed, I used to rip open a bag of potato chips and a thing of dip, and stuff my face. Or, if I was really feeling like I couldn't face the day anymore, I'd crawl back into bed and have a nap. And, of course, nothing was better for relaxing than a nice cold Sullivan's Select.

But now I couldn't eat. I couldn't drink. I couldn't sleep. There were no easy ways to modify my moods.

And I *did* still have moods. In fact, I remember reading once that "mood" was one of the definitions of human consciousness: a feeling, a tone, a flavor—pick your metaphor—associated with one's current self-awareness.

But now I was wicked pissed—"wicked pissed," that's what one of my friends liked to say whenever he was angry; he liked the sound of it. And it certainly had enough harshness associated with it to do justice to my feelings.

So, what was I supposed to do? Maybe I should learn meditation—after all, there are supposed to be time-honored techniques for achieving inner peace without recourse to chemical stimulants.

Except, of course, everything that affects our feelings, at least in our biological instantiation, *is* a chemical stimulant: dopamine, acetylcholine, serotonin, testosterone. But if you become an electrical machine instead of a chemical one, how do you mimic the effects of those substances? We were the first generation of transferred consciousnesses; there were still bugs to be worked out.

It was raining outside, a cold relentless rain. But that wasn't going to have an effect on me; I'd only be aware of the coolness as an abstract datum, and the rain would just roll off. I went out the front door and started down the walkway that led to the street. The sound of fat drops hitting my head beat out an irritating tattoo.

Of course, no one else was walking in our neighborhood, although a few cars did pass by. There were earthworms out on the sidewalk. I remembered their distinctive smell from my childhood—funny how little walking in the rain we do as we get older—but my new olfactory sensors weren't responsive to that particular molecular key.

I continued along, trying to get some perspective on what had happened, trying to rein in my anger. There had to be some way to get rid of it. Think happy thoughts: isn't that what you're supposed to do? I thought about an old Frantics comedy routine I usually enjoyed, and about naked women, and about the perfect *crack* of the bat when you hit the ball just right, and—

And the anger was gone.

Gone.

Like I'd thrown a switch. Somehow, I'd dismissed the bad feelings. *Astonishing.* I wondered what thought, what mental configuration, had produced this effect, and whether I could possibly ever reproduce it again.

As I continued to walk along, my stride was the same as before—perfect, measured. But I *felt* as though there was a spring in my step—metaphorically, beyond the shock-absorbing coils in my legs.

Still, if there was some combination that could turn off anger at will, was there another that could turn on happiness, turn off sadness, turn on giddiness, turn off . . .

The thought hit like a fist.

Turn *off* love.

Not that I wanted to turn off my feelings for Karen—not at all! But somewhere, in the patterns that had been copied from the old me, there were still feelings for Rebecca, and they still hurt because she didn't reciprocate them.

If only I could find the switch to shut off *those* emotions, to put an end to that pain.

If only.

The rain continued to fall.

CHAPTER 34

I stood at the back of the central aisle of the moonbus, and looked at my three hostages—damn, I hated that word!

"Honestly," I said, "I don't want to hurt anyone."

"But you will if you have to," said Brian Hades. "That's what you told Smythe."

"Smythe won't let it go that far," I said. "I know he won't."

But Hades shook his head, his white hair glinting in the recessed roof lighting. "He *has* to let it go that far. Immortex has hundreds of billions invested in this uploading technology—and it's all predicated on the assumption that the durable copy becomes the real you. We can't let that . . . that *conceit* . . . be successfully challenged. Not by you here, and not by anyone down there on Earth. Fortunes are at stake. *Lives*—uploaded lives—are at stake."

Hades got up out of his chair, but he seemed just to be stretching his long legs. He glanced at Akiko and Chloë, then turned back to me. "Look, there's no law up here—no police, no governments. So you haven't committed a crime. And I heard what Smythe said—there are extenuating circumstances. Your surgery—"

"Bet you wish you'd had me killed on the operating table!"

Hades spread his arms. "It's not your fault," he said. "You're not responsible. Just give me the piton gun, and walk away from this. Immortex won't do anything to you; there'll be no repercussions. You can end this right now."

"I can't do that," I said. "I'd like to, but I don't know any other way to get what I want—what I *deserve*."

"God, you are *so* selfish," said Akiko. "I can't believe they picked you."

I felt my eyes narrowing. "Picked me? Picked me for what?"

But Akiko ignored that. "What about us? Look at what you're doing to us!"

"They're not going to force a situation in which people might get hurt," I said.

"No?" said Akiko. "How long do you think they'll let you hold all of High Eden hostage? How long before the other residents start to panic? They have to put an end to this."

"It's going to be fine," I said. "I promise."

Now Chloë was speaking: "You promise? What the hell is *that* worth?"

I moved a bit closer to the two women; I so wanted to calm them, to reassure them.

Suddenly, Hades leapt. It's a myth that people move in slow motion on the moon: objects *fall* in slow motion, but if you kick off the floor with all your strength, you'll go flying like a bat out of Philadelphia. Hades was five meters away, but his leap easily carried him that distance, and when he collided with me, I went flying backwards, ramming against the moonbus's rear bulkhead.

Suddenly, the two women were in motion, as well. Akiko was out of her chair and also leaping toward us. Chloë grabbed a metal equipment case and came bounding at us, looking as though she intended to brain me with it.

I still had the gun held tightly in my right hand. But Hades had pinned that arm against the bulkhead, keeping me from getting a shot at him or either of the women.

Desperate times call for desperate deeds . . .

I swiveled my wrist as much as I could and fired a piton. Here, in the cabin, the report of the gun was deafening. Almost instantly, the piton hit its target. I'd wanted to just drill a hole through the outer hull, but I hadn't been able to aim well. The piton hit a window, going through the vinyl shade in front of it as if it were tissue paper, and breaking the glass beyond. Air started hissing out of the cabin, and a *whoop-whoop-whoop* alarm began to sound. The shade, with a small hole in it was puckering outward. From the sounds of it, the tempered glass behind it had shattered completely, and the only thing that was keeping the atmosphere from rushing out in a torrent was the little hole in the shade that it had to go through.

We were all looking at the vinyl shade now, watching it bow outward more and more. Any moment now, it would be torn loose by the rush of escaping atmosphere, exposing the whole empty window pane; when that happened, the cabin would lose all its air in a matter of seconds.

Hades looked totally furious, and his pony tail was whipping out horizontally behind his head in the breeze. He still wanted to keep me pinned, but he knew if he didn't do something soon, we'd all die. With a frustrated shout of "Damn it!" he let go of me and called to the women, "Hurry! Find stuff to cover the window with!"

The vinyl shade was visibly tearing at its edges, and air was pouring out even more rapidly. Chloë, momentarily hesitating between beating me to death with the metal box she was holding and saving herself, dropped the box, which obligingly fell in slo-mo before clanking against the floor and bouncing up half a meter, then falling again. She moved over to the nearest chair, and tried pulling up the seat cushion—but, of course, moonbuses never flew over water; their cushions weren't removable flotation devices.

Akiko, meanwhile, had gone for the first-aid kit, hanging on the wall next to the entrance to the cockpit. She scrambled to get it open, and found a package of gauze. It was doubtless less solid than she'd have liked, but she rammed some of it into the hole in the vinyl shield.

But, although the roar of escaping air diminished somewhat, that didn't do anything for the fact that the vinyl was still tearing loose at its edges. I thought about getting everybody to cram into the cockpit; the door to it looked airtight. Indeed, Hades had already gone in there. For a moment, I was afraid he was going to lock the door shut behind him, saving himself while leaving us to suffocate. But he emerged a moment later—with a large, laminated moon map! He rushed to the window, and—just as the vinyl blind blew out—spread out the map, and held it as tightly as he could against the curving bulkhead. It was being sucked up against the wall, but the fit wasn't exact; air kept hissing out.

Akiko found adhesive tape in the first-aid kit, and started sealing the edges around the map. Meanwhile, I got all the tubes of suit-repair goop, and tossed them to Chloë, who started squirting that around the map's edges, too. Hades still had his arms spread out, holding the map.

The videophone was signaling an incoming call. God knows how long it had been doing that; until the roar of escaping atmosphere abated, we couldn't have heard it. Keeping the piton gun leveled at Hades's back, I moved over and accepted the call. "Sullivan."

"Mr. Sullivan, my God, is everyone all right?" It was Smythe's voice, panic edging the cultured tones.

Chloë had almost finished sealing the edges of the map. Hades relaxed his crucifixion pose, and turned around to face me. His gray eyebrows went up as he saw the gun aimed directly at his heart.

"Yes," I said. "Everything's fine . . . for the moment. We, ah, sprung a leak."

Another voice—one I knew—came on. "Jacob, this is Quentin Ashburn. You're still plugged into High Eden's life-support system. It's not designed to rapidly repressurize a moonbus, but your air pressure should return to normal in about an hour, assuming the leak is contained."

I looked past Hades. Chloë had finished, and the map seemed to be holding in place. "It is," I said.

I heard Quentin exhaling noisily. "Good."

Smythe came back on the line. "What in God's name happened?"

"Your Mr. Hades tried to rush me, and I had to fire my gun."

There was silence for a time. "Oh," said Smythe at last. "Is—is Brian all right?"

"Yes, yes, everyone's fine. But I hope you know now that I do mean business. What the hell's happening with getting the other me up here?"

"We're still trying to reach him. He's not at his home in Toronto."

"He's got a cell phone, for Christ's sake. The number is—" and I recited it.

"We'll try that," said Smythe.

"Do that," I said, rubbing my temples. "The clock is ticking."

CHAPTer 35

Maria Lopez rose to give the defendant's closing argument on behalf of Tyler Horowitz. She bowed politely to Judge Herrington, then turned to face the six jurors and the alternate.

"The question here, ladies and gentlemen, is simple: what constitutes personal identity? There's clearly more to it than mere biometrics. We've seen that anyone can impersonate someone else, with the appropriate technology. But we understand in our beating hearts that there's something ineffable about being a person, something that goes beyond physical measurement, something that makes each of us uniquely ourselves." She pointed with an outstretched arm at Karen, dressed today in a gray pantsuit. "This robot—this thing!—would have us believe that just because it mimics certain physical parameters of the dear, departed Karen Bessarian, that it *is* in fact Ms. Bessarian.

"But it isn't. Through her writing, the real Karen Bessarian gave joy to hundreds of millions of people so, of course, we don't want to see that beloved storyteller go. But she *has* gone; she has passed from this existence. We will mourn her, we will always remember her, but we must also have the strength that her son, who loved her more than anyone, has so admirably demonstrated: the strength to let her, as the tombstone she has been denied might have so elegantly put it, rest in peace.

"The departed Karen Bessarian was the original—and humans have always put a special value on originals, on first printings, on real paintings. Counterfeit money, forged passports: they're *not* the real thing, and they should never be accorded the status of reality. You good men and women of the jury have the power here to put a stop to this nonsense, to halt this notion that a human being is nothing more than *data* that can be copied as easily as one copies a song or a photograph. We are more than that. You know it, and I know it: let's make sure the whole world knows it.

"Perhaps you agree with Dr. Poe, the philosopher we heard from, that the thing sitting over there isn't a person at all but rather a zombie. Or perhaps you think that it *is* a person." Lopez shrugged. "Maybe it is. But, even if it is, it's emphatically not Karen Bessarian; it's someone else, some new creation. Welcome it as such, if you so choose—but don't let it masquerade as someone it's not. The late, lamented Karen Bessarian deserves better than that.

"The Declaration of Independence contains some of the greatest words ever written." Lopez closed her eyes for a moment, and when she opened them, her voice was full of reverence and wonder: " 'We hold these truths to be self-evident, that all men are created equal, that they are endowed by their Creator with certain unalienable Rights, that among these are Life, Liberty, and the pursuit of Happiness.' "

She paused, letting the words sink in, then exclaimed: "Endowed by their Creator! And the word 'Creator,' dear jurors, is written with a capital C—surely meaning God, not some factory in Toronto! 'Unalienable rights'—or inalienable, the way we usually say it today, and which means precisely the same thing: rights that cannot be transferred. Such was the intent of the great, great men who wrote and signed this Declaration—luminaries such as Benjamin Franklin and Thomas Jefferson. I ask you today to honor these great men by hewing to their wisdom.

"A different physical entity—a different instantiation, to use the jargon—cannot possibly be the same person. Mr. Draper made a mockery of the Christian tradition with his cheap shots, but when Jesus Christ rose from the dead, the Bible tells us he did so bodily: the exact same physical form, coming back to life, not some new, separate entity. Indeed, we label deranged anyone who thinks they are Jesus, or any other dead person, because merely aping the behavior of someone does not make you that person. Without the same body, you're not the same individual.

"We're not talking about whether artificial intelligences created from scratch should be accorded the rights of personhood; that's a battle for another day, if anyone ever manages to make such a thing. No, what's on the table here is whether tricks of science—high-tech smoke and mirrors—should allow someone to play games with life and death. And I say no, resoundingly no.

"In this great state of Michigan, we rejected the claims of the depraved Jack Kevorkian that he should be able to move the line between life and death at his whim; you stood up against such nonsense fifty years ago, and now fate has called again upon the good people of Michigan to be the voice of reason, the conscience of a nation.

"We have drawn firm lines in this country: life beings when we cease to be potentially multiple individuals, and it ends with the cessation of biological activity in the brain. No one should be allowed to circumvent these rules for reasons of"—and here she looked directly at Karen—"personal convenience, or personal gain. Stop the madness here, ladies and gentlemen. Rule for Tyler. It's the right thing to do. Because, after all, if you don't find that Karen Bessarian died, do you not make a mockery of her life? That woman struggled, loved, gave birth, fought cancer, created art, laughed, cried, felt joy, felt sorrow. If we refuse to recognize that she died do we not also refuse to recognize that she lived?

"Don't deny her reality. Don't deny Karen Bessarian's life and death. And, most of all, don't deny her grieving son the chance to lay her to rest. Thank you."

The jury was visibly moved by Lopez's words. I'd seen two of the women and one of the men nodding repeatedly, and, although Herrington had quickly stopped it with a sharp rap of his gavel, the two men had conferred briefly once Lopez was finished.

Deshawn Draper was wearing a white rose in his lapel today, apparently a little ritual of his when giving closing arguments. "The lawyer for the defendant," he began, nodding at Maria Lopez, "made much of the Declaration of Independence. Not, you'll note, of the U.S. Constitution or the Bill of Rights, which are the documents that actually form the basis of law in this country. Ms. Lopez could not invoke those hallowed souls the 'Founding Fathers,' or the 'Framers of the Constitution,' because those terms don't apply to the authors of the Declaration of Independence, which was written more than a decade before the Constitution.

"Indeed, it's getting on to three hundred years since the Declaration was signed, and, unlike the Constitution, of which we jurists minutely examine each and every word and nuance, we've all come to recognize that the Declaration is an artifact of its times—a litany of long-ago grievances against George III, then-king of Great Britain.

"No, we must filter the Declaration through our modern sensibilities. For instance, when we hear the words 'All men are created equal,' we believe today—even if the authors of the Declaration back in the eighteenth century did not—that all *people*, not just men, are created equal; woman are just as much entitled to life, liberty, and the pursuit of happiness.

"More: when Jefferson signed that document, by men, he meant *white* men. Blacks like me were not men in his eyes; after all, he owned slaves, and therefore was directly responsible for denying them their liberty. No, it's not to the Declaration that we should look for answers; indeed, I'm sure the judge will instruct you that the Declaration of Independence has no judicial weight.

"But I *do* believe history has much to teach us. So, let me invoke another set

of great words from our past that comment on the issue of personhood."
Deshawn's voice rang out, in a credible imitation of the original. "'I have a
dream that one day this nation will rise up and live out the true meaning of its
creed: we hold these truths to be self-evident, that all men are created equal. I
have a dream that my four little children will one day live in a nation where
they will not be judged by the color of their skin but by the content of their
character.'"

Deshawn smiled at each juror in turn. *"That* is what should count! The content of one's character. And, as we have shown, the content of the plaintiff's
character is *identical* to that of the biological original.

"Still, we would be wrong to dwell too much on the past—for what we
have here is a question of the future. The Mindscan process that Karen Bessarian has gone through was hugely expensive . . . but all new techniques are.
None of you on the jury are over sixty years of age, and several of you are
much younger. By the time you are facing the difficult decisions that Karen
Bessarian recently had to face, uploading will be inexpensive—it'll be an
option available to *you*. Don't close that door. Your life can continue, just as
Karen Bessarian's has.

"The woman sitting over there—and she is a woman, in every sense of the
word—*is* Karen Bessarian, to the very life. She remembers being a little girl in
the 1960s in Georgia. She remembers her first kiss in the 1970s. She remembers
giving birth to her son Tyler, there, and feeding him at her breast. She remembers the thrill of seeing her first book published. There's a concept in the law
known as *scienter*—it refers to the knowledge that a person possesses, the
awareness. This Karen Bessarian has the knowledge of the original; she *is* the
same person.

"More than that, she has the same feelings, the same hopes, the same aspi-
rations, the same creativity, and the same desires she always did. And you
should give considerable weight to her desires—for this is *exactly* what she
wanted. The biological Karen Bessarian intended for this continuation to be
the real her, to control her assets, to live in her house, to go on enjoying her
life, to continue telling stories of the characters the whole world loves. *That's*
what Karen Bessarian wants: it's her decision, and it hurts no one except greedy
relatives. Who are we to gainsay it?

"When you retire to deliberate, you'll hold not just Karen Bessarian's fate in
your hands, but that of everyone else like her, including"—suddenly he was
pointing at me—"that man there, Karen's boyfriend Jake." He shifted his aim

slightly. "And that man, next to him, my own father—an upload whom I accept with every fiber of my being as being my dad.

"What will happen to these warm, loving, caring people if you rule for the defendant? If you believe that the woman over there is not Karen Bessarian, then she will have *nothing*. No money, no reputation, no identity, and no rights. Do we want to go back to the days when there were people among us without rights? Do we want to return to the days of yore, when the definition of who was endowed with rights was narrow—men, not women, and only white men at that?

"No, of course not. We live in an enlightened present, and want to make an even better tomorrow." He walked over to the plaintiff's table and put his hand on Karen's shoulder; Karen brought her hand up and interlaced her fingers with his. "Do the forward-thinking thing," continued Deshawn. "Do the moral thing. Do the correct thing. Recognize that this woman is Karen Bessarian. Because, ladies and gentlemen, as you've surely seen during these proceedings, she truly *is*."

CHAPTER 36

Deshawn thought the jury would deliberate for four days. The jury consultant he'd hired was estimating a full week, and the commentator on Court TV opined it would be at least eight days. Karen and I went back to her mansion and tried to keep our minds occupied by anything but worrying about the verdict. We were both sitting in her living room—we'd decided we liked sitting, even though it wasn't necessary from a fatigue point of view; it just felt more natural. I was in that leather La-Z-Boy, and Karen was in an adjacent easy chair, trying to read a paper book. While reclined in the La-Z-Boy, I could clearly see what page she was on, and noticed she kept going back to re-read the same section. I guess her inner zombie was the only one able to pay attention while we waited.

I was watching highlights of the baseball games I'd missed on a small hand-held viewer, with the sound off—I could do the play-by-play at least as well as the paid commentator.

Suddenly—is there any other way for it?—my cell phone rang; my ring tone was the theme to *Hockey Night in Canada*. The device was sitting on Karen's coffee table. I brought the La-Z-Boy to the upright position, scooped up the phone, held it in front of my face, and looked at the small picture screen, which said "Audio Only," followed by "Long Distance." I've never been good at resisting the phone; Karen says she has no trouble completely ignoring it—I suppose celebrity would do that to you. I hit a key and brought the handset to my ear. "Hello?" There was silence; I thought no one was there. "Hello?" I said again. "Hell—"

"Hello," said a man's voice with a British accent. "May I please speak with Jacob John Sullivan?"

"You've got him . . . Hello? Hello? Is there—"

"Good, excellent. Mr. Sullivan, my name is Gabriel Smythe. I work for Immortex."

"What can I do for you, Mr. Smythe. . . . Mr. Smythe . . . Hello? Hello?"

"I apologize for the delays, Mr. Sullivan. You see, I'm calling you from the moon—"

"The moon!" I saw Karen react in surprise. "Is this about—"

"—in fact, from Heaviside Crater, on Lunar Far—yes, yes, this is about the original you. As I was saying—"

"What about him?"

"I'm at Heaviside, the facility—please, Mr. Sullivan, it's very difficult talking with these delays. Perhaps if we each said 'over' when we're done. Over."

Well, I'd always wanted to do that. "That's fine. Over."

Silence, then: "There, that's better. Now, as I was saying, I'm at Heaviside, at the facility our brochures call High Eden. Mr. Sullivan, it's about your original here. He's—"

"He's passed on?" I hadn't expected to be directly informed. Karen placed a soothing hand on my arm. "I, ah, don't want to—"

"—taken three people hostage, and—what? No, he hasn't passed on. Please, wait for me to say 'over.' He's taken three people hostage—"

"Hostages! That's impossible. Are you sure—"

"—and barricaded himself inside a moonbus, along with his captives, and— Please, Mr. Sullivan; we agreed you'd wait until I said 'over.' I haven't yet—"

"Sorry."

"—finished. Your original is demanding to talk with you. There, now: over."

Karen had moved in close so she could hear both sides of the conversation. Her green eyes were wide.

"Mr. Sulli—"

"Yes, I'm here. Sorry."

"—van? Are you there? Over."

"Yes, yes. I'm here. But, look, this is crazy. I know—I know *myself*. There's just no way on God's green Earth—or anywhere else, for that matter—that I'd ever do something like taking hostages." Silence, then I remembered: "Over."

Karen and I exchanged anguished looks while the seconds past, then: "Yes, we understand that. But—um, perhaps you know this? They found a cure for your . . . for *his* condition. Over."

"Really? Wow. No, I had no idea. That's . . . well, that's amazing. Um, over."

Silence, then: "We arranged for the procedure, of course. But there have been some after-effects of the surgery. The doctor who treated him theorizes that his neurotransmitters are temporarily out of whack, and rather severely so. It's making him paranoid and violent. Over."

"Can you fix that?"

More silence, while radio waves bridged worlds, then, even though I hadn't properly terminated my last sentence, the cultured British voice came on again. "Surely—if we can get him into treatment, he'll be fine. But right now, as I said, he's holding three people hostage in a moonbus. And he's demanding his rights of personhood back. Of course, we—"

"He's *what?*"

"—explained to him why that was impossible. There's simply no legal procedure to allow . . . *repatriation* I suppose would be the word . . . to allow repatriation of personhood. Anyway, we need your help, Mr. Sullivan. We need you to come here, to Heaviside, to parlay with him. Over."

"Come to the moon? I've never even been to Europe, for God's sake, and you want me to come to the moon? Uh, over."

The maddening delay, then: "Yes. Right away. You're the only one he'll talk to. There's far more than just the three lives at stake; if he explodes the moonbus's fuel, he'll kill almost everyone here at High Eden. Over."

"Well, put him on the phone. There's no need for me to go all the way to the moon. Over."

There was silence even longer than the speed of light required. "Umm, we, ah—we tried a deception earlier, in hopes of expeditiously resolving matters. It didn't work. He won't believe he's talking to the real you unless he can see you face to face and speak to you directly. Over."

"Christ. I—I have no idea how to go about arranging such a trip. Over."

"We'll take care of all of that. You are in Toronto, right? We can have—"

"No, no. I'm in Detroit, not Toronto."

"—a driver at your door, and—oh. Detroit. Okay, we can still do this. We'll have a driver at your door within the hour to take you to Metropolitan Airport. From there, we'll fly you to Orlando, and from Orlando we'll have a small jet standing by to transfer you directly to the Kennedy Space Center. We can get you on a cargo rocket—by luck, one's scheduled for launch six hours from now to bring medical supplies to High Eden. That's not unusual; there are a lot of complex, perishable pharmaceuticals that the residents here rely on, and that are only manufactured on Earth. Anyway, there's lots of residual cargo capacity that they were going to fill with gourmet foodstuffs, but we can get that offloaded to make room for you. Over."

"Um, I've got to think about this. Let me call you back. Over."

A pause, then: "It's complex ringing the moon. Please—"

"Then you call me back in thirty minutes. I need to think. Over—and out."

I'd had to let my . . . my *guests* . . . aboard the moonbus go to the washroom. I'd worried the first two times that they might get up to something in there, but it didn't seem there was anything that could be used to their advantage. The mirror above the small sink, for instance, was polished stainless steel, rather than glass. Still, I made them keep the door open while they used the facilities.

But soon enough I myself would have to go. There was no way I would back myself into a stall, but I'd also never been good at peeing in public. I guess I'd have to get them all to turn their backs while I did it into a jar or something . . . if I could find a jar. Of course, it would be even worse when I eventually had to defecate, since that was an exceedingly vulnerable posture. If only I—

The videophone bleeped. I went over to answer it.

"We've established contact with the other you," said Smythe, appearing on the small screen. "He's in Detroit."

"Detroit?" I said. I had the piton gun in my right hand, and gently swung it back and forth between Chloë, Akiko, and Hades . . . although Akiko was currently napping, so she probably didn't pose much of a threat. "What the hell would he be doing in Detroit?" And then it hit me. The trial—he must have been curious enough, for some reason, to go watch it. "Anyway," I said, before Smythe could reply, "what's he say?"

"He says we have to call him back in thirty minutes."

"Damn it, Smythe, if you're stalling—"

"We're not stalling. We should have an answer for you soon. So, please, please, for the love of God, don't do anything desperate."

Karen and I looked at each other. She was still holding her paper book aloft; it was effortless to do so, and unless she actually told her arm to drop down, it wouldn't.

For my part, I was sitting on the La-Z-Boy, but with it upright, the mechanisms within it and the mechanisms within me both tense.

"You've got to go," Karen said. "You've got to go to the moon."

"They don't need me. They need a professional. A hostage negotiator, or a . . ."

"Or a what? A sniper? Because that's what they'll send: not someone who can talk him out of it, but someone who can *take* him out."

Damn. All I'd ever wanted was what everyone else gets: a normal life—just a normal fucking life. "All right," I said at last. "I'll go."

"And I'm going, too," said Karen.

"Where?" I replied. "To Florida?"

Karen shook her head. "To the moon."

"I'm, ah, not sure they'd pay for that."

"I can afford it."

I was taken aback for a second—but she was right; she certainly could. Even if her bank accounts were never unfrozen, the advance from St. Martin's would more than cover it. "Are you sure you want to go?"

"Absolutely. God knows how long the jury deliberations will go on, and, anyway, they don't need me here just to read a verdict. So I have to wait an extra 1.5 seconds to find out what the verdict is up on the moon; I can live with that."

Karen got up, turned, and faced me. She put out her hands and I took them, and she effortlessly pulled me to my feet. Placing her head against my shoulder, she continued: "And, bluntly, I've got too much at risk to stay here. I love—I love talking with you, Jake. I love the way you play with ideas. But you're too quick to see the other person's perspective. I don't want you to be talked into shutting yourself off. The transfer was legal and binding: *you* are Jacob Sullivan. I don't want whatever's up there on the moon playing mind games with you. The people from Immortex only care about getting their hostages back. Your original, at least in his current medical state, apparently only cares about himself. There needs to be someone up there who cares about *you*."

I drew her even closer, hugged her, feeling the soft exterior and the hardness beneath. "Thank you."

"How long till they call you back?"

"I said thirty minutes, but I doubt they'll be that patient, and—"

As if on cue, the phone rang. I glanced down at the call display, which said "Long Distance" again. I'll say.

"Hello?" I said, after touching my cell's speakerphone button.

Two seconds of digital silence, then: "Mr. Sullivan, thank you for picking up. Sorry to ring you back so soon, but we really—"

"No, that's okay. I'll come."

"—need to have an answer from you. The situation up here is—you will? Brilliant! Brilliant! I'm delighted. We'll—"

"There's one condition. Karen Bessarian gets to come with me, too. Over."

Silence, then: "You mean the Mindscan version of her? Why? Her—um, well . . ."

"We know her original has passed on. But she's my friend, and I want her with me. Over."

"Mr. Sullivan, I'm not authorized—"

"I'll pay for it myself," said Karen.

"—to make arrangements for anyone else. This is going to be—what's that? Well, if you'll cover the costs; I assume that's Ms. Bessarian speaking. But I warn you, ma'am, we're planning to use an express rocket; an extra fifty kilograms will cost . . . Anna? Give me a sec . . . approximately six million dollars. Over."

I smiled at Karen. "The six million dollar woman."

"No problem," she said.

"Well . . . all right, then," replied Smythe. "All right. But, again, we're using an express cargo rocket—fastest way to get here. They're uncrewed, and not designed for passengers. It won't be a comfortable trip. Over."

"What is comfort, anyway?" said Karen. "Neither of us need padded chairs. We're *aware* of the temperature, but indifferent to it. How long will the trip take?"

"You have to say, 'Over,'" I added helpfully.

"Um, over," said Karen.

The time lag, then: "Twelve hours."

Karen snorted—something I wasn't aware we could still do. "I've spent longer on airplane flights."

"Then it's settled," I said. "We'll go. You said you'd send a car for us? Over."

"Will do. What's the address there?"

Karen told him.

"Great," said Smythe. "We'll get it all arranged. You're on your way to the moon."

On my way to the moon . . .

I shook my head.

On my way to the fucking moon.

CHAPTER 37

The videophone in the moonbus bleeped again. "All right," said Gabriel Smythe, as soon as I'd answered. "All right. He's on his way. Jacob Sullivan is on his way here."

"By cargo rocket?" I asked.

"He will be, yes. He's *en route* to Florida now."

"When will he be here?"

"In fourteen hours."

"Well, then, there's not much for us to do until he gets here, is there?" I said.

"You can see that we're cooperating," said Smythe. "We're doing everything we can to help you. But fourteen hours is a long time. You'll have to sleep."

"I don't think so. I can still pull an all-nighter when need be. And I've taken some pills. Ask Dr. Ng. I told her I was suffering from extreme drowsiness; she gave me some uppers."

"Still," said Smythe, "things can only get more complex in fourteen hours. And three detainees is a lot to manage. Do you think you could see yourself clear to letting one of them go? A show of good faith, perhaps?"

I thought about this. Strictly speaking, I perhaps didn't need any hostages—after all, I could take out the whole of High Eden just by blowing up the moonbus. And Smythe was right: three *was* a lot of people to control. But I didn't want to change any parameters. "I don't think so," I said.

"Come now, Jake. It's going to be a lot easier for you if you only have to worry about two other people. Or one . . ."

"Don't press your luck, Gabe," I said.

"All right, all right. But surely you can let one hostage go?"

Damn it, three *was* a lot to look after. Plus, soon enough, I'd have to feed them . . .

"You probably want Brian Hades," I said. "You can't have him."

"We'll gratefully accept anyone you care to send out, Jake. Your choice."

I looked around at my crew. Hades had a defiant expression on his round face. Chloë Hansen looked terrified; I wanted to say some soothing words to her. I shut off the phone.

"What about you?" I said to Akiko Uchiyama. "You want to go?"

"You want me to beg?" she said. "Fuck you."

I was taken aback. "I—I'm not trying to be mean here."

"You're fucking us over, you son of a bitch. Not to mention everyone who cares about us."

"I was going to let you go."

"*Was.* The benevolent tyrant."

"No, I mean if you—"

"Let me go. Or don't let me go. But don't expect me to fucking *thank you* for it."

"All right," I said. "You can go. Cycle through the airlock."

Akiko looked at me for a second, no change in her facial expression.

"But when you get back home," I added, "wash your mouth out with soap."

She got up from the chair she'd been sitting in and headed for the airlock. I watched her cycle through, then went back to the videophone. "Smythe," I said.

There was a pause. "Smythe's not here just now," said the voice of the female traffic controller.

"Where the hell is he?"

"The washroom."

Lucky bastard—although I wondered if that was really true, or if they were playing more mind games with me. "Well, tell him I've just sent him a present."

The rocket's cargo hold was cylindrical, about three meters long, and a meter in diameter. It made steerage look elegant.

"How, um, how do you want to be arranged?" asked Jesus Martinez, the muscular, bald man who was overseeing the loading of cargo.

I looked at Karen. She raised her eyebrows, leaving it to me. "Face to face," I said. "There's no window, so it's not like there'll be anything to look at."

"There's no light, either," said Jesus. "Not once the hatches are sealed."

"Can't you throw in some glowsticks?" I said. "Luciferin, something like that?"

"I suppose," said Jesus. "But every gram costs money."

"Put it on my tab," said Karen.

Jesus nodded. "Whatever you say, Mrs. Bessarian." He told a man standing near him to go get the glowsticks, then, turning back to us: "You realize we'll have to strap you in for the first hour, while you're undergoing steady acceleration—although you can undo the straps later if you like. As you can

262   ROBERT J. SAWYER

see, we've already lined the chamber with padding. Your bodies are durable, but the launch will be rough."

"That's okay," I said.

"All right," said the man. "We're at T-minus sixteen minutes. Let's get you in there."

I entered the vertical cylinder of the hold, and positioned myself against the far curving wall. I then opened my arms, inviting Karen to step into them. She did so, and she slipped her arms around me. Why shouldn't we travel hugging each other? It wasn't as if our limbs were going to get tired.

Jesus and two assistants worked on positioning us just right, and then they strapped us in. "Guys like you—artificial bodies—might be the future of manned spaceflight," Jesus said as he worked. "No life support, no need to worry about prolonged exposure to high gees."

The person Jesus had dispatched appeared a few minutes later, clutching some glowsticks. "These are good for four hours a piece," he said, breaking one open now, shaking it up, and letting the—green, I guess that was also a shade of green—light fill the chamber. "You guys have normal night vision?"

"Better than normal," I said.

"Then one stick should be plenty to have going at a time, but here are the others." He put them in a webbed storage pouch attached to the inner curving wall, where Karen could easily reach them.

"Oh, and one more thing," said Jesus. He handed me something I hadn't seen in a long time.

"A newspaper?" I said.

"Today's *New York Times,*" he replied. "Well, the front section, anyway. They do a thousand hardcopies every day, still on paper, for deposit at the Library of Congress, and for a few eccentric old subscribers who are willing to pay over a thousand bucks for a printed copy."

"Yes," I said. "I've heard about that. But what's it for?"

"Instructions came through from the folks up on the moon. This'll help prove that you came from Earth today; there's no other way, except by express rocket, that a copy of this could get to the moon in the next twelve hours."

"Ah," I said.

Jesus wedged the newspaper into another storage pouch. "All set?" he asked. I nodded.

"Yes," said Karen.

He smiled. "My advice: don't talk about politics, religion, or sex. No point having an argument when neither of you can get away from the other." And with that, he swung the curved door shut, sealing us in.

"Are you okay?" I said to Karen. My artificial eyes adjusted to semi-darkness faster than my biological ones had; another difference, I suppose, between an electronic and a chemical reaction.

"I'm fine," she said, and she sounded sincere.

"Say, have you been to space before?"

"No, although I always wanted to go. But by the time they started having significant space tourism, I was already in my sixties, and my doctor advised against it." A pause. "It's nice not to have to worry about such things anymore."

"Twelve hours," I said. "It's going to seem like forever, not being able to sleep. And I can't even relax emotionally. I mean, what the hell is going on up there, on the moon?"

"They've cured the other you's condition. If you hadn't had that condition, that . . ."

I moved my head slightly. "That birth defect. Might as well call a spade a spade."

"Well, if you hadn't had that, you wouldn't have uploaded this early in life."

"I—forgive me, Karen, I'm not criticizing your choice, but, well, if I hadn't had that birth defect, I don't know that I would have *ever* uploaded. I wasn't looking to cheat death. I just didn't want to be cheated out of a normal life."

"I didn't much think about living forever when I was your age," said Karen. And then her body shifted slightly, as if squirming a bit. "I'm sorry; I shouldn't use that phrase, should I? I mean, I don't want to make you feel uncomfortable about our age gap. But it's true. When you've got decades ahead of you, that seems like a long time. It's all relative. Have you ever read Ray Bradbury?"

"Who?"

"Sigh." She said the word, rather than made the sound. "He was one of my favorite writers when I was growing up. One of his stories begins with him— or his character; as a writer I should know better than to conflate author and character—reflecting on being a school kid. He says, 'Imagine a summer that would never end.' A kid's summer off school! Just two short months, but it does seem like forever when you're young. But when you get into your eighties, and the doctor tells you that you've got only a few years left, then years, and even decades, don't seem like enough time to do all the things you want to do."

"Well, I—*Kee-ryst!*"

The engines were firing. Karen and I were pressed down hard, toward the floor of the cargo chamber. The roar of the rocket was too great to speak over, so we simply listened. Our artificial ears had cutoffs built in; the noise wasn't going to harm us. Still, the volume of it was incredible, and the shaking of the ship was brutal. After a short time, there was a great clanking as, I presumed, the rocket was released from its restraining bolts and allowed to start its upward journey. Karen and I were now ascending into orbit faster than any human beings ever had before.

I held tightly onto her, and she grasped me equally firmly. I became aware of those parts of my artificial anatomy that were missing sensors. I was sure I should be feeling my teeth rattle, but they weren't. And doubtless my back should have hurt as the nylon rings separating my titanium vertebrae were compressed, but there was no sensation associated with that, either.

But the roaring noise was inescapable, and there was a sense of great weight and pressure on me from above. It was getting warm, although not unduly so; the chamber was well-insulated. And everything was still bathed in the glow-stick's greenish light.

The roar of the engine continued for a full hour; massive amounts of fuel were being burned to put us on a fast-track to the moon. But finally the engine cut off, and everything was quiet and, for the first time, I understood what was meant by the phrase "deafening silence." The contrast was absolute—between the loudest sound my ears could register and *nothing*.

I could see Karen's face, centimeters from my own. It was in focus; artificial optics have more flexibility than do natural ones. She nodded, as if to indicate that she was okay, and we both enjoyed the silence a while longer.

But there was more to enjoy than just freedom from noise. Perhaps if I were still biological, I would have been immediately aware of it: food trying to come up my esophagus, an imbalance in my inner ear. I could well imagine that biological people often got sick under such circumstances. But for me, it was simply a matter of no longer registering the downward push from above. There wasn't much room to move around—but, then, I'm sure it had seemed to *Apollo* astronauts that they'd had hardly any room until the gravity disappeared. I undid the buckles on the restraining straps, pushed off the floor, and floated slowly the meter toward the ceiling.

Karen laughed with delight, moving effortlessly within the small space. "It's wonderful!"

"My God, it is!" I said, managing to get an arm up to stop my head from hitting the padded ceiling—although, I quickly realized, the terms ceiling and floor no longer had any meaning.

Karen managed to turn herself around—her synthetic body was shorter than mine, and, after all, she'd once upon a time been a ballet dancer: she knew how to execute complex moves. For my part, I managed to curl around the curving inner wall of the tube, becoming essentially perpendicular to my position at liftoff.

It was exhilarating. I thought about what the launch attendant had said: people with artificial bodies are perfect for space exploration. Perhaps he was right, and—

Something hit me in the face, soft, scrunchy.

"What the—?"

It took me a moment to make things out in the dim green light, especially since the glowstick was now on the far side of Karen, meaning her body was casting weird shadows across my field of view. The thing that had hit me in the face was Karen's shirt.

I looked down—across—over—up—at her.

"Come on, Jake," she said. "We may never have another chance like this."

I thought back to the one previous time we'd done this; with the stress of the trial, we hadn't tried again. "But—"

"We'll doubtless return home on a regular transport," Karen said, "full of other people. But right now, we've got an opportunity that may never happen again. Plus, unlike most people, we don't have to worry about getting bruised."

Her bra was flapping up toward me now, a seagull in our emerald twilight. It was . . . *stimulating*, watching her move as she bent and twisted, taking off her pants.

I caught her bra, wadded it up, and sent it on a trajectory that would get it out of the way, then began to remove my own shirt, which quickly billowed around me as its buttons were undone. My belt was next, a flat eel in the air. And then my pants joined Karen's, floating freely.

"All right," I said, to Karen. "Let's see if we can execute a docking maneuver . . ."

CHAPTEr 38

We had to strap in again ten hours later, as the rocket decelerated for a full sixty minutes. Although most manned flights to the moon apparently went to something called LS One, we were going to land directly at Heaviside Crater.

The landing was done by remote control and there was nothing for us to see; the cargo hold had no window. Still, I knew we were setting down on our tail fins; Jesus at Cape Kennedy had quipped, "In the way that God and Robert Heinlein meant you to," but I didn't get it.

It was near the end of the lunar day, which lasted, as I'm sure that Smythe guy would say, a fortnight. The surface temperature apparently was a little over 100 degrees Celsius—but it's a dry heat. According to Dr. Porter, whom Smythe had consulted about this, we could manage ten or fifteen minutes out in the heat, not to mention the ultraviolet radiation, before we'd have a problem; the lack of air, of course, was a nonissue for us.

The cargo rocket didn't have an airlock, just a hatch, but it was easy enough to open from the inside; the same safety rules that existed for refrigerators also seemed to apply to spaceships. I hinged the door outward, and the atmosphere that had been carried along with us escaped in a white cloud. We were inside Heaviside Crater, its rim rising up in the distance. The closest dome of High Eden was maybe a hundred meters away, and—

That must be it. The moonbus, a silvery brick with a blue-green fuel tank strapped to each side, sitting on a circular landing platform. It was attached to an adjacent building by a telescoping access tunnel.

The lunar surface was about twelve meters below my feet—far more than I'd want to fall under Earth's gravity, but it shouldn't be a problem here. I looked at Karen and smiled. There was no way for us to speak, since there was no air. But I mouthed the word "Geronimo!" as I stepped out of the hatchway.

The fall was gentle, and took what seemed like forever. When I hit—probably the first pair of Nikes ever to directly touch the lunar soil—a cloud of gray dust went up. Some of it stuck to my clothes (static electricity, I presumed), but the rest filtered back down to the ground.

There were little meteor craters everywhere within this bigger crater: some were a few centimeters across, others a few meters. I turned around and looked up at Karen.

For a woman who had been frail a short time ago, who had had one hip replaced and had doubtless lived in fear of breaking the other, she was quite gutsy. With no hesitation, she copied what I'd done, stepping out of the hatch and beginning the slow descent to the ground.

She was carrying something tubular . . . of course! She'd remembered to grab the front section of the *New York Times*, and now had it rolled into a cylinder. It was astonishing not to see her hair billow upward, or her clothes ripple, but there was no air resistance to cause any of that. I took a few quick hopping steps to the right to give her plenty of room to land, and she did so, a big grin on her face.

The sky overhead was totally black. No stars were visible except the sun itself, which glowered fiercely. I reached out a hand, and Karen grasped it, and we took huge bouncing steps together, heading for High Eden, the place we were never supposed to see.

Gabriel Smythe turned out to be a compact man of perhaps sixty, with white-blond hair and a florid complexion. He had taken up residence in High Eden's transit-control room, which was a cramped space, dimly lit, full of monitor screens and glowing control panels. Through a wide window, we could see the moonbus, just twenty meters away, attached to the Jetway. It had coverings over all the windows I could see, preventing us from looking inside.

"Thank you for coming," Smythe said, pumping my hand. "Thank you."

I nodded. I didn't want to be here—at least not under these circumstances. But I felt a moral responsibility, I guess—although *I* hadn't done anything.

"And I see you brought the newspaper," continued Smythe. "Excellent! All right, there's a videophone connection between here and the moonbus. That's the microphone, and that's the camera pickup. He's covered all the security cameras inside the bus, but we can still see him through the phone's camera, when he deigns to transmit video, and he can see us. I'm going to call him now, and let him know you're here. He's being at least partially reasonable—he let one of the hostages go. Chandragupta says—"

"Chandragupta?" I repeated, startled. "Pandit Chandragupta?"

"Yes. Why?"

"What's he got to do with this?"

"He's the one who cured the other you," said Smythe.

I felt like slapping my forehead, but that would have been too theatrical. "Christ, of course! He's also the one who started this whole damn mess with the lawsuit. He issued a death certificate for the Karen Bessarian who died up here."

"Yes, yes. We saw. We've been watching the trial coverage, of course. Needless to say, we're not pleased. Anyway, he says your, um . . ."

"Skin," I said. "I know the slang. My shed skin."

"Right. He says your skin will have wildly fluctuating neurotransmitter levels in his brain for perhaps another couple of days. Sometimes he'll be quite rational, and sometimes he'll have a hair-trigger temper, or be totally paranoid."

"Christ," I said.

Smythe nodded. "Who'd have thought it'd be easier to copy a mind than to cure one? Anyway, remember, he's armed, and—"

"Armed?" Karen and I said in unison.

"Yes, yes. He's got a piton gun—it's for mountain climbing, and it shoots metal spikes. He could easily kill someone with it."

"My God . . ." I said.

"Indeed," said Smythe. "I'll get him on the phone. Don't promise him anything we can't deliver, and do your best not to upset him. Okay?"

I nodded.

"Here goes." Smythe tapped some keys on a small keypad.

The phone bleeped a few times, then: "It better be good news, Gabe."

The picture on the screen showed the old me, all right: I'd forgotten how much gray I'd had in my hair. There was a wild look in his eyes that I don't think I'd ever seen before.

"It is, Jake," Gabe said. It was strange hearing him use my name but not be addressing me. "It's very good news indeed. Your—the other you is here, with me now, here, in the transit-control room at High Eden." He gestured for me to come into the camera's field of view, and I did so.

"Hello," I said, and my voice sounded mechanical, even to me. I'd forgotten how rich my real—my *original*—voice had been.

"Hmmph," said the other me. "Did you bring the newspaper?"

"Yes," I said. Karen, standing out of view, handed it to me. I held it up to the phone's lens, so he could read the date and see the main headline.

"I'll want to examine that later, of course, but for now, all right: I'll accept that a rocket really came from Earth today, and you might have been on it."

"Uncover the windows on the moonbus, and you'll see the rocket," I said.

"It's about a hundred meters away, and—let's see—it should be visible off your left side."

"And you've got a sniper, just waiting to pick me off if my face appears in the window."

Gabe loomed in. "Honestly, Jake," he said, "there are no snipers on the moon."

"Not unless one came with *him*," the other Jake said—gesturing at me. I had never heard myself sounding paranoid before. I didn't like it.

Gabe looked at me. He lifted his shoulders and white-blond eyebrows slightly.

"Jake," I said, gently, "you wanted to see me?"

The me on the monitor nodded. "But how do I know it's really you?"

"It's me."

"No. At best, it's *one* of us. But it could be *any* consciousness loaded into that body; just because the exterior looks like me doesn't mean that it's my Mindscan inside."

"So ask me a question," I said.

There were endless numbers of things he could have asked me, things only one of us could possibly know. The name of the imaginary friend I had when I was a kid, the one I never told anyone about. The one and only item I'd ever shoplifted, as a teenager—a handheld gaming unit I really wanted.

And I would have gladly answered those questions. But he didn't ask them. No, he picked the one I didn't want to answer. Whether it was because he perversely wanted to humiliate me, even though the revelation would presumably hurt him, too, or because he wanted to show me, so that I would convey to Smythe and the others, just how far he was willing to go, I couldn't tell.

"Exactly where," he asked, "were we when our father suffered brain damage?"

I looked at Karen, then back at the camera. "In his den."

"And what were we doing?"

"Jake . . ."

"You don't know, do you?"

Oh, I know. I know. "Come on, Jake," I said.

"Smythe, if this is another trick, I'll kill Hades—I swear it."

"Don't do that," I said. "I'll answer. I'll answer." I really did miss being able to take a deep, calming breath. "We were arguing with him."

"About what?"

"Come on, Jake. You've heard enough to know it's really me."

"About what?" demanded the other me.

I closed my eyes, and spoke softly, quickly, without opening them. "I'd been caught using a fake ID. We were shouting at each other, and he collapsed right in front of me. It was arguing with me that caused the hemorrhaging in his brain."

I felt Karen's hand alight on my shoulder. She squeezed gently.

"Well, well, well," said the other me. "Welcome to the moon, brother."

"I wish it was under better circumstances," I said, opening my eyes at last.

"So do I." He paused. "Who is that? The other upload?"

"A friend."

"Hmm. Oh, my—it's Karen, isn't it? I saw the new you on TV. Karen Bessarian."

"Hello, Jake," she said.

"You must know your skin has passed on—that came out during the trial, didn't it? What are you doing here?"

"I came with Jake," said Karen. "He's . . . we're . . ."

"What?"

I glanced over my shoulder at Karen. She shrugged at the camera a little, and said, simply, "We're lovers."

The biological me looked stunned. "What?"

"You can't picture it, can you?" said Karen. "A version of you with an old woman. You know, I remember when we met, at the sales pitch."

The other Jake seemed momentarily flustered, then: "Right. Of course you do."

"Age doesn't matter," said Karen. "Not for me. And not for Jake."

"I'm Jake," said the biological me.

"No, you're not. Not legally. Not any more than the woman who died here was me."

I could see Gabe and the others looking quite nervous, but nobody moved to stop Karen. And the other me actually looked pleased. "Let me get this straight: the two of you—Mindscan Karen and Mindscan Jake—are together, a couple?"

"That's right."

"So that means—that means, you, Jake, you aren't with Rebecca?"

I was surprised. "Rebecca? Rebecca *Chong?"*

"Do we know another Rebecca? Yes, of course, Rebecca Chong!"

"No, no. We, I—she . . . she didn't take well to my having uploaded. And, ah, neither did Clamhead—Rebecca is looking after her now."

An actual grin broke out on his face. "Excellent. Excellent." He looked at me, then at Karen, and practically laughed the words, "I hope the two of you will be very happy together."

"There's no need to mock us," said Karen sharply.

"Oh, I'm not, I'm not," said the original me, with glee. "I'm totally sincere." But then he sobered. "Still, I've been following your legal troubles, Karen. Maybe you'll both end up losing your rights of personhood."

"We're not going to lose," said Karen sharply. "My Jake hasn't just been a placeholder, looking after your life for you until you're ready to reclaim it. He's gone on, making his own life—with me. We're not going to backtrack."

The biological me seemed cowed by Karen's forcefulness. "I—um . . ."

"So, you see," snapped Karen, "it isn't just about you and what you want. My Jake has a life of his own now. New friends. New relationships."

"But I'm the *real* one."

"Bullshit," snapped Karen. "How would you ever back up that claim?"

"I'm the one with . . . the one who has—"

"What? A *soul*? You think this is about souls? There's no such thing as souls. You live as long as I have and you know that. You see people slipping away, day by day, year by year, until there's nothing left. Souls! Cartesian nonsense. There's no magic, airy-fairy insubstantial part of you. *Everything* you are is a physical process—processes that can be, and have been, flawlessly reproduced. You've got nothing—*nothing*—that this Jake doesn't. Souls? Give me a break!"

"You know that she's right," I said, gently. "You never believed in souls before. When Mom talked about Dad's soul still being in there, in that wrecked brain, you felt sorry for her not because of what had happened to Dad, but because she was *deluded*. That's the very word you thought; you know it and I know it. *Deluded.*"

"Yes, but—"

"But what?" I said. "You going to try to tell me it's different now? That you've had some sort of epiphany?"

"You—"

"If anyone should be seeing things differently," I said, "it's me. In fact, I *am*—I can see all colors now. And I know *nothing* is missing in me. My mind is a perfect—*perfect*—copy of yours."

"You wouldn't know if something is missing," he said.

"Of course he would," snapped Karen. "When you get older, you're painfully aware of things that are slipping away. Senses that are dulling, memories that can no longer be easily called up. You absolutely know when something you had before is missing."

"She's right," I said. "I am *totally* complete. And just as much as you do, I want my life."

CHAPTER 39

Two of me.

It was damned confusing, but I found myself thinking of him as Jacob, and me as Jake. It was one of those little mental tricks that we need more of as we get older. He was *Jacob*, with the *OB* at the end standing for "original body." And I was *Jake*, with the final *E* for "electronic."

I found that I, Jake, couldn't take my eyes off the videophone screen, and its image of Jacob, my shed skin. Until a few weeks ago, we'd been the same person, and . . .

And prior to that, I hadn't existed at all. He, Jacob, was the one who'd *really* had all the experiences I only thought I'd had. He was the one with the scar on his right arm from falling out of a tree at twelve, the one with the damaged ligaments in his left ankle from tumbling down some stairs, the one who'd had the arteriovenous malformation, the one who'd watched my father collapse, the one who'd made love with Rebecca, the one who'd actually seen the world with the limited palette our shared memories were painted in.

"I'm going to come over there," I said to the videophone.

"Over where?" replied Jacob.

"To the moonbus. To see you."

"No," Jacob said. "Don't do that. Stay where you are."

"Why?" I replied. "Because it's easier to deny my personhood, and my rights, when I'm just a bunch of pixels on a tiny display screen?"

"I'm not an idiot," Jacob said, "so don't treat me like one. I've got the situation contained. You coming out here will destabilize it."

"I really don't think you have a choice," I said.

"Sure I do. I don't have to open the airlock."

"All right," I said, conceding the point, "you can keep me out. But, come on, if you're only going to talk to me by phone, I might as well have never left Earth."

There was a pause, then Jacob said: "All right. Cards on the table, broski. You're here because I want you to agree to *stay* here, in my place."

274   ROBERT J. SAWYER

I was taken aback, but I'm sure nothing in my artificial physiology betrayed that. I said, as calmly as I could, "You know I can't do that."

"Hear me out," Jacob said, raising a hand. "I'm not asking for anything awful. Look, how long are you going to live?"

"I don't know," I said. "A long time."

"A *very* long time," he said. "Centuries, at least."

"Unless something bad happens, yes."

"And how long have I got left?"

"I don't know," I said.

"Sure you do," said Jacob. "I no longer suffer from Katerinsky's syndrome, so I've likely got as much time left as any male born in Canada in 2001—another fifty years, if I'm lucky. That's *everything* I've got left—and it's *nothing* to you. You'll have ten times that amount, a hundred times, maybe more. All I'm asking is you let me live out those fifty years—or less, and it could be a lot less—down on Earth."

"And—and what about me?"

"You stay here, at this wonderful resort of High Eden." He looked at me, searching for my reaction. "Spend fifty years having a holiday—Christ, let's be honest, that's what we do most of the time anyway, right? It's like the Vegas strip here, like the best cruise ship ever." He paused. "Look, I saw some of the trial coverage. I know it's not going well. Do you want to spend the next *x* number of years down there fighting legal battles, or do you want to just relax up here, and let all that get sorted out? You *know* eventually uploads will have full rights of personhood—why not just take a vacation here until that's the case, then return to Earth triumphant?"

I stared at him, at my . . . my *progenitor*. "I don't want to be unfair to you," I said slowly, "but . . ."

"Please," said the other me, an imploring note in his voice. "It's not that much to ask, is it? You *still* get immortality, and I get the handful of decades that I was being cheated out of."

I looked at Karen. She looked at me. I doubted either of us could read the other's expression. I turned back to the screen, thinking.

My mother would be happy; she'd never agree to upload herself, of course, not with her belief in souls, but this way she'd have her son back for the remainder of his life. And my father—well, I wasn't visiting him at all now. Jacob could go back to seeing him, dealing with all the mixed emotions, all the heartbreak, all the guilt. And by the time I returned to Earth, decades hence, my dad would be gone, too. Plus, if flesh-and-blood Jacob returned to Earth, Clamhead would be happy. Even, maybe, Rebecca would be happy.

I opened my artificial lips to reply, but, before I did so, Karen spoke up. "Absolutely not!" she said in that Southern-accented voice of hers. "I've got a life down on Earth, and there's no me left to return to there from here. I've got books I want to write, intellectual property I'm going to have to fight to protect, and places I want to go—and I want Jake with me."

She didn't indicate me in any way, but the simple use of my name as if there was only one entity it could possibly refer to made the other me frown. I let Karen's words hang in the air for a moment, then said into the camera, "You heard the lady. No deal."

"You don't want to push me," said Jacob.

"No, I don't. But I'm not going to keep talking like this, either. I'm coming over to the moonbus to see you. Face to face." I paused, then, with a nod, added, "Man to man."

"No," said the other me. "I won't let you in."

"Yes, you will," I said. "I know you."

CHAPTER 40

The telescoping Jetway leading to the moonbus was more solid than the ones that connect to airplanes—it had to be airtight, after all—but the overall appearance was similar. Once I'd reached its end, I was faced with a problem, though. The outer airlock door on the moonbus, set into the moonbus's silvery white hull, had a window in it, and that was uncovered. But the inner door, on the far side of the little chamber, had its own window, and that one was covered. I wasn't quite sure how to let the other me know that I'd arrived.

After standing there for half a minute, with what was doubtless a stupid expression on my face, I decided to simply knock on the outer airlock door, hoping the sound would be conducted within.

At last, the covering on the inner window was removed for a moment, and I saw the white-bearded, round face that I'd learned belonged to Brian Hades, the top Immortex official on the moon. I couldn't hear him, but he spoke to someone—presumably the other me—off to his left, and, a moment later, the outer airlock door clanged open. I stepped in, the outer door closed behind me, and a few seconds later the inner door opened, revealing the flesh-and-blood Jacob Sullivan, with a strange squat gun aimed squarely at where my heart would have been if I'd had one.

"I suppose that's one solution," I said, nodding at the gun. "If you get rid of me, there's no longer an issue about which of us is the real person, is there?"

He hadn't said anything yet, but the gun wavered a bit in his hand. The two hostages—Brian and a white woman—looked on.

"Still," I said, "you attended the Immortex sales conference. You must know that anything fired into my chest wouldn't likely do damage that Dr. Porter and his team couldn't set right. And my skull is titanium reinforced with a carbon-nanotube mesh. It's supposed to survive a fall out of an airplane even if the parachute doesn't open. I'd be mindful of the ricochet if you decide to shoot me in the head."

Jacob continued to look at me, and then, at last, he relaxed his grip on the gun. "Have a seat," he said.

"Actually," I said, "there's no need for me to sit anymore, since I don't get tired. So I'd prefer to stand."

"Well, *I'm* going to sit down," he said. He walked down the aisle and took the first of the passenger seats, the one just to the rear of the bulkhead that blocked off the cockpit. He then swiveled the chair around to face me, the gun still in his hand. Brian Hades, who had been looking on anxiously, was sitting in the second-last row, and the female hostage was sitting in another chair, eyes open so wide she looked like an animé character.

"So," I said, "how are we going to resolve this?"

Jacob replied, "You know me as well as I do. I'm not going to give up."

I shrugged a little. "I'm just as determined. And I'm in the right; after all, *I'm* not taking hostages. What you're doing is *wrong*. You know that." I paused. "We can all walk away from this. All you have to do is put down the gun."

I saw a hopeful expression pass over the woman's pretty face.

"I intend to put down the gun," Jacob said. "I intend to let the these people go—by the way, Jake, meet Brian Hades and . . . and . . ."

"You don't even remember my *name?*" said the woman. "You're ruining my life, and you don't even remember my name?"

I looked at her, and tried to make my face compassionate. "I'm Jake Sullivan," I said.

She didn't reply, and so I prodded: "And you are?"

"Chloë." She glared at Jacob. "Chloë Hansen."

Pleased to meet you didn't seem to be the right response—so I just nodded and turned back to look down on Jacob, seated in his swiveling chair. "Well?" I said.

"Look," Jacob replied, "I know, down deep, that you agree with me. You believe that biological life is more real. Let me have what I want."

I frowned. There was no point denying it. He was right; I *had* believed that. But that had been *before* I'd uploaded, before I . . . yes, damn it, yes: before I fell in love with Karen. I felt more alive with her than I'd ever felt. I looked at Jacob, wondering if I could make him understand that. Of course, he'd— *I'd*—loved Rebecca, but we hadn't ever allowed that love to blossom, to become a relationship.

"It's different now," I said. "My feelings have changed."

"Then we're at an impasse."

"Are we? You *will* eventually have to sleep."

He said nothing.

"Besides," I said, taking just the barest hint of a step forward, "I know your every weakness."

He'd been looking down at the floor for a moment—I think he *was* getting tired—but his head tilted up sharply at that.

"I know your every *psychological* weakness," I said.

"They're your weaknesses, too."

I nodded slowly. "So you'd think. But you know what I've learned, and you haven't, your poor feckless son of a bitch? I've learned that when you're in love, and someone loves you, *you have no weaknesses.* It doesn't matter what you've done in the past, it doesn't matter what you've felt in the darkest corners of your mind. Virgil said *amor vincit omnia*, and he was a pretty bright dead guy: love really does conquer all."

Suddenly, there was a bleeping sound. "What's that?" I asked.

"The videophone," said Jacob, pointing at the wall-mounted unit next to the airlock door. "Answer it."

I went over to the phone, found the answer button, and pressed it.

Smythe's face appeared on the screen. "Sorry to interrupt," he said. "But I think you'll want to hear this, too. There's a call coming in from Earth. It's Deshawn Draper. He says the jury is coming in, and—"

"Not now!" I snapped.

I turned back to Jacob, but I hadn't broken the connection. Smythe should still be able to hear everything, even if his field of view was limited. "There, Jacob, you see?" I said. "You've got my full attention. You're my number-one priority." I took a couple of steps toward him, trying to regain the territory I'd lost when I'd had to come back to answer the phone. "Let's end this peacefully, shall we?"

"Sure," said Jacob. "Just give me what I want."

"I can't. I have my own life. I have Karen." I didn't want to be cruel—really, I didn't. But he'd never seen as clearly as I did now: all the shades, all the colors, all the glory. "Besides, you wouldn't know what to do with our life back on Earth; you never have. You've *coasted*, living off family money. Christ's sake, Jacob, in many ways, you've been as disengaged from reality as Dad is. But I'm seeing now, I'm seeing it all. Life isn't about being alone; it's about being with someone."

"But there *is* someone," said Jacob. "There's Rebecca."

"Ah, yes. Rebecca. Would you like us to get her on the phone from Earth?"

"What? *No.*"

"Why? Ashamed of what you're doing? Afraid she'd never look at you the same way if she knew?"

Jacob shifted uneasily in his chair.

"'Cause I know what it's like to have her not look at you the same way. I went to see her after I uploaded. She couldn't look me in the eye; she scurried away every time I came near. She couldn't even say my name."

"That's you," he said.

"It'll be you, too, if she finds out about what you're doing here. You think she isn't going to ask what happened to the Mindscan me? You think she'll just forget about it?" I shook my head. "You can't win here; you just can't."

Jacob got slowly to his feet, but he didn't stand quite erect. "Are you all right?" I asked.

He was holding the gun in one hand, and was now rubbing the top of his head with the other.

"Jacob?" I said. He was wincing; I'd forgotten how much a flesh face could contort. "Jacob, my God . . ."

"You're part of it," he hissed through clenched teeth. "You're part of it, too."

"Part of what, Jacob? I just want to help—"

"You're lying! You're all out to get me."

"No," I said, as gently as I could. "No, we're not. Jacob, there's something wrong with your brain—but it's temporary."

Jacob swung his gun toward me; it had become like a prosthetic extension of him. "I'll kill you," he hissed.

I shrugged infinitesimally. "You can't."

"Then I'll kill them," he said, swinging the gun between Brian and Chloë.

"Jacob, no!" I said. "For God's sake—this isn't . . . isn't *us*. You know it isn't! It's an after-effect of the cure. Dr. Chandragupta can fix it. Let's just put the gun down, and we can all walk out through the airlock door."

He winced again, and doubled over a bit more. His voice was a sneer. "So they can cut into my head?"

"No, Jacob," I said. "Nothing like that. They'll just—"

"Shut up!" he shouted. "Just shut the fuck up!" He looked left and right. "I've had it with you. I've had it with all of you! You think you can talk me out of my *life?*"

I spread my arms in a placating gesture, but said nothing.

He winced again, and grunted. *"God . . ."*

"Jacob . . ." I said softly. "Please . . ."

"I can't give up," he said, as if the words were being torn from him. "There's no turning back now."

"Of course there is," I said. "Just stop what you're doing, and—"

But Jacob shook his head, lifted the gun, aimed it at Chloë's chest, and—

Whooooosh!

An enormous roar of air rushing out of—of the cockpit, behind the closed door just in front of where Jacob was standing. He wheeled around, and Chloë dove for cover behind a chair.

The door to the cockpit seemed to be air-tight; there was no danger, apparently of it rupturing, even if there was nothing now but hard vacuum on the other side. It wasn't a fancy sliding door; it was hinged, just like an airplane's cockpit door, and it seemed to be operated manually.

"Jacob," I said. "I'm not at risk if the cabin pressure blows—but you and your . . . your *guests* are. The three of you should crowd into the airlock, at least."

He made no response. I could see only whites in his eyes; sweat was beading on his forehead.

"In fact," I said, as gently as I could, "we all could just go *through* the air-lock, back into High Eden, and—"

"No!" It was more animal growl than word. "I'll kill—"

Another *whooooosh!*

Suddenly, to my absolute astonishment, the cockpit door was *swinging inward*, into the cabin. Incredible—with vacuum now on the other side, it would take enormous strength to push that door open. Chloë screamed, I think, but the scream was lost in the roar of escaping air. The door continued to open, and—

Oh, Jesus God!

And Karen Bessarian stepped into the cabin, her synthetic hair whipping backward in the wind caused by the evacuating atmosphere. As soon as she was fully inside, she let go of the cockpit door, and it slammed violently shut behind her.

Jacob swung to face her, brought up his piton gun, and fired straight into where Karen's stomach would have been. A metal spike shot into her body, but she kept moving forward, deliberate step after deliberate step.

Jacob fired again, this time aiming higher on her chest. Another spike tore into her breast, ripping plastiflesh, exposing silicone and silicon.

But Karen continued moving forward, and—

And Chloë crouched down like a cat, out of Jacob's view, then leapt, flying through the air, landing on Jacob's back, encircling his neck. Jacob fired another projectile, but this one missed—going through the cockpit door like it wasn't there, creating a two-centimeter hole through which air started pouring out again.

Jacob was undeterred. He aimed at Karen's head and squeezed off another shot. The spike hit her but ricocheted off her impenetrable skull. I instinctively followed the rebound of the spike, which smashed into the side bulkhead, lodging there without breaching it.

I swung my attention back to Karen—and opened my mouth in shock, instinctively trying to suck in breath. Her left eye socket was shattered, and the eye itself was gone. Blue metal was exposed beneath a ragged hole in her plastiskin, and some sort of yellow lubricant, like amber tears, was trickling down that side of her face.

But her voice, Georgia accent and all, was just fine. "Leave my boyfriend—and everyone else—alone," she said, still coming forward.

Brian Hades was getting into the act now. He leapt, soaring horizontally, ponytail flying, and tackled Jacob by the legs. Chloë disengaged from Jacob as he tumbled over, and she scurried away.

I was suddenly conscious of blood everywhere. It took me a moment to figure out what was happening: Jacob's nose had ruptured under the shift in air pressure, and twin geysers of crimson—God, but blood *is* bright red!—were squirting from his nostrils. Christ, if he hadn't been cured of Katerinsky's, the pressure shift probably would have killed him.

Jacob was now sprawled on the hard deck. Karen had closed the distance between him and her and was bending down. She grabbed his right wrist with her left hand, and grabbed the squat gun with her right hand. Jacob clearly didn't want to let it go, and—

And there was a *crack*, quite audible above the hiss of escaping atmosphere, and I realized that Karen had broken at least one bone in Jacob's hand as she yanked the gun from his grip. She looked at the gun with disgust and tossed it aside; it bounced high on the upholstery of one of the chairs, then fell back down in slow motion.

Jacob's hands came up, grabbing one of Karen's shins. I could see the excruciating look on his face as he did so; the broken bone in his right hand must be torturing him. But he pushed upward on Karen's shin with all his might, and, in lunar gravity, that was enough to let him toss her up and backward like a caber.

Suddenly he was scrambling to his feet and running for the gun. Brian crouched low and leapt, sailing down the cabin, colliding with Jacob, and the two of them tumbled down again. I surged forward, trying to help Brian, while Chloë ran past me going the other way. Brian made it to feet, and Jacob got up too, but he was ignoring Brian and instead had turned his attention to Chloë, who—

My nonexistent heart stopped for a second; I really think it did.

—who had picked up the gun and now fired it directly into the center of Jacob's chest.

Jacob's mouth went into one of those imperfect "O's" that biologicals make, and his defective, color-blind eyes went wide, and a new crimson stain joined the others already on his shirt, and he staggered backward, and—

Oh, God . . .

—and, in an exact repeat of what had happened to Dad, he fell back into one of the swivel chairs, and the chair rotated a half turn, and the Jacob John Sullivan born of man and woman was no more.

CHaPTer 41

"So, how did you do that?" I asked, after we'd left the moonbus, and all the hubbub had died down.

"Do what?" Karen said.

"Break into the cockpit. And then push the cockpit door open against all that air pressure."

"You know," said Karen, staring at me with her one intact eye.

"No, I don't."

"Didn't you select the super-strength option?"

"What? No."

Karen smiled. "Oh," she said. "Well, I did."

I nodded, impressed. "Remind me not to piss you off."

" 'Mr. McGee,' " said Karen, " 'don't make me angry. You wouldn't like me when I'm angry.' "

"What?"

"Sorry. Another TV program I have to show you."

"I'll look forward to—say! I cut off Deshawn. Do you know the verdict?"

"Oh, God!" said Karen. "I'd forgotten all about that. No, the jury was just coming in when he called; they hadn't read the verdict yet. Let's get him on the phone."

We had Smythe show us to the communications center, and we placed the call to Deshawn's cellular using a speaker phone so we could all hear. It turned out to be a complex process getting ahold of someone on Earth, involving actual human operators—I didn't know such things existed anymore. But at last Deshawn's phone was ringing.

"Deshawn Draper," he said, by way of greeting, then, after a second, "Hello? Is anybody—"

"Deshawn!" said Karen. "It's Karen, up on the moon—sorry about the time lag. What's the verdict?"

"Oh, so now you're interested?" said Deshawn, sounding a bit miffed.

"I'm sorry, Deshawn," I said. "A lot has gone down. The biological me is dead."

A pause, for more than just the speed of light. "Oh, my," said Deshawn. "I'm so sorry. You must—"

"The verdict!" exclaimed Karen. "What was the verdict?"

"—feel totally awful. I wish—Oh, the verdict? Guys, I'm sorry. We lost; Tyler won."

"God," said Karen. And then, more softly, "God . . ."

"Of course, we'll appeal," said Deshawn. "My dad's already hard at work on the paperwork. We'll take this all the way to the Supreme Court. The issues are huge . . ."

Karen continued to talk to Deshawn. I drifted off toward a window, looking out at the barren lunar landscape, very sorry indeed that you couldn't see Earth from here.

Brian Hades was ecstatic to no longer be a hostage, and Gabe Smythe seemed glad that it was all over, too.

Except that it wasn't over. There was still one more issue that had to be resolved.

Karen was off speaking to the biological Malcolm Draper—getting his advice on appealing the ruling against her. Although in theory the biological Malcolm and the Mindscan one should have the same views, in practice their opinions had to have diverged—although, granted, not likely nearly as much as mine and Jacob's had.

While Karen was doing that, I went over to the High Eden administration building and confronted Hades and Smythe. Hades was behind his kidney-shaped desk, and Smythe was standing behind him, leaning effortlessly, as one could in this gravity, against a credenza.

"I know," I said simply, standing in front of them, "that you've made other instantiations of me. Some down on Earth, and at least one here on the moon."

Hades turned around, and he and Smythe looked at each other, the tall man with his white beard and ponytail, and the short one with his florid complexion and British accent.

"That's not true," said Hades, at last, turning back to face me.

I nodded. "The first tactic of corporate management, on any world: lie. But it's not going to work today. I'm positive about the other instantiations. I've been in contact with them."

Smythe narrowed his eyes. "That's not possible."

"Yes, it is," I said. "Some sort of . . . of entanglement, I think." Both men reacted with surprise at my use of that word. "And I know that you've been doing things to them, things to their minds. The question I want answered is, why?"

Hades said nothing, and neither did Smythe.

"All right," I said, "let me tell you what *I* think you're up to. I learned at the trial that there's a concept in philosophy called 'the zombie.' It's not precisely like the zombies of voodoo; those are reanimated dead folk. No, a philosophical zombie is a being that looks and acts just like us but has no consciousness, no self-awareness. Even so, it can perform complex, high-level tasks."

"Yes?" said Smythe. "So?"

"'*Seems you're the only one who knows / What it's like to be me.*'"

"Sorry," said Smythe. "Were you *singing* just now?"

"I was trying to," I said. "That's a line from the theme song to an old TV series called *Friends*. Used to be one of Karen's favorite shows. And it was bang-on target: it's *like something* to be me; that's the real definition of consciousness. But for zombies, it isn't *like* anything. They aren't anybody. They don't feel pain or pleasure, even though they react as if they do."

"You realize," said Smythe slowly, "that not all philosophers believe such constructs are possible. John Searle was very much in favor of them, but Daniel Dennett didn't believe in them."

"And what do *you* believe, Dr. Smythe? You're head psychologist for Immortex. What do you believe? What does Andrew Porter believe?"

"You won't answer that," said Hades, looking back over his shoulder. "I'm not a hostage anymore, Gabe—if you value your job, you won't answer that."

"Then *I'll* answer it," I said. "I think you *do* believe in zombies here at Immortex. I think you're experimenting on copies of my mind, trying to produce human beings without consciousness."

"Whatever for?" asked Smythe.

"For—*everything*. For slave labor, for sexual toys. You name it. Religious people would say these are bodies without souls; philosophers would say they're existing without being self-aware . . . without *knowing* that they exist, without anyone being home between their ears. The market for uploading consciousness may be huge, but the market for intelligent robot labor is even bigger. No one has found a way to make true artificial intelligence, until now—and your Mindscan process does it by simplest method possible: exactly duplicating a human mind. I saw that bit with Sampson Wainwright on TV all those years ago—the two entities, behind the curtains. Your copies *are* exact—but that's not what you wanted, is it? Not really.

286 ROBERT J. SAWYER

"No, you want the *intelligence* of humans, without the sentience, without the self-awareness, without it being *like* anything. You want those zombies—thinking beings that can perform even the most complex task flawlessly without ever complaining or getting bored. And so you're experimenting with bootleg copies of my mind, trying to carve out the parts that are conscious in order to produce zombies."

Smythe shook his head. "Believe me, nothing as nefarious as what you propose is at work here."

"Gabe," said Brian Hades, softly but sternly.

"It's better he know the truth," said Smythe, "than think something worse."

Hades considered for a long time, his round, bearded face immobile. Finally, almost imperceptibly, he nodded.

But, now that he had the go-ahead, Smythe didn't seem to know what to say. He pursed his lips and thought for several seconds, then: "Do you know who Phineas Gage is?"

"The guy in *Around the World in Eighty Days*?" I ventured.

"That was Phileas Fogg. Phineas Gage was a railway worker. In 1848, a tamping iron blew through his skull, leaving a hole nine centimeters in diameter."

"Not a pleasant way to go," I said.

"Indeed," said Smythe. "Except he *didn't* go. He lived for a dozen years afterwards."

I lifted my eyebrows, which were still catching a bit, damn it all. "With a hole like that in his head?"

"Yes," said Smythe. "Of course, his personality changed—which taught us a lot about how personality was created in the brain. Indeed, much of what we know about how the brain works is based on cases like Phineas Gage—outrageous, freak accidents. Most of them are one-of-a-kind cases, too: there's only one Phineas Gage, and there could be any number of reasons why what happened to him is not typical of what would happen to most people with that kind of brain damage. But we rely on his case, because we can't ethically duplicate the circumstances. Or we couldn't, until now."

I was mortified. "So you're deliberately damaging the brains of versions of me just to see what happens?"

Smythe shrugged as though it were a small matter. "Exactly. I'm hoping to turn consciousness studies into an experimental science, not some hit-and-miss game of chance. Consciousness is *everything*: it's what gives the universe shape and meaning. We owe it to ourselves to study it—to really, finally, at last find out what it is, and why it is *like* something to be conscious."

My voice was thin. "That's monstrous."

"Psychologists have been unable to test their theories, except in the most marginal ways," said Smythe, as if he hadn't heard me. "I'm elevating psychology from the quagmire of the soft sciences into the realm of the *exact*—giving it the same beautiful precision that particle physics has, for instance."

"With copies of me?"

"They're surplus; they're like the extra embryos produced in *in vitro* fertilization."

I shook my head, appalled, but Smythe seemed unperturbed. "Do you know what I've discovered? Have you any idea?" His eyebrows had climbed high on his pink forehead. "I can shut off long-term memory formation; shut off short-term memory formation; give you a photographic, eidetic memory; make you religious; make you taste colors or hear shapes; retard your time sense; give you perfect time sense; give you a phantom awareness of the tail you used to have in the womb. No doubt I'll soon unlock addiction, making people immune to it. I'll be able to bring normally autonomic processes such as heart rate into conscious control. I'll be able to give an adult the effortless ability a child has to learn new languages.

"Do you know what happens when you cut out both the pineal gland and Broca's area? When you totally separate the hippocampus from the rest of the brain? When you do a transformation, so that what's normally encoded in the left hemisphere is mapped onto the right side of the body, and vice versa? What happens when you wake up a human mind in a body that has three arms, or four? Or has its two eyes situated opposite each other, one facing front, the other facing back?

"*I* know these things. I know more about how the mind really works than Descartes, James, Freud, Pavlov, Searle, Chalmers, Nagel, Bonavista, and Cho *combined*. And I've only just begun my research!"

"Jesus," I said. "Jesus. You have to stop. I forbid it."

"I'm not sure that's within your power," said Smythe. "You didn't *create* your mind; it's not subject to copyright. Besides, think of the good I'm doing!"

"Good? You're *torturing* these people."

Smythe looked unfazed. "I'm doing research that needs to be done."

Before I could reply, Brian Hades spoke for the first time in several minutes. "Please, Mr. Sullivan. You're the only one who can help us."

"Why me?" I said. "Is it because I'm young?"

"That's part of it," said Hades. "But only a small part of it."

"What else is there?"

Hades looked at me, and Smythe looked at Hades. "You spontaneously boot," Hades said. "No one else ever has."

I was completely baffled. "What?"

"If you, as an upload, lose consciousness, you don't stop for good," Hades said. "Rather, your consciousness comes back of its own volition. No other Mindscan has ever done that."

"I haven't lost consciousness," I said. "Not since I uploaded."

"Yes, you have," said Hades. "Almost as soon as you were created. Don't you remember? Back at our facility in Toronto?"

"I . . . oh."

"Remember?" said Smythe, standing up straight. "There had been a moment when something had gone wrong. Porter noticed it—and was amazed."

"I don't understand. What's so amazing about that?"

Smythe spread his arms as if it were obvious. "Do you know why Mindscans never sleep?"

"We aren't subject to fatigue," I said. "We don't get tired."

Smythe shook his head. "No. Oh, that happens to be true, but it's not the *reason.*" He looked at Hades, as if giving him a chance to cut him off, but Hades just shrugged a little, passing the floor back to Smythe.

"We've all been following the trial up here, of course," Smythe said. "You saw Andy Porter give testimony, right?"

I nodded.

"And he talked about competing theories of how consciousness is instantiated, remember? Of what the actual physical correlates of it are?"

"Sure. It could be anything from neural nets to, ah . . ."

"To cellular automata on the surface of the microtubules that make up the cytoskeleton of neural tissue," said Smythe. "Porter's a good company man; he made it sound like there's still a question about this. But there isn't—although we here at Immortex are the only ones who know that. Consciousness *is* cellular automata—that's where it's embodied. No question."

I nodded. "Okay. So?"

Smythe took a deep breath. "So, with the Mindscan process, we get a perfect quantum snapshot of your mind at a given moment in time: we precisely map the configuration of—to use Porter's metaphor—the black and white pixels that make up the fields of cellular automata that cover the microtubules in your brain tissue. It's a precise quantum snapshot. But that's *all* a Mindscan is—a snapshot. And that's not good enough. Consciousness isn't a state, it's a *process*. For our snapshot to become conscious, that snapshot has to spontaneously become one frame in a motion-picture film, a film that's creating its own unscripted story, unfolding into the future."

"If you say so," I said.

Smythe nodded emphatically. "I do. The snapshot becomes a moving picture when the black and white pixels become *animated*. But they don't do that on their own: they have to be given rules to obey. You know, turn white if three of your neighbors are black, or something like that. But the rules aren't innate to the system. They have to be *imposed* upon it. Once they are, the cellular automata keep permuting endlessly—and *that's* consciousness, *that's* the actual phenomenon of self-awareness, of inner life, of existence being *like* something."

"So how do you add in rules that govern the permutations?" I asked.

Smythe lifted his hands. "We don't. We can't. Believe me, we've tried—but nothing we can do gets the pixels to start doing anything. No, the rules come from the *already* conscious mind of the subject being scanned. It's only because the real, biological mind is initially quantally entangled with the new one that the rules are transferred, and the pixels become cellular automata in the new mind. Without that initial entanglement, there is no process of living consciousness, only a dead snapshot of it. Our artificial minds don't have such rules built in, so if the consciousness ever halts in a copied mind, there's no way to start it up again."

"So if one of us were to fall asleep—" I said.

"He'd die," said Smythe simply. "The consciousness would never reboot."

"So, why is this a big secret?"

Smythe looked at me. "There are more than a dozen other companies trying to get into the uploading business; it's going to be a fifty-trillion-dollar-a-year industry by 2055. They can all do a version of our Mindscan process: they can all copy the *pattern* of pixels. But, so far, we're the only ones who know that quantum entanglement with the source mind is the key to booting up the copied consciousness. Without linking the minds, at least initially, the duplicate never does anything." He shook his head. "For some reason, though, your mind *does* reboot when it's shut off."

"I've only blacked out once," I said, "and that was just after the initial boot-up. You can't know that it always happens."

"Yes, we can," said Smythe. "Copies of your mind manage to generate rules for their cellular automata spontaneously, on their own, without being linked to the original. We know, because we've instantiated multiple copies of your mind into artificial bodies here on the moon and down on Earth—and, no matter when we do it, the copies spontaneously boot up. Even if we shut them down, they just boot up again later on their own."

I frowned. "But why should I be different from everyone else in this regard? Why do copies of my mind spontaneously reboot?"

"Honestly?" said Smythe, raising his platinum eyebrows. "I'm not sure. But I *think* it has to do with the fact that you used to be color-blind. See, consciousness is all about the perception of qualia: things that only exist as constructs in the mind, things like bitterness or peacefulness. Well, colors are one of the most basic qualia. You can take a rose and pull off and isolate the stem, or the thorns, or the petals: they are distinct, actual entities. But you can't pull off the redness, can you? Oh, you can *remove* it—you can bleach a rose—but you can't pluck the redness out and point to it as a separate thing. Redness, blueness, and so on are mental states—there's no such thing as redness on its own. Well, by accident, we gave your mind access to mental states it had never experienced before. That initially made it unstable. It tried to assimilate these new qualia, and couldn't—so it crashed. That's what happened when Porter first transferred you: it crashed, and you blacked out. But then your consciousness rebooted, on its own, as if striving to make sense of the new qualia, to incorporate them into its worldview."

"It makes you an invaluable test subject, Mr. Sullivan," said Brian Hades. "There's no one else like you."

"There *should* be no one else like me," I said. "But you keep making copies. And that's not right. I want you to shut off the duplicates of me you've fraudulently produced, destroy the master Mindscan recording, and never make another me again."

"Or . . . ?" said Hades. "You can't even prove they exist."

"You think messing with the biological Jacob Sullivan was hard? Trust me: you don't want to have to deal with the *real* me."

EPILOGUE

ONE HUNDRED AND TWO YEARS LATER: NOVEMBER 2147

Oh, my God!

"What?"

Oh, my God! Oh, Christ . . .

I hadn't heard a voice in my head like this for over a century. I'd thought they were gone for good.

I don't believe this!

"Hello? Hello? Can you hear me?"

I know they said it might be strange, but—but . . .

"But what? Who is this? Jake? Is this another Jake?"

What the—hello? Who's that?

"It's me, Jake Sullivan."

What? I'm Jake Sullivan.

"So am I."

Where are you?

"Lowellville."

Lowellville?

"Yes. You know: the largest settlement on Mars."

Mars? We don't have any settlements on Mars . . .

"Of course we do, for thirty years now. I moved here over a decade ago."

But . . . oh. Ah. What year is this?

"It's 2147."

Twenty-one forty seven? You're pulling my leg. It's 2045.

"No. You're a century out of date."

But . . . oh. Really?

"Yes."

Why'd you go to Mars?

"The same reason so many people came to North America from Europe ages ago. The freedom to practice our own brand of humanity. Mars is a catch-all for those who march to a different drummer. We were being denied our identity down on Earth. We took it all the way to the Supreme Court in the U.S., but lost. And so . . ."

And so, Mars.

"Exactly. We're in a lovely community here. Lots of multiple marriages, lots of gay marriages, and lots of uploads. Under Martian law—created by those of us who live here, of course—all forms of marriage are legal, and out in the open. There's a family three doors down that consists of a human woman and a male chimpanzee who was genetically modified to have a bigger brain. We play bridge with them once a week." I shrugged, although there was no way the other me could know I was doing that. "If you can't change the old constitution, go somewhere fresh and write a new one."

Ah. That's . . . wow. My, that's something, isn't it?

"It is indeed."

I—Mars; wow. But, hey, wait! I'm not on Mars, and yet there's no time lag.

"Yeah, I encountered this before when one of us was on the moon. Whenever a new me boots up, it seems to become quantally entangled with this me; quantum communication is instantaneous, no matter how far apart we are."

And we're very far apart.

"What do you mean?"

Akiko Uchiyama said she was sending me to 47 Ursa Majoris.

"And where's that?"

Ninety light-years from Earth.

"Light-years! What are you talking about?"

She said she was sending me—you know, transmitting a copy of my Mindscan—to one of the worlds they were studying with the big SETI telescope on the moon's farside.

"Jesus. And you agreed?"

They, ah, didn't actually offer me any choice. But that must be where I am. And it's incredible! The sun—the star here—looks gigantic. It covers maybe an eighth of the sky.

"And you think it's still 2045? Is that when you were . . . were transmitted?"

Yes. But Akiko said she wasn't just sending me; she was also sending instructions for building a robot body for me.

"And are you instantiated in that body?"

Yes. It doesn't look quite right—maybe they had a hard time making some of the parts—and the colors! I have no idea if they're right, but I can see so many colors now! But, yes, I've got a humanoid body. Can't see my own face, of course . . .

"So there's intelligent life on this other world? What's it look like?"

I haven't seen it yet. I'm in a room that seems to have been grown, like it's made out of coral. But there's a large window, and I can see outside. The giant sun is a color I don't know what to call. And there are clouds that corkscrew up vertically. And—oh, something's flying by! Not a bird; more like a manta ray. But . . .

"But no intelligent aliens yet?"

Not yet. They must be here, though. Somebody built this body for me, after all.

"If you really are—my God—ninety light-years away, then the aliens took twelve years to reinstantiate you after receiving the transmission."

It might have taken them that long to figure out how to build the artificial body, or to decide that it was a good idea to resurrect me.

"I suppose."

Can you contact Dr. Smythe? He'll want to know . . .

"Who?"

Gabriel Smythe.

"That rings a vague bell . . ."

He's with Immortex. The head psychologist, I think.

"Oh, right. *Him.* If he hasn't uploaded, he must be dead by now; I'll see if I can find out."

Thanks. I'm supposed to try to send a radio signal back; I'll have to ask the natives about that. Proof of concept: Akiko and Smythe wanted to show that human consciousness could be transmitted, that . . . that ambassadors *could be sent to other worlds at the speed of light.*

"Are you going to send the radio signal?"

If the natives here—whoever they are—let me, sure. But it'll be ninety years before it'll get back to . . . what the heck do you call it? 'Sol system,' no?

"I guess. So, tell me: what else can you see?"

Man, this is weird . . .

"Jake?"

Sorry. It's a lot to absorb at once. Connecting with you; full-color vision; where I am; the passage of time.

"What else can you see?"

Vegetation—I guess that's what it is. Like umbrellas turned inside out.

"Yes. And?"

Some vehicle going by, shaped like a pumpkin seed. There's something alive inside, under a transparent canopy . . .

"My God! An alien! What's it look like?"

"Dark, bulky, and—damn, it's gone."

"Wow. An actual alien . . ."

Are you going to tell people? Tell humanity that you're in contact with a distant world?

"I—I don't know. Who would believe me? They'd say it was a hallucination. I've got nothing to show them, and any confirming signal you send won't get here for the better part of a century."

I suppose. Too bad. I've a feeling this is going to get interesting.

"There is *one* person I can share it all with."

One's better than none. Who?

"Karen Bessarian. You actually met her. She was the old woman we spoke to at the Immortex sales pitch."

That was Karen Bessarian, the writer?

"Yes. And she's still writing. In fact, she's back to writing *DinoWorld* novels—the characters went public domain thirty years ago, but readers recognize that Karen is their creator, and the books she's doing about them now are selling better than the originals."

Good for her. But what's happening with us? How's the family business?

"Fine. They even brew Old Sully's here on Mars now."

Great! What else? Are we married?

"I am, yes."

Oooh, I know! To Rebecca Chong, right? I knew that eventually—

I smiled. "No, not to Rebecca. She's been dead for over fifty years, and, um, she didn't think much of uploads."

Ah, well, then I guess I don't know who we—

"It's Karen," I said simply. "Karen Bessarian and I are married. The first Mindscans ever to tie the knot."

"Her? But she's so old! I never would have thought . . .

"Yes, her. But we can talk about that later. Tell me more of what you're seeing."

I must be under some sort of observation; I can't imagine they'd activate me otherwise. But so far, there's no sign of the natives here, except that vehicle that went speeding by the window. The room is big, and it has something that must be a door, but it's almost twice as high as I am.

"Any other clues about the aliens?"

Well, there are markings on the walls. Spirals, circles. Writing, I suppose. God knows what it says. There's an elevated work surface in the room, but nothing that looks like a chair.

"Sitting is overrated."

Yeah, perhaps. I'm standing myself. It's all very—the door! The door is opening, crumpling aside like an accordion, and—

"Yes? Yes? What do you see?"

Hello? Hello! Um, my name is Jake. Jake Sullivan.

"What do you see? What do they look like?"

I guess we'll have to learn each other's language, eh? That's okay . . .

"Jake! What do they look like?"

We're going to have some interesting times together, I can see that . . .

"Jake? Jake?"

Like I said, my name is Jake, and I guess I'm here to tell you a little bit about what it means to be human.

There was a pause, presumably while the other me thought things that weren't articulated in words, then:

But, you know, I'm in contact with somebody else, and I think he knows even more about being human than I do. Let's see what he has to say . . .

FUrTHEr READING

Consciousness is back, baby! For most of the twentieth century, brain studies avoided any discussion of consciousness—the feeling of subjective experience, the apprehension of qualia, the sense that it is *like* something to be you or me. But in the last decade, the issue of consciousness has very much moved to center stage in the exploration of the human brain.

Although I touched on the nature of consciousness in my 1995 novel *The Terminal Experiment*, and again in 1998's *Factoring Humanity*, I find myself drawn back to this fertile ground once more, in large part because consciousness studies are so multidisciplinary—and I firmly believe it's the interplay of disparate elements that makes for good science fiction. Whereas twenty years ago, you'd be hard-pressed to find *any* academic talking seriously about consciousness, these days quantum physicists, evolutionary psychologists, neuroscientists, artificial-intelligence researchers, philosophers, and even lowly novelists are engaged in the debate.

(Indeed, one could argue that novelists were the *only* ones who took consciousness seriously for much of the last century: we strove, however ineffectually, to capture the stream of consciousness in our narratives, and to explore the limitations and richness of constrained points-of-view and subjective experience . . . all while the Skinnerian behaviorists were telling the world that such things were meaningless.)

The resurgent interest in consciousness is perhaps best summed up by the existence of the essential *Journal of Consciousness Studies*, published by Imprint Academic. *JCS* is subtitled "Controversies in Science and the Humanities," and refers to itself as "an international multidisciplinary journal." You can learn more about it at www.imprint.co.uk/jcs.

I own a complete set of this journal, which is now in its twelfth year, and consulted it extensively while writing *Mindscan*. However, the papers in it are often very technical; for those interested in popular discussions of consciousness, I recommend the following books, which also influenced me while I was working on this novel.

※

Carter, Rita. *Exploring Consciousness*. Berkeley: University of California Press, 2002. An excellent introduction.

Carter, Rita. *Mapping the Mind*. Berkeley: University of California Press, 1998. A good overview of how the brain works.

Crick, Francis. *The Astonishing Hypothesis: The Scientific Search for the Soul*. New York: Charles Scribner's Sons, 1994. Crick—the co-discoverer of the helical structure of DNA—believed that consciousness didn't really exist.

Dennett, Daniel C. *Consciousness Explained*. New York: Little Brown, 1991. Often referred to by those who think there's something special about human self-awareness as "Consciousness Explained Away."

Freeman, Anthony. *Consciousness: A Guide to the Debates*. Santa Barbara, California: ABC-CLIO, 2003. A fascinating look at the various controversies.

Jaynes, Julian. *The Origin of Consciousness in the Breakdown of the Bicameral Mind*. New York: Houghton Mifflin, 1990 [reissue; originally published in 1976]. An enchanting, if ultimately unprovable, hypothesis that true human consciousness didn't emerge until Classical times; utterly fascinating.

Kurzweil, Ray. *The Age of Spiritual Machines: When Computers Exceed Human Intelligence*. New York: Viking, 1999. A fascinating, optimistic look at thinking machines and uploaded minds; see also my dialog with computer scientist A. K. Dewdney about this book at www.sfwriter.com/brkurz.htm.

LeDoux, Joseph. *Synaptic Self: How Our Brains Become Who We Are*. New York: Viking, 2002. A good look at the neuronal nature of human minds.

Moravec, Hans. *Mind Children: The Future of Robot and Human Intelligence*. Cambridge, Massachusetts: Harvard University Press, 1988. A classic about artificial intelligence.

Ornstein, Robert. *The Evolution of Consciousness: The Origins of the Way We Think*. New York: Touchstone (Simon & Schuster), 1991. Makes clear that Darwin has a lot more to teach us about consciousness than Freud.

Penrose, Roger. *The Emperor's New Mind: Concerning Computers, Minds, and the Laws of Physics*. Oxford: Oxford University Press, 1989. A classic proposing that human consciousness is quantum mechanical in nature.

Penrose, Roger. *Shadows of the Mind: A Search for the Missing Science of Consciousness*. Oxford: Oxford University Press, 1994. Among many other fascinating things, explores the possible relationship between microtubules and human consciousness.

Pinker, Steven. *How the Mind Works.* New York: Norton, 1997. A fine overview of modern cognitive science, mostly from an evolutionary-psychology perspective.

Richards, Jay W., ed. *Are We Spiritual Machines?: Ray Kurzweil vs. the Critics of Strong A.I.* Seattle, Washington: Discovery Institute Press, 2002. Precisely what the title says.

Searle, John R. *The Mystery of Consciousness.* New York: New York Review of Books, 1997. The originator of the "Chinese Room" problem cited in this novel spells out his beliefs about the ineffable nature of human consciousness.

ACKNOWLEDGMENTS

Many thanks to **John Rose, Salman A. Nensi,** and **Kristen Pederson Chew,** for creating *The Bakka Anthology,* and to **Stanley Schmidt** of *Analog Science Fiction and Fact* magazine. My short story "Shed Skin," which inspired this novel, was commissioned for that limited-edition anthology, and later also appeared in the January/February 2004 issue of *Analog.*

Thanks also to artificial-intelligence pioneer **Ray Kurzweil,** whom I had the pleasure of meeting when we gave joint keynote addresses at the Twelfth Annual Canadian Conference on Intelligent Systems in Calgary in 2002; Ray subsequently provided me with a whack of very useful printed material. Thanks, also, to **Greg Armstrong,** Senior Research Technician, Robotics Institute, Carnegie Mellon University, who gave me a wonderful tour of their facilities. And thanks to **Gregory Benford** and **Elisabeth Malartre,** who provided me with an advance manuscript copy of their brilliant nonfiction book *More than Human,* forthcoming from Tor.

Many thanks also to **Dr. Hal Brian Scher** of Scher Psychology Professional Corporation, Thornhill, Ontario, who went above and beyond the call of duty in discussing brain injury and the nature of consciousness with me. **Jerome M. Siegel, Ph.D.,** Brain Research Institute, University of California, Los Angeles, and **Robert P. Vertes, Ph.D.,** Professor of Neuroscience, Center for Complex Systems and Brain Sciences, Florida Atlantic University, both provided excellent research refuting the notion that sleep was required for memory consolidation. And neurologist **Dr. Isaac Szpindel** of Toronto and neurosurgeon **Dr. Lou Jacobs** of Garden City, Michigan, both kindly vetted the manuscript.

For advice on the legal aspects of the plot, I thank **Russell J. Howe** and **Darcy Romaine** of the law firm Boland Howe Barristers LLP in Aurora, Ontario; **Victor A. Coen,** a specialist in probate litigation at the Michigan law firm of Sommers Schwartz Silver & Schwartz; **Richard M. Gotlib,** senior corporate counsel, Hudson's Bay Company, Toronto; and **Ariel Reich, Ph.D.,** senior corporate counsel, Hewlett-Packard Company, Palo Alto.

For advice on the theological aspects of the plot, I thank the **Rev. Paul Fayter,** historian of science and religion, York University, Toronto.

Many thanks, also, to the friends and colleagues who let me bounce ideas off them or otherwise provided input, including **Ted Bleaney, Linda Carson, David Livingstone Clink, Lily Sazz Fayter, Kim Howe, Al Katerinsky, Howard Miller, Kirstin Morrell,** my brother **Alan B. Sawyer, Gordon Smith, Elizabeth Trenholm, Hayden Trenholm,** and **David Widdicombe.**

Parts of this novel were written while I was writer-in-residence at the Toronto Public Library's Merril Collection of Science Fiction, Speculation, and Fantasy. Many thanks to collection head **Lorna Toolis,** and to the Toronto Public Library Board and the Friends of TPL's South Region, which jointly funded my residency.

Thanks also to **Danita Maslankowski** who organized the Spring 2004 "Write-Off" retreat weekend for Calgary's Imaginative Fiction Writers Association, at which much editing and polishing of this manuscript were accomplished.

Huge thanks to my wife, **Carolyn Clink;** my editor, **David G. Hartwell,** and his associates, **Moshe Feder** and **Denis Wong;** my agent, **Ralph Vicinanza,** and his associates **Christopher Lotts** and **Vince Gerardis; Tom Doherty, Linda Quinton, Nicole Kalian, Irene Gallo,** and everyone else at Tor Books; and **Harold** and **Sylvia Fenn, Janis Ackroyd, Melissa Cameron, David Cuthbertson, Marnie Ferguson, Leo MacDonald, Steve St. Amant, Heidi Winter,** and everyone else at H. B. Fenn and Company.

Finally, thanks to the 700 members of my online discussion group, who followed along with me as I created this novel. Feel free to join us at:

www.groups.yahoo.com/group/robertjsawyer/